S0-AEW-682

Linda Lael Miller

WANTON ANGEL

POCKET BOOKS
New York   London   Toronto   Sydney

An *Original* Publication of POCKET BOOKS

 POCKET BOOKS, a division of Simon & Schuster, Inc.
1230 Avenue of the Americas, New York, NY 10020

This book is a work of historical fiction. Names, characters, places and incidents relating to nonhistorical figures are products of the author's imagination or are used fictitiously. Any resemblance to actual events or locales or persons, living or dead, is entirely coincidental.

Copyright © 1987 by Linda Lael Miller

ISBN 978-1-4516-1114-4

First Pocket Books printing July 1987

10 9 8 7 6

POCKET and colophon are registered trademarks of Simon & Schuster, Inc.

Illustration by Matthew Frey—Wood Ronsaville Harlin Inc.

Manufactured in the United States of America

For information regarding special discounts for bulk purchases, please contact Simon & Schuster Special Sales at 1-800-456-6798 or business@simonandschuster.com.

For Irene Goodman, my agent and my friend.
Thank you for sharing this dream with me,
and for helping to make it come true.

Dear Readers, Old and New,

It is with joy that I give you one of the novels written earlier in my career. Some of you have read it, and will feel as though you're meeting old friends; to others, it will offer a completely new reading experience.

Either way, this tale is a gift of my heart.

The characters in this and all of my books are the kind of people I truly admire, and try to emulate. They are smart, funny, brave, and persistent. The women are strong, and while they love their men, they have goals of their own, and they are independent, sometimes to a fault. More than anything else, these stories are about people meeting challenges and discovering the hidden qualities and resources within themselves.

We all have to do that.

We are blessed—and cursed—to live in uncertain times.

Let us go forward, bravely, with our dearest ideals firmly in mind. They're all we have—and all we need.

May you be blessed,

Linda Lael Miller

Books by Linda Lael Miller

Banner O'Brien
Corbin's Fancy
Memory's Embrace
My Darling Melissa
Angelfire
Desire and Destiny
Fletcher's Woman
Lauralee
Moonfire
Wanton Angel
Willow
Princess Annie
The Legacy
Taming Charlotte
Yankee Wife
Daniel's Bride
Lily and the Major
Emma and the Outlaw
Caroline and the Raider
Pirates
Knights
My Outlaw
The Vow
Two Brothers
Springwater

Springwater Seasons series:
  Rachel
  Savannah
  Miranda
  Jessica
A Springwater Christmas
One Wish
The Women of Primrose
  Creek series:
    Bridget
    Christy
    Skye
    Megan
Courting Susannah
Springwater Wedding
My Lady Beloved
  (writing as Lael St. James)
My Lady Wayward
  (writing as Lael St. James)
High Country Bride
Shotgun Bride
Secondhand Bride
The Last Chance Café
Don't Look Now
Never Look Back
One Last Look

PROLOGUE

Northridge, Washington Territory
April 1886

THE CHILD RAN, scrambling, wild dark hair tumbling over a tear-streaked face, past one tar-paper shack after another, captive sobs burning in her throat. Reaching the farthest shanty, the one closest to the raging green river, she stumbled over the shoe-scuffed wooden crate that served as a stoop and hurled herself into the tiny, dimly lit room beyond.

"Gran!" she wept, in fury and in pain.

The shanty had but one room, twelve feet square, and there was no window to let in the spring sunlight. Gran stood at the cookstove sandwiched in between a narrow bed and an even narrower cot, an iron-gray tendril escaping an otherwise severe hairstyle at the nape of her neck.

The steam whistle in the smelter works up on the hill rose over the thunderous din to tell the time: twelve noon and too soon by three hours for Bonnie Fitzpatrick to be back from school.

Gran was a gentle woman, but she brooked no nonsense and now her lips thinned. "What is it, child, that sends you runnin' home before lessons is through, and lookin' as though the Devil himself were right behind you?" The old

1

woman paused to cross herself with the quick deftness of the very devout.

Bonnie swallowed, suddenly ashamed. The Mackerson twins had triumphed, not by their torment, but by making her run away. Now she'd be in trouble right and proper, not only with her teacher, but with Gran and maybe Da, too, when he got home from his shift up at the smelter. And, on top of that, she'd have to go back and face those pampered hellions, the daughters of the smelter's resident manager, with them knowing they'd bested her.

"Well?" Gran demanded, not unkindly but not charitably, either. With a sigh, she left her wooden spoon in the soup kettle and sat down on the edge of the rickety bed she and Bonnie shared, patting the worn quilt with one work-roughened hand.

Obediently Bonnie sat down beside her grandmother, full of remorse and anger. "The Mackerson twins called me a stupid Mick, Gran," she confessed miserably. "They said I'm nothin' and I'll never live anyplace better than Patch Town."

Bonnie had half expected punishment, for outbursts of the sort she'd just indulged in were rarely tolerated, but instead she felt her grandmother's strong, thin arm encircle her shoulders. "You know you're a daughter of Erin, Bonnie, and that's something to be proud of, then, isn't it?"

Bonnie had endured enough prejudice to shake that belief, if not rout it entirely. What good was being a daughter of Erin, if the one dress you had was so old that you couldn't make out the pattern of the cloth anymore, or even the color? What good was it, if your shoes were pointy at the toes and too small for your feet in the bargain, so that you limped like a cripple?

"Bonnie Fitzpatrick, you'll be answering me, and straight away, too," Gran prompted.

"Maybe the Mackersons are right," Bonnie reflected with a sigh.

There was a charged silence in the room, and Bonnie's stomach leaped in alert just before Gran wrenched her around to face her, one hand raised to administer a sound slap.

But Gran's hand fell back to her lap, and her bright blue eyes twinkled with a mischievous humor entirely out of keeping with the lot that had fallen to the proud Fitzpatrick family. "It seems, then, colleen, that I've never told you about the day of your birth," she said, and her brogue, faded by time and hardship to just a hint of the Irish, was suddenly thick and rich again.

Bonnie's smoky violet eyes widened in their dense, dark thicket of lashes and she pushed a tangle of mahogany hair from her face with a dirt-smudged hand. "Did something special happen that day?" she whispered, hoping against hope that something had.

Gran nodded importantly and lowered her voice to tell the secret. "Indeed it did, then. The Lord Himself was there at your birth, Bonnie. He took you into his strong, carpenter's hands, He did, and you just a wee baby, of course, fresh from Heaven. He smiled and held you up for the Father Himself to see, and His beautiful face was all alight with the joy of you, it was." Here Gran paused to cross herself again, and she closed her eyes for a moment, her thin lips moving in a prayer that Bonnie couldn't hear. " 'Look, then, Father,' He says, says He, 'isn't she a fine babe, a wondrous fine babe?' "

Bonnie could barely breathe. "Go on with you," she whispered, her heart thudding against the inside of her chest with the splendor of such a vision.

" 'Tis true," Gran insisted, crossing herself once more and then rising swiftly to go back to the stove and the pot of stew bubbling there, its fragrance pushing back the stench of Patch Town just a bit. After a while she added, over one sharp-bladed shoulder, "You go on back to school, then, Bonnie Fitzpatrick, and don't be disappointing the Lord, Himself thinkin' you turned out just the way He wanted and all."

Bonnie's strong little legs trembled slightly as she stood up. She smoothed her dark tangled hair and squared her shoulders, peering at Gran's rod-straight back in the half-darkness. "Is this one of your tales, Gran?"

"Seen Him there with me own two eyes," Gran said firmly. "Off with you, then, and mind you don't dally along

3

the way. I'll not be overlookin' any more foolishness and neither will the Lord."

Bonnie's heart got away from her then, racing ahead in sheer jubilance, and she turned on one rundown heel to chase after it, dashing past the shanties, past the outhouses stinking in the sun, past the piles of refuse and the curious stares of the neighbors.

From that day forward, Bonnie Fitzpatrick was changed. There was a deep and tender joy within her that could not be moved, for whenever she thought of the Lord holding her up in delight for the Father to see, it took the sting out of living in Patch Town and wearing the same ugly calico dress day after day. The Mackerson twins couldn't hurt her and soon gave up trying, though Forbes Durrant, a boy who lived just two shanties from the Fitzpatricks, was more persistent. He laughed at Bonnie's story and dubbed her "the Angel," and the name stuck, first because Bonnie Fitzpatrick claimed the Lord Himself had been present at her birthing, later when she blossomed into a beauty the likes of which Northridge proper, let alone Patch Town, had never seen. Not for a moment was her fairness lost on Forbes, who teased her mercilessly but would have faced Goliath himself to protect her.

At seventeen, Bonnie caught the eye of Eli McKutchen, heir to the McKutchen Smelter Works at Northridge and an empire that reached from one coast to the other as well. A tall man, naturally forceful in his opinions and broad in the shoulders, Eli had glossy, wheat-gold hair that was forever in a fetching state of disarray, along with his grandfather's amber eyes. As far as Bonnie was concerned, he was near perfect, and therein lay the seeds of future grief.

The townswomen were outraged, for it did seem that Eli McKutchen, with his glowing prospects and his good looks, was as enamored of Bonnie as she was of him. "Uppity snit. Has a fly in her nose, that one," they muttered into their teacups and their delicately painted fans. How could Josiah, Eli's grandfather and a man highly respected in Northridge, permit such an unsuitable alliance?

The men of the town focused their jealousy on Eli instead

4

of Bonnie. "Lucky bastard," they grumbled, into their warm beer and their poker hands.

Josiah, impressed by Bonnie's spirit as well as her beauty, dashed the town's best hopes for justice by approving wholeheartedly of the match. Bonnie's humble beginnings did nothing to dissuade him; he'd been poor once himself, after all. He loved his grandson, and he saw in Miss Bonnie Fitzpatrick an indefinable something that made him feel quietly joyous. To celebrate Eli's good fortune, for any good fortune of Eli's was also his own, he built a two-story mercantile and handed it over to Jack Fitzpatrick, lock, stock and barrel.

Fitzpatrick, hungry for half his life and in debt for the other, was overwhelmed that the giving up of a single, troublesome daughter could yield such bounty. After the ceremony, conducted in the McKutchens' fragrant garden, Jack had a mite too much to drink and waxed sentimental, weeping because his dear old mother had died just the year before, too soon to share in the joy of it all, and of course his own sweet Margaret Anne had gone on to glory, too, long since. He'd rarely thought of his lost wife, once the first terrible grief had passed, but this fortuitous turn of events brought her back to his mind and his heart. What a delight it would have been had that sainted woman lived to see her girl wed to such a fine promising lad as Eli McKutchen, with all the world at her feet. And here was himself, with a store all his own—filled with goods it was—and his name painted right on the window for all heaven and earth to see! Why, the pleasure of it was enough to swell a kind heart to the breaking, and a broken heart was cause for a good man to slip into his cups a bit, now, wasn't it?

Indeed, when night had fallen and the wedding was over and the bride and groom were alone in their marriage chamber, there was only one person in all of Northridge drunker than Jack Fitzpatrick, and that was young Forbes Durrant, who knew a thing or two about heartbreak himself.

Part One

ANGEL
IN DISGRACE

CHAPTER *1*

"... a splendid little war ..."

SPOKANE AND THE surrounding wheat fields were far behind now; the train, with its burdened freight cars and near-empty passenger section, labored slowly, clamorously along the banks of the fierce Columbia River, making its way ever upward into the high country of eastern Washington State.

Bonnie McKutchen sat with weary stiffness in her seat, a small, soot-covered bundle of quiet despair. Days of travel had left her dark hair lank and rumpled, and the smells of cigar and wood smoke clung to her clothes. Her blue broadcloth traveling suit and matching hip-length capelet, with its smart trim of jet beads, were both wrinkled, and her hat, despite repeated shakings, was rigid with dust.

Beyond the grime-streaked window rolled the wild Columbia, and Bonnie turned her attention to the torrent. Rushing and tumbling from its headwaters high in the Cascade Mountains of Canada, slicing through Washington, the river formed the boundary between that state and Oregon for some three hundred miles, until it reached Astoria and the Pacific.

Before the coming of the railroads, steamboat pilots had braved the treacherous river, with its stair-step rapids and vicious currents, but now, in early May of the year 1898, the great paddle wheelers, along with their captains, were mere

9

memories. The primeval waterway, though tapped by its mighty tributaries, the Kootenay, the Willamette and the Snake among them, thundered on, still relatively unchanged by man, toward the sea that had summoned it for millennia.

Bonnie sighed. Mr. Theodore Roosevelt, often a guest at her table back in New York and, until his sudden resignation just a week before, Assistant Secretary of the United States Navy, had repeatedly and forcefully stated that the nation must take more care in protecting its rivers and conserving its wilderness lands. Such resources, Mr. Roosevelt maintained, while vast and bounteous, were not inexhaustible.

Bonnie agreed, of course, yet as the train bore her relentlessly away from what meant most to her in all the world, the thought of Mr. Roosevelt sent a dizzying jolt of resentment through her. But for his radical views concerning the current conflagration with Spain, after all, she might not be on this train and Eli might not be on his way to Cuba.

According to the newspapers, the Spanish were inflicting unspeakable atrocities on the "childlike" natives of that hellish island of jungles and disease-bearing mosquitoes. Bonnie brought herself up short. She must not think of Cuba, or of Eli being there, until she was stronger.

In order to distract herself, she surreptitiously inspected the few other souls riding in the railroad car. Sitting directly across the aisle was a lone man, hidden for the most part behind a crumpled and probably outdated copy of Mr. Hearst's New York *Journal.* Toward the front, a family of four got up to stretch, colliding with one another as they moved into the narrow aisle.

Bonnie studied the quartet from beneath lowered lashes.

The man and boy, both fiery redheads, wore cheap ready-made suits of checks and plaids, designs that did battle upon the person of each and then proceeded to arouse hostilities with their counterparts on the opposite body. The woman's hair was yellow, elaborately coiffed and quite possibly populated; her dress was a scanty tatter of pink taffeta.

The daughter, whom Bonnie judged to be about twelve years of age, seemed oddly out of place in that busy vortex

10

of tattersall and houndstooth and sickly taffeta. Uncommonly pretty, with shiny brown hair streaming down her back, green eyes, and flawless skin, she wore a simple brown dress, trimmed in braid of a cocoa color, and the garment, though frayed, was crisply clean. Momentarily, as her family tried to return as a bumbling unit to the soot-encrusted seats, the girl's gaze met Bonnie's in a sort of resigned desolation that was heartbreaking in a person so young.

Saddened, Bonnie bit her lower lip and looked down at her hands.

"They're vaudevillians," a masculine voice confided suddenly, in low and wholly charitable tones.

Bonnie lifted her eyes as the man from across the aisle moved toward her. Tall and well-built, with bright chestnut hair and mustache, and royal blue eyes, he wore a gray suit with an embossed satin vest. His golden watch chain bounced against a middle that looked hard and fit. With neither ceremony nor permission, he sank into the seat beside Bonnie's, giving the newspaper he had been reading an authoritative snap, and the pleasant scents of Castile soap and mint rose around him with the motion.

"Vaudevillians?" Bonnie echoed, careful to keep her voice down. She had a fascination with show people and their performances, though admittedly this enthrallment had brought her to dire regret on one tragic occasion.

The stranger nodded and there was a spark of amusement in his eyes. "My guess would be that they're booked at the Pompeii Playhouse in Northridge. Most vaudevillians travel with a troupe, but there are exceptions, of course."

Bonnie was wildly curious and thus willing to overlook the patent impropriety of speaking, let alone sharing a seat, with a man she didn't know. She stole one more glance at the family of thespians and then turned widened, gray-violet eyes to the face of the gentleman sitting beside her. "My goodness! Northridge must have grown and prospered since I was there last—certainly there was no playhouse."

The man smiled, revealing a set of enviably white teeth. "The theatre is the benevolent work of the Friday Afternoon Community Improvement Club, which, curiously enough, invariably meets on Tuesday mornings. They've started a library, too, and have poetry readings on alternate Thursday evenings."

For a moment, Bonnie remembered how she had yearned for books to read during her childhood. After she learned to make sense of the printed word, she still had only a dog-eared copy of McGuffey's *Reader*—until Miss Genoa McKutchen befriended her and changed her life forever, that is.

"I grew up in Northridge, you know," she said, frowning slightly and stiffening to keep her balance as the train careened around a particularly sharp curve of track and the loosely bolted seats threatened to come unfastened from the floor. "I don't remember meeting you, Mr.—"

"Hutcheson. Webb Hutcheson." The name was supplied with gruff pleasantry. "I've only lived in Northridge for a few years. My misfortune—if I'd been there earlier, I might have met you."

Bonnie colored slightly and looked down at her hands, which were knotted together in her lap. Unable to deal with the larger tragedy of her life, for the moment anyway, she despaired over the smaller: Her best gloves were so stained and smudged that they would surely be unsalvageable.

The silence lengthened as Mr. Hutcheson awaited her name. Bonnie didn't like saying; anyone who was the least bit familiar with Northridge's history would recognize it immediately. The smelter works had been built by Eli's grandfather, Josiah McKutchen, and Eli's sister, Genoa, was a prominent resident. Still, her arrival wouldn't be a secret for long in any case, and she could hardly withhold her identity when her companion had so forthrightly offered his.

"I'm Bonnie McKutchen," she said.

Mr. Hutcheson sat up just a little straighter, with no pretense of interest in the newspaper he held or anything but what Bonnie had said. "Eli's wife?"

Bonnie swallowed and nodded her head, her eyes averted. A feeling of aching loneliness washed over her, as though there weren't a whole world full of people all around her, and she came near to weeping—something she hadn't done since that cold December afternoon when she and Eli stood beside the grave of their infant son, Kiley, together and yet apart, each swathed in their dense and separate griefs.

They had traveled back from the cemetery at the head of a procession of carriages hung with crepe, plumes of black feathers nodding and bobbing on the horses' heads, and Eli had stopped loving Bonnie that day.

Mr. Hutcheson cleared his throat, bringing Bonnie back to the here and now, and gave the headline on his bedraggled newspaper an emphatic thump with one forefinger. "What do you think of this war with Spain?" he asked, a mite too loudly.

Bonnie flinched, inwardly at least. Her traveling companion had unknowingly struck a subject almost as painful as the death of her child. It was a struggle not to crumple in upon herself, not to cover her face with both hands and wail. Through the shifting blur of the present, she saw the past: the cold distance in Eli's eyes as he'd told her that he meant to go to Cuba with his friend Teddy Roosevelt. If she needed anything, he'd pointed out dismissively, she had only to ring up Seth Callahan, his attorney, and ask for it.

"I need you!" Bonnie had wanted to scream, but, of course, she hadn't. She'd drawn herself up, using her pride as a handhold, and offered the argument that Eli was a businessman, not a soldier. Her calmness and logic had changed nothing.

Bonnie blinked her eyes and the misty vision faded. Conscious of leaving Mr. Hutcheson's question suspended in midair, she drew a deep breath and sat up a little straighter. "The Spaniards did express a desire to avoid armed conflict," she said. "Mr. McKinley put that fact before Congress, but they insisted on fighting, not only in Cuba, but in the Philippine Islands, too."

Webb Hutcheson's handsome face was expressionless; Bonnie could not read his convictions in his eyes or the set of his chin or a rising of the blood beneath his skin. "They did sink the *Maine*, Mrs. McKutchen," he reminded her blandly.

"That has not been proved," Bonnie insisted, warming to the subject. "It is possible, you know, that the Spanish forces were not responsible for the tragedy." And a tragedy it had been, that explosion in Havana harbor, back in

13

mid-February. Two hundred sixty American seamen had perished in the blast.

They sat in stricken silence for a moment, the two of them, both as horrified and baffled as if the incident had just taken place before their eyes.

"Public sentiment demanded some form of retribution," Mr. Hutcheson offered.

Bonnie cast a contemptuous glance at his copy of the New York *Journal* and scowled. "Public sentiment," she said, "was created out of whole cloth by men like Mr. Hearst and Mr. Pulitzer." She paused, tugged at the tops of her soiled gloves in an unconscious display of annoyance. "Two days ago our navy destroyed the entire Spanish fleet at Manila Bay. Wasn't that retribution enough, Mr. Hutcheson?"

He sighed and laid a finger thoughtfully to his mustache, then looked away. Perhaps he was hiding a smile; men could be so damnably superior when a woman spoke of international affairs. Once, months before, when Bonnie had ventured to offer an opinion on the growing crisis between the United States and Spain, Eli had laughed and shaken his head, disregarding her remarks as he might those of a child.

She simmered at the memory, starting when the train whistle shrilled to alert the populace of Northridge to an imminent arrival. Mr. Hutcheson looked quite sober, although one side of his mouth appeared to quirk almost imperceptibly as he said, "You are well-informed, Mrs. McKutchen. Tell me—will you be in Northridge long?"

Bonnie cleaved to her dignity, even though her cheeks were throbbing and her heart was beating too fast at the prospect of making a new start in a town that might well take open delight in her reduced circumstances. "It is my plan to take up permanent residence there," she replied. "Why do you ask?"

Mr. Hutcheson arched one chestnut eyebrow and hesitated for some moments before answering. "Expressing sympathy for the Spanish position might not be the wisest course, if you hope to have friends. The prevalent view in Northridge is 'Remember the Maine, to hell with Spain.'"

The train seemed now to be pitching forward at a furious rate, like a foot racer flinging himself across a finish line. Reflexively, Bonnie reached out for an armrest and found herself clutching Mr. Hutcheson's muscular knee instead. She drew back her hand with a cry that elicited a throaty chuckle from the man beside her.

"My readers will be most interested to hear about your plans to settle in Northridge," he said.

Bonnie instantly recoiled, as though he had flung a hissing snake into her lap. "Your readers?"

His smile was blandly polite. "I publish the *Northridge News*," he explained. "I would like to print a short article—"

Perhaps it was the expression on Bonnie's face that silenced him, for surely it conveyed horror. She felt betrayed, wondered if Mr. Hutcheson had known who she was all along. Had he only struck up this conversation to obtain material for the pages of his newspaper? If he knew the truth, what a story it would be!

She envisioned a headline. PATCH TOWN UPSTART PUT IN HER PLACE. The ladies of Northridge would cluck and shake their heads as they read, secretly pleased that Jack Fitzpatrick's little girl was no longer living above her station, no longer the cherished darling of their favorite son, Good Prince Eli.

"No," she said, in a firm and quiet voice. "There will be no article about me."

Mr. Hutcheson said nothing, so Bonnie turned her attention to the window again, staring out at the tattered beginnings of Northridge. The town sprawled beneath a mountain thought to be an extinct volcano, bounded on the opposite side by the river. The horse-drawn ferry Bonnie had loved as a child was still in operation, she was pleased to see. How often had she stood at one of the rough-hewn wooden railings, having gladly paid the penny fare, pretending that the angry Columbia was an exotic sea and she a pirate princess? She could almost feel the cool river mist on her face again, hear the bleating of sheep being hauled across to market. The backs of her legs tickled, even now, as though touched again by shifting, woolly creatures.

Mr. Hutcheson spoke with quiet diplomacy and, despite the screeching of the train wheels along their tracks, Bonnie heard him clearly.

"My horse and buggy will be waiting at the depot," he

said. "I would be happy to drive you to the McKutchen place."

It was over a mile to Genoa's grand house, not a distance that would ordinarily have given Bonnie pause, but she was tired and there was her baggage to consider. She had brought little enough, heaven knew, compared to all that she had left behind, but it was still more than one person could carry. There would be no one waiting at the depot, for though Bonnie had wired Genoa that she was coming, she had not been able to say exactly when she would reach Northridge.

"You are very kind," she said in soft acceptance. "Thank you."

While Webb fetched her baggage, Bonnie stood on the footworn platform between the train and the small station, steam from the engine hissing in the air and swirling around her in clouds. For all her misgivings, she was glad to be back in Northridge. In New York, she had always felt out of place, ever conscious of her background and the Cinderella quality of her life with Eli. Here she would not be a usurper or a pretender, but simply Bonnie. Nothing more would be expected of her.

Heartened, she wondered if wild asparagus still grew along the railroad tracks beyond Patch Town, and who lived in the shack that had been hers and Gran's and Da's during the early years. She hoped that her father's business had not fallen into serious disrepair by its neglect. Underneath all this wondering was one pulsing, elemental question: Would Eli come looking for her once he learned that she was gone?

There was bedlam all around her, a familiar and temporary excitement stirred by the arrival of the train. Speckled, short-horned cattle were being driven out of a stock car farther back, through a chute and into a holding pen adjoining the livery stable next to the depot. The frightened beasts bawled and scrambled against one another, and the men herding them along shouted colorful oaths. Women in bright dresses and painted faces muttered with disappointment that the train had brought them no customers, and the family of vaudevillians were bumping into each other in vacuous confusion, except for the girl, who stood apart.

Finally Webb Hutcheson reappeared, driving a smartly

tended though modest buggy. Bonnie's belongings had been
crammed into the narrow space behind the seat and the
fancy women watched with renewed enthusiasm as the
editor of the *Northridge News* helped his passenger step
from the platform into the rig.

"Dances are still only a dollar, Webb honey," a redhead
sang out. "Come by the Brass Eagle tonight and ask for me.
The name's Dorothy, if you don't recall."

Webb grinned and reddened slightly, then brought the
reins down with a brisk movement of his wrists. His
sturdy-looking sorrel horse bolted forward and the buggy
lurched into motion.

Bonnie bent around the black bonnet of the rig for one
last look at the women in silks of sapphire blue, emerald
green, pink, and amber. Their gowns gleamed like gaudy
jewels in the late afternoon sunshine. "They like you," she
said. Perhaps it was the expansive relief of being off that
train that caused her to be so outrageously forward.

Webb laughed. "Hurdy-gurdies like any man with a dollar
in his pocket," he answered.

Hurdy-gurdies! Bonnie just had to look back again, and
the stretch was so great that she nearly fell out of the buggy.
It was only Mr. Hutcheson's swift hand on her arm that
saved her.

Bonnie blushed when she looked into Webb's face and
saw the gentle laughter in his eyes. There were so many
questions that she wanted to ask about hurdy-gurdy dancers. Did they sell their favors as well as their dances? Was it
true that some of them amassed fortunes and went on to
marry well or engage in respectable businesses?

Bonnie certainly couldn't ask Webb Hutcheson things
like that, but she made a mental note to put the questions to
Genoa at the first reasonable opportunity.

The familiar brick smokestack still loomed above the
fenced confines of the smelter yard, far up on the hill, but
the fancy building down the road, near Patch Town, was
new. Before they started up the steep road leading to the
main part of town, Bonnie saw the courthouse jail and the
bank and Webb's newspaper office.

The road was strewn with sawdust and dappled with
horse dung, and there were loaded wagons traveling up and

down the hill. On one side was the undertaker/furniture-maker's establishment; on the other was new addition, the suspiciously fancy structure with a façade and a sign that read EARLINE'S.

"Earline's what?" Bonnie presumed to ask.

Webb seemed reluctant to answer, and he cleared his throat once before doing so. "Rooming house," he said. "As a matter of fact, I'm living there myself—just until my place is built, of course."

"Of course," agreed Bonnie, who couldn't have cared less where Mr. Hutcheson chose to live. Now that she'd escaped that jarring, stultifying train, and her head was clearing, she was anxious for a look at her father's store. At the same time, she felt a pang that Jack Fitzpatrick wouldn't be there to greet her, as a sort of cushion to break her fall from grace. But Jack had returned to Ireland in haste, just a year after Bonnie's marriage, and though he'd stopped in New York to bid his only child a rather hurried and furtive farewell, he hadn't explained. He'd thrust the deed to his general store into his daughter's hands and trudged up the ramp of a steamer bound for London, and that had been the last Bonnie had seen of him, from that day to this. There had been one mysterious, badly spelled letter—Jack Fitzpatrick, bless his soul, could barely read or write—conveying the news that he'd found work in a Dublin saloon and reminding Bonnie that the store in Northridge was hers now.

Although her father's state of mind and curious behavior had worried Bonnie greatly at the time, she had not taken the matter up with Eli, for he was less charitably inclined toward Jack Fitzpatrick than his late grandfather had been; he would surely have ascribed his father-in-law's actions to an undeniable weakness for rye whiskey. So, for reasons of pride, Bonnie had engaged in a series of small deceptions in order to contribute to her father's livelihood without her husband's knowing.

"Mrs. McKutchen?"

Bonnie started in the buggy seat, felt a pang at finding herself nearly three thousand miles from what had once been her very own Camelot, alone, unloved and quite nearly penniless. She forced herself to smile. "I guess I was wandering," she said. "I'm sorry."

"You looked so—bereft for a moment there," Webb replied, with gentle bluntness. "What's wrong?"

Bonnie looked away quickly, lest the tears stinging behind her eyes betray her. "I wonder," she ventured, after a moment or two, "if we could drive by my father's store—if it wouldn't be too much trouble."

"Your father's what?" Webb asked, and he sounded so puzzled that Bonnie turned to stare at him, the imminent tears forgotten.

They had come to Northridge's main street now, and Webb had stopped the buggy to let a wagon loaded down with lumber have the right of way.

"My father's mercantile," Bonnie said, feeling strangely alarmed. "It's just down this way, on the other side of the Union Hotel."

Webb averted his eyes and a muscle flexed in his jawline, but when the lumber wagon had passed, he turned from his straight course to Genoa's house and headed toward the Union Hotel without saying a word.

Just beyond that well-kept and reputable establishment stood the narrow two-story building Jack Fitzpatrick had once taken such pride in. In just a few years, it had fallen into a state of dishonor the likes of which Bonnie had never seen. The paint, once a pristine white, was now peeling, the windows were filthy and cracked, and the beautiful sign bearing her father's name had been replaced with an ugly board, sloppily lettered with the damning words COMPANY STORE. MCKUTCHEN ENTERPRISES.

"McKutchen Enterprises?!" Bonnie demanded of no one in particular and everyone in general, gathering her skirts to leap out of the buggy.

Mr. Hutcheson stopped her by again clasping her arm, just as he had earlier, when she'd nearly fallen out, staring after the hurdy-gurdy dancers. "Bonnie, wait—"

Bonnie had no more strength to fight, but she trembled with rage and the tears she'd struggled so hard to control filled her eyes and spilled down her cheeks. "That bastard— that smug, self-righteous *bastard*—he stole my store!"

Apparently unmoved by Bonnie's lapse into smelter-brat vernacular, Webb sighed. "What are you talking about?"

"That store belongs to me, that's what I'm talking about!

19

And if Eli High-and-Mighty McKutchen thinks he's going
to get away with this—"

Webb arched his eyebrows. "It would seem that he
already has," he said quietly. "Mrs. McKutchen, let me take
you to Genoa's house now. You're tired and overwrought."

Bonnie sat up straighter and dashed away her tears with
the back of one gloved hand. She'd already betrayed the true
state of her legendary marriage to Webb Hutcheson and
now people on the street were beginning to stop and peer at
her, with questions and dawning recognition in their eyes.
"Yes—please—take me to Genoa's."

Deftly, Webb turned the buggy around in a broad sweep
and drove onto a quiet, tree-lined street, where there were
few houses.

Soon they came to a familiar wrought-iron gate set into a
low brick wall. The horse's shod hooves made a clippity-
clop sound on the cobbled driveway.

The house, Bonnie was pleased to see, had not changed in
her absence. The sight of it, with its gables and white-
painted brick walls and long, graceful verandas, was a
restorative. The grounds were green with springtime and
lilacs, both purple and white, bloomed everywhere, their
delicious scent easing Bonnie's weary muscles and broken
heart.

There was a frosted oval window in the front door, etched
with the image of a ghostly swan, and even before the rig
had come to a full stop, the door flew open. As Webb
secured the brake lever and spoke soothingly to the horse,
Genoa McKutchen scampered down the limestone walk,
her skirts bunched in her hands, her face alight.

Nearly forty years of age, Genoa was seven years older
than her brother, Eli. She was not a pretty woman, for her
face was too long and too sharply featured for beauty, and
her wildly curly hair was too sparse. It was, however, the
same shade of butternut-gold as Eli's hair, and the way the
sunshine caught in it caused a keen ache to swell in Bonnie's
throat.

Genoa literally pulled her sister-in-law down from the
buggy seat and then enfolded her in a bony hug. Tears of
delight shimmered in her thinly lashed, light blue eyes.

20

"You must be tired, dear—was the trip too dreadful? I must have Martha fetch lemonade—won't you join us, Webb?"

Webb smiled, and so, however wanly, did Bonnie, remembering an observation of Eli's that his sister talked the way telegrams were written.

"I'd better get to the office," Webb demurred, tipping his round-brimmed hat in a gentlemanly fashion and turning to pry Bonnie's baggage from behind the seat of his buggy. A plump maid came out of the house with a gangly boy, and they whisked the two valises and the twine-bound box inside.

Both Genoa and Bonnie thanked Webb, and they lingered on the walk for a few moments, each with an arm around the other, as he drove back along the driveway and through the gate.

"Are you hungry?" Genoa asked gently.

Bonnie shook her head. "Could we walk for a few minutes, Genoa? Down by the pond?"

Genoa nodded, linked her arm through Bonnie's, and started toward the sparkling water, with its fringe of willow trees. Two fanciful small boats, carved and painted to resemble swans, bobbed beside a wooden dock.

The two women sat down on a shaded marble bench, the breeze ruffling their hair.

Genoa spoke first, and that after a long interval of sweet silence. "Why did you leave Eli, Bonnie?" she wanted to know. "It seems so sudden, so rash—"

Bonnie pulled off her gloves and set them aside, then removed her hat, too. As calmly as she could, she told about the cold Kiley had caught in early December, how it had developed into pneumonia, how the child had perished as Eli paced the nursery floor with him.

She did not mention that she'd been out when it happened, watching a frivolous vaudeville revue, for she wasn't ready to think of that, let alone speak of it.

"Eli blamed me for what happened," she finished bleakly, watching the lapping water at the edge of the pond. "He went to live at his club the day after the funeral, Genoa, and I have reason to believe that he took a mistress." Bonnie paused, sighed. The worst, from Genoa's point of view and

21

her own, was yet to come. "He's gone to war, Genoa. Eli has gone to Cuba, with Mr. Roosevelt."

Genoa raised one hand to her breast and her face went white. With her grandfather gone and her parents far away in Africa, Eli was all the family she had, and Bonnie's heart ached for her.

"Eli isn't a soldier!" she fretted, after a long moment of grappling with the shock.

Bonnie took Genoa's hand and squeezed it in her own. "No, he isn't. But he is very strong, Genoa, and I'm sure he'll be safe." She thought of the high-handed manner in which Eli had absorbed her father's store into McKutchen Enterprises. Her anger buoyed her, sustained her, kept her own fears and heartbreak at bay. For these reasons, Bonnie clung to that unworthy emotion and fanned it to full flame every time it threatened to die.

Soon it became a habit.

CHAPTER 2

THE *AMERICANO* WAS a big, golden man and, even with his sickness, Consolata Torrez liked to touch him. When she was not working in the cantina of her Uncle Tomás, she hovered in her room upstairs, where the patient lay tossing and muttering upon a cot too narrow for his powerful frame. With cool water and a clean cloth, she bathed his jaundiced, fevered flesh and whispered, over and over again, the holy petition of the Rosary.

Consolata left her charge only to serve wine and food in the cantina or to say novenas for the señor's recovery in the small stone chapel across the road. It was not safe to keep the stranger here, for there was still trouble in the town of Santiago de Cuba and, if the Spaniards were to find him, they would surely kill him.

Consolata sighed as she soaked the cloth in water that had grown tepid, wrung it out in strong brown hands, and continued to bathe the handsome *Americano*. Two days he had been here, two days out of his mind with *la calentura amarillo*, the yellow fever. When Uncle Tomás returned from Havana, he would be furious with his niece for sheltering this soldier. Consolata had endangered all of them, he would say, and no amount of candle lighting or saying of novenas would save them from the wrath of the Spanish should her foolishness be discovered.

23

Consolata had seen the fruits of angering the Spaniards many times during her life of seventeen years, and her sigh turned to a shudder. Edmondio, her uncle's friend, had spoken out against the invaders once, and now he had but two fingers remaining on his right hand, the disfigurement being his punishment for sedition.

Frowning, Consolata lifted one of the *Americano's* hands, strong and sun-browned, the palm uncallused. The fingers, one encircled by a golden wedding band, and the back of the hand were dusted with fine hair, just the color of brown sugar. This soft, glistening mat covered his broad, deep chest and his arms and legs as well, lying in moist sworls against his yellowed flesh like the scribbles of a child.

The man began to toss and call out again. "Bonnie," he moaned, "Bonnie?"

Consolata bit down on her lower lip for a moment, silently begging the Virgin's forgiveness for the hatred she felt toward the woman Bonita. Carefully, gently, she washed the strong-featured face once more.

"Bonnie!" the man rasped in his delirium.

Tears welled in Consolata's eyes. She rose from her knees, a slender, shapely girl with dark hair that tumbled well past her waist and a face that brought many extra customers into the cantina. Leaving the cloth and basin on the floor, she reached for the finely made suitcoat hung so carefully over the back of a chair.

In one pocket, Consolata well knew, there was a wallet, with much currency of *los Estados Unidos* inside, but she cared nothing for money. It was the folded papers that both intrigued and alarmed her, for they bore the golden man's unpronounceable name and the names of those who should be told of his illness.

She tucked the papers into the pocket of her skirt and, after smoothing a lock of brown-sugar hair from the señor's forehead, crept out of the room on bare and silent feet.

Downstairs the cantina was empty, because of the siesta, and there would be no customers to tend until the oppressive heat of the day had lifted. The street, too, was deserted, for all the villagers were resting, and the warmth settling over the valley of the Sierra Maestra was so dense as to be

24

almost tangible. Resisting her conscience, Consolata paused to gaze at the sun-sparkles dancing on the bay. Steep bluffs rose above the waters on three sides, making Santiago de Cuba virtually impregnable by sea, and on the tallest of these was the Castilla del Morro, a grim fourteenth-century fortress.

Consolata shaded her eyes to look up at the stronghold and silently cursed all men who made war.

Finally she crossed the road, the dust hot and dry beneath her naked feet, and slipped into the cool and shadowy chapel. After proper greetings to the Virgin and the Blessed Savior, Consolata sought out the padre.

Like the golden man, the padre was an *Americano*, though he spoke swift and effortless Spanish, and he was young. He had blue eyes with laughter in them and hair the color of fire, and he smiled at Consolata even though it was clear that she'd interrupted his siesta.

"Do they have siesta in Kansas?" Consolata asked guilelessly, trying to put off the moment when she would have to give up her terrible secret.

The padre, who had drawn his feet down from the top of his desk on Consolata's entrance, cleared his throat and sat up very straight in his chair, then laughed. "No, my child, they do not," he answered in faultless Spanish. "And that is their misfortune. What brings you out in the heat of the day?"

Consolata could not find words to answer, so she drew the papers from her pocket and extended them in one hand. The padre accepted the documents and read them in one rapid sweep of his eyes.

"My goodness," he said, after a few seconds of thought. "Consolata, do you know this man? Why do you have his papers?"

Consolata lowered her head. "He came to the cantina two days ago," she mumbled in reply. "He has the fever—"

The padre looked alarmed. "Where is your uncle, Consolata?"

"Uncle Tomás is away in Havana. When he comes back, he will be very angry."

The missionary muttered something in English and rose

25

decisively from his chair. Knowing that he wanted to see the stranger, Consolata led the way outside, across the hot and dusty street, into the cantina. The beautiful man from the North slept fitfully in Consolata's bed, his flesh covered with a fine sheen of sweat.

"How in the name of heaven did you get a man this size upstairs?" the priest asked, bending over the cot to touch the man's fevered forehead with the fingers of one hand.

Consolata explained that the *Americano* had roused, at least partially, after his collapse, and that she'd been able to keep him on his feet long enough to reach her bed.

"You should have come to me immediately, Consolata," the padre said, but the reprimand was a gentle one and there was understanding in his eyes. "This situation is extremely dangerous, not only for Señor McKutchen, but for you and your uncle."

Consolata could only nod.

"You've told no one that this man is here?"

"Only you," Consolata managed to answer.

"That is good. After dark, you and I will move him to my chambers in the church. In the meantime, I'll go to the American forces and ask for their help."

Consolata was very conscious of the wicked thoughts and feelings that had possessed her from the moment she'd brought the handsome stranger to her room. She'd undressed him, after all, and bathed him, and she despised this woman he cried out for, without even knowing her. She clenched her hands together and lowered her head. "Padre, have I sinned?"

Gently, the holy man from Kansas touched her tangled hair. "No, child. Kindness is never a sin."

Consolata's uncle was of a different opinion when he returned from Havana and learned of the man hidden in his niece's room. That night, when the cantina was filled with Spanish soldiers and there was no sign of either the padre or the *norteamericanos* he had promised to fetch, Tomás threatened, in his anger and fear, to turn both his sister's child and her half-conscious charge over to the enemy.

CHAPTER *3*

BONNIE ENTERED HER father's store and swiped at a fly buzzing furiously near her left ear. Smells of spoilage and general sloth assaulted her on every side, and the chiming of the little bell brought no shopkeeper to attend her.

Fighting to control the nausea that had troubled her since her arrival in Northridge nearly a week before, Bonnie raised her chin and took in the full scope of the mercantile's descent into neglect.

The stairs, leading to spacious apartments on the second floor, were littered with all manner of trash, their sturdy banister gone. The tilting bins, built directly into the walls, stood agape, and Bonnie knew without looking that weevils and possibly even mice frequented the sugar and flour they contained. A layer of grime covered the giant coffee grinder that sat on a table in the middle of the shop, and the potatoes and onions, in their bushel baskets, were not only sprouting but rotting as well. The framed photographs of smelter workers and miners, which Jack Fitzpatrick had cherished, were all but obscured by flyspecks and dirt.

The windows, scrubbed and glistening when Bonnie had last stood inside this store, were coated with mud and the excrement of birds on the outside and yellowed by cigar smoke on the inside. The shelves were dusty and the solid wooden floor was covered in sawdust and strewn with elements Bonnie preferred not to identify. She stepped up to the counter and saw that the pickle barrel was uncovered, and there was something floating inside that had never, at any point in time, been a cucumber—Bonnie closed her eyes tightly and willed her stomach to calm itself when she realized that the object was a discarded cigar, swollen and wet.

She shuddered and then started when a querulous voice behind her demanded, "Help you, missus?"

Bonnie turned, one hand to her breast, to see an unkempt little woman staring at her through a white film of cataract. "No, thank you—I mean, yes—"

"Make up your mind, honey!" the hag crowed, tugging at a clump of long hairs that sprang from her chin. "Either I can help you, or I cain't!"

Bonnie sighed. "I assume you work for McKutchen Enterprises?"

"In a roundabout way, I reckon I do. But I gets my pay from Mr. Forbes Durrant." The crone gave Bonnie's fancy Eastern clothes a suspicious once-over. "Don't get many ladies in here. Who are you, anyways?"

"Might I see Mr. Durrant, please?" Bonnie countered, drawing herself up.

"Oh, you want a dancin' job! I shoulda figured, with looks like yours, that you weren't no pot-tender's woman. Mr. Durrant's down at the Brass Eagle most times—hardly ever comes in here."

In addition to her nausea, Bonnie now had a headache. "I don't wonder," she answered, turning to leave. Now she knew, at least partially, why Genoa had skirted all her questions about the store, pretending to the vapors every time the subject had arisen.

"Fine piece like you could earn a pretty penny down at the Brass Eagle!" the shopmistress called after her, in a burst of jubilant generosity.

The bell made a tinny clatter when Bonnie slammed the door behind her. She stormed along the street, barely glancing at the Pompeii Playhouse across the way, a place that would have intrigued her greatly at any other time.

She walked rapidly down the hill, passing Earline's board-

28

inghouse and the undertaker's place, her face hot with rage. She'd known, of course, that Forbes Durrant managed the smelter works and mining operations at Northridge—he'd been plucked out of Patch Town and groomed and educated for the job by Josiah McKutchen's own hand—and she'd never thought to question the choice. Now that Bonnie had seen Forbes's neglect of the mercantile, however, she had opinions aplenty.

Reaching the bottom of the hill, Bonnie turned to the right, passing the marshal's office and the courthouse, which shared a framework building of minuscule proportions. She hurried past Webb Hutcheson's newspaper office lest he see her and come out to speak—better to meet with Forbes without delay, while her ire was running high enough to provide impetus for the confrontation.

The Brass Eagle Saloon and Ballroom stood alone on the very border of Patch Town, a huge place built of white limestone. Blue velvet curtains trimmed with gold braid and tassels showed at every window, both on the upper and lower floors, and the steps beneath the double front doors were made of rich gray marble. A beautifully wrought eagle of shimmering brass was inlaid along the front of the top step.

Furious that such a place could have been erected within a stone's throw of dismal poverty, of tar-paper huts and seeping sewers, Bonnie stomped up to the doors, tried one shining knob, and walked in. One did not knock at the door of a saloon, did one?

Inside she found herself in an entryway that could only be described as grand. There was an Aubusson rug on the floor, and a cherrywood clock stood to one side of the carpeted stairs leading up to the second story. Bonnie did not want to think about the things that probably went on up there.

To her right was a beautifully appointed saloon with a carved mahogany bar and dozens of round, felt-topped game tables. She caught glimpses of good paintings and polished mirrors. To the left was a ballroom, as large as any Bonnie had seen in New York. The orchestra platform was carpeted in plush sapphire blue, and there were brass fixtures on the walls between mirrored panels that stretched from the floor to the ceiling.

While Bonnie was still full of righteous wrath—people were all but starving within shouting distance of all this luxury, after all—she was intrigued, too. For a moment she even imagined herself wearing one of the fine gowns she had left behind in New York, whirling around this smooth oaken floor in Eli's arms. How dashing he would look in his cutaway coat and tails, his tailored trousers with their black satin strips down each crisply creased leg . . .

"We don't need no more dancers right now, sweetie," a female voice announced.

Bonnie turned in the doorway of the ballroom, startled. Just behind her stood one of the fancy women she had seen at the train depot the day of her arrival—the red-haired one who had been flirting with Webb.

Bonnie squared her shoulders. "I am not here to inquire after—after a position. My name is Mrs. Eli McKutchen and I want to see Mr. Durrant immediately."

The redhead, clad in a scandalous blue satin wrapper that barely covered her thighs, looked alarmed. "Mrs.—oh my God—Forbes!" She scurried to the base of the stairs and shouted up, "Forbes!"

A squirrelly little man, who looked as though he might be some relation to the creature working at the company store, appeared on the upper landing, his face red with proprietary umbrage. "Hush up, Dottie—Mr. Durrant's working!"

Dottie gestured toward Bonnie. "This lady right here is Mrs. Eli McKutchen. Did you hear me, Walter? Mrs. *Eli McKutchen.*"

Walter paled and turned to scurry away. Moments later he was back, more composed this time, asking for the pleasure of escorting Bonnie to Mr. Durrant's private office.

So the Angel was back.

Forbes Durrant checked his reflection in the glass surface of his desk, straightened his ascot, and smiled at himself to make sure there was nothing caught in his teeth. His light brown hair was in place, his shave was fresh, and his dark eyes betrayed none of what was written in the account books spread out before him. He closed the ledgers briskly and settled back in his chair just as Bonnie swept into the room.

The years away from Northridge had been good to her. Bonnie had always been a beauty, but now she was a woman grown, and maturity gave her an intriguing refinement that appealed to Forbes. She'd developed curves that made a man's hands ache to touch them, and Forbes let his gaze run over her contours with audacious leisure, thinking of the fortune he could make if Bonnie were willing to dance the hurdy-gurdy.

Bonnie's eyes were still wide and violet and fringed with coal-black lashes, of course, but they were no longer too large for her face. Her dark hair, always tumbling down her back when she was in pinafores, just begging to be pulled or dipped into the nearest inkwell, was bound softly into a knot atop her head so that the weight of it billowed out around her ivory face in a lush, glistening fluff of muted ebony. Forbes knew that the sun could catch in those sable tresses and turn them to fire.

"Don't stand up, Forbes," she said wryly. "You were never a gentleman."

Forbes laughed even though a surge of heat passed through him, followed by a chill. "I never claimed to be a gentleman, did I, Angel?" He gestured toward a velvet upholstered chair facing his desk. "Sit down."

The scent of her—French lavender—carried across the room to further upset Forbes's reeling senses. "There is no need for me to sit, Forbes. I don't plan to stay long." Bonnie's fine breasts rose enticingly beneath the elegant ivory fabric of her dress as she drew a deep breath. "You will remove your—your merchandise from my store, Mr. Durrant. I am giving you exactly twenty-four hours to accomplish this purpose."

Forbes reached out, took a cheroot from a crystal box on his desk, lit it with a wooden match. "What happens, Angel, if I don't meet your terms?"

"Please do not refer to me by that name again." Bonnie squared her shoulders and lifted her chin. "You will meet my terms, Mr. Durrant, because that store is legally mine and we both know it."

Forbes was wondering what would make the wife of one of the richest men in America want to reclaim a shoddy, rundown storefront. Could it be that all was not bliss in the fabled marriage between the princess of Patch Town and the well-bred industrialist?

Forbes felt a rush of satisfaction. So many things weren't what they seemed, and if Bonnie McKutchen was in some kind of disgrace, her predicament could easily be turned to profit. No doubt, her tastes were on a level far beyond what the income from one paltry general store could meet.

He sighed. This would have been a good time to stand up, but his involuntary response to the reality that was Bonnie McKutchen rendered the act inadvisable. "Upon your marriage—by the way, belated congratulations on your dramatic social advancement—the store became Eli's. As did everything else you owned, Angel—pitiably little as it was."

Bonnie's cheeks flushed a lovely apricot pink. God, Forbes thought, Eli McKutchen is a lucky son of a bitch.

"I will not dignify that remark with a reply, Forbes Durrant," Bonnie said coldly.

Forbes chuckled, then sobered. He'd heard all the gossip about Bonnie over the years, and he knew that her little boy had died during the winter just past. That was an experience that would have broken a lot of women, but Bonnie still had her spirit and he admired her for that. Besides, there was always the possibility that she had Eli's blessing in coming back to Northridge, and he couldn't risk offending the lady's powerful and probably indulgent husband. "The store is yours, of course," he said calmly, though his mind raced through a sheaf of possibilities.

If Bonnie wasn't here with Eli's blessing, if he'd thrown her out, for instance, or if she'd flown the coop of her own accord, her husband might not be inclined to protect her. It went without saying that she would fail in business—she hadn't the experience required for any sort of enterprise. When that happened, the Angel might just be open to other possibilities, like dancing downstairs in the Brass Eagle Ballroom.

As though reading his mind, Bonnie gave Forbes a look that would have seared an elephant's hide and swept out of the office, leaving him to memories he'd been trying to hold off throughout the interview.

Since it was safe to stand up, he did so, and strode to the liquor cabinet, where he poured himself a double shot of brandy. The potion didn't wash from his mind the pictures of Bonnie as a bride, any more than it had the night he'd irrevocably lost her to Eli McKutchen.

Forbes smiled, despite the lingering pain. Bonnie was here and McKutchen was elsewhere. If his employer and unknowing benefactor had been in Northridge, he would have been among the first to know it—and maybe the loss wasn't irrevocable after all.

He sat down at his desk again and began making a list of the colors that would look best on Bonnie. He'd already estimated her measurements with a practiced eye.

When the pertinent statistics had been recorded, he cupped his hands behind his head and settled back in his chair. He had only to see that the Angel's little venture failed. That was all.

In the meantime, he'd have the gowns made up and delivered to the Brass Eagle.

CHAPTER 4

Bonnie was gone.

Eli had had more than a month to absorb that fact, but the house that had once been so full of her laughter and her quick temper and her outrageous political opinions was a constant and merciless reminder. He was sick and he needed his wife and she was gone.

Seth Callahan, Eli's lawyer and closest friend, had given his assessment of the situation often enough: It was Eli's own fault that Bonnie had taken flight like a scared bird. Hadn't he virtually deserted her after Kiley's death? Hadn't there been that string of nameless, faceless women to whom he'd turned for a comfort that eluded him even now? Hadn't he gone off to war with no real thought for Bonnie's feelings? Eli knew now that he'd been throwing an emotional temper tantrum from the moment his son's life had slipped away.

He closed his eyes tightly against the memory, his hands clasping the arms of the invalid's chair he'd been confined to even after his return to the States. Before that, he'd lain in a Cuban hospital for nearly six months.

Kiley filled Eli's mind, despite efforts to keep him out, and he could feel the warmth and substance of the baby against his shoulder again, feel the gentle trembling that had preceded the child's death.

Eli opened his eyes again, to replace the images with the ordinary accoutrements of a sickroom—the basin, the carafe containing the icy water he expected to crave for the rest of his natural life, the books and the newspapers and the chair where that blasted nurse sat, twenty-six hours a day, just staring at him.

The doctors said that yellow fever, when one was fortunate enough to survive it, that is, required a long period of recovery. There was one consolation: Eli would now have a lifelong immunity to the disease.

Bonnie crept into his mind. Why didn't she come back? She should be here with her husband, not three thousand miles away in Northridge, doing whatever she was doing.

Eli sighed and wheeled himself over to the small desk between the windows. He reached out for the latest chatty and innocuous letter from Genoa and read it again, troubled by the sense of some unspoken inference that all was not well where Bonnie was concerned.

He crumpled the letter in one hand. He was imagining things, that was all. He missed Bonnie, he loved her more deeply than he had ever realized, but he was willing to permit her this episode of independence if that was what she needed. On the other hand, if she was up to some foolishness . . .

Eli tossed the crumpled letter across the room and it bounced off a photograph of Bonnie, Kiley and himself, taken at Fire Island the summer before the boy's death. For a moment, his grief returned full force, so intense that Eli was dazed by it.

He was very glad when the door suddenly opened to admit a blustering Seth Callahan.

A small man with red muttonchop whiskers and gold-rimmed spectacles, Seth was overdressed for the weather as usual. Under one arm, he carried a thick packet, wrapped in paper and bound with twine.

"Good day," he said, with a slight nod. Seth was always proper.

Eli was not. "How the hell can you go around in a starched collar in weather like this?" he demanded testily.

Seth sputtered and fussed with the packet. "Never mind that. It is imperative that you read these papers!"

35

Frowning, Eli unwound the twine and tore away the wrapping. Inside, he found bundles of letters from citizens of Northridge and smiled. Ah, yes, the busybody contingent. He could depend on them for up-to-the-minute information.

The members of the Friday Afternoon Community Improvement Club had written a twelve-page discourse concerning Bonnie's behavior, all twenty-seven of them signing with a flourish. Indeed, in form if not content, the document was reminiscent of the Declaration of Independence.

The entire diatribe boiled down to one disturbing statement: It was a scandal for a woman in Bonnie McKutchen's condition to live alone over a storefront and entertain unmarried callers such as Webb Hutcheson and Forbes Durrant.

The paper rattled a little as Eli set it aside on the bureau. "What the devil do they mean by 'her condition'?" he demanded of a flushed and nervous Seth, who was now stationed a full six feet away and had the air of a man about to run for his life.

"Read the others," Seth urged.

One by one, Eli read the remaining letters. Many didn't concern Bonnie at all; they were from men who worked in the smelter yard and had solid complaints about their wages and working conditions. Others only touched on Bonnie, but the phrase "her condition" turned up over and over again.

And then there was the letter from the doctor. He stated outright that his fee for attending Mrs. McKutchen was fifty-six dollars, which should be remitted in total before her delivery.

What Eli had not allowed himself to suspect before was distilled to brutal fact by the doctor's words. Bonnie was pregnant.

How could she stay in Northridge when she knew what another baby would have meant to the both of them? There was only one explanation and Eli wasn't sure he could bear it.

The child wasn't his.

He gave a cry of rage and pain and moved to fling all the

papers off his lap, all except a fat envelope that probably contained more bad news.

"It appears we've made a mistake," Seth put in hoarsely, "in appointing Mr. Durrant to manage the McKutchen holdings at Northridge. According to my inquiries, he's been abusing his authority for some considerable time and the workers despise him."

Eli had a blinding headache, and his stomach roiled. "Do you think I give a damn what that pissant does?"

"Eli, you read the workers' letters. There's a strike brewing, for God's sake!"

"I don't care."

"Eli—"

"I want to divorce my wife, Seth," Eli said, meeting his lawyer's eyes.

Seth flushed and lowered his own gaze to the envelope that remained in Eli's lap. "I'm afraid that won't be necessary," he said.

"What?"

Prying at his high collar with three fingers, Seth edged toward the bedroom door, opened it, stood poised in the chasm. "Mrs. McKutchen," he said, "has already divorced you."

At first Eli was quiet, too stunned to react; he simply watched Seth Callahan's Adam's apple try to fight its way free of that constricting collar. But then, as he thought of Bonnie's baby and traced it back to conception, he gave a bellow of rage and proceeded to clear every surface in the room. He overturned most of the furniture, shattered every lamp, reduced the basin and pitcher to shards of glass, destroyed the mirrors and even the windows.

Only the picture taken on Fire Island, before the end of the world, remained unharmed.

In early October, Eli sailed for Europe. He visited England and Scotland, France and Italy, Germany and Belgium, lingering as long as he could bear to in each country, recuperating, gathering strength with every passing day.

For over a year, cables from Seth kept him apprised of the havoc Forbes Durrant was wreaking with the holdings at Northridge and, in the spring of 1900, Eli could no longer ignore his responsibilities toward his grandfather's company.

He dreaded seeing Bonnie again, at the same time craving the sight of her, and for all this he decided that, since she was no longer his wife, she would be easy to ignore.

When Eli's ship docked in New York, Seth was waiting with evidence to the contrary.

CHAPTER 5

"Where the hell is Forbes?" hissed Dottie Thurston, standing beside Bonnie on the marble steps of the Brass Eagle Saloon and Ballroom. A train whistle keened in the distance; the four-fifteen was rounding the last bend in the river, drawing nearer and nearer.

For some reason, the sound compounded the wire-tight tension that charged the spring air. Bonnie kept her eyes on Menelda Sneeder and her hatchet brigade and tried to smile companionably. "I don't know," she answered, barely moving her lips, "but somebody had better find him. And fast."

Dottie turned and, with a quick gesture, dispatched Eleanor on the mission. According to Bonnie's hasty calculations, that left roughly a dozen be-rouged and perfumed troops to face the petulant multitudes gathered behind Menelda.

"Step out of our way," challenged Mrs. Sneeder, member in good standing of the Friday Afternoon Community Improvement Club, her eyes sweeping over Bonnie's green silk dress and lingering, for one contemptuous moment, at her feather-fluffed bosom.

Bonnie stood her ground and smiled harder. "Let's be reasonable, Menelda—"

"Don't you dare address me by my Christian name, you—you shameless floozy!"

Bonnie's patience was ebbing fast. She was vaguely conscious of a growing crowd of spectators, men and boys who would not lift a hand to prevent a full-blown conflagration, should matters come to that. Perspiration prickled between her breasts and on the palms of her hands—Lord in heaven, wasn't it hot for an April afternoon? She drew a deep breath and began again.

"Is it 'Christian,' Mrs. Sneeder, to threaten innocent people—"

The word "innocent" had been a foolish choice but, by the time Bonnie realized her folly, it was too late. The mob of corset-bound, ax-bearing townswomen was stirred to a new level of vexation.

"Innocent?!" shrilled Miss Lavinia Cassidy, who worked in the public library three afternoons a week and was known to cherish hopes that a certain handsome smelter worker would give up his rascal's life to court and marry her.

Bonnie might have argued that she and several of the other women congregated behind her only danced with men, declining to do anything more, but she knew that the effort would be futile. These angry wives, mothers and sweethearts believed the worst, and nothing short of a miracle would change that fact.

"It is against the law," Bonnie went on, stalling for time now, praying that Eleanor would find Forbes in time to avert total disaster, "to destroy private property. Now if you ladies would just go home where you belong—"

The calico crowd buzzed like a swarm of bees and Bonnie closed her eyes for a moment, silently berating herself for once again choosing exactly the wrong words.

Menelda Sneeder lifted her hatchet high in the air, rousing her followers to a fever pitch of righteous wrath with the motion. "This place of iniquity and sin shall not stand! Step aside, Bonnie McKutchen, you and the rest of those whores!"

That did it. Bonnie lunged off the step, a crimson fog shimmering before her eyes. At her lead, Dottie and the others waded in and the resulting melee delighted the cheering spectators.

Bonnie went directly for Menelda, wrenching the hatchet from the woman's hands with a strength she hadn't dreamed she possessed. After dropping the weapon to the muddy ground, she gave Mrs. Sneeder a push that sent her stumbling backward to land bustle first in the muck.

With murder in her eyes, Menelda shrieked a war cry and struggled to her feet, her legs tangling in her voluminous skirts. She knotted muddy hands in Bonnie's hair and pulled hard.

Bonnie brought one fist up under Menelda's chin, breaking the woman's painful hold on her scalp, and was about to follow through with a right cross when an arm as hard as a horseshoe suddenly curved around her waist and gripped her against an indurate midsection.

Startled at first, Bonnie went limp. Menelda Sneeder put out her tongue and hissed, "Now you'll suffer for your sins, you painted hussy!"

The jibe electrified Bonnie; she kicked and struggled and cursed, but the arm that restrained her was immovable, a manacle of bone and muscle. She tried to look back at her captor, but he held her so tightly that she couldn't even turn her head.

The mayhem of drab calico and brightly colored taffeta continued all around, but Menelda, for all the splotches of mud on her face and dress, held her chin high. She smirked, her beady eyes flashing with sweet triumph. "Surely God will smite you for what you've done, Bonnie McKutchen!"

The voice grated past Bonnie's ear, low and fierce and audible only to her. "God," said Eli McKutchen, "will have to wait His turn."

Every muscle in Bonnie's body tensed, suddenly and painfully. "Oh, no," she breathed.

"Oh, yes," countered her former husband.

Just then, Forbes arrived with his hired henchmen and the marshal of Northridge. The men began dispersing the mud-flinging, hair-pulling faction, but Bonnie couldn't think about that, couldn't think of anything but the granite-like body against which she remained hopelessly pinioned.

"Put me down," she managed to say, after some time had passed, assuming a pretense of dignity. "This instant."

Bonnie was not released, but the arm loosened enough

41

that she could turn her head—it took a moment more to gather the courage for that—and look up into Eli's face.

"If it isn't the mayor of Northridge," he drawled ominously, apparently unconcerned that half the population of the town was gathered in that boggy, dung-dappled street, looking on. "Who would have thought that august office would be held by a whore?"

All Bonnie's terror or, at least, most of it was displaced by a fury that coursed through her veins, stinging like the venom of a snake. She struggled to free her arms for attack, only to have them crushed against her sides. "I am not a whore!" she screamed.

"And *I'm* not a Presbyterian!" taunted Menelda Sneeder.

Bonnie squirmed, wild with bloodlust, making a trapped animal sound in her throat, but she could not free herself.

At that moment a man wearing thick spectacles and carrying a battered valise appeared in front of Bonnie, a savior with red muttonchop whiskers and very kind eyes. Bonnie recognized Seth Callahan, the family attorney. "Put Mrs. McKutchen down, Eli," he said reasonably. "You are making a scene."

Eli's arm tightened reflexively, then relaxed. Released so abruptly, from a position that had not allowed her feet to touch the ground, Bonnie lost her balance and tumbled to her knees.

Outraged, terrified and humiliated, all of a piece, Bonnie filled both hands with mud and bounded back to her feet, hurling the sodden dirt at Eli as she rose. In the second of grace granted her by his reaction, one of seething shock, Bonnie lifted her ruined skirts and broke into a dead run.

Eli caught her easily, again with that flint-hard arm, then turned toward the Brass Eagle, carrying her against his hip the way a schoolboy would carry books.

"Let me go!" Bonnie wailed, in fear for her very life.

Eli strode inside the Brass Eagle, pausing at the base of the stairs, and neither Bonnie's cries of protest nor her struggles slowed his pace by one whit. He started up the stairway, Seth hurrying to keep up and adding his protests to Bonnie's.

The cabbage-rose pattern on the carpeted steps seemed to

42

rush past Bonnie's eyes like pictures in a nickelodeon. "Eli," she croaked, as they reached the upper floor, "I beg of you. Put me down."

Eli's dusty black boots covered the length of the hallway in mere seconds; there was no answer but for the opening of a door.

Bonnie squeezed her eyes shut, for this was Forbes's private apartment and there was no telling what sinful sight might present itself.

"Eli!" shouted Mr. Callahan, with spirit and a contrasting note of hopelessness. "I must insist that you listen to me!"

"Later," Eli retorted, and slammed the door of the suite, probably in Mr. Callahan's face. There was a resolute sound of metal meeting metal—the shooting of the bolt, no doubt.

Bonnie opened her eyes in an effort to regain her equilibrium and forestall the motion sickness that was quivering in the pit of her stomach.

Pausing only momentarily, Eli strode into a bathroom of luxurious proportions. He shifted Bonnie so that he held her upright again, as he had in the street below, then reached down to insert the plug in an enormous marble bathtub. Deftly, he opened one spigot.

Steaming hot water began to gush into the deep tub and Bonnie knew fresh terror. He meant to parboil her!

She began to flail and wriggle against her captor, her heart pounding in her throat and filling it so that she could not scream.

In the meantime, someone was hammering thunderously at the door of the suite, jarring it on its hinges.

"Eli!" bellowed Mr. Callahan's voice, regrettably far away, and the doorknob began to rattle. "Damn you, open this door or I'll get the sheriff! I'm not bluffing!"

"Neither am I!" Eli shouted back, grappling with Bonnie while he bent to add cold water to the boiling tub. "Go ahead and get the marshal—they don't have a sheriff here. Tell him I'm giving my wife, the mayor, a badly needed bath." He paused and chuckled speculatively before adding, "Care to place any bets whose side he's going to take, Seth?"

"I am not your wife!" Bonnie found the courage to point out. "For the last time, Eli, let me go!"

He tested the water with a vigorous swish of one hand. "If you say so, dear," he responded, and then he dropped Bonnie, dress, feathers, mud and all, into the tub.

The water splashed high, covering Bonnie's face, filling her nostrils. She sputtered and choked, infuriated beyond all bearing, and let loose a stream of Patch Town invective that would have given the members of the Friday Afternoon Community Improvement Club collective heart failure.

Eli sighed as the door of the suite finally gave way with a whining crash, stepped back from the side of the tub and folded his arms across his chest. His fine clothes were muddied, Bonnie was pleased to see, and behind the mockery in his golden eyes snapped a controlled rage that was better left unnoticed.

"Are you through bathing, dear?" he asked sweetly, as Forbes, Mr. Callahan and the marshal all wedged themselves into the doorway like vaudevillians in a comedy revue, their mouths agape.

Bonnie's dignity was entirely gone. She rose from the water like an Independence Day rocket, hair and clothes dripping, makeup doubtless running down her face. She didn't care how she looked; at that moment, her one aim in life was to tear Eli McKutchen apart with her own hands.

Her voice, as she moved toward him, was a low, throaty monotone. "You self-righteous, overbearing, *store-stealing—*"

Eli stood still, unafraid, unmoved, a maddening grin curving his perfect lips, but the three rescuers backed out of the doorway, their eyes wide.

After one quick glance about, Bonnie selected the toilet brush as a weapon and it seemed to fly into her hands. Holding it baseball-bat fashion, she took a hard swing and struck Eli's chest a bristly blow. The slight spray of water didn't bother Bonnie, considering the sodden condition of her person, but it made Eli's jaw tense and intensified the quiet ferocity in his eyes. With one swift motion of his hand, he wrenched the brush from her grip and flung it aside, sending it clattering against the wall.

There was a short, ominous silence as Bonnie and Eli stood facing each other, neither willing to give so much as an inch.

44

Forbes, apparently the bravest of the three, edged his way past Eli's massive frame. His brown eyes laughed at Bonnie briefly before fastening themselves to the face of her oppressor. "Mr. McKutchen, if there's anything I can do to straighten out this—er—matter—"

"You've done quite enough," Eli replied, his eyes never leaving Bonnie's face. "And don't delude yourself, Durrant: I won't forget the favor."

Forbes shuddered visibly, but he was never off balance for long and he quickly recovered his obnoxious aplomb. "You seem to misunderstand the situation, Eli—Mr. McKutchen. Bonnie—Mrs. McKutchen—is a hurdy-gurdy dancer, not a—a—"

"Whore?" Eli supplied, with biting clarity.

Lacking the toilet brush, Bonnie had no recourse but to kick her estranged husband soundly in one shin. He gave a howl of pain and during that precious moment of distraction, Bonnie dodged past him, past Forbes, and fled for her life.

She ran into the hall, bathwater dripping from her hair and her clothes, her shoes sodden and squishy, and down the rear stairs, through the kitchen. There, with the cooks and serving girls staring at her in utter amazement, she paused to catch her breath and think.

She couldn't very well go dashing through the streets in this state of disarray, and yet every moment she tarried in the Brass Eagle increased her dire risk. The thought of facing Eli McKutchen again, before he'd had time to recover his reason, was a horrifying one.

Bonnie stood on the far side of a worktable, trembling with cold and fear and fury, trying to think. If she could just reach the newspaper office and Webb Hutcheson, she would be assured of safety.

"If Forbes or—or anyone else comes in here," Bonnie whispered, through chattering teeth, "you haven't seen me. Do you understand that? You haven't seen me!"

With that, spurred by a clatter in the fancy dining room beyond, Bonnie dashed out the rear door and cautiously rounded the building. Menelda and her battalion of do-gooders were gone; there was only the usual late afternoon traffic in the streets.

Huddled near a corner of the Brass Eagle Saloon, Bonnie drew a deep breath and scurried down the street toward the humble offices of the *Northridge News.*

"I hope you know," Seth Callahan blustered coldly, "that you have made a complete fool of yourself."

"I'll drink to that," chimed Genoa, lifting her wineglass in the air and her wry eyes to Eli's face.

Eli looked around the once-familiar parlor, feeling crowded by the army of Dresden figurines, the false mantels, the portieres and plants, the displays of wax fruit and the tasseled curtains. He suppressed an awesome urge to spread his arms in an attempt to clear some space and give himself room to breathe. "Why didn't you tell me that Bonnie was—dancing—at the Brass Eagle?"

Obviously delighted by the whole situation, Genoa took a leisurely sip of her wine and savored it properly before answering. "You didn't ask."

Eli's hand tightened around a snifter of brandy, all but crushing the delicate crystal to shards. "As my sister, it was your duty—"

Genoa shot out of her Morris chair, her pale blue eyes flashing, her narrow face red with incensed conviction. "Don't you dare to talk to me about duty, Eli McKutchen. You suffered a tragedy when you lost Kiley, but your actions after the fact were hardly admirable, were they? You shut Bonnie away when you might have given her comfort, as was your *duty,* and then you went off to a silly war, where you had no business being! And if that wasn't enough, you proceeded to carouse through Europe, like the prodigal son, completely ignoring your responsibilities not only to Bonnie, but to our grandfather's company!"

"Here, here," muttered Seth, hefting his glass, apparently emboldened by its contents. His eyes glittered with admiration as he watched Genoa.

Eli was taken aback—much of what Genoa said was true, though he wasn't willing to admit that yet—and by the time he'd thought of a response, the petulant wail of a child filled the cluttered parlor.

The prettiest nanny Eli had ever seen stood in the tasseled and beaded doorway, a squalling toddler riding on one hip, addressing Genoa: "Pardon, Miss McKutchen, but little Rose Marie is some fretful and I wondered if she shouldn't start her nap early, even though the schedule says—"

Eli stared at the child, setting his glass down among a half dozen china shepherdesses, and she stared back with eyes exactly the same color as his own, falling silent in mid-wail. Her hair, like his, like Genoa's, was wheat-brown with a mingling of gold, and her identity fell on his spirit with the weight of a house. "My God—Bonnie's child?"

Out of the corner of one eye, Eli saw his sister nod. "Yes."

"I'd forgotten—" His voice fell away. It was a lie; he'd never forgotten, not for a moment. He'd been torn apart by the knowledge that Bonnie had borne another man's child, and he'd never dared hope—

"A startling resemblance," observed Seth. "Uncanny, isn't it, Miss McKutchen?"

"Absolutely striking," agreed Genoa, in tones of saucy gentleness, before speaking crisply to the nanny. "You may give Rose Marie her nap now, Katie, but let's not let Mrs. McKutchen find out. You know how she is about the schedule."

Katie, a lovely, dark-haired imp with a look of dignity about her that ran completely counter to her station in life, nodded and smiled, then turned to go.

Both Eli and the child protested at the same moment, the child with a cry, Eli with a quick "Wait—"

Genoa touched his arm. "Later, Eli," she said softly. "There will be plenty of time for you and Rose to get to know each other."

Reeling with a curious mixture of wrath and pure delight, Eli relented and sank into an overstuffed chair, reaching blindly for his brandy snifter. Seth had to find it and put it in his hand, and, after a good look at his employer's face, he refilled it in the bargain.

Webb was away from the newspaper office, as luck would have it, and Bonnie couldn't wait for him. She finally waylaid a goggle-eyed messenger boy passing on the street and sent him to the Brass Eagle, with a hastily scrawled note for Forbes.

Instead of sending a reply, Forbes came in person, his

brazen brown eyes humorously sympathetic as they took in Bonnie's ruined clothes, smudged face and tangled hair. "Oh, Angel, you've got us all into a mess this time, haven't you?"

Bonnie swallowed, cold and miserable and deeply shamed. Forbes's opinion didn't matter but, if she were to be honest with herself, she had to admit that Eli's did. "I suppose I'm fired," she said.

Forbes paused long enough to draw a cheroot from the inside pocket of his coat and, leaning against the jamb of Webb's open door, he struck a wooden match against the sole of his boot. "Eli McKutchen is the one man I can't afford to tangle with," he said, with uncommon forthrightness. "On the other hand, nobody draws business into the Brass Eagle the way you do. And you're not legally his wife, are you?"

Bonnie had divorced Eli rather impulsively, angry because he'd gone off to war and because her father's store had fallen into such ruin. She shook off the regret that possessed her whenever she thought of her action and, lifting her smudged and rouge-stained chin, announced, "Eli McKutchen has no legal hold over me, Forbes. None whatsoever."

"He has a few over me, Angel," Forbes reflected, his eyes in the far distance now. "He has a few over me."

"He isn't going to approve of your management of the smelter," Bonnie agreed. "It seems to me that since we're both in trouble, we might as well stand our ground."

Forbes chuckled. He was a rounder and every other sort of scoundrel, but Bonnie had to admire his spirit. "So you admit that you're in trouble, too, do you?"

Bonnie lowered her head for a moment, and then nodded. She thought of her daughter and her store and her position as mayor, joke that it was, and felt a new determination surge through her. "I'm not going to let Eli bully me, Forbes. I have reasons to fight and, by God, fight I will!"

As if in wonder, Forbes shook his head. "Are you forgetting how powerful Eli is, Bonnie? We're not dealing with a spurned pot-tender or a lumberjack, you know—your ex-husband is a man the likes of Vanderbilt, Rockefeller and Astor."

"I've met them all," Bonnie sniffed and in that moment, if she was forgetting anything, it was the ridiculous state of her appearance, "and they're only men."

Forbes's perfect teeth were bared in an insufferable grin. "Well, Angel, if you're game, so am I. We'll beard the lion and all that."

Despite everything, Bonnie laughed. With the demeanor of a queen, she swept past Forbes and started walking down the street toward the Brass Eagle Saloon and Ballroom. "Why didn't you tell me you had a bathtub like that?" she demanded. "My word, it's so luxurious as to be sinful, Forbes Durrant!"

Forbes looked unaccountably happy as he strode along beside her. "That's the way I like my sin, Bonnie-my-sweet. Luxurious."

A shiver crept up Bonnie's spine, a shiver that had no connection whatsoever to her wet clothing. It was all very well to whistle in the dark, but the truth was just as Forbes had pointed out—Eli *was* one of the most powerful men in America. If his temper didn't cool and his natural good nature failed to come to the fore, he might well crush not only Forbes, but Bonnie herself.

Dottie Thurston assessed Bonnie's fresh dress and neat, if somewhat dewy, coiffure with slightly envious eyes. "Forbes never lets nobody else use his bathtub," she complained in an undertone, as the ballroom began to fill with token-bearing miners, smelter workers and sheep farmers. Soon the orchestra would play, the dancing would begin, and Bonnie found herself dreading the evening as never before.

"It was something of an emergency, you know," Bonnie whispered back, her eyes anxiously scanning the rough crowd of men awaiting the first strains of music and the feminine contact the dancing would allow them.

"Don't know why you'd want to leave a man like that anyhow," Dottie fussed, her hands on her round hips now, her eyes, like Bonnie's, moving over the night's crop of dancing partners. "Eli McKutchen's good-lookin' enough to stop a girl's heart, and he's got all that money, besides."

Blessedly the music began before Bonnie had to give a reply. She danced first with Till Reemer, who worked as a foreman at the smelter, and then with Jim Sneeder, Menelda's husband. Jim had a habit of wrenching his partner a little too close during a waltz—and all the dances were waltzes—so Bonnie kept her arms stiff to hold him at his distance.

"Heard Menelda got a little out of hand today," he commented, trying all the while to draw his dancing partner nearer.

"Yes," answered Bonnie, remembering the upraised hatchet and the hatred—perhaps not entirely unjustified— flashing in Menelda's eyes. "We did have words."

"I keep tellin' that woman to stay home and mind her knittin', but she don't listen."

"Indeed," Bonnie agreed, absentmindedly, her eyes sweeping the room over Jim Sneeder's shoulder.

At last the music stopped and Bonnie turned gratefully away, only to come face to shirtfront with Eli McKutchen. Her gaze slipped from the tasteful diamond stud on his tie to his squared, almost imperceptibly cleft chin, to his golden eyes.

Taking one of her hands firmly in his own, he turned it palm up, then dropped so many tokens into the hollow that the small brass chips overflowed, falling to the floor in a tinkling cascade.

Bonnie looked up into Eli's impassive face and was possessed of the unnerving realization that she was in even more trouble than she had admitted to Forbes earlier, on the way back from the newspaper office. She was still in love, and with a man who could easily destroy her.

The music began to play and Bonnie, heedless of the tokens scattered over the ballroom floor, allowed herself to be taken into Eli's arms. As they danced, she watched his face for any expression that might indicate his mood, but his features were unreadable, neither stony nor tender.

For the rest of the evening, Bonnie's every dance was Eli's, and no one dared to complain.

At midnight the music stopped and the magic ended. Eli draped Bonnie's wrap over her shoulders—a light blue cape

50

left over from more prosperous days in New York—and ushered her most forcefully down the front steps of the Brass Eagle Saloon and Ballroom and into a carriage waiting in the road.

"You," he said, as the elegant vehicle lurched away into the night, "have some explaining to do."

CHAPTER 6

BONNIE MCKUTCHEN WASN'T about to explain anything. She sat stiffly in a corner of the lushly upholstered carriage seat, her wrap drawn close against the chill of an April evening. Whatever spell Eli had woven earlier, inside the Ballroom, had evaporated.

With a raspy sigh of irritation, Eli sat back in his own seat, facing Bonnie's, and folded his arms across his chest. His face, turned toward the window, was draped in shadow, but Bonnie could make out the tense line of his jaw. "My daughter," he said, after several moments had passed. "Rose Marie is my daughter."

Bonnie remembered her humiliation in the street that day, her ignoble bath in Forbes's suite, her sodden flight to Webb Hutcheson's newspaper office. And beneath these remembrances were others, those of the hurt she'd suffered in New York when Eli had blamed her for Kiley's death. He had betrayed her, scorned her, in fact, and ultimately deserted her. "If you say so, darling," she said sweetly.

She felt Eli's glare, rather than saw it, and a dangerous silence fell between them. The carriage groped and slid over a road made muddy by yesterday's rain.

Bonnie broke the impasse by tartly demanding, "Where are we going?"

Eli took his time in answering; it was his nature to be downright cussed when he chose. Finally, after stretching vastly and making a startling sound similar to a yawn to accompany the motion, he replied, "Why, to your store, of course. It is true, is it not, that you and my daughter live in the apartment upstairs?"

Bonnie was simmering at the emphasis he'd put on the phrase "my daughter"—of course Rose Marie was Eli's child as much as her own! How galling that he had so obviously expected circumstances to be otherwise. "Rose and I do indeed live above the store," she said with quiet dignity. "Do you plan to try and steal it again?"

"From what information I've been able to gather, the place isn't worth stealing," came the immediate response, carrying a soft and wounding bite.

Bonnie felt the attack sorely, though she did her best not to give any outer indication of that. Had the mercantile flourished as she had hoped, what a sweet triumph it would have been, but in truth the enterprise was a dismal failure, just as Forbes and even Genoa had predicted it would be. Only sheer stubbornness made Bonnie open the doors for business each morning, and it was with the deepest regret that she closed them each afternoon in order to spend the evening dancing at the Brass Eagle Ballroom. Too proud to accept help from Genoa or demand it from Eli, Bonnie needed the money she earned by dancing to survive. "I had no idea," she countered coldly, "that thieves were so choosy."

The carriage was moving up the steep incline leading to the main part of town. "I didn't steal your store, Bonnie."

Bonnie felt color rise into her cheeks. "Perhaps not personally," she said and, though she spoke quietly, there was a challenge in her words.

"Not personally, not impersonally. In fact, I don't know what the hell you're talking about!"

"I'll tell you what I'm talking about, Mr. McKutchen. When I returned to Northridge two years ago, I found my father's mercantile in a disgusting state. Furthermore, there was a sign over the door that read "Company Store, McKutchen Enterprises!"'"

Light from a street lantern spilled muted gold over Eli's

face. He stiffened in his seat, in order to keep from being thrust, by gravity, into Bonnie's. "You sound as though your dear and much revered father had built that store himself. If you will remember, it was a gift to him from my grandfather —a sort of reverse dowry, if you will."

"McKutchen Enterprises giveth and McKutchen Enterprises taketh away—is that what you're saying?"

Just then the carriage reached level ground and swung into a right turn, heading toward Bonnie's store, where Katie would be waiting with Rose Marie.

"Good God, woman, you are impossible to talk to!" Eli thundered. "That isn't what I am saying at all! I'm merely trying to understand your attachment to the place—"

"You could never understand," whispered Bonnie with proud despair.

The carriage drawing to a halt, Genoa's driver and general handyman got down from the box and opened the door. Bonnie stepped out with his help, comforted by the width and substance of her store, standing so sturdily in the kindness of night, and by the bright light beaming from the upstairs windows.

She would look in on a sleeping Rose Marie, exchange a few words with Katie, have a cup of tea. This dreadful day, for all its shocks and upsets and humiliations, was blessedly over.

Except that Eli was looming in the opening of the carriage door, his voice quiet. "Bonnie—"

She turned with great effort to face him, glad that the darkness would hide the pain in her bearing, just as it hid the imperfections of her mercantile. "Please go," she said, her voice barely above a whisper.

Eli hesitated, then withdrew to the shadowy interior of his sister's elegant carriage and departed.

Bonnie rounded the side of the plain frame building and climbed the outside stairs, letting herself into the kitchen. Katie, poring over a thick book, looked up at the sight of her employer and smiled. "You look all done in, ma'am. I've set tea on to brew, but I think maybe you should just go straight to bed."

Bonnie hung her wrap rather carelessly over a peg beside

the door, thinking of the first time she'd seen Katie Ryan. It had been aboard a train that long-ago day; Katie had been traveling with her family of vaudevillians to perform at the Pompeii Playhouse. When her parents were ready to move on, Katie refused to go with them and somehow prevailed against their authority, turning up at Genoa's door to ask for a position.

Genoa hired the girl as a companion, taking an instant liking to her just as Bonnie had, and at Rose Marie's birth Katie became the child's nurse. Half her salary was still paid by Genoa, a circumstance that nettled Bonnie's pride but could not, for the time being, be avoided.

Bonnie poured herself a cup of tea and ignored Katie's concern. "How is Rose? Did she eat her supper?"

Katie looked a bit guilty, it seemed to Bonnie. "She's fine, ma'am, and she did eat."

"And?"

Katie lowered her beautiful green eyes for a moment. "It was her papa that fed her, ma'am," she admitted in a rush. "Rose took to him right away, and I didn't see how I could say anything—"

Bonnie sat down at the kitchen table, curving her hands around the teacup for warmth. "It's all right, Katie," she said gently. "I suppose it was inevitable that Eli would see Rose and—and recognize her."

"He didn't know about her at all, did he?" Katie asked, her eyes looking off into the distance, her mouth quirking at one corner in just the merest smile.

Bonnie knew that the sight of Eli feeding a year-old child must have been a humorous one, given his size and inexperience, but she felt a twinge of envy, rather than amusement. "He knew," she said in reply, not adding that Eli had assumed Rose to be another man's child.

Katie was back in the here and now, and slightly flushed. Despite her stage experience, she was not an outgoing or daring person, and she probably regretted mentioning Eli at all. She closed her book and stood up. "I'll be off to bed now," she said. "Miss Rose will be up early, I'm sure."

Bonnie put her teacup in the deep iron sink and went to the windows overlooking the street to turn down the wick in one of the two lamps that burned. A half dozen rough-looking men were passing below; even in the darkness, Bonnie could see that they were reeling drunkenly. Their words were muffled, of course, but they held a petulant note.

A chill unrelated to her own problems trembled its way up and down Bonnie's spine. The men were smelter workers, she knew, and she could guess at their conversation: they were unhappy about their wages, their working conditions and their hours. Only weeks after Bonnie's return to Northridge, there had been talk of a strike and scattered incidents of violence, but Forbes, in his capacity as manager of the McKutchen Smelter Works, had been able to appease the workmen temporarily. Now, rumor had it that there were union organizers in Northridge again, conducting secret meetings.

Perhaps, given the state of his grandfather's company, Eli couldn't have chosen a better time to return to Northridge.

Bonnie took up the unextinguished lamp and made her way to the rear bedroom she shared with Rose Marie, considering the terrors that a full-fledged conflict between the different factions could incite, and realizing that, on the contrary, Eli could not have chosen a *worse* time to come back.

Holding the flickering kerosene lamp with care, Bonnie paused to admire her sleeping daughter. Curled up in her crib, Rose Marie was a cherub with wheat-gold hair and pink cheeks, and just the sight of her somehow made every annoyance unimportant. She set the lamp down on her bedside table, bending to kiss Rose Marie's forehead and tuck her blankets securely into place.

Bonnie turned from the crib with reluctance, went to the bureau to pour water into the basin and wash the paint from her face. That night she couldn't bring herself to meet her own gaze in the small mirror affixed to the wall above the bureau until she'd taken the fancy clips from her hair and brushed away the flamboyant coiffure.

Her gown was cut low against her bosom and Bonnie drew in her breath at the sight of herself. She had always been able to justify dancing the hurdy-gurdy, but that night her doubts were more difficult to settle. She cast another look back at the slumbering Rose Marie and for the first time it occurred to her that, knowing the child was his, Eli might well lay claim to her. He might try to take Rose away.

Of all the dangers that confronted Bonnie, this newest was by far the most frightening. Trembling, she struggled out of her dancing gown and put on a long flannel nightdress. She kissed Rose again and got into bed. As she lay there thinking of all the things Eli could offer their child that she could not, Bonnie's fear deepened until it was nearly unbearable, and the heavy quilt that covered her could not keep her warm.

Eli had not slept well, for there were too many apparitions haunting Genoa's house, and not all of them were specters of the departed. He heard and saw his parents everywhere, remembered the pain of losing them. He was thirty-three years old and still bewildered that his mother and father had left their children and gone off to Africa, seeking souls to save.

But the ghost Eli found most difficult to confront was Bonnie's. She was everywhere in the house, that younger, laughing, less confident Bonnie, the girl who had been his bride.

Needing space, needing air, Eli left the house as soon as he'd washed and dressed. He stood beside the pond, flinging small stones into the water. It was as though his grandfather stood with him, so he had not really escaped, but Josiah's presence was one he could deal with.

His mind slid back to the day his parents had announced their intention to leave "the things of this world" behind. He'd stood just here that day, ten years old and stricken to the core of his soul, and Josiah had joined him.

"It's a sad day for the McKutchens, boy," Josiah had said. "You go ahead and cry if that's what you feel like doing. I know I feel like it."

The young Eli had held himself in iron control. "These rocks won't skip," he'd said. "They just sink to the bottom."

Josiah had bent and searched until he found a flat stone; when he'd offered that, the sobs Eli had been holding back

57

had broken free and the boy had flung himself into his grandfather's arms.

Eli wrenched himself back to the present, missing the old man no less for the effort. He was almost relieved to see Genoa standing a few feet away, watching him with mingled love and caution in her eyes.

For a time, brother and sister stood in silence, bound in spite of longstanding differences by their affection for one another.

It was Eli who broke the stillness. "If you're going to tell me again that I should have been here, Genoa—"

As his words fell away in midsentence, Genoa approached and took her brother's hand. "You're home now, that's what's important." She drew a deep breath and sighed. "What are you going to do, Eli? About the problems at the smelter, I mean?"

Eli was tired. He'd traveled cross-country on a train, after all, and then spent half the night dancing with Bonnie and the other half mourning the loss of her. Before he could make any intelligent decisions regarding the smelter works, he would have to talk to the workmen, to Seth, and to Forbes Durrant. In addition, he would need to have a firsthand look at the plant itself and to examine the books. "Seth warned me about Durrant," Eli muttered, in place of answering Genoa's question.

"I never understood Grandfather's confidence in that man," Genoa said quietly, her gaze, like Eli's, fixed on the sparkling waters of the pond. "He said Forbes was a 'scrapper.'"

Remembering Bonnie's accusation the night before concerning her father's store, Eli felt a cold rage toward Forbes Durrant. The appropriation of that insignificant store, a place unaccountably precious to Bonnie, had surely been his doing, since Eli had had no knowledge of the matter. "Grandfather told me often enough that Forbes would bear watching. I just didn't listen. I was too busy with other things."

"You mean Grandfather didn't trust Forbes?" Genoa's eyes rounded.

Despite everything, Eli had to grin. "He told me that a mind as quick as Durrant's was as likely to be devious as loyal. I imagine a good look at the company books will show Forbes to be a most inventive man."

"I should have done something," Genoa fretted. "I knew Forbes was living beyond his means—why, no one on a salary could afford to build an edifice the likes of the Brass Eagle Saloon!"

Eli sobered again, reminded of the ballroom and the woman who danced there every evening, in exchange for dollar tokens. He was going to have to do something about that: The thought of Bonnie being held so intimately by any bastard with a buck to spend was unbearable. He'd bought up all her dances the night before, but that had been a short-term solution, to say the least. "It does seem that Grandfather's fair-haired boy has been skimming the profits, but if he's as smart as the old man thought, it's going to take some digging to prove anything."

"Surely you're going to ask him to resign!"

Eli tossed another stone into the pond. "At some point, I'll probably have to fire Durrant. Right now, I'd rather he went on believing that I'm too distracted by the situation with Bonnie to be concerned with the smelter."

Genoa's shock had not subsided. "Eli, you can't be serious! The man has probably been stealing from us for years, and there are rumors that he's been hiring toughs to drive out the union people and the workers that support them!"

Eli hurled the last stone into the pond. "The responsibility for this godawful mess is mine, Genoa, and I'll straighten it out. But it's going to take time, and it'll be done my way."

"I just hope it isn't too late," Genoa replied and, in a swish of cambric skirts, started back toward the house.

Menelda Sneeder entered the mercantile with understandable reluctance and, despite her street encounter with the woman the day before, Bonnie felt her sympathies rise. According to Forbes, it was those very leanings toward forgiveness that caused her business to teeter on the brink of bankruptcy.

"Good morning, Mrs. Sneeder." Wearing her hair in a soft, billowing topknot, clad in a modest, sprigged-calico dress instead of a low-cut silk, her face unpainted, Bonnie might not have been the same person who danced the hurdy-gurdy at the Brass Eagle and, for Menelda's sake as well as her own, she pretended this to be so.

"Good morning, Mrs. McKutchen," Menelda replied miserably, her eyes catching on Rose Marie, who was sitting in a highchair near the counter, busily chewing on her favorite rag doll. In that moment, Mrs. Sneeder's unhappy expression faded to a certain guarded wistfulness.

"Is there something I can help you with?" Bonnie asked, with a brisk kindness meant to preserve Menelda's pride.

"It's about my account," Menelda said after a long pause, and she cast anxious eyes in one direction and then the other, to make sure that no members of the Friday Afternoon Community Improvement Club were about. "I can't pay anything this week, but my little one needs some of that cough medicine—"

Bonnie took a sizable bottle of the concoction from the shelf behind the counter and extended it without a word. The fact that Menelda had appeared in the store in broad daylight, and after the events of the day before at that, was an accurate measure of her desperation.

Menelda clasped the medicine in both hands and swallowed, her eyes averted, but there was angry color in her cheeks, too. "You'd think my Jim would take care with his money—they say there's a strike coming and our Zoë is so poorly—but he spends half a day's pay to dance with a fancy woman."

The barbed words snagged Bonnie's spirit, just as they were meant to, but she couldn't very well protest Menelda's remark when there was so much truth in it. It was wrong for Jim Sneeder to spend his wages in such a way, and it was wrong for Bonnie to profit by his foolishness.

She didn't bother to say good-bye when Menelda turned and hurried out of the store.

Almost simultaneously Webb Hutcheson appeared, handsome in his neat broadcloth suit, his round-brimmed hat and manly mustache. He removed the hat and glanced at the window, taking note of Menelda's swift leave-taking, then turning his attention back to Bonnie.

"I hear I missed a major battle in front of the Brass Eagle yesterday afternoon."

"Some newspaper man you are, Webb Hutcheson," Bonnie answered, pretending to be busy aligning bottles of laudanum and vegetable tonic on a shelf.

All the same she knew that Webb was very near, probably leaning against the other side of the counter. "I've also heard that your husband is in town."

Bonnie stiffened and then went purposefully on arranging and rearranging. "My *former* husband," she corrected.

Webb gave a patient sigh. If there was one hallmark of the man's character, it was patience. "Aren't you going to write down whatever it was Menelda Sneeder just bought on credit?"

The senseless moving and clinking of bottles stopped abruptly; Bonnie's shoulders stooped and she lowered her head slightly. "I'll thank you not to meddle in my business, Mr. Hutcheson. Menelda needed that medicine and she didn't have money to pay for it."

"Of course," Webb replied evenly, "just yesterday she was ready to chop you to bits with a hatchet."

Bonnie whirled to face Webb then, her eyes full of tears. "She might have had the money if her husband hadn't danced with me."

Webb, who had indeed been leaning against the counter, straightened and backed away a step. "We've had this conversation before, Bonnie. I have sympathy for you, but you know I can't tell you that dancing the hurdy-gurdy is right."

Rose was fond of Webb, who paid her proper court on almost every occasion, and she began to bounce in her highchair, plump arms extended. Her chortling laugh deepened Bonnie's guilt, for she couldn't help thinking of Menelda's little girl. Zoë was sickly, and she needed the medicine her father couldn't afford because he spent so much at the Brass Eagle every night, when his shift at the smelter was over.

Webb laughed at Rose's antics and deftly freed her from her chair, lifting her high above his head. Shrieking with delight, she spread her chubby arms out like the wings of a bird and, fate being what it is, Eli walked in at exactly that moment.

His golden eyes darkened to deep amber as he watched,

and Bonnie saw his jaw tighten, but before Eli could speak, Rose Marie surprised everyone by whooping, "Papa! Papa!"

Instantly the strain in Eli's face was gone, replaced by a blinding grin. "Hello, princess," he said, holding out his arms.

Webb surrendered the child without speaking, and the stricken look in his blue eyes compounded Bonnie's miseries. He'd made it clear enough that he hoped to marry Bonnie and raise Rose Marie as his own, and this sudden encounter with Eli was an understandable shock to him.

After a moment of struggle, Bonnie found her voice and introduced the two men to each other. Webb nodded, offering a hand, and Eli took it, shifting Rose Marie into the curve of his left arm.

Reminded of Kiley, and Eli's easy way with him, Bonnie ached. She had forgotten how children took to this man.

As soon as it was politely possible, Webb made an excuse and left the store.

Despite the child's protests, Eli put Rose back into her highchair. She'd taken his hat during the process and he allowed her to keep it, chuckling when she put it on and virtually disappeared inside, but his face was solemn when he turned his attention to Bonnie.

"I presume it's Mr. Hutcheson's main aim in life to—take you away from all this?"

Bonnie tried to ascertain Eli's mood and failed. His words had not been barbed, as far as she could tell, but that didn't mean he wouldn't follow that remark with one designed to cut. "I would not say that marrying me is Mr. Hutcheson's 'main aim in life.' Publishing his newspaper keeps him quite busy."

Eli leaned against the counter, just as Webb had done, and while there was no threat in his manner or bearing, Bonnie retreated a step.

"Are you going to marry Hutcheson, Bonnie?"

The shelf containing the bottled medicines and tonics was pressing hard against Bonnie's back. She met his question with one of her own. "Why should you care whether I marry Webb or not?"

Eli did not move, and yet Bonnie sensed a change inside

him, a quickening. "I have the best reason in the world—this little girl. Your decisions—and so far they've been something less than conventional—affect Rose."

Despite an effort to remain cool and aloof, Bonnie felt a flush rise into her face. She kept her chin high, but there was a perceptible tremor in her voice when she replied, "Rose is always my first concern, Eli. Always."

"Even when you're dancing the hurdy-gurdy?"

The tremor that had begun in Bonnie's voice spread into her very soul. "Yes, believe it or not, even then. It takes money to support a child."

"Don't use money as an excuse, Bonnie. The bank drafts Seth sent to you over the last two years added up to a considerable sum, and you returned them all. Furthermore, Genoa would do anything for you, but except for a few dollars here and there, you don't allow her to help. Let's be honest. The real issue here, dear heart, is your cussed Irish pride, and while it's all very well to turn up your nose at McKutchen money and make your own way, I'll be damned if I'll let you drag my daughter through hell in the process!"

Rose, sensing the discord between the adults, gave a wail and floundered out from under Eli's hat.

Katie, ever alert, came dashing down the stairs to collect her charge, crooning, "There, there—you're just needing your lunch, now aren't you?"

Rose was squalling by the time Katie lifted her out of the highchair and hurried back upstairs, without so much as a word or a glance for either Bonnie or Eli. They stood in silence for some seconds, then Eli retrieved his hat from the floor and slapped it against one thigh.

"I'll repeat my question, Bonnie. Do you intend to marry Hutcheson or not?"

Bonnie did not love Webb—God help her, it was Eli McKutchen she cared for, even after all the heartache and all the time that had passed—but plenty of people married without that worthy emotion and lived happy lives. Liking and respecting Webb as she did, knowing that becoming his wife would solve many of her problems and give her a fresh start in the bargain, Bonnie was suddenly tempted. The risk of losing Rose to Eli would not be nearly so great if she

63

married a solid citizen like Webb, and she wouldn't have to dance the hurdy-gurdy anymore. Wouldn't have to serve as mayor or try to keep the mercantile going.

"I might marry Webb," she said thoughtfully, speaking more to herself than to her former husband. "I just might."

When Bonnie looked up, several pensive moments later, Eli was gone.

CHAPTER 7

THE INNER CORE of the smelter works was a place of noise and stifling heat. Grimy steam billowed from the quenching pots, accompanied by a loud sizzling sound that made a man's insides quiver against the rounding of his rib cage, and the blast furnaces glowed red-hot. Men stooped with age and hard work bent over the conveyor belt leading from the dry crusher, sorting lead ore from plain rock, while boys hardly out of short pants tended dross pots full of molten lead, skimming away the waste that boiled to the top with long steel paddles.

I hate this place, Eli thought, but he walked on, Seth scrambling along on his right side, Forbes Durrant keeping a more sedate pace at his left. Finally they entered a small, cluttered office, and the soul-shaking noise was muted by the closing of a heavy door.

Seth dragged a handkerchief from the pocket of his suitcoat and dabbed at his forehead and his neck, which was as usual encased in a high, rigid collar. "Great Zeus, this place is as near an approximation of hell as I've ever seen!"

Eli glanced at Forbes and silently agreed. The smelter not only looked like hell and felt like hell—in all probability, it had its own devil.

"The refinement of metal," Forbes said, with a spreading

of his clean white hands, "is and always has been a nasty process. These men know that and, believe me, they're glad of the work."

Eli leaned back against the edge of the desk, which was all but buried in papers and ledger books, and folded his arms. In essence, what Forbes said was true, and except for the youth of some of the pot tenders, Eli had seen nothing to which he could take serious exception. Still he sensed something brewing, something hotter than the contents of the dross pots and furnaces. Genoa and Seth were right—there was going to be trouble.

"Those kids tending the pots—how old are they?"

Forbes shrugged. "Ten, twelve, fourteen maybe. Why?"

Eli exchanged a glance with Seth, who was still mopping his face and neck with his handkerchief, and fought to keep his temper. Between his most recent encounter with Bonnie and Durrant's blithe attitude, his control was stretched thin as ice on a shallow puddle. "I want them out of here. They should be in school, not risking their lives skimming dross."

Forbes looked affably indulgent. "Many of them are supporting sisters and brothers, Mr. McKutchen, as well as widowed mothers. Would you have me tell them to study arithmetic and spelling while their families starve?"

"Surely some arrangements could be made for the unfortunates," Seth suggested fitfully, flushed and obviously in need of fresh air. "Why, if one of those nippers were to fall into that molten metal, gentlemen, the responsibility would be our own!"

Eli shuddered at the picture that rose in his mind, but Forbes simply smiled, again with that damnable indulgence. "There are always risks," he insisted. "These boys have hungry mouths to feed and they don't expect to be mollycoddled, nor do they need special treatment—"

"I want them away from the dross pots and the furnaces," Eli interrupted, his voice low and even, yet clearly audible despite the din pounding at the very walls of that cramped little office. "Let them sweep up or carry messages or whatever, at the same wages, but keep them away from the hot ore."

Forbes opened his mouth to argue, had second thoughts, and closed it again.

There was plenty more Eli wanted to say to Forbes Durrant, but most of it could wait. "Mr. Callahan here will be wanting to review the company records," he began, when the door of the office burst open.

A lanky, soot-blackened figure filled the chasm, the glow of the furnaces providing an eerie backdrop. "Mr. Durrant," the man croaked, "there's been an accident—a bad one—"

"Where?" Eli demanded.

The worker's eyeballs were startlingly white in the mask of filth that covered his face. "Out by the tracks—rails gave way on one of the ore cars. Mike Farley's been crushed under the rocks—"

"Has anybody sent for the doc?" Forbes snapped, pushing the workman aside to bolt through the door.

As Eli passed by the dross pots on the way to the smelter's private railroad spur, he reached out and caught one adolescent worker by the shirt collar, forcing the boy to drop his skimming paddle and stumble along ahead, wide-eyed.

Outside, in air so much cleaner and cooler that it was like a restorative tonic, Eli released the boy with a brusque "Wait here," and sprinted toward the train tracks, where a crowd of muttering men were gathered.

The wooden rails of a cattle car had splintered and a pile of rock destined for the dry crusher had cascaded out onto the ground, burying at least one man under its weight.

Eli pushed his way through the workmen, forgetting Forbes and Seth, and helped clear away the last huge chunks of rock. They needn't have hurried, for Mike Farley was dead.

Eli straightened, wanting to bellow a protest to the skies. One of the other men gathered Farley's crushed, bloody corpse into his arms and wept in furious despair. "My boy! Oh, God, my boy!"

Seth materialized at Eli's side, looking worried and not a little ill. "Why would anyone haul rock in a railed car?" he fretted. "Steel would certainly be called for, since wood couldn't be expected to hold—"

The sense of Seth's remark brought Eli out of shock. He assessed the car with one lethal sweep of his eyes and then strode toward Forbes, catching the man's shirt in both hands and flinging him backward into the crushed slag covering the ground.

The boy entered the store nervously, just as Bonnie was about to close for the day, the filth that marked him as a smelter worker still covering his face and the clothes he was rapidly outgrowing.

Bonnie smiled, reaching back to untie the strings of her storekeeper's apron. Whatever this young man's business was, it couldn't take long. "May I help you?"

"M-Mr. McKutchen sent me here. He—he done whomped Mr. Durrant good, right in the smelter yard— Mike Farley's been mashed up fine as cornmeal—I ain't supposed to tend pot no more, Mr. McKutchen says, so I came here to sort spuds and such—"

Bonnie's smile was long gone, and she held up both hands. "Wait—you're not making sense. Slow down and speak clearly."

"Mike Farley's dead. 'Bout a ton of rock fell on him out by the tracks. I was told to come here and work for the same wages as I was gettin' at the smelter—"

Just then Katie rushed in, returning from her every-other-day trip to the library, her arms loaded with books. "Ma'am, it's dreadful—there was an accident at the smelter and a man was killed! It was Susan Farley's husband and now she's having her baby too early!"

Bonnie was already reaching for a shawl. She remembered Susan Farley, a shy, slender blonde who lived in a Patch Town shanty. Whenever Mrs. Farley came into the store, she looked hungrily at the yard goods and the pretty threads but bought single potatoes or onions. With a pang Bonnie recalled the most extravagant purchase Susan had ever made: a penny's worth of candy lemons.

"I'm going down to the Farley place to see if there is anything I can do," she said to Katie. "Please look after Rose, and be sure to lock the store carefully before you get to reading."

The boy's dirty hand caught at Bonnie's sleeve as she started outside. "Beg pardon, ma'am, but I'm supposed to work—"

What on earth could Eli have meant by sending this poor

urchin to "sort spuds and such" in a store where whole days passed without a single sale being made? It was a mystery that would have to be solved later. "You'll have to get yourself a bath if you want to work in my mercantile," Bonnie said, not unkindly, and then she hurried along the street. Anxious to help Susan Farley if she could, she raced down the steep hill toward Patch Town.

The place was as wretched as ever, the tar-paper shacks sitting squalid in the April sunshine, the paths littered with every sort of refuse, the stink of community outhouses all but overwhelming.

Bonnie identified the Farley shack by the gathering of women standing outside, twisting their shabby, colorless skirts in work-reddened hands and shaking their heads.

"If it ain't her ladyship, the mayor," one woman said, curling her lip and looking Bonnie up and down.

"Leave her be, Jessie," put in another of the helpless vigil-keepers. "Time's been that my babies would have gone hungry if Miz McKutchen hadn't give me credit at her store."

"How the devil did she get to be mayor, anyhow?" someone else wanted to know, as Bonnie made her way toward the shanty and boldly walked in.

The Farley shack was incredibly small, housing only a tiny stove, a table, and a bed. Clothes hung on pegs, and Bonnie thought she saw a mouse peering out of a hole in the five-pound sack of flour sitting among chipped crockery and cooking pots on the one shelf the cabin boasted.

She quickly turned her attention on Susan and the woman who was trying to soothe her: Genoa.

Eli's sister barely looked up, patting Susan's hand as a hard contraction wrung a breathless cry from the patient. "At last, someone who can follow simple directions," she said. "Bonnie, fetch some clean water and put it on to boil. This baby is determined to be born, with or without our permission."

Bonnie rolled up the sleeves of her dress, took the two largest kettles from the shelf, and went outside. The crowd of women parted for her, and some trailed after as she made her way to the well in the middle of Patch Town and began pumping water into the kettles.

"Is Susan going to be all right?" implored the woman who had stood up for Bonnie earlier.

"Of course she ain't going to be all right!" snapped someone else, before Bonnie could answer. "She's got no man to look after her now! No amount o' fancy women comin' down here and fussin' is gonna change that, neither!"

"There'll be bad trouble over this, you mark my words!" spouted still another. "The union fellers will raise hell and our men'll go out on strike. Then we'll *all* be hungry!"

Staunchly, Bonnie went back to the shanty with the water Genoa had asked for. Her sister-in-law had started a flickering fire in the tiny stove, but this being April, there was very little wood on hand for burning.

As Susan Farley arched on her bed, in the throes of labor and despair, Bonnie went to the doorway of the shanty and addressed the onlookers in a clear and forceful voice. "We need wood to keep the stove going. Please go and gather whatever you can find."

Several of the women hurried away toward the riverbank, hoping that the Columbia might spare them some of the broken tree limbs, scraps of bark and bits of driftwood she sometimes carried over her swirling currents. Since it was spring, the water would be high from the snows melting in the Canadian Cascades, and small trees torn from their rooting places along the way would be plentiful.

"Genoa," Bonnie asked softly, when she'd found a basin and a cloth and begun to wash Susan's pale face with cool water, "what are you doing here?"

"I might ask the same thing of you, Bonnie McKutchen." Genoa smiled a brief, rueful smile. "Or should I address you as 'your ladyship, the mayor'?"

"So you overheard that woman out there, did you?" Bonnie asked. "And you didn't even come to my defense!"

"I knew you could take care of yourself. Besides, when I arrived those women out there called me a skinny spinster! And worse! I do hope they're not pawing and poking at my brand-new carriage."

Bonnie couldn't help a slight chuckle, despite the grimness of the situation. She hadn't noticed Genoa's elegant rig outside, but she wasn't really surprised to find her sister-in-

70

law in a Patch Town shanty. Miss McKutchen visited often, though some of the families proudly refused her "charity."

Susan began to toss wildly on the cot, crying out for her lost husband, and it took both Genoa and Bonnie to settle her. The young widow's travail went on for several hours until, at sunset, Susan Farley's baby was born, a boy surely too small to survive. Genoa was not prepared to admit defeat.

"Bonnie, do you remember my telling you about Mama —how she was so tiny when she was born? The midwife put her in a shoebox and kept her warm in a slow oven."

Bonnie nodded thoughtfully. She and Genoa had washed the baby and wrapped him in the warmest covering available, Genoa's bright plaid capelet, but the child was blue with cold. "It's worth a try, isn't it, little one?" she said, remembering what Gran had told her so long ago about her own birth, the words drifting through her mind. Even after all this time, and all that had happened, the story still inspired her whenever she thought of it. *He took you into His strong, carpenter's hands, He did . . .*

She knew, of course, that Gran had been speaking figuratively, in order to make the point that every life was precious to God and should therefore be valued. Bonnie held the little fellow wrapped in Genoa's cape very close for a moment, her eyes burning, and clearly imagined the Galilean raising him up for the Father to admire, face shining with proud delight.

Genoa, a most perceptive woman, patted Bonnie's shoulder. "We'll take the poor child to my house and do our best to save him," she said gently, but her eyes took in the shadowy little hut, the bereft, half-conscious woman lying motionless on the narrow bed. "I do wonder if it's a kindness, though. His life won't be an easy one."

Bonnie drew a deep breath and sniffled. "No life is easy, is it, Genoa?"

Genoa sighed. "You're right, of course," she said, and before she could add anything, there was a stir outside and a tall man with spiky white hair and dirty clothes came into the shanty, followed by a somber Eli.

"This is John Farley," he said quietly. "The man killed today was his son."

71

Farley edged closer to the bed where Susan lay, his face wan with concern and the hopelessness of grief. "The babe?" he asked brokenly.

Bonnie gave Mr. Farley a view of his grandson, careful to cover the child again quickly. It wouldn't do for the poor little creature to catch a draft.

"Awful small," Farley said.

Genoa was standing very straight, her fine dress soiled, her hair a fright, and yet there was an innate dignity about her that no one could ignore. "Mr. Farley, there is a chance that your grandson might survive, if he has the proper care. Susan, too, will need warmth and good food to recover. I would like to take them both to my house, where they can be properly looked after."

"Your house, ma'am?" Mr. Farley echoed, disbelieving. "Why would you want to do that?"

Genoa flung just the briefest look of challenge in Eli's direction before answering resolutely, "I am a McKutchen and therefore must bear some responsibility for the results of your tragedy."

Eli turned abruptly and went outside, and Bonnie followed on instinct, the Farley baby still held securely in her arms. She had to hurry to catch up, for Eli's strides were long, carrying him swiftly across the mushy grassland that curved upward from the banks of the river.

"Eli!" she finally called breathlessly, and though he stopped, his broad shoulders stiff in the twilight, he did not turn to face her.

The wet of the boggy grass and sod was soaking through Bonnie's shoes, chilling her feet, but for the moment she paid that no mind. "Eli, what happened today was terrible, but it wasn't your fault."

The great shoulders relaxed a bit, but Eli still kept his back to Bonnie. "The river's rising," he said, after a long and pulsing silence.

Bonnie couldn't bear the pain she sensed in him. "Eli McKutchen, you turn around and look at me!" she ordered.

Slowly, and with an effort that conveyed the true depths of what he felt, Eli turned. In the gathering darkness, Bonnie could see that his golden eyes were suspiciously bright. "Oh, God, Bonnie," he breathed, running one hand through his already rumpled hair, "how could I have ignored this? How could my grandfather?"

Bonnie knew that he was speaking of the conditions at the smelter and in Patch Town, where so many of the workers had to live. "The past can't be changed, Eli," she said gently, "so there's no use in suffering over it."

"Bonnie!" Genoa's voice rang through the deepening twilight. "We'd best get that baby out of the night air!"

Biting her lower lip, Bonnie turned to go, her wet shoes making a squishing sound as she walked.

Reaching the carriage where Genoa stood waiting, Susan and Mr. Farley already inside, Bonnie surrendered the baby to her sister-in-law. "It's kind of you to look after Susan, Genoa," she said.

Genoa took in the whole of Patch Town in a sweeping gaze of despair. "I wish I could help them all," she answered, and then she got into the carriage and the vehicle rolled away.

Bonnie was very much aware of Eli's presence; indeed, without looking she knew that he was standing just behind her and slightly to her right. "You'll have to walk home," she said, because the silence was unbearable.

"I'll survive that," Eli responded, his voice low and still somewhat stricken. "Shouldn't you be at the Brass Eagle, painting your face?"

Lamps flickered behind the oiled-paper windows of the shanties all around. Usually, even here, there would have been the nightfall laughter of small children playing outside before supper, but that evening the place was glumly still, the only sounds being the occasional chime of a cooking pot against an iron stove top and the rush of the nearby river. Possessed of a lonely, empty feeling, Bonnie sighed and started walking. She had no spirit to spar with Eli.

He fell easily into step beside her. "I'm sorry," he said.

Bonnie glanced at him out of the corner of her eye. She couldn't rightly remember Eli ever having apologized to her before, for anything—not his coldness after Kiley's death, not the women, not the impulsive journey to Cuba—and she was strangely moved. To hide that, she changed the subject.

"What was Cuba like, Eli? Were you a Rough Rider?" she

asked, belatedly remembering that her skirts were trailing in the mud and filth on the ground and lifting them with a delicacy acquired in New York.

Eli laughed, though there was no real humor in the sound, only a hollow weariness and a raspy catch that made Bonnie's heart ache. "The term 'Rough Rider' is something of a misnomer. We charged San Juan Hill on foot since the War Department had neglected to provide horses. The Spaniards shot at us for a while and then dropped their guns and ran; I've since thought that they were undone by our stupidity rather than our valor."

"I suppose it was all Mr. Roosevelt's idea," Bonnie sniffed. She had not forgiven that man for persuading Eli to fight in Cuba and she wasn't sure she ever would.

There was a richness to Eli's chuckle that meant he was recovering from the shocks of the day. "T.R. was in his element," he said, with respect and a certain affection. "God, you should have seen him—heard him!"

"If I never see Mr. Theodore Roosevelt again," Bonnie said shortly, "it will be entirely too soon."

Patch Town was behind them now. As they were passing the Brass Eagle Saloon and Ballroom, Eli suddenly reached out and caught Bonnie by the arm, swinging her around to face him and at the same time drawing her into the privacy of the tentlike shadows sloping from the wall of Forbes's saloon to the wooden sidewalk. Caught off guard, she collided with Eli's rock-hard chest and bounced backward against the wall. Before Bonnie could catch her breath, Eli bent his head and claimed her mouth with his own, his tongue playing skillfully around her lips until they opened for him.

A jolt of need went through Bonnie McKutchen, turning her sturdy knees to vapor. With any other man, including Webb Hutcheson, that kiss would have been an affront—but this was Eli. For two years she'd ached for his touch, his kiss, and the reality was far better than the memory. In fact, it brought on a surge of emotion so heated that Bonnie feared to melt away like a penny candle.

The kiss ended, but Eli's hard frame still imprisoned Bonnie against the cold limestone wall of Forbes's building, and she felt like the moon, freezing on one side and

74

sun-parched on the other. She struggled to catch her breath, strained to regain her composure.

Eli braced himself against the wall, one hand on each side of Bonnie's head, and gave an exasperated sigh. "I don't know why I did that, Bonnie. I'm sorry."

Two apologies in the space of a few minutes! Bonnie was amazed—and just a bit insulted—and to make matters worse, all kinds of memories of the ferocious levels of passion this man had been able to carry her to during their marriage were springing to mind. They were also working mischief in less seemly places.

"I don't know why you did it, either!" Bonnie snapped, slipping beneath Eli's right arm and striding furiously down the sidewalk.

Eli did not pursue her, and that was at once a good thing and a bad one. Indignantly, undone by her own responses to that impossible, arrogant man, Bonnie stormed up the marble steps of the Brass Eagle Saloon and reached for the handle of one of the two doors. It was locked.

It wasn't like Forbes to close the Brass Eagle and, even though Bonnie was secretly hoping that she needn't dance that night, she was puzzled, too.

She tapped somewhat timidly at the door and, when there was no answer, she went to one of the windows to peer inside. The blind was partway down, and Bonnie had to bend to look beneath it. When she did so, she felt a firm pinch on her bottom and leaped in anger and surprise, giving a startled cry at the same time.

Eli stood behind her, arms folded in innocence, lip twitching. "The temptation," he confessed, "was my undoing."

It had been a difficult day and if there was one thing Bonnie would not endure from anyone, including Eli McKutchen, it was the indignity of being pinched. She raised her hand, intending to slap him soundly across the face, but he stepped back quickly, probably guessing that next she'd resort to a painful meeting of her shoe and his shin.

"Go away, Eli!" Bonnie hissed, completely forgetting the kiss and her earlier feelings of sympathy. "I've got work to do."

"There won't be any dancing tonight," Eli responded.

"Forbes is recuperating from the emotional strain of today's tragedy."

Bonnie's eyes widened as she remembered the boy who'd come to her store with news of the Farley accident. He'd said something about Mr. McKutchen "whomping" Mr. Durrant. "Eli, you didn't—"

"I'm afraid I did."

"You beast! When did violence ever solve anything?!" Bonnie stomped back to the door and pounded on it with both fists.

Eli was grimly amused. "Ask the woman who has kicked me, struck me with a toilet brush and tried to slap me, all in the space of forty-eight hours."

"Dottie!" Bonnie yelled, pounding harder. "Open this door!"

It was Laura, one of the new girls, who unlocked the door at last and peered cautiously out. Her eyes widened at the sight of Eli, and she moved to close the crack of space but not quickly enough. Bonnie pushed from the opposite side and prevailed.

"Where is Forbes?" she demanded of poor Laura, who was gulping anxiously, smoothing her brown hair and watching Eli all at the same time.

Laura managed to answer that Forbes was feeling "poorly."

Flinging a scathing look at Eli, Bonnie hurried up the stairs and down the hallway to the rooms she had been carried into so unceremoniously two days before. She knocked once and then entered without waiting for a call to come in.

Forbes was lying on a settee near the windows of an elegantly decorated parlor, his right eye swollen completely shut. He was wearing trousers and a satin smoking jacket, and he grinned at Bonnie as a fluttering Dottie fluffed the pillows that had been propped behind his back.

"Sweet Angel," he said ruefully, looking Bonnie up and down with his one eye. "How I'm going to miss you."

Bonnie frowned. "What do you mean, you're going to miss me?"

"You're fired," he replied.

WANTON ANGEL

In a curious mixture of relief and high dudgeon, Bonnie whirled on one heel and marched out, racing down the hallway and the stairs, in search of the man who had ended her career as a hurdy-gurdy dancer. Kicks, slaps and toilet-brush blows were nothing compared to what she was going to do to Eli McKutchen now.

CHAPTER 8

THOUGH THE ROOMS above Bonnie's store were empty, a lamp flickered in the center of the kitchen table, and a neatly penned note had been tucked beneath its base. Katie had gone to Genoa's house for the evening and, of course, taken Rose Marie with her. No explanation was given, but then none was needed, since Bonnie knew well enough how Katie enjoyed Genoa's vast collection of books. Added to that attraction were seemingly infinite supplies of cookies and cakes and, best of all, a concert roller organ; Katie loved that tabletop mechanism and would stand turning the handle for hours, if allowed, while interchangeable cylinders scratched out such favorites as "Lead, Kindly Light" and "You Look Awfully Good to Father."

Despite annoyance that Katie had left a lamp burning unattended, despite all the tragedy of that day and the losing of her job—she was sure the responsibility for that lay at Eli's feet—Bonnie was glad of an opportunity for silent reflection.

She ate a light supper of warmed-over stew and biscuits, then heated water for a bath. Her own quarters lacking the luxuries of a stationary tub and indoor plumbing, such as both Genoa and Forbes Durrant enjoyed, Bonnie dragged the oversized washtub reserved for purposes of personal hygiene from the pantry to the kitchen and sprinkled pink carnation bath crystals into it. While the water heated on the wood-burning stove, she went into her bedroom and took off her dress and underthings, donning a blue flannel wrapper in their stead, taking her hair down and brushing it. Once the sable-ebony tresses shone and crackled with electricity, Bonnie braided a single plait and returned to the kitchen.

Three large kettles of water, laboriously pumped at the sink, were now steaming on the stove top. Bonnie carried them one by one to the tub, pouring their contents onto the rippled bottom of the tub. The pink crystals melted and released the luscious scent of carnations into the room.

Bonnie added cool water to the bath, tested it with one expert toe and found it perfect. She shed her wrapper, laying it over the back of a chair, and sank blissfully into the tub, closing her eyes and sighing as she settled back to enjoy the warmth and the fragrance.

She did not think of the trials and tribulations of the day just past, or of the very real possibility that Katie and Rose Marie might be a bother to Genoa, who was no doubt busy with Susan Farley and her baby. She did not think of losing the job she badly needed and she did not think of Eli McKutchen.

Not, that is, until he boldly walked into her kitchen, his golden eyes sweeping over Bonnie's naked and heat-pinked flesh in one insolent foray. "You should lock your doors at night," he observed.

For a moment Bonnie just stared at him, unable to believe his audacity, but when good sense returned, she made a dive for her wrapper.

Eli had anticipated this most natural move and pulled the chair that held the robe out of reach. In fact, he turned that chair backside-front and sat in it, his arms resting across its back and effectively pinning Bonnie's wrapper beneath them.

Bonnie sank back into the tub, her arms folded across her bare breasts and her thigh drawn up in such a way as to cover the nest of her femininity, which was beginning to ache in a most disturbing way. "Get out," she managed to say, closing her eyes tightly in the ostrich hope

79

that if she could not see Eli he would not be able to see her.

"You beautiful dreamer," Eli responded smoothly. "You can't actually think that I'm going to leave?"

"I do indeed think you are going to leave," Bonnie said, eyes still closed, arms still clasped across her bosom. "This is highly improper. In fact, you are intruding!"

"Ummm-hmmm."

Bonnie's eyes flew open at his lazy drawl. The water was growing chill and so was her heart, although her blood raced hot beneath her skin. "Have you no decency, Mr. McKutchen? What kind of influence will this have on Katie and Rose Marie?"

Eli smiled. "You know from experience that I have no decency, and influencing Rose Marie and Katie will be quite impossible, since they aren't here. I just saw them at Genoa's."

Bonnie sighed, determined to keep her head. Eli was clearly trying to annoy her, but he needn't have the satisfaction of knowing just how thoroughly he had succeeded. "If you won't behave as a gentleman, then kindly give me my wrapper. I'm cold."

"You're cold?" The words were crooned in a tone of mock sympathy and Eli's chair made a scraping sound as he rose from it and slid it farther out of reach in almost the same motion. He took the kettles from the stove and carried them to the iron sink, the muscles in his arms and shoulders moving beneath his shirt, stretching it taut, as he pumped water into each one. The pots made a clink-sizzle sound as they were placed on the stove again. While Bonnie watched with wide, disbelieving eyes, her former husband returned to his chair and again sat astraddle of its seat, his arms propped along its sturdy back. "There will be more hot water soon—darling."

Bonnie wished that the water she already had, now very tepid and inadequate stuff, were deep enough for her to drown in. Beyond leaping from the tub and dashing, naked as the day she was born, for the bedroom, Bonnie was at a loss for a strategy.

"Why are you doing this?" she asked in a small voice.

Eli ignored her question entirely, giving a sigh and gazing off into the distance with a dreamy expression on his face. For a moment, the only sounds were the surging of heat moving through the water on the stove and the traffic in the street below—more that night than usual, because the Pompeii Playhouse was offering an evening's entertainment.

"Remember that night when all the servants were out—it was raining and we—"

Bonnie remembered all right, and she gave a little cry, shifting in a whoosh of water and outrage so that she sat cross-legged like an Indian in her bathwater, her arms still shielding her breasts. Their tips were pulsing now, at the memory of the delightful attentions they'd gotten that night "when all the servants were out and the rain was falling."

"Eli McKutchen, you wretch, I know what you're doing and I demand that you stop this instant!"

Eli gave a throaty chuckle, his eyes still fixed on the long ago and faraway, his chin propped on one steel-corded forearm. "Ah, yes. They can have their central heating—every parlor should have a fireplace with a bearskin rug on the hearth—"

Heat was surging through Bonnie now, just as it was surging through the water warming on the stove. She found her sponge, after a moment of frantic one-handed groping, and hurled it at Eli in fury and desperation. It missed its mark, splattering against the railed back of the chair and bringing nothing more than a chuckle from her tormentor.

Inwardly Bonnie cursed herself for every kind of fool. Why hadn't she locked the door when she'd come in? Why had she allowed herself to forget how skillful Eli was at arousing her? From the very first day of their marriage he had been able to stir her deepest passions with a word or even a look. What if he reminded her of that time in the carriage, on the way home from dinner at the Astors'?

Too late, Bonnie realized that she had reminded herself. Her body trembled in delicious memory of that scandalous encounter, her breasts growing heavy and her secret place expanding painfully in need of its natural counterpart. "Oh, Lord," she wailed softly, letting her chin rest on her knees.

Eli was back at the stove, testing the water in the kettles with an index finger. "It's ready," he announced blithely, taking one pot by its handle and carrying it to the side of the tub. "Look lively there," he said, "I don't want to burn you."

Bonnie instinctively shifted to one side, and the water Eli poured into the tub swirled around her bottom like a warm cloud. As if that part of her *needed* warming! "Eli, please— if you'll just—"

"More water. Heads—er—bottoms up."

Another stream of liquid heat moved around Bonnie in a sweet current, lulling her, permeating her. The aching need spread into the deepest parts of her, demanding fulfillment.

As though he had every right to be there, causing her such sinful anguish, Eli returned the kettles to the stove and recovered the sponge. He squeezed it out right where he stood, with no regard whatsoever for the carefully polished linoleum, and then approached.

Bonnie knew that she was lost when he paused to roll up one shirtsleeve and then the other, his movements methodical and unhurried. Though a lot of people would have said otherwise, there was but one man in all the world who knew how to turn Bonnie McKutchen into a wanton, one man who had ever gotten the chance to try, and that man was standing next to her bathtub with a sponge in his hand.

Bonnie closed her eyes and allowed the back of her head to rest against the edge of the tub and her strong arms to sink, powerless, into the freshly warmed water that smelled of carnations. She felt his hand brush past her hip, heard the soft scratching sound of soap being lathered against the sponge.

Deftly the sponge circled the outer part of Bonnie's left breast, moving ever so slowly inward toward the center. She gasped involuntarily when the nipple was reached and gently lathered.

"I've never bathed a mayor before," Eli remarked in a low voice, now washing her right breast. "How did you come to hold that office, may I ask?"

Bonnie opened her eyes and was about to make a stand when Eli's free hand slipped beneath the water and parted her legs, seeking the bud that would bloom to passion, finding it. As he dallied, Bonnie's protest lodged in her throat, then slipped out as a moan.

Eli chuckled and continued to stroke Bonnie even as he filled the sponge with water and then squeezed, letting the scented liquid wash the soap from her breasts. "You were saying?" he teased.

Bonnie's knees drew upward and then fell wide of each other, even though she had ordered them to close tight together. "Ooooo," she whimpered.

"You can tell me how you got elected later," Eli conceded charitably. "Right now, you're a lady much in need of pleasing."

Bonnie was a lady in need of pleasing, a healthy woman who had not been made love to in two years, and her need was a searing thing, immune to reason and propriety, flowing through her entire being with all the elemental force of the river surging past Northridge in the darkness. She felt Eli's breath on her breast and arched her back, muttering, "Yes, oh, yes." Her wet hands clasped at his broad shoulders and then the back of his head, and when his lips closed around her nipple in a teasing nibble, a great trembling went through her.

And all the while his fingers worked, driving Bonnie on and on toward what she knew would be only the first of many savage crescendos, for Eli had never been one to give quarter in that respect. No, he would love Bonnie again and again, satisfy her again and again, until they both fell into exhausted sleep.

Bonnie's hips rose and fell in shameless response as Eli attended her, now trailing kisses along her collarbone, now nibbling at her earlobe, now taking greedy suckle at her breast. Water splashed over the sides of the tub as though set to boiling and with a keening cry of abandon and release, Bonnie rose high above its surface, trembling as the tumult within her had its primal way and then, long moments later, allowed her to sink back into the tub. She was shivering when Eli lifted her from the water into his arms, and it seemed perfectly natural to rest her head against his shoulder as she had done on so many other occasions.

He didn't seem to mind that her wet flesh was soaking his shirt and trousers; his voice was gravelly as it grated past her ear. "The bed, Bonnie. Where is it?"

Still languorous from her release, Bonnie mumbled directions.

He laid her very gently on the bed, crosswise, and, using a towel taken from atop the bureau, dried her with tenderness before shedding his boots and clothes and kneeling on the floor. His strong hands moved up and down Bonnie's naked thighs, bringing back the gooseflesh he had toweled away so carefully. He touched her breasts and her slender waist and her satiny stomach, his golden eyes wondrous, as though he had not loved her a thousand times before, in a thousand unconventional places.

"Oh, Bonnie," he muttered once, as he eased her knees far apart and then put his hands on her waist to draw her forward for full and unrestrained enjoyment, "how I've needed you—wanted you—"

Bonnie knew the pleasure to come and was not sure that she would be able to bear it, after wanting so long. She trembled as he parted the nest of curls at the joining of her thighs to unveil what he would so thoroughly consume.

"Sweet Bonnie," he said, his voice throaty and gruff and close enough to warm a part of Bonnie that could belong only to him, whether he chose to love her or to discard her when he had had his fill. He was an expert at heightening her need with words, and now, over her whimpers, he wove his singular spell. "Remember that restaurant at Newport, Bonnie?" he asked softly. "We had a private dining room and I kissed you—just like—this—"

Bonnie was fevered as he kissed her again; her fingers tangled frantically in his hair and a low, primitive wail came from her throat, senseless and yet telling the story of all womanhood. He burrowed close to take full suckle and covered her breasts with his strong hands, fondling them, kneading them, encouraging their pink tips until they became hard points thrusting against his palms.

For all the intensity of Eli's loving, Bonnie's climax came slowly, slowly, extracting every passion, calling every muscle and every sense into play. She fretted and pleaded and

84

when, at last, satisfaction overtook her, she knew an anguish of repletion.

Eli lay beside her then, turning her so that they lay lengthwise on the bed, and she stroked his broad, solid chest with one hand for a time, waiting for her breathing to settle into evenness again, for the quivering beneath her flesh to cease. Despite twice reaching the sweet pinnacle, there was yet a need within Bonnie: a need to be taken, to be filled with this man. Only so would she truly be appeased.

She whispered the words she'd never expected to say again, as long as she lived. "Have me, Eli. Take me."

A chuckle moved through the sturdy flesh beneath her hand. "You were always persuasive," he said, but to Bonnie's surprise he sat up instead of poising himself above her.

Her expression of wide-eyed worry made him smile. "Don't worry, love—I need you very badly. It's just that if I lie down to take you, I may never be able to stand up again." Eli paused and assessed the beauty of her with a slight, marveling shake of his head. "Come here," he said.

She moved to stand before him and for a time he caressed her. At last Eli drew her down to sit astraddle of his lap, easing inside her with the gentleness that had always marked his lovemaking. Never, no matter what heights their passion had reached, had he ever hurt her.

Their mutterings became one tangled sound as Bonnie raised and lowered herself upon Eli, both soothed and driven by his possession. When the pace did not suit Eli, he slowed Bonnie to an excruciatingly tender meter, and periodically he took time to sample each of her breasts, to kiss her deeply, to caress her face and her shoulders and her bottom. She was eager to please and be pleased, but Eli kept her in check until a moment of his choosing, when he finally gave Bonnie the freedom to move as he moved, in a wild search for fulfillment that ended in a fusion so explosive that new universes were surely created.

They rested and loved, rested and loved, until the world was quiet and the night was deep. Bonnie slept then, curled close to Eli, her body no longer fevered but wholly appeased.

* * *

It was nearly dawn and Eli lay awake. Through Bonnie's window, he could see the stars blinking out like silver flames over the roof of the Pompeii Playhouse. The distant sparks of light shifted and blurred and Eli wiped his eyes with the back of one hand, shamed even though Bonnie wasn't awake to see his disgrace.

He should not have come to Northridge, even though Rose Marie was here, and the smelter. After this night, he might never be able to deal with Bonnie rationally again.

She nestled close to him in her sleep, her flesh soft and fragrant, and Eli ached to know that she had been one of Forbes Durrant's women, selling herself. He couldn't afford the luxury of believing her assertions that she did nothing more than dance, though God knew he wanted to believe it.

More tears followed those he had wiped away, silent, masculine tears, but tears nonetheless. Eli eased out of bed, found his clothes, slowly got into them. He paused for a long look at Bonnie, one that cost him a part of his already wounded spirit, memorizing the way the moonlight washed over her curves, glimmered in her hair, caught in the thick eyelashes that rested on alabaster cheeks. The anguish he felt was unlike anything he had ever endured before.

He had to remember who Bonnie was, what she was. She had given herself to him as she would have to any man who could pay the price. Her fierce yielding had been a practiced thing, a part of her trade, and so had her cries of pleasure, her soft pleas and that special way of satisfying him. She had never done that during their marriage and he had not asked it of her. So where had she learned it?

The answer to that question rocked Eli McKutchen to the core of his soul. With resolution, he drew a sizable bill from his wallet, laid it on Bonnie's nightstand, and crept out of her bedroom.

Bonnie awakened slowly, stretching her thoroughly sated body in systematic motions, like a cat. She sensed that Eli was no longer in bed but was not concerned by that, for he had always been an early riser. He was probably well into his day's work, in fact.

Normal morning sounds came from the kitchen—stove lids clattered and clanked and water was pumped. Bonnie sat up in bed, yawning behind one hand and smiling as Katie's voice rose in a crystalline rendition of "Take Me Back to Home and Mother." Rose Marie teetered into the room and, with a cry of glee, thrust her plump little body up onto the bed, nestling close to Bonnie.

In those precious minutes to come, Bonnie McKutchen was supremely happy. During the night, she had been loved to near madness by the one man she cared for and now, on this bright sunny morning, she had the luxury of giggling with her daughter. Oh, it was easy to be optimistic, when one's life seemed to brim with love, so perilously easy.

The scent of fresh-brewed coffee filled the room and Bonnie, seeing her wrapper draped neatly over the footboard of the bed, reached for it and put it on. She was smiling as she tied the belt, but her smile faded when she saw the folded bill tucked beneath the lamp on the bedside table.

At first Bonnie could not accept the meaning of that money. Eli had been a generous husband, where finances were concerned at least, and he had often left cash for Bonnie before going off to his place of business in the mornings.

She sank to the side of the bed, her hands lying numb in her lap, her throat thick with a growing misery. After some moments Bonnie reached for the bill, her fingers shaking, and unfolded it. Fifty dollars.

Feeling ill, Bonnie closed her eyes and swallowed. Eli was no longer the indulgent if somewhat overbearing husband, leaving money behind of a morning for his pampered darling to spend on trinkets and hats and vaudeville tickets. The brutal truth was that Eli was a stranger now, and the fifty dollars constituted payment for services rendered.

The bill wafted, forgotten, to the floor. Bonnie rose from her seat on the edge of the bed, crossed the room and quietly closed the door, muffling Rose's giggles and Katie's expert rendering of "Two Little Girls in Blue."

Tears slipped down Bonnie's cheeks as she washed and dressed and arranged her hair in a soft knot atop her head, but she made no sound, and by the time she joined Katie and Rose Marie in the kitchen, her eyes were dry, if swollen and red.

Having no appetite, Bonnie drank coffee while Rose and Katie ate their eggs and toasted bread. She ignored Katie's worried looks and dodged her artfully presented questions, and when the meal was over and the table had been cleared, she went back to the bedroom and collected the fifty-dollar bill from its resting place on the rug.

The first order of business would be to return it to its rightful owner.

"Please leave those dishes," Bonnie said, when she returned to the kitchen and found Katie up to her elbows in steaming water. "I'll take care of them later. I have an errand to attend to, but I won't be gone long."

Katie dried her hands on her apron, looking puzzled and not a little concerned. "Is there something wrong, ma'am?"

Bonnie could not reply honestly. She feared that she would dissolve in misery if she tried. "I would like you to open the store for business," she said, averting her eyes.

Blessedly, Katie did not press for an answer to her question. "Rose and I will see to the shop. Take as much time as you need."

"Thank you," Bonnie managed to say. And then, with dignity, she walked out the door, down the stairs, onto the wooden sidewalk. There were more people on the streets than there should have been on a workday, she thought distractedly, as she walked toward Genoa's house, and something else was different, too, though she couldn't quite decide what it was.

With no memory of the walk, Bonnie arrived at the McKutchen gate, entered it, and made her way up the driveway. Eli was standing on the broad veranda at the front of the house, engaged in a volatile if hushed conversation with Seth Callahan and eating from a plate at the same time.

Seth saw Bonnie first and greeted her cordially, his eyes lighting. "Good day, Mrs. McKutchen," he said, for he and Bonnie had always been friends, though their relationship was a formal one.

"Mr. Callahan," Bonnie responded politely, but her gaze had already attached itself to Eli and his plate of corned beef hash, and she wondered that the food didn't scorch under it.

Though Eli remained absolutely still and quite silent, Seth cleared his throat and beat a hasty retreat into the house, closing the swan-etched door behind him.

Bonnie held her skirts as she climbed the steps leading onto the long porch, the fifty-dollar bill rolled in one hand and moist with perspiration. She approached Eli, her bearing and facial expression revealing nothing, and stood before him, tilting back her head to look up into his face.

Stubbornly, for he was nothing if not mule-obstinant, Eli stared back, his plate in one hand, his fork in the other. His jawline was tight and there was a snapping flash in the depths of his golden-amber eyes, but it was clear that he would not be the first to speak.

"Good morning," Bonnie said sweetly. "Enjoying your breakfast?"

Eli looked down at his corned beef hash and swallowed visibly, even though he hadn't taken a bite since he'd caught sight of Bonnie.

With a delicate and decorous motion, Bonnie lifted her right hand and tucked the rolled fifty-dollar bill neatly into Eli's food. "You may eat this, Mr. McKutchen, along with your meal."

Eli's mouth dropped open for a moment, but he forcefully closed it. For once in his illustrious life, he was at a loss for words.

Bonnie smiled at Eli, smiled at the corned beef hash with the fifty-dollar bill sticking out of it like a candle on a birthday cake, and sweetly shoved the plate against Eli's chest. Then, all dignity, she turned and marched down the steps, back up the drive. The plate clattered belatedly to the floor of the veranda.

Just when she thought she would get away unmolested, Eli caught up to her and stopped her queenly flight by grasping her arm in one hand and whirling her about. Bits of fried potato and corned beef were sticking to his elegant linen shirt.

"Unhand me this instant, you rogue," Bonnie breathed, through clenched teeth. In another moment, she would not be responsible for her actions.

Eli's fingers tightened, then went lax and fell away. The merest hint of shame moved in his features and was quickly

89

overcome. "Did I underpay you, Angel?" he asked, and his voice was stone cold. "I meant to be generous."

Blood rushed into Bonnie's face at such speed that she swayed slightly on her feet. Eli caught her wrist in a grip that left her fingers numb and forestalled the blow. "How cruel you are," she breathed, after long seconds of glaring up into his eyes. "How utterly, miserably cruel. It's no wonder that the workers hate you, that Patch Town is what it is. You have no heart, Eli McKutchen, and I pity you."

Those words seemed to wound Eli as no blow of hand or foot could have done, and he released Bonnie's wrist with a slow movement of his fingers. When she turned to walk away, he called Bonnie's name, but she did not stop or even look back.

Eli had just created the worst kind of enemy: one who has loved and then been shamed for that loving.

Part Two

ANGEL
OF VENGEANCE

CHAPTER 9

BONNIE WAS HALFWAY back to her store when she realized what it was that had eluded her before. The dry-crusher at the smelter yard, a source of constant din, had fallen silent, and the muffled, whooshing roar of the blast furnaces had been stilled.

She stopped alongside the road and turned her full attention toward the brick smokestack towering against the blue spring sky. There were no traces of the gray burgeoning puffs that usually rose from its rim.

So it had happened, then. The union organizers, strangers to Northridge and its people, had gotten their way. The smelter had been closed.

Bonnie bit her lower lip and walked on, so deep in thought that she was hardly aware of the world around her. Her feelings about the strike were mixed, for while the workers had legitimate complaints against McKutchen Enterprises, few of them had the means to live without their wages. There would be hunger and discontent, and conditions in Patch Town would go from wretched to intolerable, in short order.

By rote, skirts in her hands, Bonnie crossed the street and made her way toward the mercantile. A crowd of men and women had gathered in front of the Pompeii Playhouse and, though Bonnie knew most of them, there were strangers present, too.

One of these, a heavyset man with a pockmarked face and dark pouches beneath his mournful eyes, stood facing the gathering from the theatre porch. He was not a prepossessing fellow, but his voice carried well enough that Bonnie could hear him clearly, even from the other side of the street.

"Such travesties as what occurred yesterday can no longer be overlooked," the speaker called out dolefully. "A man is dead, ladies and gentleman. Mike Farley is dead!"

Seeing Webb Hutcheson among the onlookers, pencil and paper in hand, Bonnie went to stand beside him.

"There is a strike, then?" she asked.

Webb was writing rapidly. "Of sorts," he answered. "Half the men still want to work."

There were mutterings in the crowd, but Bonnie kept her eyes on the sad-looking stranger standing on the porch of the Pompeii Playhouse.

"Your brothers have decided that enough is enough," he went on. "McKutchen Enterprises has filled its coffers on the fruits of your labor, gentlemen. Your blood and sweat have made its owners rich, and what do you have? You have shacks to live in! You are paupers!"

"At least we have what to eat!" shouted a man Bonnie couldn't see. "Or we did have, afore all this union foolishness got foisted off on us!"

"I'll be there for the start of my shift!" agreed another worker. "I got a family lookin' to me to feed 'em!"

Other men grumbled and shouted their support for this point of view, while still others dissented. The forlorn stranger lifted both hands in a call for peace. "There will be a strike. It has already begun. And if anyone tries to cross the lines, there will be violence. Bloodshed. We can avoid that by standing together!"

Bonnie closed her eyes and swallowed. She had read about other strikes in other places, and she knew that men on both sides would die if some accord wasn't reached.

Terrified, reminding herself that she was mayor of Northridge and thus had a responsibility to keep the peace if she could, Bonnie left Webb's side and made her way through the throng, up the steps of the Pompeii Playhouse, to stand beside the union man. He was perched on an upended soapbox and this certainly gave him the advantage of height, though in reality Bonnie guessed him to be much shorter than she.

"If you'll step down, please," she suggested reasonably, as the women in the assemblage, Menelda Sneeder among them, began to whisper behind their hands.

Looking baffled, the speaker stepped down from his soapbox and Bonnie ascended it gracefully, her chin high even though she was quaking inside.

"I address you," she said bravely, "as your mayor."

There was a hush, followed soon enough by mutterings from the women and stifled laughter from the men.

"I grant you that my appointment to this office was unconventional—"

"That it was, Angel," one of Bonnie's most devoted dancing partners called out good-naturedly. "The town council was drunk to a man that night, and they chose you to fill poor Mayor Hawley's shoes as much to rile their wives as anything!"

"I have no illusions as to why I was selected," Bonnie answered, in a clear if slightly tremulous voice. "Nonetheless, I *was* selected and I was sworn into office. If you'll just listen—"

"Women don't even vote in this state!" some querulous masculine soul bellowed out. "You ain't really mayor, Bonnie, so you just get yourself back to the Brass Eagle Ballroom, where you belong!"

"I *am* the mayor," insisted Bonnie, shoulders back, chin high, eyes flashing. "And unless you call a special election, I will remain mayor until November. Now stop your prattling about the Brass Eagle and women not being able to vote in this backward state, and listen to me!"

"You tell 'em, Angel!" called Jim Sneeder, who was promptly elbowed by Menelda for his trouble.

Webb, his royal blue eyes shining with mingled amusement and admiration, gave a slow nod of encouragement.

Bonnie drew a deep breath. "Your complaints against

95

McKutchen Enterprises are valid ones, but you must be reasonable." There was a stir at this, and the mayor of Northridge paused to let it pass. "A strike is dangerous. Men will be injured, maybe even killed. Women and children will go hungry and be without homes. Why don't you approach Mr. McKutchen, since he's here in town, and try to reach some agreement with him? He has been neglectful, I grant you, but Eli is a rational, intelligent man—"

"You ought to know what kind of man McKutchen is!" taunted a woman near the front. A glance told Bonnie that her heckler was Miss Willadeen Severs, the schoolmarm.

Bonnie stopped herself from reminding Miss Severs publicly of her overdue account at the mercantile and finished her first and probably last speech as mayor. "Please don't let a few troublemakers, outsiders, make your decisions for you! Meet with Mr. McKutchen and state your grievances as reasonable men! Why risk injury and hunger and even death if you don't have to?"

The applause began with Webb Hutcheson and spread through the crowd, though only scattered men took it up. The women, without exception, stood stony-faced, hating Bonnie for dancing with their husbands, for daring to call herself the mayor, and maybe for reminding them that they could not vote. Of course, in all of the country, only the ladies of Wyoming Territory were allowed a say in government, and everyone knew that the men there had conceded suffrage for a selfish reason: to lure unattached females into their towns, their kitchens and their beds.

Bonnie stepped down from the soapbox and made her way through the mob, across the street, and into her store, Webb Hutcheson close on her heels.

Inside the mercantile Rose was playing happily on the floor with one of the many toys Genoa had bought for her, a doll with a compartment in its stomach to hold its now bunched and wadded wardrobe. Katie was behind the counter, pretending to read, while a scrub-faced, shoddily clad boy diligently swept the floor.

Bonnie stared at the young man for a moment, baffled, then remembered him as the smelter urchin whom Eli had sent to "sort spuds and such." She had never questioned her former husband about this odd arrangement, and she blushed to recall why the subject had not been raised. "Your name?"

"Tuttle," the boy responded brightly, his smile wide. Without all the dirt and soot, he was really quite handsome, if raw-boned and gangly. "Tuttle P. O'Banyon, ma'am."

Katie giggled behind her library book.

"You have a most impressive name, Tuttle," Bonnie said in his defense, for he was of a tender age and she knew what it was to be hoping for better things, having lived in Patch Town herself. "Did Mr. McKutchen happen to mention how you were to be paid? I'm afraid we're not exactly thriving, as far as trade is concerned."

Tuttle had reddened at Katie's giggle, but his dignity was innate. He squared shoulders that would one day be of impressive width and ran a hand through his shaggy red-gold hair. "Mr. McKutchen said I'd still be working for the company, so I reckon he'll see to my wages."

Bonnie wanted no truck with Eli McKutchen, even indirectly, but she hadn't the heart to send Tuttle P. O'Banyon away. He obviously had high hopes for his position and, if he lost it, he would surely end up smack in the middle of the labor controversy. "Very well, then," she said, "if you'll just wash the front windows when you've finished the sweeping? And Katie, I'll be wanting you to help me with the accounts."

Webb, whom Bonnie had entirely forgotten, cleared his throat at this point.

Embarrassed, Bonnie turned to face him. "Webb! Was there something—"

He smiled, an infinitely patient man. "I've got to spend today getting out this week's issue of the *Northridge News,* but I wondered if you and Rose wouldn't consent to a picnic tomorrow, over across the river."

Bonnie's heart ached within her, although she kept her answering smile firmly in place. If she accepted Webb's invitation, which she very much wanted to do, he might misinterpret her reasons. She knew that he wanted to show her the house he'd been building on his land across the river, that he hoped they would share it one day, as man and wife. That disturbing fact aside, Bonnie enjoyed picnics in the country and she needed the distraction of an outing.

Perhaps this would be an opportunity to have a serious talk with Webb and make her position clear. "I would enjoy that," she said gently.

The look of quiet delight on Webb's face depressed her. Why couldn't she love this fine man, become his wife, bear his children? She would be happy with him, she knew, and the ladies of Northridge might even accept her, since Mr. Hutcheson was so well-respected in the community.

Bonnie bit her lower lip and watched solemnly as Webb left the mercantile to return to his ramshackle press. Oh, to love that man, instead of one who despised her, as Eli did!

By the end of the day, the grim results of tallying her accounts had given Bonnie a throbbing headache. She felt somewhat at loose ends, too, having nowhere to go now that Forbes had banned her from the Brass Eagle Ballroom.

Worries pressed in around Bonnie even as she fed and bathed Rose Marie and put her daughter to bed for the night. Katie, as usual, sat at the kitchen table, poring over a book. Unlike most young girls, she did not read saucy French novels or poetry; instead, Katie consumed treatises on philosophy, science, politics and religion. She was determined, as she had repeatedly stated, to "amount to something."

Bonnie remembered the similar aspirations she'd cherished as a young girl and felt sadder still.

"Why don't you go and watch the entertainments over at the Pompeii tonight?" Katie suggested. "You're a bit down in the mouth, if you don't mind my saying so."

Bonnie had to smile. She did love to watch vaudevillians perform—in New York it had been almost an obsession, she'd been alone so much—but there was rarely time or money for such pursuits now. What with losing her job at the Brass Eagle and the state of her accounts, it was a time for economy, not self-indulgence. "I couldn't. Things are going to be stretched very thin around here, Katie. If the trouble at the smelter yard lasts any length of time, we'll have even fewer customers than we do now, and those who owe us won't pay."

"They don't pay anyway," Katie responded cheerfully. "Go on and see the turns, Mrs. McKutchen. There's a magician—we used to work on the same circuit with him, my family and I—and there's a singer, too."

Bonnie thought with yearning of an evening in the Pompeii Playhouse. She could do with a little laughter, a little wonder, and perhaps a few tears that could not remotely be ascribed to the hurt Eli McKutchen had done her. "Well—"

"Thunderation," persisted Katie, "it only costs ten cents, now doesn't it? Surely you can spare that? It's not as though Miss Genoa would let us starve—"

Bonnie gave the dish towel a brisk, snapping shake and hung it on its peg. "We aren't Genoa's responsibility, Katie. At least, Rose Marie and I are not."

"I've gone and hurt your pride, now, haven't I?" Katie fretted sadly, cupping her chin in her hands. "I didn't mean to, Mrs. McKutchen. I really didn't."

"I know," Bonnie said quietly. She could hear music coming from the Playhouse, rolling atop the summer breeze to float through the open windows of her apartment and call to her. "I would so like to see the entertainments."

Katie had returned to her book, and she was totally absorbed in it, although Bonnie knew that the girl would hear and respond to even the slightest fuss from Rose.

Feeling very lonely and certain that she would not sleep if she retired early—how could she, in that room where Eli had made such tender love to her and then dismissed her as a whore—Bonnie went downstairs and helped herself to a dime from the till. She smoothed her dress and checked her face and hair in one of the shaving mirrors displayed with gentlemen's grooming aids and then called up to Katie, "I'll be across the street if you need me."

Katie's voice was like a chiming bell. "Have a grand evening, ma'am," she answered, "and mind you keep clear of rowdy sorts when you're coming home afterward."

Bonnie grinned as she let herself out through the main door and carefully locked it behind her. For such a young girl—she was barely fourteen—Katie was a motherly sort.

The program had already started by the time Bonnie bought her ticket, found a seat near the back of the spacious Pompeii Playhouse and settled in to forget her troubles for all too brief a time.

She saw the magician Katie had mentioned, along with an act consisting of six remarkably intelligent dogs and a somewhat slower trainer. She wept as an enormous woman sang "In the Shade of the Old Apple Tree," laughed at the bawdy stories told by a homely young man named William Fields. All in all, the evening was most restorative, and Bonnie was in better spirits when she left the theatre, hurrying because Genoa's familiar carriage was parked in front of the store.

Her sister-in-law sat at the kitchen table, sipping tea. She had been chatting with Katie, who smiled uncertainly at Bonnie, closed her book with a thump and vanished into her room.

"Have you ever seen a brighter child than Katie?" Bonnie asked, sensing that something was terribly wrong and wanting to put off knowing what it was.

There was true affection in Genoa's gaze, along with a certain reluctance. "I seem to recall one who was equally precocious," she said.

Bonnie sat down at the table and poured a cup of tea, inwardly bracing herself for bad news. Genoa looked wan and thinner than ever, and she was not in the habit of calling at such a late hour. "The Farley baby—"

Tears sprang into Genoa's pale blue eyes, glistening on her sparse lashes. "Bonnie, Susan and her baby are both fine. I'm here because—because of Eli."

Bonnie's heart stopped beating, then began again, with a pounding lurch. "Something h-has happened to—to—"

"No," Genoa said quickly, reaching out to cover Bonnie's trembling hand. "Eli is fine." She paused a moment, then went on. "Bonnie, he means to take Rose away from you if he can. He said the most dreadful things and he's having poor Mr. Callahan draw up papers to declare you a—a poor influence."

A poor influence. Bonnie suspected that Eli had used considerably stronger words, but she couldn't take offense now because she was too frightened. "He really hates me," she said softly, to herself as much as to Genoa. "Dear Lord, to take my child away!"

"Both Mr. Callahan and I have tried to reason with him,

Bonnie," Genoa hastened to say. "Eli wouldn't listen to a word we said."

Bonnie left her chair like a sleepwalker and went to stand at the sink, her back to Genoa, near to doubling over with the pain. "I can't lose my baby. Eli must not take my baby."

Genoa said nothing, for there was nothing to be said. After a few moments she rose from her chair, pausing behind Bonnie to lay a sympathetic hand on her shoulder. She left soon after, without saying good-bye.

Bonnie slept that night, but fitfully, caught in one nightmare and then another. She awakened at intervals, shaken and sick, to plot her escape and Rose's, but she knew in her heart that she wouldn't have the shadow of a chance against Eli if he took her to law. What judge would take her side?

Webb arrived at midmorning with his horse and buggy, having prevailed upon his landlady to prepare a picnic basket. Bonnie wondered distractedly how Earline Kalb, a woman with a reputation almost as tarnished as her own, had reacted to the request. According to gossip, Earline wanted to make Webb a permanent boarder and, on the rare occasions when she encountered Bonnie, she made a point of snubbing her.

For all that, Webb's devotion was unwavering. "Good Lord," he muttered at the sight of her, "you look as though you haven't slept in a month! Are you all right?"

Bonnie could not explain, at least not immediately. There would be time enough for the terrible truth later, when they were away from the prying eyes of Northridge. She shook her head and allowed Webb to help her into the buggy seat. He placed Rose Marie carefully in her lap and then rounded the rig to climb up himself and take the reins into his hands.

They were waiting to board the small ferry that would carry them across the Columbia, when Bonnie finally spoke, and then it was only to say, "The river looks high."

"It's perfectly safe," Webb assured her gently, as the sturdy craft, built of heavy logs, was drawn toward them by ropes wound around great horse-powered spindles.

The boat drew smoothly up to the riverbank and Webb drove his rig aboard, greeting the grizzled old operator with a smile.

Hem Fenwick had been reading the new issue of the *Northridge News* and he waved it for emphasis as he said, "This here front page article of yours is bound to bruise a few toes, Webb." He spared a polite nod for Bonnie as he closed the gatelike railing behind them and then signaled his helper, stationed on the other side of the river, to set his team of horses to pulling.

Webb grinned. "How about your toes, Hem? Did I step on them?"

"Not me," replied Hem. "But them union fellas might do a little howlin' and hoppin' around."

Bonnie was holding Rose Marie so tightly that the child squirmed in protest, and she made a conscious effort to relax a bit. The gray-green water swirled against the sides of the ferryboat and splashed up over its worn decks, but since neither Hem nor Webb seemed concerned, Bonnie was determined not to worry. She smiled and tried to take an interest in the conversation, a decision she was soon to regret.

"You don't lack for nerve, Hutcheson," Hem observed pleasantly, settling back against the boat's railing and folding his arms beneath his bushy white beard. Overhead, twin ropes suspended from one side of the river to the other squeaked on their pulleys as the craft was hauled through currents powerful enough to carry it away, should it ever break free. "No, indeedy, you surely don't."

Webb looked uncomfortable, not for his own sake, but for Bonnie's. He tried to ignore what Hem had said, turning to smile at Rose and tickle the underside of her chin.

"Ain't afraid of the union, ain't afraid of Eli McKutchen!" Hem crowed in exuberant wonder.

Webb paled, and a muscle in his jawline bunched. "Why would I be afraid of Eli McKutchen?" he asked, in a voice that could have frightened Bonnie, had it been directed at her.

Hem, who was either heroic or stupid, spat over the side of the rail and beamed. "Everybody knows that the Angel is his woman, Webb."

Such fury coursed through Bonnie that she was sickened by it. She hated being called "the Angel" and, more than that, she hated being referred to as Eli's woman, but somehow she managed to keep her temper in check. "Don't talk about me as though I weren't here, Hem," she said in a clear voice. "And I am not Eli McKutchen's 'woman.'"

Hem's grin widened for a moment, but it faltered when he saw the warning in Webb's gaze. He turned away and busied himself with a series of unnecessary signals directed toward shore.

"I'm sorry," Webb said quietly, his hand venturing shyly to cover Bonnie's.

She did not withdraw it. "So am I, Webb. So am I."

It was a relief to Bonnie when the ferryboat finally came ashore and Webb was able to drive his rig up the bank. The road above was muddy and narrow, but Webb navigated it with his usual skill, turning the horse and buggy north toward the plot of land he'd bought some time before Bonnie's return to Northridge. He'd been building the house all that time, putting in a wall here and a floor there, whenever he could spare the time. Now, Bonnie suspected, the place was finished and ready to accommodate a wife.

Dismally, Bonnie watched the horizon.

"Smile," Webb reprimanded softly, just as the sturdy white house came into view. Standing on a gentle rise overlooking the river, it gleamed in the bright sunlight.

"Oh, Webb," Bonnie whispered, "how beautiful!"

The pride in his face shamed her. He slapped the reins down to make the horse move faster, and soon they were turning onto the rutted path that served as a driveway.

Bonnie drew in her breath when they finally came to a stop in front of the house. The windows all had shutters, painted green, and there was a swing on the porch, where a man and his wife could sit of an evening, watching the river roll by. Beyond that river, Northridge was clearly visible.

Sheer despair swelled into Bonnie's throat. "You've done a fine job, Webb," she said, speaking with a difficulty that was not lost on her friend.

Webb took Rose from Bonnie's lap and set the child on her feet, then helped Bonnie down. He did not release her hand, but instead drew her around the side of the house, past a pretty bay window that would offer a grand view to the rear. Here, though no yard had been planted, a sizable plot had been marked off for a garden.

Bonnie wanted, for one wild moment, to live here with Webb always, to plant vegetables and flowers in that garden. A quiet joy filled her at the thought of weeding and watering, of cutting flowers to set out in vases, of preserving tomatoes and carrots and peas for her family to enjoy on cold winter days.

Some dreams, she thought sadly, are so beautiful that we just want to reach out and grab them, even though we know they weren't meant to be our own.

"Would you like to see the inside of the house?" Webb asked gently.

Bonnie didn't think she could bear to walk through those carefully planned rooms, knowing that she would have to disappoint Webb, but she could hardly refuse. "Certainly," she said, catching hold of Rose's hand.

Webb took the other, and Rose Marie swung gleefully between them as they went up the back steps and entered a spacious kitchen. The room hadn't been painted, and there was no linoleum on the floor, but the cabinets had been put up and there seemed to be dozens of them. Their glass windows glistened with newness. The stove was large, larger even than Genoa's, with a long warming oven across its top and a pretty brass woodbox standing beside it.

The room smelled pleasurably of new wood, and Bonnie could imagine herself baking bread there, washing dishes, brewing fresh coffee for a tired husband.

Rose studied herself in the gleaming chrome trim on the stove front and laughed at her distorted reflection, while Bonnie examined the sink, with its shiny water spigots, and felt real yearning. "Oh, Webb—indoor plumbing!"

Webb looked very pleased and proud, but modesty kept him from bragging about such modern conveniences. He said only, "There's a well house out back."

The next room was a dining room—the bay window they had passed outside graced this chamber—and beyond this was the front parlor, a place filled with light and affording a view of Northridge and the river. The fireplace, made of new red brick, was there for the sake of charm, apparently, for the vents in the floor indicated that this house had a central heating system.

Adjoining the parlor was a study that ran the length of the

house. The walls were lined with bookshelves and there were plenty of windows to let in the sun. Through them, Bonnie could see the snow-capped Cascade Mountains in the distance.

"I could work here," Webb said shyly. "And if someone wanted to sew or read—"

Bonnie looked away.

Upstairs there were four bedrooms, the largest at the front of the house boasting its own fireplace with built-in bookshelves on either side. And as if the place weren't already a miniature heaven, there was a bathroom, too, with a flush toilet, hot and cold running water and an enormous tub.

"We could be very happy here, Bonnie," Webb ventured to say.

Bonnie's conviction that one should never marry without love was beginning to waver. "I know," she said.

CHAPTER 10

ELI WAS ANNOYED and distracted. He'd spent hours behind closed doors at the Brass Eagle, wrangling with the union organizers and their more devoted followers, but very little had been accomplished. Now, entering Genoa's kitchen, he cursed himself; it was no wonder that he hadn't been able to achieve anything as far as negotiations were concerned— he'd been able to think of nothing but Bonnie. She'd become an obsession.

Genoa was bent over the open door of the oven, fussing with a shoebox that rested there. The papers Eli carried, which contained Seth's astute opinions on the smelter situation, fluttered to the floor as the muscles in his hands went slack.

"Good God!" he boomed, and the impossibly small infant nestled in the shoebox squalled a pitiable protest. He lunged forward and snatched the baby, box and all, from the oven door. "Genoa, have you taken leave of your senses?!"

Genoa's pale blue eyes widened for a moment, then filled with quiet laughter. "Give me the child, Eli," she said reasonably. Even sweetly.

Eli stepped back in horror, holding the baby protectively. He gaped at his sister, incredulous.

Genoa extended her arms. "Eli," she said, the soul of patience. "The child."

Eli stared, appalled. How could his sister's mind, once so formidable, have degenerated to such a state in a few short years? He supposed it was the loneliness of a spinster's life, the lack of cultural stimulation. He took another step backward and collided with Seth, who bent, muttering, to gather up the notes that were spread out all over the floor. All the while the lawyer dabbed at his neck and forehead with the ever-present handkerchief.

"What is going on here?" he fussed, light glittering on his spectacles as he looked from Eli to Genoa in puzzlement.

"That," blustered Eli, holding the box firmly and squaring his shoulders, "is what I'd like to know! By all that's holy, Seth, I just walked in here and found my own sister about to roast this baby like a suckling pig!"

Genoa's laughter erupted at this, and so, surprisingly, did Seth's. He rose from his crouching position on the floor, forgetting the scattered papers, and carefully pried the shoebox from Eli's grasp.

Genoa took the child, her skinny shoulders shaking, and tucked the toweling that served as a blanket more closely around its squalling little body. "There, there, little one," she said gently, before putting the box back on the oven door.

Eli bolted forward, was ably restrained by a still-chortling Seth. "Eli, relax—"

"Relax?!" bellowed Eli, trying to round his friend and save the child.

Seth caught Eli's shoulders in surprisingly strong hands. "Will you listen to me, you hulking idiot? Your sister is not about to roast this infant; it was born prematurely and it needs to be kept warm!"

Eli closed his eyes, feeling every inch the fool. Memories of the night his son had died swept over him, and he swayed under their impact. The grief, which had never truly left him, followed its wake, and he groped for a chair and then sank into it, his hands rising to cover his face.

"It's Kiley," Seth explained to Genoa in a low voice, and then he left the kitchen.

Eli struggled to control his emotions, stiffened when he

felt Genoa behind him, her hands resting gently on his shoulders.

"I'm so sorry," his sister said in a soft voice.

Eli drew one deep breath after another, willing the trembling, based in the very core of his spirit, to cease. Finally it did. "I should be able to deal with what happened, Genoa," he said miserably. "It's been more than two years."

Genoa's fingers moved, strong and capable, forcing the taut muscles in Eli's shoulders to relax. "The death of one's own child is not an easy thing to come to terms with, Eli. For all that she has Rose Marie to love now, I don't believe Bonnie has managed it either."

Eli lowered his hands. He still felt a need to weep and rage at the injustice of Kiley's death, though the anguish was subsiding again. Involuntarily, he trembled, knowing that the pain would return as fierce as ever.

Genoa swept into the chair beside his and caught one of Eli's hands in both of her own. "I'll never forgive myself," she said quietly, "for not coming to New York when Seth wired me of Kiley's passing. You needed me then, and so did Bonnie."

"There was nothing anyone could have done, Genoa," Eli said, his voice bleak. Bitterness filled the raw hollow in his soul where the pain had been. "And Bonnie recovered very nicely, it seems to me."

"Bonnie did nothing of the sort," Genoa responded immediately with brisk kindness. "She's broken to pieces inside, just as you are. I declare, when I think of how you failed each other, both of you, I could spit!"

Eli stared at his sister. "What are you saying?" he demanded. "I didn't fail Bonnie—"

"You did," Genoa insisted. "And Bonnie failed you. For God's sake, Eli, and for your own, face the truth!"

Eli remembered the distance that had arisen between Bonnie and himself that horrible night and ached. She'd come to him, shattered by the loss of her child and his, and he'd turned her away. Blamed her. There had been a strange, irrational comfort in blaming Bonnie. "What truth is that, Genoa? That my son is dead? That I'll never see him again?" Unmanly tears were dangerously near; Eli choked them back. "Believe me, I've come up against that unholy reality often enough. It haunts me every minute of every day."

"Your son?" Genoa emphasized the words quietly. "Eli, Kiley was Bonnie's son, too. Her loss was as profound as yours, don't you see?"

As the room seemed to be closing in on Eli, he shoved his chair back and shot to his feet, all but smothering. "Enough," he growled, striding toward the door and the fresh air and freedom beyond it.

But Genoa caught his arm in one hand and held on. "Go to Bonnie," she urged her brother desperately. "Tell her how you're hurting and let her tell you what she feels. It's the only way you're ever going to get past this, Eli. The only way!"

Eli wrenched the door open, his lungs dragging in clean summer air in despairing gasps. The pain was back, threatening to crush him. He shook his sister's hand away with a vicious wrench of his arm and hissed, "In the name of God, Genoa, let me be—"

Genoa followed him into the yard, tears of frustrated compassion slipping down her face. "Stop running away, Eli, and let yourself mourn," she begged. "Don't you see that you're poisoning your very soul by holding all that pain inside?"

"There is no pain!" Eli bellowed the lie, and then he stormed away toward the pond, driven by the very anguish he denied.

"How long has Eli been this way?" Genoa asked despondently, as Seth Callahan returned to the kitchen and began collecting his papers.

"From the first," Mr. Callahan answered, his tone glum. "Emotionally he's a volcano. The ground fairly shakes around Eli sometimes, but he will not allow himself to erupt."

Genoa's heart broke within her. "He's afraid?"

Seth shuffled the papers into order, tapping their edges against the tabletop for something to do. "I believe Eli fears that if he lets himself fall apart, he'll never be whole again. The problem is, of course, that it takes all his energies—and they are formidable, Genoa—to maintain the mere semblance of sanity. The longer Eli refuses to give way, the more perilous the situation becomes."

"And now there is the smelter—"

Seth sighed. "Yes. And Bonnie."

Genoa took a handkerchief from the pocket of her skirt and dried her eyes. "Yes. Bonnie. Whatever can we do to help them, Seth?"

Seth removed his spectacles and rubbed his myopic eyes with a thumb and forefinger. "Very little, I fear. I pray that when Eli reaches the breaking point, Bonnie will be there for him. He needs her desperately."

Genoa shuddered, hugging herself. "I do believe the world is collapsing around our ears, Mr. Callahan. Bonnie is very, very strong, but for all the brave show she puts on, she's just as badly wounded as Eli. I'm not sure she has the strength to help anyone else."

Mr. Callahan sighed again and put his spectacles back in place. "You may be right, my dear," he said, his voice husky and distracted. "May heaven help us all."

They sat quietly on a blanket spread over the ground, Webb and Bonnie, Rose Marie sleeping soundly between them. Her heart in her throat, Bonnie busied herself putting leftover food back into the picnic basket, having already washed the plates and utensils inside the house, at the kitchen sink.

Webb stopped her nervous motions by cupping one hand under her chin. "Bonnie," he said, with gruff gentleness. "Look at me."

Bonnie trembled and raised her eyes to Webb's kind, handsome face. Again she willed herself to love him, again she failed. Her whole soul hungered for Eli McKutchen, much as she wished things to be otherwise.

"You don't love me," Webb guessed, without bitterness or rancor.

Miserably Bonnie shook her head. "Not the way a wife should love a husband, Webb."

A short silence fell. Rose Marie fretted in her sleep and Webb touched her little back with one hand, settling her.

"You still love Eli," he said after a few moments.

Bonnie nodded. "Against all good sense and all reason."

She paused, the pain and fear and despair nearly overwhelming her. "H-he hates me, Webb. He's planning to take Rose Marie away from me."

Webb tensed. "Did Eli tell you that himself?"

"No. Genoa did," Bonnie confessed, and her dignity, so long her strength, was broken at last. One tear slid, tickling, down her cheek. "I'll die without Rose. She's all I have."

Rose whimpered in her sleep as Webb smoothed the child's tangled hair. "You won't lose her, Bonnie. I won't let that happen."

"There isn't anything you can do to stop it," Bonnie insisted, dashing at her wet cheek with one hand. "Eli will win. He has money, power, influence—"

"And he knows that Rose Marie is his daughter?"

Webb's question surprised Bonnie. "Yes."

"Suppose we said that she was mine? Suppose you married me, and we told the world that Rose Marie was my child?"

Bonnie's eyes widened, even though she had considered this approach herself. "You would do that? You would claim Rose—you would still want to marry me, even knowing that I don't love you?"

Webb shrugged and, though he smiled an ingenuous smile, his blue eyes were dark with pain. "You might come to love me, Bonnie—someday. Stranger things have happened, you know."

Bonnie lowered her head, stricken. Under the circumstances, Webb looked very good to her; he was a warm, dry place to run to while rain lashed at the ground, but he was truly a wonderful man who deserved so much more than Bonnie could give him. "I would be cheating you, Webb. Suppose—suppose I never forget Eli?"

"I'm willing to take that chance, Bonnie. Marry me—let me prove that I can make you happy."

Impulsively Bonnie reached out and grasped both his hands in hers. "Webb, will you think of yourself just once? Suppose I don't make you happy? Suppose you end up hating the sight of me?"

"I could never hate you."

"Yes, you could!"

A cool wind was blowing up from the river, and Bonnie

shivered. The sky had clouded over and a light spattering of rain began to fall, ending the conversation and sending both Webb and Bonnie into frantic activity. While Bonnie snatched up the picnic basket, Webb roused Rose Marie and hurried toward the shelter of the house.

They waited in the living room, hoping the rain would let up. It didn't.

"Unless you want to be stranded here," Webb said diplomatically, "we'd better leave."

Involuntarily Bonnie's eyes lifted to the ceiling. Webb's bedroom was directly above. For all that she was considering marrying this man, she had not once imagined sleeping with him. How could she have overlooked something so fundamental? She blushed hotly when she saw that Webb was watching her, reading her thoughts.

"Let's go," she said, too hastily.

"Damn," Webb replied, with good-natured disappointment. And then he bundled Rose tightly in his suitcoat and bolted outside, leading the way to the buggy.

The road, if it could be called that, was already a mass of muddy goo, and it was barely visible for the pounding rain. When they reached the ferry landing, Hem and his helper were unhitching the team that worked on that side of the river.

"Water's too damned high to cross!" the old man informed them. "You'll have to wait till morning!"

Bonnie cast one frantic glance at Webb and saw that he was more than content to accept the situation. In fact he was grinning a cocky grin.

"Hem Fenwick!" Bonnie yelled over the din of the rain. "You take us across that river right now!"

"No, ma'am!" Hem shouted back.

Webb looked damnably smug. In the last analysis, it seemed, all men were alike. "We'll drown if we try it, Bonnie!"

"Webb Hutcheson, people are going to talk!" Bonnie shrieked, and Rose, startled, began to wail and struggle in her arms.

Webb took the child onto his lap, soothing her. "That has never bothered you before, now, has it?" he retorted.

Hem looked delighted. "Whoo-ee, I'd like to be there when McKutchen hears about this!"

"It might lend a lot of credence to our story," Webb reasoned quietly. Hem was frowning now, trying to hear what was being said. "We could even say that we've been secretly married for months—"

"Webb!" Bonnie wailed.

Webb patted her knee. "Now, now, dear, let's be calm. Reasonable. We can't cross the river without a ferry, now can we?"

"There's a bridge downriver—" Bonnie speculated anxiously.

"Ten miles downriver," Webb pointed out. "Bonnie, we'd never make it through. It's getting dark and there isn't much of a road even in the best of weather. Imagine how it would be now, in this rain."

Sizing Hem Fenwick up in a long glance, Bonnie considered piracy. Following that, she weighed the possibility of swimming across the river.

"Think of Rose," Webb said, spoiling everything.

Bonnie sighed, wholly defeated.

Chuckling, Webb turned the buggy back toward his house.

It was a night for surprises, Forbes Durrant thought to himself. He wouldn't have expected McKutchen to patronize the Brass Eagle after all that had happened, but there he was, swilling whiskey as though he might be trying to put out a fire in his belly. Forbes could have told him, from bitter experience, that whiskey wasn't going to cure what ailed him, but why extend the favor? Let McKutchen learn for himself that nothing could extinguish the Angel's blazes, once she'd set them.

The second surprise was seeing Earline Kalb storming toward him. Even for a woman of her questionable reputation, entering a saloon alone was unthinkable.

Forbes gave her a mild assessment as she approached. She was a shapely piece and he wondered what it would be like to bed her.

"Earline," he said with a nod.

113

She took in his bruised and battered face and smiled. "Forbes," she returned cordially.

After refilling McKutchen's glass, Forbes turned back to the woman. She was drawing stares all around. "How can I help you?" he asked.

"I'm looking for Bonnie McKutchen."

The whole saloon went silent. Out of the corner of his swollen eye, Forbes saw Eli's glass stop midway between the bar and his mouth.

"The Angel doesn't work here anymore," Forbes said moderately.

"She's no angel," Earline shot back, "and we both know it."

Forbes shrugged.

"How about Webb Hutcheson? Has he been in tonight?"

Forbes allowed himself a quick glance in Eli McKutchen's direction and saw that he was listening. Intently. "Sorry. Webb isn't a regular customer. I don't know where he is."

"Maybe you don't," Earline allowed, "but you always know where the Angel is and what she's doing, Forbes, and don't try to deny it."

"I'm not denying anything."

"Pa took Webb and Mrs. McKutchen across the river this mornin'," put in young Walt Fenwick, from beside one of the billiard tables. "Reckon they're stuck over there for the night, 'cause of the rain. Don't nobody need to worry, though—Webb's got himself a fine house yonder and they'll stay warm and dry."

Forbes closed his eyes and drew a deep breath. When he looked again, he saw Earline grab a billiard ball and fling it at Walt's head. Poor Walt dodged that, a baffled expression on his face, and whirled, only to collide with Eli McKutchen.

Eli caught the hapless ferryman by the lapels and lifted him clear off the floor. "Where exactly is this fine house?"

Forbes sighed and started to round the bar. He couldn't afford any trouble; now that he was no longer managing the McKutchen holdings, the Brass Eagle was his only source of income. All the same he didn't know what he was going to do once he reached Eli and the man he was about to strangle.

114

He was saved by that scrawny little lawyer Callahan, who left his own place at the bar and craned his neck to look into his client's face and say with authority, "Eli, that will be quite enough."

Eli released his hold on Walt's coat and thrust him onto the billiard table. Forbes winced, remembering what it would cost to replace the felt that covered it.

"Where is it?" the giant demanded, his gaze shifting to Forbes.

Forbes swallowed. "Where is what?"

Eli advanced a step, looking dangerous. "The house, you idiot. Hutcheson's house."

"Two miles due north of the ferry landing," Earline supplied helpfully. "But you'll never get across that river in this rain."

I wouldn't bet on that, Forbes thought, careful to keep a straight face.

Thunder cracked in the sky as Eli McKutchen turned and strode toward the door. The lawyer slapped a bill down on the bar and ran after him.

For the Angel's sake, Forbes hoped some stupid son of a bitch wouldn't offer the use of a rowboat.

The house was snug against the cold and the rain, and Webb had lit lamps all around. They'd made supper of the leftovers from the picnic and a warm fire was blazing on the living-room hearth.

Rose slept comfortably in a corner, Webb having made her a bed of his coat and the lap robe from the buggy.

Bonnie was miserable. "I'm ruined," she said to the flames in the fireplace. "Ruined!"

Webb returned from the barn just then, his hair dripping wet, his shirt transparent. He chuckled as he sat down beside Bonnie in front of the fire. "This is ironic," he said. "The Angel, worrying about her reputation!"

"I do have morals, you know!"

Webb grinned and planted an innocuous kiss on the tip of Bonnie's nose. "Be honest. It isn't the talk you're worried about at all. It's what you think I expect of you."

Bonnie blushed. "What exactly do you expect?"

Webb gave a heavy and rather exaggerated sigh. "Nothing you don't want to give, Bonnie, so calm down."

Bonnie drew a deep breath. Of course, she knew that Webb would never force her, but she had to worry about something, it seemed. "Suppose it rains for days and days, Webb," she fretted, gazing into the flames again.

Webb took the newest edition of his paper from the picnic basket and handed it to her. There was just the merest hint of sadness in his voice as he said, "If it does, I'll build an ark. Read the paper, Bonnie, while I look around for something we can sleep on."

Bonnie had no intention of sleeping, but she did need something to distract herself. She unfolded the latest issue of the *Northridge News* and tilted the paper toward the fire in order to see the print. Webb's article about the troubles at the smelter caught her eye immediately, and she read with growing concern. Hem Fenwick had been right when he'd said this piece would squash a few toes.

Knowing Webb as a gentle, caring man, Bonnie was always struck by the blunt manner in which he wrote. The article was a scathing indictment of outsiders who stirred up trouble for their own purposes, and it urged the workers of Northridge to give Eli McKutchen a fighting chance to right the wrongs that had been done them. If he refused to meet their demands for higher wages, and better conditions in which to live and work, then and only then should they strike.

Bonnie was staring thoughtfully into the fire when Webb returned with an armload of work clothes. Of these, he made a makeshift bed on the floor in front of the fireplace.

"I'm afraid this was the best I could do," he said. "Next time I come out here, I'm bringing food and blankets."

Bonnie could only think of the article. "Webb, Hem was right. The union people aren't going to thank you for this piece."

"I don't write to please them, Bonnie."

She drew her knees up and rested her chin on them. "Frankly, I'm surprised that you took Eli's side the way you did. You've always been critical of the way the smelter has been managed, and you've waged a one-man campaign against Patch Town."

Webb sighed and, after one cautious look at Bonnie, removed his sodden shirt. Only then did she notice that he was shivering. "I'm no friend of Eli McKutchen's, Bonnie—he knew about Patch Town and all the other problems connected with the smelter, and he took his sweet time looking into things."

"But still you defended him." Bonnie took up a heavy coat from the pile of work clothes and gently draped it over Webb's broad shoulders.

"I wasn't defending McKutchen," Webb insisted quietly. "I was only trying to avoid more trouble. If he's willing to make things right, then the town ought to give him that chance. I just hope it isn't too late."

Once again Bonnie sat with her chin on her knees. She thought of the men already out on strike, and a shiver ran up her spine. "In a way I blame myself," she said. "For the conditions in Patch Town, at least."

Webb was silent, thoughtful.

"No one knew better than I did how it was—how it is—to live there. I should have pressed Eli to make changes."

"You were young, Bonnie. And how much influence would you have had?"

Bonnie wanted to cry, but she held back. "There was a time when I had a great deal of influence with Eli, Webb. He loved me very much. Until—until—"

Webb's hand came shyly to cover Bonnie's. "Until your baby died?"

Bonnie cast a quick look at the sleeping Rose Marie, in an unconscious attempt to reassure herself that this child was indeed safe. "Everything went wrong after that. Eli blamed me, you know."

Webb nodded and his grip on Bonnie's hand tightened for a second. "I know."

In spite of herself, Bonnie trembled at the memory. "I thought it would pass, that it was his grief making him act that way. But things just went from bad to worse and finally everything fell apart. Eli ran away, and so did I."

Webb glanced at Rose Marie. "There must have been moments when you could reach out to each other."

Bonnie would have been embarrassed to speak of such intimate matters with any other man and most women, but this was Webb. Her friend. No matter what she said to him, he always seemed to understand. "Eli moved out of our house the day after the funeral, the very day. I know he took at least one mistress. I—I was desperate to reach him somehow—"

"You don't need to tell me, Bonnie."

"I need to tell someone, Webb—I so need to tell someone!"

Webb put one strong arm around her shoulders and held her close. Bonnie sensed that he had braced himself against whatever she might say, but she was unable to keep her peace.

"J-just before Eli left for Cuba, I telephoned him at—at his club. I begged him—oh, Webb, I actually *begged* him—to come home. I thought we could talk—"

Webb waited in silence for Bonnie to go on.

"I th-threw myself at him, Webb. I was so afraid and so desperate—"

"And he made love to you."

Bonnie shivered and tears sprang to her eyes. "That's putting it kindly. I've never seen Eli like that—he tore my clothes, Webb. It was as th-though he hated me."

Webb stiffened, and Bonnie could feel the quiet fury coursing through his big frame. "Did he hurt you?"

"Oh, yes. But not in the way you think. The pain wasn't physical, Webb." Bonnie ached to remember that afternoon in the sumptuous room she had once shared so happily with her husband. Eli had used her, driven her to one shameful response after another, and then left her. "It was the contempt. Webb, he was so cold. So brutally cold."

"It's over now, Bonnie," Webb pointed out, after a very long time. "I know you were hurt, but that part of your life is behind you."

Bonnie thought of a night just past, when she had lain with Eli McKutchen. She'd forgotten everything, every hurt, every insult, and responded to him with an abandon that could only be described as wanton. And in the morning she'd awakened to find a fifty-dollar bill on her bedside table. For all of that, Bonnie couldn't be certain, even now, that if Eli crooked one finger, she wouldn't go to him. Her need of him was that consuming, that danger-ous.

She sighed.

"It's over," Webb said again.

Solid, substantial Webb. How Bonnie hoped and prayed that he was right.

CHAPTER 11

THE BACK OF Eli's head throbbed, and the thin light flowing in through his bedroom window was an assault on his eyes. He drew the covers up over his face and groaned.

"I don't remember getting drunk enough to deserve a hangover this bad," he muttered, the words muffled by several layers of bedding.

Seth's voice came from somewhere near the foot of the bed. "You didn't. I clubbed you over the head with a bottle."

Slowly Eli drew his covers down to the middle of his nose and tried to focus on the man who claimed to be his friend. "What?"

"You were bound and determined to swim the Columbia River," Seth huffed. "I had to do something."

Eli grimaced as he touched the back of his head and found a goose egg the size of a croquet ball. "You might have tried reasoning with me, you know," he complained.

"I might have tried reasoning with a stump, too. Get out of that bed, Eli, and get dressed. We've got to meet with the union people again."

"Talk about reasoning with stumps," Eli sighed, squinting up at the ceiling until his vision came right. "We tried that yesterday, remember?"

120

"Yes, and we'll try again today. We'll try tomorrow, if we have to, and the day after that and the day after—"

"Talk isn't going to accomplish anything, Seth. We need action."

"What do you suggest?"

"Those poor bastards in Patch Town must be up to their knees in river water, after last night's storm. Get them out of there."

Seth made a rude harrumph sound. "And put them where, Eli? In your sister's parlor?"

Eli ignored Seth's questions, sensible though they were. "Get some lumber and start building those new cabins we talked about. On that stretch of land south of town. I want sewers and washrooms and be sure to leave room for kitchen gardens and the like—"

"Am I to hire help or just make a morning of it all by myself?"

In spite of his goose egg and the niggling knowledge that Bonnie had spent the night with another man, Eli laughed. "Hire help." He tried to sit up, groaned and fell back to his pillows again. "What did you say you hit me with?"

Seth chuckled and left the room without answering.

After a very long time, Eli managed to maneuver his way out of bed. Cleaning up and dressing were interminable processes, and by the time he'd gotten himself downstairs, he was in a foul mood.

Genoa was in the kitchen again, with the shoebox baby, and she smiled at her brother, undaunted by his scowl. "You've missed breakfast," she said.

"I'm not surprised," grumbled Eli, opening the icebox and peering inside. He found a milk jug there and pulled off its top, drinking directly from the bottle in a calculated effort to annoy his sister.

Just then Eli noticed the small person sitting at the table, huddled inside a blanket. Genoa rolled her eyes as she spoke to it. "You must overlook my brother's rudeness, Susan," she said. "He has the manners of a warthog."

"Damnation!" Eli thundered, slamming the icebox door. First Bonnie had gone off to spend the night with some ink monkey on the other side of a raging river, then Seth had hit him with a bottle, and now his own sister was consigning

121

him to the social status of a warthog! "Hellfire!" he roared, as an afterthought.

The blanketed figure trembled.

"Now, now, Susan," Genoa said kindly. "Drink your tea and don't be afraid of Eli. Despite appearances, he's really quite harmless."

"Harmless," Eli muttered, storming out of the kitchen and back through the house. They'd see how damned *harmless* he was when he got his hands on Bonnie and that lover of hers.

Five minutes later, Eli entered the dining room of the Union Hotel and ordered breakfast. He made sure his table was near a front window, which afforded him a clear view of the street. If anybody approached Bonnie's store, he would see them.

His head injury having had no discernible effect on his appetite, Eli consumed two plates of fried ham, four eggs and six biscuits by the time a muddy buggy drew to a halt in front of the mercantile. With some help from her sweetheart, Bonnie alighted from the rig. She carried Rose Marie in her arms and smiled wearily, shaking her head at something Hutcheson had said.

Eli tossed a bill onto the table and abandoned his breakfast, striding out into the sunny, rain-washed new day.

"Papa!" Rose Marie crowed, extending both arms and wriggling in her mother's arms.

Both Bonnie and her swain stiffened. Bonnie tightened her grasp on the child and retreated a step, but Hutcheson turned and faced Eli squarely, and there was no fear in his bearing or in his eyes.

Rose Marie began to squirm and shriek. "Papa!" she screamed, furious.

Bonnie calmly unlocked the front door of the mercantile and disappeared inside.

Hutcheson's clothes were wrinkled, like Bonnie's—they'd probably both been caught in the rain—and his hair stuck out all over his head. Despite all this, there was an unwavering air of dignity about him, and Eli liked him for it.

"Maybe we'd better talk," Eli said.

Interested passersby were pausing in front of the mercantile's spotless windows, pretending fascination with the goods displayed there. "Not here," Webb replied with a long sigh. "Let's go over to the hotel. I could use a cup of hot coffee."

Eli felt a muscle in his jawline jump, brought it under firm control. "Whatever you say."

"If you don't stop screaming for your papa, young lady," Bonnie hissed, shaking one finger in Rose Marie's outraged face, "I'm going to give you the spanking to end all spankings!"

Katie, always the peacemaker, made haste to interest Rose Marie in the oatmeal she'd prepared. "There now, our Rose won't be needing a spanking, now will she. She's such a good girl!"

"She's such a McKutchen!" snapped Bonnie. Her hair was tangled and her clothes were rumpled, and she wanted nothing so much as to take a hot bath and sleep, but she wouldn't be permitted the luxury because Eli and Webb were probably facing off in the street at that very moment. She had to get to them before yet another disaster could take place.

Muttering, she stomped out of the kitchen and down the outside stairs, only to find the sidewalk empty except for normal traffic. She looked up and down the street, running one hand over her matted hair. Dear Lord, where had those two great oafs gotten to? She had to find them.

Tuttle P. O'Banyon was busily sweeping the sidewalk, and Bonnie spoke to him three times before he reluctantly gave her his attention.

"Have you seen Mr. Hutcheson and Mr. McKutchen this morning, Tuttle?"

Tuttle reddened and his Adam's apple moved up and down the long column of his neck. Clearly, he'd heard that Mrs. McKutchen had spent the night beyond the river with Mr. Hutcheson. There probably wasn't a single person in all of Northridge who hadn't been told the grisly tale. "Yes, ma'am."

It was all Bonnie could do not to stomp her feet. "Where?" she hissed.

Tuttle gestured toward the Union Hotel with one bony hand and went back to his work.

Walking into that hotel with her hair and clothes in such a damning state and the last shreds of her reputation gone was one of the most difficult things Bonnie had ever had to do, and she managed it only because there was no real alternative.

She felt the eyes of waitresses and diners alike boring into her as she crossed the spacious dining room. Webb and Eli were seated at a table near the front windows, glaring at each other over steaming mugs of coffee.

They sensed Bonnie's presence at exactly the same moment and both of them stood out of deference to her, though Webb's rising was the more mannerly. Eli looked wryly explosive, and Bonnie wanted to crawl under the rug when his eyes swept over her, taking in every wrinkle in her dress.

"If you make a scene," she said under her breath, as Webb drew out a chair for her, "I will kill you both. Is that understood?"

"Perfectly," replied Eli, staring down into his coffee cup.

"We will work this through," Webb insisted, "like rational adults."

"Dreamer," Bonnie muttered.

"I was just telling Mr. McKutchen here about our house," Webb immediately announced.

A sidelong glance at Eli put Bonnie on alert. "Our house?" she croaked, praying that Webb wouldn't just leap into the deception they'd spent the night planning.

"Yes, indeed," Webb answered, beaming. His hand moved to cover Bonnie's but withdrew under the instant heat of Eli's gaze. "Bonnie and I have agreed that it's time we stopped keeping our true relationship a secret."

Eli reached out for a table knife and Bonnie's stomach did a triple backflip, relaxing when he only turned the utensil from end to end. "After last night," he said in a dangerously polite voice, without looking at either Bonnie or Webb, "there can be no question of your 'true relationship.'"

Bonnie flushed. She hadn't come to the decision to marry Webb easily—they had talked all night long—but she wasn't

124

prepared to feel shame. Fear, yes. Dread, yes. But not shame. "Eli—"

His golden eyes swung to her face, full of menace. And the profoundest sort of pain.

Bonnie would have called the whole charade to a halt, then and there, if Webb hadn't cut her off.

"For reasons of our own, Bonnie and I thought it best to keep our marriage a secret. The fact of the matter is that we've been husband and wife for a long time."

Only Bonnie could have seen past Eli's cold manner. He was humiliated. Wounded. "How long?" he asked.

"Two years," Webb answered kindly. Bonnie couldn't have spoken if her very life had depended upon doing so.

"Two years." Eli sighed the words and, after a moment or so, his eyes linked with Bonnie's. It was like looking into a nickelodeon; she saw his thoughts so clearly. He was remembering the night he'd bathed Bonnie, carried her to her bed, made love to her. He was remembering her responses and his own.

Only the memory of the fifty-dollar bill he'd left behind in payment kept Bonnie from shouting that Webb was lying.

Eli's chair moved soundlessly over the carpet and, as he rose, Webb did, too.

"Two years," Eli marveled distractedly but, when his gaze locked with Webb's, the air between the two men fairly sizzled with electricity. "You poor, misguided bastard," he said in a low voice, and then he turned and walked out of the dining room and Bonnie covered her face with both hands and swallowed hard. She felt dizzy, almost to the point of fainting.

"There was no other way," Webb said gently.

It was a long moment before Bonnie dared to speak. "Go away, Webb. Just go away."

"At least let me see you back to the store—"

"You've done enough. We've done enough. Just go—I can get back to the store on my own."

Reluctantly, Webb left and, after a few more minutes, Bonnie slipped out of her chair and somehow made her way across the dining room, through the small lobby, into the street. She climbed the outside stairway of the mercantile— she might have crawled for all she remembered of the journey—stumbled into her bedroom and collapsed onto the bed.

"Bullfeathers," Genoa said briskly, turning from the blue vellum invitations she'd been addressing at her desk in the rear parlor. "If Bonnie and Webb were married, I would have known it. The whole town would have known it."

Considering the way he felt, Eli was strangely calm. "Why would they lie about something like that?" he asked, leaning against the mantel, gazing at his own reflection in the mirror above it but seeing images of Bonnie instead. Bonnie, lying beneath him, her face transfigured as they made love.

Genoa's answer was startling. "You forced them to lie, Eli. And I must confess that the fault is partly mine, too."

Eli whirled. "What?"

"You were going to take Rose Marie away," his sister reminded him. "Bonnie would do almost anything to prevent that."

"You told her?"

"Of course I told her. Bonnie is my dearest friend."

"And I'm your brother!"

Genoa closed her eyes for a moment and, when she opened them again, they were bright with blue fire. "Yes, Eli, you are my brother and I love you dearly. But what you planned to do to Bonnie was just plain cruel and I had to give her warning!"

"Cruel? Has it ever occurred to you that I might have been trying to protect my daughter?"

"You weren't trying to protect Rose Marie, Eli—be honest with yourself if you won't be honest with me. You wanted to hurt Bonnie because of Kiley, because she wasn't waiting for you when you came home from Cuba."

Eli lowered his head. Much as he might want to, there was no way he could deny what his sister had said. He cared for Rose Marie, but there hadn't been time for any sort of bond to develop between himself and his daughter. "They'll say that Hutcheson is Rose's father," he despaired.

"Of course they will. It would do Bonnie and Webb no good whatsoever to pretend they've been married all this time if they said otherwise."

A horrible thought possessed Eli. Bonnie would have

been lonely and frightened when she arrived back in Northridge two years before. Maybe she'd turned to Webb Hutcheson. Maybe—

Genoa shook her head, obviously reading her brother's mind. "Eli, you oaf, you know that child is your own. Rose Marie has your hair, your eyes and, regrettably, your temper."

Eli remembered how Rose had squirmed in Bonnie's arms back there on the sidewalk, shrieking for her papa. Yes, she was his, all right. He smiled.

"Eli McKutchen," Genoa demanded suspiciously, "what are you planning to do?"

Apparently Genoa's mystical abilities had deserted her. "Nothing," Eli answered. "Nothing at all."

"But—"

"I've got work to do, Genoa. Must be going." He slipped his hands into his trouser pockets and grinned, feeling better than he had in a long, long time. The beads and tassels of Genoa's portiere, usually a source of vast annoyance, hardly bothered Eli as he went through the parlor doorway.

"Eli!"

He paused, just over the threshold. "You have your hands full around here," he called back, as an afterthought, "what with that young widow and her baby. Seth and I will be taking rooms at the Union Hotel."

The beaded portiere clattered as Genoa shot through the doorway. "The Union Hotel? Nonsense—Eli, this is your home!"

Eli bent his head and planted a brief, blithe kiss on Genoa's furrowed forehead. "I'll send someone for my things," he said.

Genoa looked despondent. "I don't understand. Eli, if you're angry with me—"

Eli laughed. "I'm not angry, Genoa. But it's time I took hold and started straightening out my life and, to do that, I have to be in the center of things. In more ways than one."

Genoa's eyes widened. "You want to be near Bonnie!" she speculated, on a long breath.

"That's part of it," Eli replied. And then he turned and walked out of the house. At sunset, when the second shift

127

fought its way through the growing picket lines outside the smelter works, Eli was among them, dressed the way the workmen were dressed and carrying a dinner box.

The work was harder than Eli would ever have imagined, but he stationed himself at one of the blast furnaces and shoveled coal into its hell-hot belly until his shirt was soaked with sweat and his muscles were screaming.

The other men watched him surreptitiously as they tended dross pots and quenchers and sorted ore, and by the time the whistle signaling the dinner break finally blew, they were all but hopping with curiosity.

Holding a sandwich in soot-blackened hands, Eli forced himself to eat. He knew the men were thinking that he'd drop any minute and he wondered if they weren't right.

By the time the shift ended, a full twelve hours after it had begun, Eli was so weary that he could barely walk. Somehow he managed to sign out, put his shirt back on, and stagger through the picket line. Seth was waiting on the smelter road with a buggy, but Eli pretended not to see him. The other men made it as far as their beds unaided, and he would do that, too.

He was half blind with fatigue by the time he reached his room at the Union Hotel. Without taking the time to wash up or even remove his clothes, he collapsed onto the bed and slept like a corpse.

Hours later, Eli was awakened by the grinding pain in his own muscles. Muttering to himself, he thrust himself off the bed and stumbled into the bathroom, where he ran a bath so hot that he couldn't see his hand in front of his face for the steam. He sank into the scalding water with a grimace, willing to endure the burning heat because of the relief it gave his knotted ligaments.

Soon enough, there was a discreet tap at the bathroom door.

"Go away, Seth," Eli moaned.

"I have brandy," Seth cajoled. "Imported. A double shot."

Eli reconsidered. "Come in," he called back.

Seth brought the brandy in and extended it to Eli in a crystal snifter, his eyes politely averted. "You're a madman," he said, not unkindly.

128

"So I've been told," Eli replied, after several gulps of brandy. "How long before I have to go back to that hellhole?"

Seth drew his watch from a special pocket in his vest and consulted it with raised eyebrows. His spectacles were so fogged with steam that he had to look down his nose to see. "Approximately two hours, though whether or not you truly have to go back is certainly a debatable subject."

"I have to," Eli confirmed grimly.

"Why?"

"Because I'm not going to have any credence with those men unless they know I can do what they do every damned day of their lives, that's why. Don't you see, Seth? To them, I'm just Josiah's spoiled grandson. They know I've got money and they know I've never had my hands dirty before today."

Seth sighed. "I see what you mean."

"Good," Eli snapped in reply. "That's a comfort to me, Seth. A real comfort. Now, get out of here and let me die with dignity, will you?"

When Seth had gone, Eli finished his drink and his bath and reluctantly got out of the bathtub. The chambermaid was going to curse him when she saw that the pristine white porcelain tub had been turned to a greasy black, but that was the way of it.

Every muscle throbbing in protest, Eli dressed himself in fresh clothes, pulled his filthy boots back onto his feet and went downstairs, dinner box in hand. He consumed a fried chicken dinner in the hotel dining room and was back at the smelter in time to pass the grumbling strikers with the other men who worked the second shift.

That night was worse than the night before. The air seemed hotter and every lift of the coal shovel sent searing pain streaking across the small of Eli's back, but he worked on until the first whistle blew. This time he couldn't make himself eat, even though he needed food almost as much as he needed rest. His throat closed over every bite he tried to take and he knew that he'd be violently ill if he did manage to swallow something. That would certainly undo everything he was trying to accomplish.

"Better eat, Mr. McKutchen," urged the young man who

shoveled coal into the other furnace. "A body can't hold up under twelve hours of work without somethin' to keep the fire goin'."

Eli dropped the sandwich, made in the kitchen of the Union Hotel, into his dinner box. His colleague resembled a blackface minstrel, he was so dirty, and Eli figured he probably looked about the same himself. "What's your name?"

"Benjamin Rollins."

"How long have you been working here?"

Rollins swelled up with pride. "Nigh on five years now, I guess. I was ten when I started."

"Ten," Eli muttered. At ten, he'd been building boats to sail on the pond behind his grandfather's house.

"Yes, sir. I was a pot tender first, but I got real strong, real fast, so they put me on the furnaces soon enough. Twice the wages."

Eli only nodded, too tired to carry the conversation further. He looked down at his blackened, blistered hands and smiled ruefully, remembering his grandfather's iron-fast belief that a man should never ask his workers to do anything he couldn't do himself.

"Some of us are wonderin' what you're doin' here, Mr. McKutchen," Ben Rollins choked out. His eyes were on the sandwich in Eli's dinner box. "Fancy man like you don't usually do such as shovelin'."

Eli extended the sandwich, ignoring the boy's remark. The more the men wondered why he was feeding furnace along with the rest, the better.

"Well, if you ain't gonna eat," Rollins conceded, his eyes round and white in his black face. He snatched the sandwich from Eli's hand and literally stuffed it into his mouth.

At six the next morning, when Eli again saw daylight, he was surprised to find Bonnie waiting for him at the gate. She looked fresh and pretty in her pink and white gingham dress, and the sunlight glimmered red in her hair. For a moment, Eli considered hurling his arms around her out of sheer spite. At least he tried to convince himself that that would be his motivation.

"Have you gone mad?" she demanded, in a whisper, falling into step beside Eli as he strode along the road. Every nonchalant swing of his dinner box cost him an agonizing price, but he was damned if he'd let Bonnie know that. "You can't go on doing this kind of work!"

"Thank you for your concern," Eli replied. "Does your husband know you're out?"

Bonnie bit her lip and lowered her head, and Eli was moved to a painful sort of tenderness by the wispy tendrils of mink-soft hair that danced along the nape of her neck. He wanted to kiss her there.

"Eli—"

He felt a sweeping sort of triumph and deliberately hid the fact. "Yes, Mrs.—Hutcheson?"

Bonnie stopped in the stream of curious workers, her arms folded, her eyes snapping as she glared up into Eli's sooty face. "Building a new place for the families to live is enough, Eli. The other concessions are enough. You don't have to kill yourself to do penance for having money!"

"I'm not trying to do penance for anything, Bonnie," Eli answered with a sigh. "I care about these people and I want them to know it."

"Look at you! You're so tired you can barely stand, and you're filthy in the bargain! Is that caring?" She drew in a deep shaking breath. "I'll tell you what it is, Eli McKutchen —it's madness!"

Eli had to start walking again. People were staring and, besides, his muscles were beginning to cramp. "I really don't think you should be here," he said. "It's highly improper, you know."

"I don't give a— I don't care whether or not it's proper! Someone has to get some sense through that cast-iron head of yours before you hurt yourself!"

He tossed her a sidelong grin. "If you're worried about my safety, Mrs. Hutcheson—"

"Stop calling me Mrs. Hutcheson!"

"That's your name, isn't it?"

Her glorious purple-gray eyes rounded and then shot sparks. "Yes! Yes, you lout!"

The other workers had gone ahead, though a few of them were brave enough to risk a subtle look back over their shoulders now and again. Eli kept his voice down.

"You didn't mention your husband the other night when

we made love. Are you in the habit of whoring behind Hutcheson's back, Bonnie?"

She stopped again and her hand lashed out, making sharp contact with Eli's face and coming away black with soot. Her eyes turned almost as dark and her cheeks were a bright, enticing shade of apricot.

Eli kept walking, swallowing a grin. He shook his head, as if in wonder. "I guess I'm just old-fashioned. I wouldn't want my wife letting other men bathe her."

Bonnie scrambled to catch up, so mad that she could barely contain herself. There wasn't a damned thing she could say without confessing that she and Hutcheson had invented their marriage and that knowledge was, to Eli, as sweet as new cream.

He tried to sound ingenuous, though in truth he wanted to drag Bonnie into the bushes and make slow, sweet love to her. "Do you carry on with Webb the way you did with me?" he asked.

"C-carry on?" Bonnie was double-stepping to keep up, and the color glowed bright in her face.

"Yes," Eli replied clinically. "You make a yelping sound—"

"A yelp—I do *not!*"

"Oh, but you do. And the things you say!"

It didn't seem possible, but Bonnie blushed even harder. She made a strangled sound in her throat, caught her skirts up in both hands and ran back to her store as fast as she could go, Eli's delighted chuckles following after her.

CHAPTER *12*

"I DON'T THINK Eli believes that we're married," Bonnie said to Webb without preamble, the moment she entered the store.

"Good morning to you, too," Webb retorted with weary humor. There were shadows of fatigue under his eyes and he leaned against the counter as though he might need it to hold him up.

Bonnie looked down at her hand, which was splotched with soot from Eli's face, and scowled. Why had she done such a foolish thing as to approach that man anyway? She might have known that he wouldn't listen to reason. "That hardheaded—"

Webb drew a deep breath and released it loudly. "Bonnie."

She sighed and her shoulders slumped. "I'm sorry. Was there something you wanted?"

Webb stood straighter and there was a reprimand in his blue eyes, albeit a gentle one. "I want you to be my wife, Bonnie. I want to make the lie true."

Marrying Webb had seemed such a good idea two nights before, when they had worked out the plan. But there were so many things Bonnie hadn't fully considered then, not the least of these being the powerful attraction she felt toward

Eli, notwithstanding all the pain he'd caused her. Suppose he tried to seduce her again? Would she be able to resist? With any other man, resistance was a certainty, but Eli McKutchen wasn't just any man. Suppose she married Webb and then turned right around and betrayed him? Webb would be destroyed by that.

And there was Rose Marie. Was it fair to make her live a lie, to make her believe that Webb was her father, and not Eli, whom she already knew as Papa? Bonnie could not bear to lose her daughter, but she didn't want to deceive her, either. And yet, if this crazy plan were to work, she would have to do just that. She would have to lie to Rose, as well as the rest of the world.

"Oh, Webb, I don't know what to do," she confessed, barely able to meet his eyes. Memories of that recent night when Eli had made love to her seared her mind. What would Webb say if he knew about that? Would he still be so anxious to make Bonnie McKutchen his wife?

"I thought we'd already decided what to do," Webb pointed out quietly.

Bonnie raised the shades that covered the store's front windows and found a rag to wipe the soot from her hand. "We can't live a lie, Webb. We can't tell Rose that you're her father. It wouldn't be fair to her."

"I would be a very good father."

Bonnie knew that that was true; she'd seen how gentle Webb was with Rose, how caring and patient and kind. Yes, he would be a good father, and he would be there for Rose all the time. Should Eli take the child to live with him, he would almost certainly consign her to the care of nannies and housekeepers, sparing little or no time for her himself. And when she was older, he would send her away to boarding school—that was the way the rich raised their children. "I'm not sure I have the strength to be a proper wife to you," Bonnie dared to say, hoping that Webb would read between the lines.

Webb did not understand; how could he? "I can't wait forever, Bonnie," he said gruffly, then put on his hat and left the store.

Despondent, Bonnie began the day's business, if it could be called that. Now that she was no longer dancing at the

Brass Eagle, there was almost no money. She couldn't keep the store going much longer; soon she would have to marry Webb just to survive.

She was thinking these dismal thoughts when Seth Callahan entered the store and smiled at her.

"Good morning," he said with conviction.

Bonnie stiffened, instantly suspicious. Perhaps Mr. Callahan had come to serve legal papers, regarding Rose's custody. "I'm not sure it *is* a good morning, Seth. Are you here about my daughter?"

Seth took out his handkerchief and dried his brow and the back of his neck, something Bonnie had seen him do a thousand times. Winter or summer, Seth always seemed to be overheated, and it was little wonder since he always dressed so warmly. "I'm here on business, Mrs. McKutchen. You've heard, I suppose, that Patch Town is to be demolished?"

Bonnie had heard about the new cabins that would be built on the southern end of town. Everyone knew about it; in a town the size of Northridge, such news always traveled fast. "Yes. It's about time, don't you think?"

Seth removed his spectacles and gave the lenses a thorough wiping with his handkerchief. "I do indeed. But better late than never, no?"

"No." Bonnie swallowed hard. "I mean, yes."

"I'm here to order various and sundry goods, Mrs. McKutchen—paint, nails, tools, fixtures, things of that nature. Everything except the lumber."

Bonnie's mouth dropped open. She was so used to failing where the general store was concerned that she couldn't quite grasp what Seth was saying, what he was offering.

"Have you catalogues?" Seth prompted. "I'm certain that you don't stock the goods we'll need in the necessary volume."

Bonnie brought a stack of catalogues from beneath the counter, her eyes wide, and Seth immediately began to peruse them.

"A pencil and paper, if you will," Seth said, already absorbed in one of the books. The instant the requested items had been provided, he began listing lengths of pipe.

135

"The cabins are going to have indoor plumbing?" Bonnie marveled, watching in wonder as Seth wrote.

The lawyer did not look up. "Oh, yes. We plan to wire for electricity, too, though I imagine it will be quite some time before there is power available in these remote areas."

Bonnie was agog. "Was this your idea, or Eli's?"

"Building the cabins was Mr. McKutchen's notion," Seth replied. He looked up and the light in his eyes was downright impish. "However, he gave me no directives as to acquiring the necessary materials."

She could have kissed Seth for choosing to give her the business. He was handing Bonnie her first real chance at success. "I appreciate this, Seth. I really do."

"Of course, you'll need a substantial deposit," Seth said, embarrassed by Bonnie's gratitude. "I doubt that your suppliers would be willing to extend this kind of credit."

That, Bonnie thought, was an understatement of classic proportions. Her suppliers were growing testy over accounts already overdue. A possible snag occurred to her, and she frowned. "Eli may be very upset about this," she warned.

"Eli is not your enemy, Mrs. McKutchen," Seth said, looking up from his list at last. "I know it sometimes appears that he is, but the truth, I feel, is something quite different."

Bonnie was curiously uplifted by Seth's words, but she wasn't willing to give them any real weight. She knew, after all, that Eli held her in contempt. The fifty-dollar bill he'd left on her bedside table had been proof of that, and when he was kind to her—a rare enough occurrence—it was only because he wanted something.

The silence seemed to bother Seth; again he removed his glasses and gave them a thorough polishing. "Eli is more than my employer, Mrs. McKutchen," he began reluctantly. "He is my friend. And I am very concerned about his well-being."

Bonnie leaned forward slightly, a little alarmed. "You mean the way he's working so hard in the smelter?"

Seth dismissed the theory briskly. "After an initial adjustment period, I'm sure Eli will be able to handle smelter work. He has the constitution of a bull, you know. No, it's his emotional state that worries me."

136

"His emotional state?"

"He has never really come to terms with the death of young Master Kiley, Mrs. McKutchen. He grieves as deeply now as he did when the boy first passed on, and that is not healthy."

Any mention of Kiley wounded Bonnie, and she still wept for him sometimes in the privacy of her room, but she had Rose Marie now and that was a vast comfort. One Eli couldn't share. "Eli never cried," she recalled softly. "I knew he was hurting, but he never cried."

"I know," Seth said, and he seemed embarrassed again, very uncomfortable. Probably, he felt that he had said too much, that he had somehow betrayed his friend. "Mrs. McKutchen, if you don't mind, I'd like to take these catalogues along to my room at the hotel. It might take hours or even days for me to make out a proper order."

Bonnie was glad to be distracted from thoughts of the worst time in her life and from the new worry aroused by what Seth had said about Eli's mental state. "I couldn't refuse such a valued customer," she said brightly.

Seth gathered the catalogues into a neat stack, lifted them off the counter, and then set them down again. "Oh, yes—I almost forgot. Miss Genoa asked me to give you this." He pulled a bright blue envelope from the inside pocket of his suitcoat. "She's planning a lawn party for the Saturday following next, and she does hope you'll come."

A lawn party. How like Genoa to plan a frivolous entertainment when the rest of the world was in utter turmoil! Smiling, Bonnie took the envelope and broke the fancy wax emblem that sealed it.

"Good day, Mrs. McKutchen," Seth said politely, as he opened the door to leave.

Bonnie looked up from Genoa's neatly penned invitation. "Good day, Seth. And thank you very, very much."

Seth reddened. "You are most welcome, of course," he replied, and then he was gone.

Bonnie went about her work happily, singing as she dusted shelves and at the same time assessed her inventory. She needed to restock so many items, and perhaps she could expand her business by putting in a line of women's clothing. The members of the Friday Afternoon Community

Improvement Club, having gone to great lengths to avoid buying their groceries from Bonnie, might not be able to resist the latest fashions.

While Bonnie worked and dreamed, Tuttle helped by giving the front windows a good cleaning, and Katie took Rose Marie out for a bit of fresh air.

The door had barely closed behind them when Tuttle said, "That Katie is a smart one. I asked her how come she don't go to school, and she said she knows more than the teacher does."

High on a ladder, dusting cans of peaches and pears with a rag, Bonnie smiled. "Katie is very bright. I fear the world is going to run out of knowledge before she learns all she wants to know."

"She reads too blasted much," Tuttle said, and this time his voice carried a note of complaint. "It's God's own wonder she ain't blind already."

Aha, Bonnie thought. "What about you, Tuttle? What do you want to learn?"

Tuttle thought for a moment, then went purposefully back to polishing the window. "I don't know, ma'am, but I will say that I'd admire to be like Mr. Hutcheson or Mr. McKutchen or Forbes Durrant, even. I'd like to earn my way by thinkin' instead of tendin' pots or shovelin' ore at the smelter."

Bonnie considered. Eli had been born to the life he led, and Forbes was hardly an exemplary model for a young man just starting out, but there might be something in Tuttle's admiration for Webb. "You might speak with Mr. Hutcheson, Tuttle, and ask him if he needs an apprentice. He may be willing to teach you his trade."

Tuttle looked delighted for a moment, but then the glow faded. "I don't read too good, and my spellin' is worse yet. How could I ever write articles and such as that?"

Bonnie climbed carefully down the ladder. "There are a lot of other factors involved in publishing a newspaper, Tuttle. Typesetting, for instance. You could learn to do that. And maybe Katie and I could help you with your reading and spelling."

Tuttle climbed down out of the window, nearly squashing a straw gardening bonnet in the process, and his face fairly shone with new hope. "I reckon Miss Katie might fancy a newspaper man, don't you?"

With great effort Bonnie managed not to smile. Indeed, she even looked stern. "Tuttle, if you become a journalist, you must do it because it's work you enjoy doing, not just to catch a lady's fancy."

"Could I go and see Mr. Hutcheson now? Please, ma'am? I've done a right fair job on the windows and—"

"Yes, Tuttle, you may go. And when you see Webb—Mr. Hutcheson—please tell him that I'd like him to come for supper tonight. Around six o'clock, if that's convenient for him."

Tuttle smoothed his hair and bolted toward the door. "Yes, ma'am. I'll tell him. And thank you!"

Bonnie sighed, wondering if she had set Tuttle up for a serious disappointment by arousing his hopes. While Webb was known to be well-fixed, he did put out the newspaper by himself and it was possible that he'd never hired help for reasons of economy.

The little bell over the front door rang, startling her, and Bonnie looked up to see Earline Kalb standing just inside the store. Earline took in only male boarders at her rooming house and, for that reason, she was only slightly higher on the social scale than the hurdy-gurdy girls dancing in the Brass Eagle Ballroom.

Earline had a womanly figure and mounds of rich, chestnut brown hair, and her green eyes were round and thickly lashed. She was attractive and still young, and Bonnie found it surprising that she had never been married.

"May I help you?" Bonnie asked. Earline, being above her, if only by half a rung, had never bought so much as a paper of pins in the mercantile.

"It's all over town that you and Webb Hutcheson are secretly married!" Earline thundered, bearing down on Bonnie at such speed that Bonnie felt called upon to put the width of the counter between herself and her visitor.

"If it's all over town, then it isn't much of a secret," Bonnie dared to say. She was annoyed at being accosted in such a manner, and in her own store, too.

"So it's true?" demanded Earline, wrenching off her gloves as though to prepare for fisticuffs.

139

Bonnie didn't know how to answer that. "Well—"

"Of course, the gossips are having a heyday, between that and the night you and Webb spent together over across the river!" Earline paused to draw a deep and shaky breath. "You're messin' around with my man, Bonnie McKutchen, and I don't like it!"

"How can Webb be your man if he's married to me?" Bonnie was careful to speak in a roundabout way to avoid saying right out that Webb was *indeed* her husband.

"I'll tell you how he can be my man," Earline hissed, bending forward so that her enormous breasts touched the counter and keeping her voice low. "He's been sleeping in my bed for three years, that's how he can be my man!"

Bonnie was shocked, although she supposed she shouldn't have been. After all, Webb was a healthy, vital man and, as such, he had certain needs. Needs Bonnie had certainly never supplied. "Oh," she said lamely.

"Thought you were all Webb needed, did you? Well, Angel, you were wrong. Now, maybe Northridge believes that you and my Webb are married, but I've got reason to think it's Eli McKutchen that's liftin' your skirts, and I want to know the truth. Right now!"

Bonnie's cheeks pounded with the hot color of outrage. "Get out of my store, you crude woman, before I throw you out!"

"That's liable to be a tall order, Mrs. McKutchen, you being such a scrawny little thing!"

Bonnie was rounding the end of the counter, bent on showing Earline the error of her ways, when she caught sight of Eli standing just inside the door. He was grinning, and Bonnie knew then that he'd heard the worst of what Earline had said. She was so mortified that she stopped cold.

Earline, on the other hand, was decorum personified. She took her time putting her gloves back on and assessing Eli's impressive frame. He was wearing the rough clothes of a working man, his shirt open almost to his midriff, and he still managed, damn him, to look like the refined New Yorker he was. "When you get tired of living at the hotel, Mr. McKutchen," Earline said sweetly, "you come on down to my rooming house." She cast one look back at Bonnie before adding, "All the comforts of home. I look after a man right and proper."

Eli had stopped grinning, but a corner of his mouth twitched slightly and his eyes danced. "I'll keep the offer in mind, ma'am," he said, with a polite inclination of his head.

Satisfied, Earline swept past him and out the door, her nose high in the air.

"You do have a gift for making enemies, Mrs. Hutcheson," Eli observed, when they were alone again.

Bonnie put both hands to her cheeks in a desperate attempt to cool them. "That hussy! She had her cap set for Webb, that's all!"

Eli approached the counter, set his dinner box down with a thump and did his best to look pained at the state of modern morals. "Sounds like your secret husband is about as faithful to his vows as you are."

Bonnie could hardly say that she had been "faithful" to Webb; Eli knew she hadn't. Neither could she swear indignantly that Earline had been lying about her relationship with Mr. Hutcheson. It was all a terrible mess, one that could never be untangled. "If you have business here, Mr. McKutchen," Bonnie said stiffly, "I would like to know what it is. If, on the other hand, you simply want to harass me—"

"I came about the materials Seth plans to order for the cabins."

Though Bonnie kept her chin high, she also clenched the counter's edge for support. Now it would happen, now another dream would be dashed. "I see."

"Judging by the total dearth of color in your face and the whiteness of your knuckles, I'd say that you *don't* see. You're expecting me to rescind the order, aren't you?"

Bonnie swallowed. If he did that, she would be ruined, and she had no real hope of mercy. Eli could be a very ruthless man, and it was entirely possible that he was out to destroy her. "I guess I am," she admitted.

"Well, then, you're wrong, Mrs. Hutcheson. The order stands—on one condition."

Bonnie held her breath. Of course there would be a condition. She only hoped it wouldn't be too terrible.

"You are not to involve my daughter in this lie you and Hutcheson have concocted."

"L-lie?"

Eli laughed—it was a bitter sound, completely void of humor—and shook his head. "By God, you never quit, I'll say that for you. You're not married to Hutcheson any more than I am, Bonnie, and we both know it. You can tell the town whatever you like, but don't you dare tell that little girl that she's anyone but who she is, or you'll spend the rest of your life regretting it. Do you understand me?"

"I don't know what you're talking about!"

"You little liar, you know exactly what I'm talking about. You delight in driving me crazy, that's all—I have half a mind to take you across my knee right here and now!"

"That's your problem, Eli McKutchen—you have half a mind! And if you so much as touch me, I'll—I'll—"

Eli was, incredibly, unbuttoning his cuffs. Rolling up his sleeves. "You'll what?" he prompted, in a deceptively soft voice.

"I'll report you to the marshal!"

"And he'll charge me with spanking the mayor—a dire offense, and there's probably no precedent. Be serious, Bonnie."

Eli was edging along the counter as he spoke and it looked as though he meant to carry out his threat. Bonnie was enraged at the prospect of such humiliation, but she was scared, too. This was no time to throw oil on the fire.

"You don't believe in striking women!" she blurted out, as a desperate reminder.

"I don't believe in blacking their eyes and breaking their bones," Eli conceded evenly, still advancing, "but I'm not the least bit opposed to blistering their—"

"Eli! Bonnie!" Genoa swept into the store, in a rustle of skirts and sunny goodwill. "How nice to see you talking together! It's almost like old times!"

Bonnie closed her eyes and breathed a silent prayer of thanks, and when she dared to look again, she saw the golden sparkle in Eli's eyes that told her, better than words ever could have, that he'd only been teasing her. With a nod to Genoa, he took his dinner box from the counter and left.

Genoa beamed. "You're such a handsome couple," she said, with a delighted sigh. "It's a pity Eli had to rush off—"

"Yes, isn't it?" Bonnie replied, forcing a smile. "He's working at the smelter now, you know."

Genoa's joy faded. "Yes, I know."

Bonnie wanted very much to make her friend feel welcome and at ease. She put aside her irritation over Eli's trick and asked, "Do you have time for tea? I was just about to close the store for the day."

"I'm sorry, I'm in a dreadful rush—just went for the mail, don't you know—are you planning to attend my party?"

Bonnie's smile was a genuine one. "I wouldn't miss it for the world, Genoa."

"Excellent. Well, I must be off—oh, yes, I forgot—Katie and Rose Marie are at my house. They are having quite the best time with the roller organ and I wondered if they mightn't spend the evening with me?"

Bonnie nodded. "Will you see them home in your carriage? I wouldn't want them walking in the dark, with so many strangers in town."

Genoa looked offended, though only moderately so. "Why, Bonnie, of course I wouldn't allow them to take such a chance! How can you even suggest that I would?"

"I'm sorry," Bonnie said. "It's been a very long, exciting day and I'm not thinking very clearly."

"Poor dear," crooned Genoa. "You work much too hard." Having made this pronouncement, Miss McKutchen took her leave.

Bonnie pulled the shades down over the windows and carefully locked the door. Between Eli's bluff and that messy confrontation with Earline Kalb, she'd had enough of this day.

Upstairs Bonnie searched her tiny icebox for something to make for supper. Perhaps she'd been impulsive in inviting Webb over tonight, but it was important that they talk, especially after Eli's demand that Rose Marie must not be presented as anyone's child but his own. Eli had joked about the spanking, but Bonnie knew that he was dead serious when he warned her not to lie about Rose.

He had not said that he would try to take Rose away, and for now, that was enough.

Bonnie pumped water into the tea kettle and set it on the stove, then built a fire. If Eli wasn't planning to raise Rose Marie himself, then there was no reason to marry Webb . . .

There was a tap at the rear door as the clock struck six and Bonnie smiled at Webb's promptness. "Come in!" she called.

The door opened and Webb entered, looking wan and just a bit harried. He forced a smile, however, and said, "Let's have supper at the hotel. You've been working all day and you shouldn't have to cook."

For the millionth time Bonnie wished that she'd had the plain good sense to fall in love with this man. How many others would be so considerate and kind? She thought of Eli, threatening to spank her like a child, and simmered.

"I think that's a wonderful idea, Webb," she said. On the way down the side stairs, she remembered Tuttle and his hoped-for apprenticeship. "Did young Mr. O'Banyon pay you a call this afternoon?"

Webb smiled, still looking very pale and tired, and took Bonnie's elbow in a gentlemanly manner, helping her to navigate the stairs. "Yes, and I hired him. I've been needing someone to help out for a long time."

Bonnie felt pleased. All in all, it had been a grand day, what with Seth's plan to order enough goods to build an entire town and Tuttle finding a trade that would provide him with a comfortable livelihood.

Webb and Bonnie were seated in the dining room of the Union Hotel, their dinners ordered, before Bonnie mentioned her own good news. Instead of looking pleased that Seth was going to buy thousands of dollars' worth of goods through her store, however, Webb scowled.

"When we're married, you won't be running the store anymore, Bonnie. I hope you understand that."

Bonnie understood but was annoyed that Webb was taking such an arbitrary attitude. He might at least have been happy for her! She unfolded her napkin and placed it neatly in her lap, letting Webb's comment go unchallenged.

Momentarily he sighed and took her hand in his. "Bonnie, I'm sorry. It's wonderful that you'll be making such a sale, of course, and I'm happy for you."

"What's troubling you, then?" Bonnie asked softly, all her ire displaced by concern.

"You and Hem were right about that anti-union article I wrote—I've had some threats, Bonnie."

Bonnie's eyes rounded. "Threats?"

"Letters," Webb confessed. "Unsigned, of course. I'm not afraid for myself, Bonnie, but some of those people threatened you. They're demanding that I print a retraction."

"You aren't going to do that, are you?"

Webb assessed Bonnie with worried eyes. It was going to be very hard to tell him that she couldn't become his wife. Very hard indeed. "I couldn't back down that way, Bonnie. McKutchen is doing everything he can to make things right, and I mean to point that out in the next issue of the paper. Still, if anything happened to you—"

"Nothing is going to happen to me, Webb. I can look after myself."

"All the same, I wonder if you and Rose would be safe out at the house, all alone. Bonnie, I think it might be better if we put the wedding off for a few weeks—just until things calm down a little. Until those new cabins are built and the strike is over."

Inwardly Bonnie sighed with relief. There being no need to hurt Webb now, she could put off dashing his hopes. "Earline Kalb came by to see me today," she said, with a mischievous smile.

Webb dropped his coffee cup.

CHAPTER 13

Standing at the liquor cabinet in his office, Forbes poured brandy for himself and McKutchen. A light rain was spattering the windows and the river was rising; there had been a great deal of snow during the winter just past, and Forbes could picture the stuff melting off the high peaks of the Canadian Cascades, swelling all the streams that poured into the Columbia. Fleetingly he wished that he'd built the Brass Eagle on higher ground.

He handed McKutchen his glass and sat down in the chair behind his desk. He wondered what it was that Eli wanted of him. A woman? Information about Bonnie? What? He waited.

McKutchen looked fit, though there were burns and small blisters on his hands. Even in his working clothes he had an air of authority. "I need your help, Durrant," he said, after staring into his brandy snifter for some seconds.

Forbes settled back in his chair, his brandy in one hand, and smiled to himself. "In what way?" he asked moderately.

The look McKutchen gave him was sharp enough to pin anybody to the wall. "I want you to manage the smelter again."

So the job was too tough for McKutchen, was it? Forbes

146

knew better than to say this aloud; he let the silence say it for him.

McKutchen tossed back his brandy and set the snifter down on Forbes's desk with a thump. "Well? Will you take the job or not?"

Forbes pretended to consider. In truth he needed the income that management of the smelter works would provide. He could live well on what the Brass Eagle Saloon and Ballroom brought in, of course, but he had certain financial goals that could only be met if he continued to invest and for that he required the sizable monthly bank draft from McKutchen Enterprises. "What changed your mind?" he stalled. "I got the definite impression that you didn't care for my management methods."

"I didn't and I don't, but Seth doesn't have time for a job like this and neither do I. It might be months before I can bring in someone else, so I'm giving you a second chance—at a higher salary—if you want it."

Forbes was galled. "Why should I help you, McKutchen, if you're planning to replace me when you can?"

Josiah McKutchen's grandson smiled. "I won't bring in anybody else if you can do the job, Durrant. This time, just do it correctly. I'll be looking over your shoulder, and so will Seth. You might want to keep in mind that I'm being generous here—considering some of the discrepancies Seth found in your bookkeeping system. A few of them were just blatant enough to land you in prison."

Prison. Forbes swallowed hard. He was too good-looking for prison.

McKutchen spread his hands. "I'm willing to overlook past transgressions, Durrant—we can start fresh."

The offer now seemed more than generous. Why, it was downright bighearted. "What do you want me to do first?"

"Call another meeting. Make it clear that every worker is welcome, whether he's still doing his job or out on strike. In the meantime, I want you to have some bills printed and passed out, saying that from now on, there will be three shifts at the smelter, instead of two. Each man will work eight hours, instead of twelve, for the same wages he's getting now."

Forbes's mouth dropped open for a moment. "That's financial suicide!" he protested.

McKutchen rose from his chair. "I hardly think so, Forbes. The profits we've been making in the past five years were enormous. We can well afford to give something back to the men. What we can't survive is a prolonged strike."

"Then you'll give in to the union's demands?"

McKutchen sighed. "If the men want a union, I won't try to stop them from having one. But I won't subsidize the organization, either. Make sure the workers understand that any dues they dole out to the union boys will come out of their own pockets, not mine."

"You won't raise wages."

"I've decided to make other concessions instead—I'm providing those cabins free of charge. I'm cutting back hours. For now, that's all I'm willing to do."

Privately Forbes thought the company was conceding too much. After all, they could have hired Chinamen to replace the workers that were out on strike and made greater profits than ever. In the final analysis, however, he was certainly in no position to argue. "Very well," he said with a shake of his head.

McKutchen paused at the door. "That woman who came in here the other night—the one who runs the rooming house—"

"Earline?"

"Yes. What's her claim on Webb Hutcheson?"

Forbes shrugged. "She's his landlady and probably his mistress."

"I'm surprised Bonnie was willing to overlook a mistress, considering that Hutcheson is supposed to be her husband."

Forbes laughed then. "I've heard the rumor, but the Angel isn't married to Hutcheson and never has been. For one thing, Webb wouldn't have permitted any wife of his to dance the hurdy-gurdy—I guarantee you that."

"I see," McKutchen replied, with a half-smile on his lips. At that, he opened the door and left.

The rainy weather might have put a damper on Bonnie's spirits if it hadn't been for the pages and pages of neatly printed merchandise orders Seth brought to the store. Even considering past-due accounts and shipping costs, Bonnie's own profits would be huge. To save time, she decided to travel to Spokane and meet with her suppliers in person, rather than trusting her orders to the mails. She would go that very day, and she said as much.

Seth nodded distractedly. "I've done my best to anticipate what goods will be needed," he said, in businesslike tones, as he watched Bonnie scan and rescan the lists. "However, there are always variables in any undertaking of this magnitude, so we'll probably require the odd item, here and there."

Bonnie set down the papers she'd been devouring with her eyes and tried to be calm, though inwardly she felt like jumping into the air and kicking her heels together for glee. "Of course," she said. "I've been wondering, though— where are you going to get workers for this project?"

"Some of them will have to be brought in from outside, I suppose," Seth answered confidently, "but since Mr. McKutchen is cutting back the shift hours at the smelter from twelve to eight, I daresay some of the men will be glad of an opportunity to use those four free hours to earn some spare money."

Bonnie was sure that that was the case, and she hoped that some of the families would bring their store accounts up to date on the proceeds. Perhaps business would pick up, too, and the mercantile would become a paying proposition for once. "That is a wonderful idea, Seth," she said.

"Well, yes. Yes, indeed," Seth sputtered, gripping the lapels of his coat in his hands. "You will be attending the public meeting on Sunday afternoon, I presume?"

"Public meeting?"

"Mr. McKutchen has hired the Pompeii Playhouse for the purpose."

Bonnie squared her shoulders. "Of course I'll attend. After all, I'm the mayor of this town."

Seth blushed at the reminder; it was as though Bonnie had told him some silly and intimate secret. "Yes, well— good day, Mrs. McKutchen."

"Good day, Mr. Callahan."

The moment Seth had gone, Bonnie rushed to put a CLOSED sign in the front window and lock the door. "Katie!" she called.

Katie came cautiously down the stairs. "Yes, ma'am? What is it?"

"I'm going to Spokane on business. I would like you and Rose Marie to stay with Genoa until my return."

Katie loved visiting Genoa's grand house, and she beamed at the prospect. "How long will you be away, ma'am?"

"Two or three days at the most—I must be back by this Sunday."

"What about the store? Don't you want me to keep it open and all?"

"There would be absolutely no point in that, but I'll leave a note in the window, telling people where to find you in case someone needs medicine or something."

Katie nodded and scurried upstairs to pack for herself and Rose Marie. Meanwhile, Bonnie stuffed dresses and clean underthings into a satchel and tried to figure how much money she would need for food and lodging while in Spokane. Seth had given her a large bank draft as a deposit on the goods ordered, but that, of course, would go to the suppliers.

Downstairs, she checked the till and found that she had seven dollars and fourteen cents to her name. She would have to eat sparingly and take a room in the cheapest hotel to be found, for a round-trip railroad ticket would take fully half her money, but Bonnie was undaunted. This was her big chance and, if she had to, she would go hungry and sleep sitting up in the railroad station rather than let such an opportunity pass her by.

As it happened, Genoa guessed the situation when the reason for the trip was explained to her. Not only was she willing to take Katie and Rose Marie under her wing while Bonnie was away, but she had the carriage brought around and rode with Bonnie to the depot. Just before Bonnie boarded the afternoon train, Genoa pressed a twenty-dollar bill into her hand.

Bonnie tried to protest, but Genoa would have none of that. "You can pay me back when you're rich and successful," she insisted, fairly shoving Bonnie up the steps of the one passenger car the train boasted.

Her vision blurred by a sheen of grateful tears, Bonnie did not notice the solitary passenger at the back of the car until Northridge was far behind.

He was cowering behind the current issue of the *Northridge News*, but Bonnie recognized him all the same. She would know those strong, gold-dusted hands anywhere.

"Are you following me?" she demanded, once the conductor had taken up tickets and disappeared into another car.

Slowly, the newspaper descended, revealing a familiar face. Eli smiled broadly. "How could I have known that you would be on this train?" he countered reasonably.

"I think it's entirely possible that Genoa sent word to you at the hotel!"

Eli smiled and gave his newspaper an insolent snap. "You flatter yourself, Bonnie. It so happens that I have business in Spokane. Business that has nothing whatsoever to do with you."

It would be fruitless to argue with the man. Biting her lower lip, Bonnie turned in her seat and forceably fixed her attention on the trees and the river slipping past her window. The rain had relented a little, but it was still coming down steadily, and the river looked higher and wilder than ever before. To keep from thinking about Eli, Bonnie fretted over the residents of Patch Town. They were too near the water, too vulnerable to it, and so were a number of other people. Webb, for one; his newspaper office would be swept away if the river rose to flood stage.

Bonnie shivered and, just as she did, Eli sat down in the seat beside hers. She did not turn to look at him, even when he said her name. Perhaps, if she ignored him, he would go back to his seat at the rear of the car and leave her alone.

There was a long silence, then Eli made a sound like a sigh of exasperation.

"I lied," he said.

Bonnie was so surprised by his confession that she turned to face him, completely forgetting her earlier decision to ignore Eli McKutchen no matter what he did or said. "What?"

"I have no business in Spokane."

Bonnie didn't know how to respond to that. She felt just like the first time she'd ever come face-to-face with Eli; she had a sense of sweet alarm and a queer feeling in the pit of her stomach. "Genoa did send word, then."

"No. You told Seth and Seth told me."

Bonnie could not find it within herself to be angry with Seth, not after he'd saved her business from certain failure. She bit her lower lip again and dropped her eyes. "Don't spoil this for me, Eli," she said softly. "Please."

"I don't want to spoil anything. I merely want a chance to talk to you without Seth or Genoa or Webb Hutcheson hanging around. And then there's Forbes. Are you aware that he almost always knows where you are and what you're doing?"

Bonnie remembered a certain night, when she'd tried to take a simple bath in her kitchen, and blushed. She wouldn't want Forbes or anyone else to know about that. "Forbes and I grew up together," she said. "Other boys liked to collect spiders or play marbles, but Forbes had a different hobby. Watching me."

"I can't say I blame him for that," Eli muttered, though from his tone it sounded as though he did after all blame Forbes. "You'd think he would have taken up another interest by now, though, wouldn't you?"

Bonnie smiled in spite of herself. "Yes," she replied. "But there is no explaining Forbes."

There must have been something in Bonnie's smile or tone that Eli didn't like, for he frowned. "You know, I think that bastard wants you for himself."

"Forbes might have entertained a notion or two along those lines at one time, but he's long since accepted the fact that he and I aren't destined to be together."

"Unlike you and Webb, you mean."

Bonnie felt color rising in her face. "I declare, Eli Mc-Kutchen, if you start ragging me about that again, I'll get off this train at the very next stop!"

"You're not really married to Hutcheson, are you?" Eli persisted, and there was no trace of insult in his voice, only a certain vulnerability.

Bonnie sighed. She had never been a very good liar and

152

this particular falsehood was just too cumbersome to manage. "No. I'm not married to Webb."

Eli's look of smug relief was irritating.

"But that doesn't mean I *won't* marry Webb," Bonnie pointed out quickly. "He has asked for my hand in marriage, and I may say yes."

"Why?"

"Why?" Bonnie echoed, annoyed. "Because Webb Hutcheson is a very good man. A very gentle and honest man. He could give Rose and me a real home."

Mentioning Rose had been a mistake; Bonnie knew that an instant too late. Golden fire snapped in Eli's eyes. "You don't love him," he said.

"How do you know that?" Bonnie snapped. The pompous ass! Did Eli think he was the only man she could ever love? If he did think that, he was right, of course, but Bonnie had no intention of letting him find out. Ever. "It may be that Webb and I share a grand passion."

Eli subsided slightly, scowling, his arms folded across his chest. "A grand passion," he muttered.

Bonnie was warming to the subject. She became reckless. "You asked me the other day if I 'carry on' with Webb like I did with you. Well, I do. I not only yelp, I howl!"

Behind them, the conductor cleared his throat. Bonnie was instantly mortified, for it hadn't occurred to her that anyone would overhear what she'd said. Why couldn't she learn to bridle her foolish and impulsive tongue? Why?

Eli chuckled and shook his head as if in awe of Bonnie's capacity to embarrass herself.

"Next stop, Colville," said the conductor, whom Bonnie recognized as the husband of one of the members of the Friday Afternoon Community Improvement Club. He had only to relate Bonnie's rash words to his wife and the gossips would have another tidbit to brandish over their interminable cups of tea.

Eli was laughing inside himself, Bonnie knew, but she couldn't face him any more than she could face the conductor.

"I hate you," she hissed, when she and Eli were alone in the car again.

"We'll see about that."

Bonnie looked around, to make sure the conductor wasn't nearby again. When she saw that the car was truly empty, she muttered, "What I just said was the truth! Webb drives me wild with passion!"

Eli rose from his seat, but there was no rage in his face and no jealousy. Only a certain self-satisfied confidence that Bonnie was lying. Which, of course, she was.

Eli disappeared for several minutes and Bonnie was just beginning to hope that he had decided to ride in the engine room when he returned, his golden eyes bright with an alarming sort of mischief.

He sat down in the seat beside Bonnie and immediately caught her face in both his newly callused hands, forcing her to look at him. "We'll see, my angel, who drives you wild with passion."

His lips were descending toward hers. She wanted to struggle but all she could think about was Eli's mouth coming closer and closer. A shiver went through her, and the peaks of her breasts, hidden beneath her dress and camisole, suddenly burned.

"You can't do this—the conductor—we'll be in Colville soon—"

Eli chuckled and Bonnie felt the sound against her mouth, he was so close. "We won't reach Colville for another half an hour," he replied, "and you needn't worry about the conductor. I bribed him to busy himself elsewhere."

Simultaneously Eli claimed Bonnie's mouth with his own and his hand closed over one of her breasts. Bonnie felt her nipple quicken beneath his palm and stiffened, but she couldn't break away. She made a whimpering sound of protest and of need as Eli's kiss mastered her and brought her rebellion swiftly to heel. He continued to kiss and caress her until she was not only assenting but responding.

Breaking the deep kiss to nibble at her lips, Eli opened the front of Bonnie's dress and boldly slid his hand inside, beneath her camisole, to take her nipple between his fingers. At the same time, using his other hand, he was slowly raising her skirts.

Bonnie trembled. What if the conductor comes back? she

154

asked herself wildly. What if the train makes an unexpected stop? I can't let this happen here, in a railroad car, in the broad light of day! So said Bonnie's mind, but her body was of a different opinion, a primitive opinion. It craved the luscious attentions Eli was giving it and far more besides.

"Oh," she moaned, as she felt the strings holding her drawers in place give way under one tug of Eli's fingers. "Oh, no—"

"Oh, yes," Eli said, his lips against hers again, and his hand slid down inside her muslin drawers to find what he sought. "I'm going to have you, Bonnie. Right here, and right now."

"You can't—you mustn't—oooooh—"

Eli chuckled and went right on fondling Bonnie. She tried to sit staunchly, but it was all she could do to restrain her hips. They wanted to fly. "We're all alone, Bonnie. Just you and me and our—wild passion."

Bonnie pulled away from his kiss, gasping. His fingers were driving her crazy. "Eli—please stop. I'm sorry for saying what I did about Webb—honest—"

"Too late," Eli mumbled, and then he bent his head and took full, leisurely suckle at the breast he had bared minutes before.

Bonnie put one gloved hand over her mouth to stifle a cry of frenzied delight and her hips took full flight while her knees widened. She was in a fevered daze by the time Eli turned her so that she was kneeling astraddle of his lap. Blithely, as though such things were done every day, he tore her drawers away and opened his trousers.

The warm prodding of his manhood was more than Bonnie's body would allow her to resist. With a throaty cry, she took him inside herself.

At this Eli moaned. He let his head fall back and closed his eyes, his hands firmly on Bonnie's hips, guiding them, setting a slow pace. She watched as the cordlike muscles in his neck tightened, thinking not of scandal or shame but of how very desperately she loved this man.

They moved slowly together for long minutes—the friction was a delicious ache in Bonnie—until the train suddenly began to rattle and shimmy. The unexpected motion

155

brought both Bonnie and Eli to an instantaneous release. For Bonnie the climax was brutal in its intensity, convulsing not only those muscles that cosseted Eli, but those in her toes and her shoulders and all points between. Eli endured his own triumph in absolute silence, though Bonnie could see ferocious spasms of emotion and sensation in his throat and along his jawline.

The moment Bonnie's body had sated its greed, she moved to leave Eli, shamed to the very core of her being, but he held her firmly in place, his hands warm and strong on her soft hips. His eyes held her as much a prisoner as did his hands, for there was a quiet power in their depths that caught at something deep within Bonnie and would not let her go.

"Stay," he said gruffly. "Please stay."

His hands left Bonnie's hips and came to her bodice, opening it fully, drawing down her camisole. Bonnie shivered with involuntary pleasure as Eli gently caressed her bare breasts.

"The conductor!" she reminded him desperately in a soft whine.

"Don't worry, Bonnie. He wouldn't come near this car even if it burst into flame."

Bonnie thought it might be she that burst into flame, rather than the passenger car; the heat was already rising within her as Eli touched and weighed and toyed with her breasts. Sheathed deep inside her, his manhood flexed itself, exerting a singular power.

"Lean back, Bonnie. I want to taste you."

Bonnie was far beyond reason by then, and far beyond the boundaries of propriety, too. Allowing her head to fall back and her breasts to thrust forward, she crooned as Eli enjoyed one sweet peak and then the other. At times he was greedy, at other times he was incomparably gentle, but at all times he controlled Bonnie's every reaction.

He grew more and more fierce within her, filling her, heating her, tormenting her. When her release came, it was so strong that Bonnie's legs flew out from her sides in order that she might take him as fully inside her as possible.

Eli was caught in the throes of his own approaching crisis and, as such, he was temporarily powerless. That gave an already fulfilled Bonnie a delicious opportunity to give Eli back a little of his own.

She opened his spotless linen shirt one button at a time, tangling her fingers in the dense hair that covered his chest, caressing him, grazing his nipples with the tips of her fingers. He watched her face with glazed golden eyes as she loved him, groaned when she bent and took a nubbin of masculine flesh between her lips.

Finally Eli's hips rose in a fierce, powerful thrust and he released his passion at last, his magnificent body shuddering with the force of his satisfaction. His hands moved upon Bonnie's bare breasts the whole time, molding them, clutching and caressing, and his wonderful amber eyes went blank as his whole being convulsed.

Too pleased by her victory to feel shame now, Bonnie removed herself, buttoned her bodice, and did what she could with her torn drawers. With luck the ties would hold them together until she could change clothes.

Eli sat gasping in his seat, apparently unable to move. Still flying high on the wings of her triumph, Bonnie gave him a little pat and then buttoned his trousers for him. She'd done that many times before their divorce, and in places far less conventional than a railroad car, too. Soon after their marriage, in fact, Eli had told Bonnie that he would have her when and where he wanted, and though they'd never been caught, there had often been an element of risk. That daring had always intensified their passion and at least, Bonnie thought with a bittersweet smile, that hadn't changed.

Her body lulled to a sweet sense of sleepy languor, Bonnie looked for regret within herself and could find none. She only hoped that Eli would not spoil things by making some cruel remark or, worse yet, trying to pay her again.

She closed her eyes against that idea and felt Eli's hand gently cup her chin. He turned her away from the window and toward him.

"Stay with me in Spokane, Bonnie," he pleaded hoarsely. "If Hutcheson is going to have you all the rest of his life, let me have you for these few days."

Bonnie felt an unbearable sadness at his words and at the defeated emotion behind them. Was it possible that Eli really cared for her, just as Seth had implied in recent days? Could it be that, beneath all that anger, he still loved her just a little?

She decided that she didn't dare hope for such a miracle. The disappointment would be unbearable if it turned out that she was mistaken. She had every reason to believe that Eli was using her and none to feel that he bore her any goodwill, yet she couldn't resist his attentions. What had just taken place was proof enough of that.

And she needed more of Eli's loving; her body and her soul cried out for it.

"I won't be called a whore, or paid for my love, Eli McKutchen," she warned. "And I will not be mocked when this is over and we're both back in Northridge."

Eli lifted his right hand in a pledge, and a slight smile curved his lips. "You have my word, Bonnie. Once we get back to Northridge, it will be as if nothing had happened."

Bonnie wasn't sure she wanted exactly that—the suggestion made her feel a little sad, in fact. Even bereaved. But she nodded her assent to share Eli's bed because she knew she was bound for it anyway. This way she could at least tell herself that it had been a deliberate choice.

CHAPTER 14

THE HOTEL WAS a grand place, its huge lobby filled with potted greenery and handsome leather furniture. Heavy crystal chandeliers, powered by electricity, twinkled against the impossibly high ceilings, shedding their light over lush Persian rugs and the elegantly clad guests who walked upon them.

Bonnie drew in her breath; she'd forgotten that such sumptuous beauty existed since her return to Northridge. Thinking these thoughts helped to distract her while Eli spoke to one of several clerks stationed behind the registration desk, but the trick didn't work for long because Bonnie knew that she didn't really belong in a place like this anymore. If she ever had.

She paced, clutching the handle of her shabby valise, her conscience suddenly sore and smarting. She was no longer Eli McKutchen's wife, in the eyes of either God or the law, and yet she had allowed the man to make love to her in a railroad car and then bring her to this hotel! What was the matter with her? What had happened to her principles, to her ideals, to her morals?

Bonnie was about to walk out of the hotel and find a place that she could afford on her own, when Eli reappeared at her side, taking a gentle but firm hold on her elbow. The

159

expression in his whiskey-colored eyes conveyed both amusement and a tender understanding.

She was defeated, without Eli's saying so much as one word, because for all the papers she'd signed and all the dreams that had died, Bonnie still felt as much married to this man as she ever had. Her mind might know that the union had been legally dissolved, but Bonnie's soul was still cleaving to him as husband, and all her emotions took its part. Her intellect was left to struggle alone.

"You swear you'll never tell?" she asked tremulously, a part of her already anticipating the singular joys that lay ahead.

Eli arched one butternut eyebrow. "As long as you want this to be a secret, Bonnie, it will be. Now let's get settled and find a decent restaurant—I'm starved."

Bonnie gave a sigh of such relief that Eli chuckled as he took her valise in one hand and her forearm in the other, ushering her toward the elevator.

"Did you think I planned to hurl you onto the bed and have my way with you the moment we entered our suite, my love?"

Bonnie eyed the elevator dubiously. She disliked the things, was always dizzied by the swiftness of the ride. She would have felt safer, too, if the door had been sturdier, but it was only iron grillwork, and it made an alarming clanking sound when the elevator operator opened it. "No," Bonnie lied coolly, hoping that the small, uniformed man who ran the apparatus knew what he was about. "I did not."

Eli only grinned, saving his reply until they had reached the top floor of the hotel and were standing outside the door of their suite. "We can have our supper right here, if you'd like," he said.

Bonnie made a face at him, hating his teasing but at the same time taking an odd comfort from it. "I don't know that we can go anywhere fancy," she conceded. "I haven't the clothes for it, you know."

"Being a humble storekeeper from Northridge," Eli added, unlocking the door of their suite with a brass key and stepping back, so that Bonnie might enter first.

She swept ahead of him, chin high, on a wave of pretended elegance, but the simple beauty of the suite's sitting room dissolved her act. The last of the day's sunlight streamed through a western window, pooling on a carpet of the palest blue. There were two cream-colored sofas, facing each other, along with a small ivory fireplace polished to a glistening patina. Bonnie would not have believed that such an exquisite room existed in Spokane, outside some of the fine houses on the city's South Hill, that is.

The suite also boasted a bathroom with a giant tub of gray marble, a small dressing room, and, of course, a bedchamber, decorated in burgundy and pale pink. The bedstead was of glistening brass, and the sheets—Bonnie pulled back the wine-colored counterpane just a wee bit to investigate—looked and felt like real silk. As shy as any virgin bride, Bonnie turned a shade of pale fuschia well-suited to the decor and fled back to the sitting room.

Eli had just dismissed the bellhop, who had brought his suitcase up from the registration desk. He grinned at the high color in Bonnie's cheeks. "Do the rooms meet with your approval, my dear?"

"They do," Bonnie confessed in a choked mockery of dignity.

"Bonnie." Eli took her upper arms gently in his hands. "Please relax—I was only teasing before, when I talked about having my way with you. We won't make love at all, unless that's what you want."

"Then why did you go to all the trouble of following me?" Bonnie demanded, angry with Eli and angrier still with herself. "Why did you make love to me in—in a railroad car, for pity's sake—and then persuade me to come here?"

Eli chuckled, bent to kiss the tip of her nose. "I made love to you? Tell me, Bonnie, was I alone responsible for what happened on board that train?"

Bonnie knew that he wasn't completely to blame, though he had, of course, instigated the thing in the first place. Honesty forced her to concede, at least to herself, that she had been a willing and even eager partner. "I can't believe we did that," she muttered.

"It was tame, compared to that time—"

Quickly Bonnie pressed gloved fingers to Eli's mouth, silencing him. But even through her gloves, the warmth of his lips triggered some response within her, and she drew her hand back as rapidly as she had sent it forth. "It is unfair of you to remind me of past indiscretions, sir," she said, only half in jest. For good measure, she stepped back, out of Eli's reach. "I'm very hungry," she added. "Can we go and have something to eat now?"

They dined in a darkened corner of the hotel's enormous restaurant, by candlelight. The mood, for all Bonnie's efforts to the opposite, was intimate.

"This is almost like old times," Eli observed over the rim of his wineglass. "Sometimes I wish we could go back to those days, when we were first married and all was right with the world."

"We can't," Bonnie said flatly, wishing that she had never agreed to do this mad, scandalous thing. She would probably be damned for her sins, and here she'd tried so hard to be good.

But trying to behave herself had never been any help when it came to Eli McKutchen. This was the man who had always been able to take outlandish liberties with her person and get away with it. For instance, there was that time when he had brought her to a sweet, fierce release in the dark privacy of their box at the opera, using only his expert touch and words of gruff, challenging love that no one else could hear . . .

Bonnie turned pink just remembering.

Eli smiled but said nothing, apparently intent on finishing his steak.

Bonnie, on the other hand, felt a heated despair that wasn't entirely unpleasant and could hardly eat a bite of her own dinner of fresh trout, fried potatoes and glazed beets, no matter how she tried. The fine food had all the allure of stewed cardboard.

"Would you like to see a play or something?" Eli asked, once he'd finished his dinner and the dirty dishes had been taken away. "It's early."

Bonnie ached to be alone with her former husband even as she castigated herself for giving in to his charm so easily. It was no great wonder, was it, that he had left her fifty dollars in payment the other night. Perhaps she'd deserved that, just as she would deserve the pain and remorse she would almost certainly feel when this enchanted time-out-of-time was over. "I have to see all my suppliers tomorrow," she said remotely, "so perhaps it would be better if I got some sleep."

To his credit, Eli said nothing; he allowed Bonnie to fool herself that there would be no more to the evening. But she knew better, and so did he.

When the check had been signed, Eli graciously drew back Bonnie's chair and offered her his arm. It was easy to pretend that they were still married, still a part of New York society. For a moment their divorce was not real to Bonnie, nor was her flight to Northridge or her time as a hurdy-gurdy dancer, mayor and storekeeper. It was as though none of those things had ever taken place.

They rode the elevator in silence, neither of them noticing the balding and watchful operator, who knew that these two strangers loved each other and smiled to think that there was still romance in the world.

Bonnie's feet seemed to glide an inch or so above the floor, rather than making solid contact with it, and when Eli unlocked the door of the suite and handed her inside, she was quite unprepared for his courteous "I could use a walk in the fresh air. Make yourself comfortable, Bonnie, and try to relax."

Try to relax? Didn't he know that she was about as relaxed as it was possible to be? Why, if he'd wanted to make love on the sitting-room floor, she wouldn't have protested. "You're not angry?"

With one finger, he touched her nose. "I'm not angry. I just want to take my time, Bonnie, and savor this night."

A delicious tremor went through Bonnie's tired body. Her knees were still weak from that torrid episode on the train and her drawers were still hanging from her waist in ribbons, and here she was wanting Eli to take her again. Well, she too would savor this night, for it and the one to follow might have to last her all her life. Instinctively, Bonnie knew that there would never be another man, Webb or anyone else, who could stir in her the kind of passion that Eli did.

Wanting to seduce the man, there and then, Bonnie instead turned away with sweeping grandeur and made her way into the bathroom.

163

She closed and locked the door behind her and began running water into the impressive tub for a bath. Oh, yes, she was a paragon of poise and deportment, she told herself. No one would ever guess, to see her lounging in that luxurious tubful of water, that Bonnie had any self-doubt at all.

She did have, however. What she did not possess, having forgotten to fetch one from her valise, was a wrapper. That was no matter for concern, for the bathroom quite conveniently and sensibly adjoined the bedroom. When her bath was over—and Bonnie stretched it out to a sinful length of time because it was so very pleasant—she wrapped herself in one of the hotel's thirsty white towels and ducked into the next room.

Had she known that Eli would be there, sitting on the side of the bed, undoing his cufflinks as any husband might do after an evening out, she would certainly have remained in the bathtub for a little longer, giving herself a chance to gather her courage.

When she saw a bottle of champagne on the bedside table, couched in a silver wine cooler, she trembled inside her towel.

"H-how was your walk?" she managed to ask, painfully conscious of her dripping-wet hair and her nakedness beneath that scrap of fluffy cloth.

Eli only smiled, setting his cufflinks aside. They made a musical, tinkling sound against the base of the wine cooler.

Bonnie swallowed hard, drawing the towel more tightly around her. She was cold—that was it, she was cold—and she began to shiver.

"Come and get into bed before you catch your death," he said. Inadvertently, Eli had reminded himself as well as Bonnie of Kiley's fatal bout with pneumonia, and his wonderful flax-colored eyes reflected an almost fathomless grief, though only briefly. He even managed to smile as he rose from the bed and approached Bonnie.

He settled her beneath the covers and took away the towel in almost the same motion. Briskly, while Bonnie sat with the silken covers drawn up to cover her breasts, Eli towel-dried her hair until she knew it must be standing out around her head like the mane of a lion.

Finally Eli tossed aside the towel and stood up to round the bed. There he uncorked the champagne with a practiced motion of his thumbs and the liquid bubbled enticingly as he poured it into one crystal glass and then another.

He extended the first glass to Bonnie, his eyes bright and changeable as molten gold as they made their way over her face, her wild tangled hair, her bare shoulders. Bonnie drew the covers up a little higher, though not even a hint of cleavage was showing.

Eli smiled at her breathless, wide-eyed suspense and lifted his glass. "Here's to us, my love. May this be a night we never forget."

Bonnie was certain that the night would be memorable. Perhaps at some future time, while lying sleepless in her own lonely bed, she would recall the minutes and hours to come and weep for them, for Eli, for herself. Her throat felt thick and her eyes burned as she lifted her glass high, took a long sip and then set her champagne aside.

She watched shamelessly as Eli removed his clothes and turned down the lights. Through the window above the bed came the silvery glimmer of moonlight, as pleasing to the eye and the spirit as champagne to the tongue. Bonnie felt a ferocious sort of contentment; hang Northridge, the Friday Afternoon Community Improvement Club, the conventions of the day. For tonight, she was still Eli McKutchen's wife and she had the right to his tender pleasuring and the primitive passion that would follow it.

She did not resist, could not have resisted, when Eli caught one of her hands in his and pulled her upright, so that she knelt in the middle of the bed. Lifting her easily by her waist, he brought her to the very edge of the bed and then sank to his own knees on the floor.

Bonnie shivered with anticipation and unguarded need as he slowly stroked her hips, her bottom, her back, his hands conveying a sort of reverence by their touch, rather than any sort of command. The points of Bonnie's breasts swelled and then tightened as Eli ignored them to caress the rest of her thoroughly, and she made a soft yet savage sound as he traced the tender flesh of her inner thighs with the tips of his fingers, urging them to part for pleasures yet to be relished.

Presently Eli's fingers circled the peaks of her breasts, in a touch so light as to be something more nearly imagined than experienced as a reality. Bonnie moaned and her long, damp hair tickled the backs of her calves as she lifted her face to the ceiling, abandoning her body to pleasures that would be almost unendurable for their keenness and power.

And Eli continued to tamper with her distended nipples, now shaping them, now soothing them, now causing them to ache with the need to nourish one impossible, magnificent man. Throughout, a second hand was moving down over Bonnie's rib cage, over her quivering middle, to the spot where a bud of flesh pulsed in its silken hiding place, waiting to be found.

The finding was not swift; no, the search was wondrously slow and deliberate, causing Bonnie such delicate anguish that she made a sound that was half groan and half whine when the tender treasure was at last uncovered and conquered. Her back arched still further as Eli consumed his prize, now tentatively, now with voracity.

Bonnie tangled her fingers in Eli's hair, but her hands fell to his shoulders when her gratification came, for it was the shameless response of a savage's woman, convulsing her again and again, with a biting keenness that tore a low groan of lust from her throat.

The satisfaction had been brutal in its might, but it still left a hollow place inside Bonnie. For her the act would not be complete until Eli entered her and made her fully his own.

She fell backward on the bed, drawing him with her by her desperate grip on his shoulders and by his great need for her, and the weight of his body upon hers was a welcome dominance.

Eli took her in one thrusting motion of his steel-like hips; instinctively her legs wrapped themselves around him in a claiming as old as the stars at the farthest border of the universe.

Bonnie was fevered, flinging herself at Eli as though to batter him, but in reality, of course, she was surrendering herself. Smoothly, fiercely he lunged and withdrew, lunged and withdrew, until Bonnie was tossing her head back and forth in delirium and groaning senseless, desperate pleas.

"All right," Eli conceded gruffly, as he let his own measured restraint fall away. "All right, Bonnie. I'll give you what you want . . ."

Bonnie rose high off the bed to meet his final stroke, a wailing moan coming from her throat as her body shuddered in glorious defeat. Only moments behind her, Eli growled as he caught her bottom in strong, lifting hands and plunged into her depths in a series of long, explosive strokes that ended with a warrior's hoarse shout of conquest.

Eli sank, gasping, to Bonnie's side, his head pillowed on her dampened, tingling breasts, one of his legs curved over her thighs.

"That," she managed to say, "will be fifty dollars."

Eli laughed and gave what he could reach of her bottom a smart slap. Mere minutes later, he had recovered his considerable virility, and he seemed determined to make up for every session of lovemaking lost because of the years apart.

He washed Bonnie and himself with a cloth soaked in champagne, then, with his fingers, he sprinkled droplets of the sparkling wine over her full breasts. His method of clearing away the nectar left Bonnie insensible with need.

Bonnie awakened early the next morning, with Eli sprawled beside her in sated sleep, and she scrambled from the bed, her cheeks pounding. She needed a bath, in water instead of champagne, but she filled the tub slowly because she didn't want to wake Eli. She had important business to see to, and none of it would get done if he decided to make love to her again.

She was settled in the bathtub, the embarrassment over her wanton behavior the night before almost under control, when the door opened and Eli came in, naked as the day he'd entered this world, and climbed blithely into the tub with her.

Instantly Bonnie's cheeks were hot again, throbbing in time with the beat of her heart. "Don't you touch me, Eli McKutchen," she hissed. "I have work to do!"

"You certainly do," he said, in a crooning undertone that was as smooth and rich as the finest brandy and just as intoxicating. And then he drew Bonnie up, far enough out of the water that she sat astraddle of his thighs, fully vulnerable to him.

"I mean it, Eli—" she sputtered, pushing at his broad shoulders with her hands, but her words were cut off when his mouth closed over her own. Only a moment later, her hands stopped their fruitless pushing and moved to the back of his head, where they tangled in the richness of his wheat-gold hair.

Bonnie called on her suppliers alone, walking from one office to another and placing her orders. The wholesalers were all gracious and eager to accommodate her requests for piping, plumbing fixtures, paint and hardware. They were goggle-eyed at the size of the deposits she put down and solicitous in a way that made Bonnie wonder if the thorough loving she and Eli had engaged in showed in her eyes or some aspect of her person.

The very thought mortified her.

When her business had been concluded, Bonnie treated herself to a hearty luncheon in a sandwich shop—thanks to Eli, she'd never gotten around to having breakfast—and then shopped for small gifts for Katie, Genoa and Rose Marie.

Doing this was the closest Bonnie came to admitting to herself that Northridge even existed. Regardless of the true state of affairs, in fact, she felt quite deliciously, completely married to Eli.

It was late afternoon when she returned to the suite and found it empty. Yawning from the combined exertions of making love, tending to her business and then shopping, Bonnie was content to be alone. She removed her hat, took her hair down, and brushed it thoroughly. Then, with more yawns, she stripped down to her drawers and camisole and stretched out on the neatly made bed for a nap.

Some hours later, she felt cool air on her breasts and turned from her side to her back, still half asleep. "Ummm," she said, as warm hands gently caressed the plump, pink-tipped bounty. Oh, it was a nice dream indeed, sweetly erotic . . .

She even felt the ribbon ties of her drawers being pulled,

so softly and so slowly. Liking the dream more and more, Bonnie stretched, making a purring sound deep in her throat, her arms reaching above her head.

When they were caught there and held tenderly captive by a strong masculine hand, Bonnie opened her eyes. She gasped with sleepy pleasure as, simultaneously, Eli's mouth claimed one swollen nipple and his hand slid down inside her drawers to seek, caress and madden.

It was a wonderful way to be awakened, Bonnie thought, even as her body began to thrash about in its own involuntary response. Her nipple blossomed in the warm, suckling moistness of Eli's mouth, her hips delighted in the slow pace he set for them, and her arms made no effort to be free of the forceful hand that held them so gently at the wrists.

Freshly bathed, Bonnie huddled in the corner of one of the twin sofas in the sitting room, clad only in her practical corduroy wrapper—was there a less glamorous garment to be found anywhere on the face of the earth?—watching as a bellhop wheeled a dinner cart into the suite. The young man's eyes never touched her, even when she extended the small bill Eli had provided for his tip.

It was a relief when the waiter-bellhop found his way out of the suite and closed the door behind him. In the bathroom, Eli was taking a noisy bath, singing for all he was worth and splashing so much water around that Bonnie was sure it must be seeping through the floor and dripping onto the heads of the people in the room directly below theirs.

Eli's merriment gave her a forlorn feeling, and she bit at one fingernail for a moment before slapping her own hand.

Strangely distraught, Bonnie got up and padded over to the serving cart, lifting one silver lid to reveal steaming roast beef, neatly sliced and pink at the center. Under another lid was a vegetable dish, and under still another, mashed potatoes drenched in butter. Suddenly, Bonnie was fiercely hungry.

"Eli!" she called, out of fairness. "Dinner is here!" Then, having given him adequate notice, she took a plate and began to fill it with a meal more suited to a smelter worker than herself.

She was nearly through eating when Eli joined her,

wearing a robe made of royal blue velvet. After casting one mocking glance from the slim pickings remaining on the serving cart to Bonnie's plate, he dished up a dinner of sorts and sat down on the sofa opposite hers to eat.

"What did you order for dessert?" he asked after some time, his eyes on the one serving dish Bonnie had not uncovered and plundered.

Bonnie shrugged indifferently. After all, she had consumed most of the roast beef, most of the mixed carrots and peas and all but a dollop of the mashed potatoes. She was full.

Eli arched one eyebrow. "Since you devoured more than your fair share of the main course, I would think you might at least have the courtesy to check and see if there is anything for dessert. Man does not live by breast alone, you know."

Bonnie flushed at the wicked reminder and flounced off the sofa to lift the lid from the unexplored serving dish. There was nothing to fill out Eli's scanty repast; only a small, hinged box with a beautiful Renaissance angel painted on its lid.

Charcoal-violet eyes lifted to laughing golden ones, then returned to the delicate little box. With a slightly tremulous hand, Bonnie unfastened the tiny catch and lifted the beautifully painted lid.

Instantly, tinkling notes of music flowed into the mundane world, seeming to have had their beginning in another, better place. Bonnie didn't recognize the tune, but that didn't matter. She lifted the music box carefully, her hands cupped beneath it. Her eyes rounded in wonder as she watched the miniature works turn beneath a layer of glass.

Bonnie had owned beautiful things before in New York—all of them given to her by this same man—but she had left them all behind when she fled her marriage and since then she had not possessed such a frivolous, splendid treasure. Now, she was moved almost to tears, though a pragmatic thought saved her from disgrace at the very last second.

"Is this payment? Like the fifty-dollar bill?" she demanded. Oh, Lord, if he said yes, she was going to die. Just die.

But the expression snapping in Eli's twenty-four-karat

eyes was angry, not mocking. "It's a gift," he said, and the fury in his voice spoiled the gentle melody of the exquisite music box.

Somehow his words were more like a slap across the face than the reassurance they should have been. Unwilling to part with the music box, Bonnie clutched it close, turned and walked into the bedroom.

She locked the door behind her, but Eli only came undramatically through the one leading into the bathroom. He undressed and Bonnie finally undressed, too, and got into bed beside him.

They made love that night with a ferocity unequaled by any previous joining, but their union was more a battle of souls and bodies than a celebration of human passion, and for that reason Bonnie perceived it as a sinful act. Memories of that fevered skirmish, which left them both exhausted and damp with perspiration, were to weigh heavily on her spirit in the difficult days to come.

CHAPTER 15

THE HOTEL DINING room was busy, as dozens of guests enjoyed their breakfasts. For all the sound and fury, for all that she was sitting directly across a table from Eli McKutchen, Bonnie felt very much alone.

"There will be talk, Bonnie," Eli said, in a moderate voice, "whether we go back to Northridge separately or together."

Seeing the truth of that didn't make matters any easier for Bonnie. The dream was over. Indeed, it had ended the night before, when things had gone sour between the two of them. "I still think we should take different trains. I'll go today and you can follow tomorrow. That way, we can both arrive in time for the public meeting on Sunday and there will be less gossip."

Eli's shoulders moved in a shrug, and there was a somber look in his eyes. Still, his lips were trying to smile as he said, "Seth tells me that you plan to attend the meeting in your capacity as mayor."

Bonnie's face and throat heated. Now that the topic of Northridge had been brought up, she was remembering things she would have preferred to forget: her time as a hurdy-gurdy, the struggles of running a mercantile, her temporary engagement to Webb Hutcheson. She stiffened in

172

her chair, stunned to realize that she had not given so much as a thought to the proposal or to Webb himself in the past two days. Even more startling, Eli had not asked a single question about that rainy night she'd spent across the river, in Webb's house.

"Close your mouth, dear," Eli said quietly.

Bonnie obeyed. "You never asked about that night on the other side of the river—"

Eli took his time before answering, taking a sip of his coffee, smiling at the waitress when she came to remove the dirty plates. "I don't need to ask. I know what happened between you and Hutcheson—nothing."

Bonnie was both relieved and insulted. It was good to know that Eli credited her with a measure of morality, but did he perchance think that no other man would want her? "How can you be so certain?"

He grinned but, for the sake of discretion, he at least kept his voice low. "You let me make love to you in a railroad car, Bonnie, in the bright light of day. And you didn't quibble when I asked you here to the hotel. Those things, among others, tell me that you've been—shall we say—chaste for a long time. You needed me as badly as I needed you, and that wouldn't have been the case if someone else had been taking you to bed."

Bonnie cupped her hands around her water glass and then lifted them to her face, trying to cool her stinging cheeks. There was nothing she could say in reply, so she kept her peace.

"Don't marry Hutcheson, Bonnie," Eli warned, suddenly and in a grave tone of voice. "You won't be happy with him."

Something kept Bonnie from confessing that she had no plans to marry Webb, now that there seemed to be no immediate danger of her losing Rose Marie. "I don't know about that," she reflected, almost blithely. "I think Webb is the kind of man who could make a woman very happy. He's solid and dependable, you know, not to mention handsome."

There was an almost imperceptible change in Eli's color; he turned a shade paler even as a pink flush crept up his neck and glowed just beneath his jawline. "Meaning?"

173

"Meaning that if we should ever suffer a family tragedy, Webb would still be faithful to me. He wouldn't allow his private pain to drive him to someone else. And he would certainly never go rushing off to some silly war, leaving me to face my grief alone."

The jibe struck Eli with an obvious impact, but he kept his composure. "Hutcheson will be as faithful as a lap dog—there's no denying that," he said evenly. "But don't look for the kind of passion we've shared, Bonnie—he's not going to be able to give you that."

"You could not possibly know such a thing!"

"Yes, I could. I know human nature, Bonnie, and I know you. You need fire and excitement. Hutcheson is a decent sort, but he's not going to try to please you in bed because it will never occur to him that you want to be pleased. The wives of men like that see sexual intercourse as a duty, Bonnie, and that's the way their husbands like it." He paused, sighed. "Hell, you'd be happier with Durrant than with that plodding print jockey."

Enough was enough. Bonnie grabbed for her handbag and stood up. "I won't listen to another word!" she hissed, snatching her valise from the seat of the extra chair at their table.

Eli caught her by the wrist and deftly forced her back into the chair nearest his. The valise thumped to the carpeted floor. "For God's sake, Bonnie, stop reacting to all the things I've done to you and hear what I'm saying now!"

"I don't want to hear any more!" Bonnie snapped, folding her arms across her bosom and thus adding an unspoken "and I won't." "You've done nothing but insult the man I—the man I—"

"The man you love, Bonnie? The man you want to spend the rest of your life with? You want to be safe and respectable, but you're paying one hell of a price for those things, Bonnie! Your spirit will wither away to nothing!"

Bonnie trembled. For some reason, she could not give ground, could not admit that she had these same doubts about any union with Webb Hutcheson. She couldn't say that she had changed her mind about marrying the man, though that would have made things so much easier. "Let me go!" she whispered.

Eli's fingers slowly loosed themselves from around her wrist. "Hutcheson is a good man, Bonnie. But he's dull as dishwater and he'll expect you to have no more interest in lovemaking than the baby you might get from it. And he'll be disgusted if you make him think otherwise."

"Webb is a passionate lover!" Bonnie argued in a whisper. "Why would Earline Kalb be so jealous of me if he didn't p-please her?"

"In his eyes, Earline is a whore, Bonnie. She's supposed to like being tossed into the long grass. But you'll notice that Webb isn't looking to marry his landlady—he's only using her."

Bonnie stood again, hauling her valise along, and this time Eli made no effort to detain her. That was a good thing, for if he had, she would certainly have fetched him up alongside the head with her satchel. "I'm going back to Northridge right now," she said. "I'll thank you to wait and catch tomorrow's train."

Eli nodded a grim and vaguely menacing agreement. "Very well. After all, we wouldn't want Hutcheson to find out that I've been bedding his lady love while he slaved over the presses. He'd be shocked, you know."

Bonnie swallowed, too stricken to be angry. "You wouldn't tell him, would you? I mean, you did promise—"

"I gave you my word, Bonnie, and I mean to keep it. I won't tell anybody that we've been together, but there will be those who guess what's been happening between us." Eli stood up, leaving money behind to pay the breakfast tab and taking Bonnie's valise from her. "The least I can do is see you safely aboard the train."

They walked to the depot, since it was only a short distance from the hotel. Bonnie was furious with Eli, but she also felt as though a cherished part of her life was ending—for a second time—and she was distraught. The years ahead looked infinitely long and empty. Whether she married again or not, a part of her would be hollow. Raw.

Bonnie was standing on the railroad platform, bracing herself for an awkward good-bye, when Eli bent his head to encircle the rim of her right ear with just the tip of his tongue. "I'll see you in Northridge," he said.

Bonnie knew what Eli meant, and a delicious shiver went

through her before she turned and fairly hurled herself into the passenger car. The train was so crowded that Bonnie had trouble finding a seat, but she didn't give much thought to the matter, assuming that the other passengers were bound for Colville, where there were several sawmills and a man could find work.

For a time she mourned the joys of the two days just past, but when the train finally shuddered and rolled into Colville, making its customary stop, none of the rough-looking men disembarked. Bonnie began to wonder about them and watch them surreptitiously.

They were a coarse lot, swearing over card games and filling the car with swirls of blue-gray cigar smoke, but they didn't look like sawmill workers or even people Seth might have sent for to help build the new cabins. It was their clothes that made them different, Bonnie thought; they wore cheap, ill-fitting suits—but suits, all the same—and bowler hats. They were city men, from far away, and they had to be on their way to Northridge.

What would such men find to do in that small town?

Bonnie raised one hand to her throat as the answer occurred to her. These were union men. Professional troublemakers.

One of them was starting toward the vacant seat beside Bonnie's when suddenly a small blond woman came sweeping down the aisle, fanning herself with a magazine as she moved, and fell into that same seat.

Bonnie gave a sigh of relief. "Hello," she said.

Eyes as dark and velvety as the center of a pansy returned the greeting. "I nearly missed the train, you know," the young woman announced breathlessly.

Bonnie thought of the huge, smelly male that had been making his way toward her and shuddered. "Thank heaven you didn't," she answered as the train chugged out of Colville again, whistling its farewell.

"I'm Lizbeth Simmons," the blonde offered brightly, setting her magazine in her lap. She was about Bonnie's age and dressed in a gray flannel skirt and a pristine white shirtwaist, and her pale hair was a fluff of softness around her flawless oval face. The pansy eyes widened. "Who are you?"

176

Bonnie thought sadly that this woman would make an excellent friend, whoever she was. But once she reached Northridge and was taken under the collective wing of the Friday Afternoon Community Improvement Club, Lizbeth Simmons would be shown the error of her ways and henceforth refuse to speak to the likes of Bonnie Mc-Kutchen.

Reluctantly Bonnie gave her name and mentioned that she owned Northridge's only mercantile.

"How admirable—a woman in business for herself!" observed Lizbeth, very pleased by the idea. "I'm a teacher, so I barely manage to keep alive, from a financial standpoint. Of course, I do feel that one can accomplish much in my profession, given the proper chance."

Bonnie hadn't known that a new teacher had been hired for Northridge's one-room schoolhouse, and she was surprised, especially since the term was about to end. "May I ask who engaged you?"

Lizbeth smiled warmly, showing a row of small, pearl-like teeth. "Of course. A Miss Genoa McKutchen—why, she must be a relative of yours!"

"She is—was—my sister-in-law."

A slight frown, one of puzzlement, wrinkled Lizbeth's alabaster brow, then smoothed away. "I'm to teach adult classes over the summer—there is a problem of illiteracy in Northridge, according to Miss McKutchen's letters. In the fall, she—Miss McKutchen, I mean—plans to open a new school, just for the children of the smelter workers. She seems to feel that they're getting short shrift under the present system."

Bonnie was delighted, though a little miffed that Genoa hadn't confided this ambitious plan to her. "It's a fine idea," she said sincerely. "The Patch Town children are regarded as second-class citizens by the more—prosperous residents."

"Those who don't work at the smelter, you mean?"

Bonnie shook her head. "Practically everyone depends on the smelter for a living in one way or another, but there is a social hierarchy all the same. Some of the crew bosses and shipping clerks and such have their own homes." An old bitterness tightened Bonnie's lips for a moment and sparked

177

in her eyes. "They look down on those who have to live in Patch Town."

"Patch Town? Miss McKutchen didn't mention such a place in her correspondence—"

"It isn't a place that anyone—especially the McKutchen family—could be proud of." Bonnie sighed, suddenly feeling very dispirited and very much an outsider. Now, through some strange mental alchemy, Northridge and all the people there were real again, while the time in Spokane seemed but a fantasy. With the toe of her slipper, she nudged the side of her valise, tucked beneath the seat ahead, to remind herself that the music box was packed away inside, solid proof that Eli, for two days and two nights at least, had loved her as a husband loves a wife. "In all fairness," she added belatedly, "the McKutchens are making an effort to correct the things that are wrong."

The man in the seat just ahead—he wore the standard dusty bowler and dung-colored suit—turned to glare at Bonnie. His eyes were accusing brown beads, looking out of an acne-scarred face.

Bonnie felt threatened, though she met the ugly man's gaze with an intrepid stare of her own. When he had turned around again, she said in a voice meant to carry, "Northridge's problems will be worked out fairly, provided there is no more interference from outside factions."

The union man stiffened, but did not look back at Bonnie again. Nevertheless, she was very much aware of the sudden heavy silence that filled the car. "I'm forever saying imprudent things," she confessed to Lizbeth, in a near whisper.

Lizbeth laughed. "Oh, but you're honest, and I like that in a person. Isn't it fortunate that we had each other to ride with? I fear I might have turned and gotten right back off this train if I hadn't spotted you sitting here, a port in a storm." She wrinkled her pert little nose and added in an undertone, "The smell! Mercy me, it's insufferable, don't you think?"

"There is a certain air," Bonnie answered pointedly, and the ears of the odious man in front of her turned crimson at their tips.

For the rest of the trip, Bonnie and her temporary friend chatted about fashions, the pros and cons of living in

Northridge, and the virtues of Miss Genoa McKutchen's plan to upgrade the local system of education.

It was a sad relief to reach Northridge, to part with Lizbeth Simmons, who would have made an exemplary friend, to return to the realities of daily life. There would be no more staying in gracious hotels, no more elegant restaurant meals, no more ecstasy in Eli McKutchen's arms.

On the cheerful side, though, Bonnie was looking forward to seeing Rose Marie again, for she had missed her daughter terribly. It would be nice to chat with Genoa—though she would have to be very careful not to let on what had really happened in Spokane—and have tea with Katie, who would no doubt be able to give a full accounting of all that had taken place during Bonnie's absence.

The mood in Northridge was suspenseful; Bonnie sensed that the moment she stepped down from the train. The river looked to be swollen well beyond its normal levels and the sky was a formidable, glowering charcoal color. Mud sucked at the soles of Bonnie's shoes and stained her skirts as she stepped down from the platform. Samuel, the son of Genoa's cook, was on hand with the carriage, to fetch Lizbeth, but Bonnie didn't want to ride. She needed time to gather her thoughts and feelings and drive them back into their proper places.

"Would you mind bringing Rose Marie and Katie to the store as soon as you can?" Bonnie asked Samuel, after politely refusing his offer to drive her home to the mercantile.

Samuel, a homely adolescent who would one day be a homely man, nodded. "Yes, ma'am, Mrs. McKutchen. I'll do that."

Was there a hint of a smirk on Samuel's face and lurking in his tone?

Bonnie couldn't decide and didn't really care, one way or the other. There would be speculation, just because she and Eli had left town on the same train, but she couldn't help that, so she wasn't going to worry about it. She set her course for the top of the hill, the mercantile, home.

The board sidewalk leading up to the main part of town was slippery with streaks of mud, and the grain of the wood showed clearly, wetted by a recent rain.

Uneasily Bonnie looked back over one shoulder, toward the temperamental river. When she turned her face forward again, she saw Webb Hutcheson's buggy, headed down the hill, make a broad turn in the street and come to a stop beside her.

Even though she didn't look directly at Webb's face, Bonnie sensed his quiet fury. He'd heard, then, that she and Eli had left Northridge on the same train. God knew what he was thinking, but whatever it was, it couldn't have been worse than the truth. Bonnie's throat ached and she shifted the handle of the heavy valise from one hand to the other and back again.

"Hello, Webb," she finally managed to say.

The answer was stony. "Climb in, if you want a ride."

Bonnie hadn't wanted a ride when Samuel had offered one at the depot and she didn't want a ride now, but she felt so guilty over her rendezvous with Eli that she put the valise behind the buggy seat and got in.

Webb did not say a single word during the brief journey to the mercantile, but he followed Bonnie up the side stairs and waited behind her as she rummaged through her handbag for the key and opened the door.

The darkened kitchen had that musty smell that comes of emptiness, and Bonnie quickly opened the small window over the sink to let in some fresh air.

A chair scraped behind her and she knew that Webb was sitting down at the table. He meant to stay.

She closed her eyes for a moment and then started putting wadded pages of the *Northridge News* into the stove. She added kindling to this and lit a fire, then pumped water into the teakettle. All this was accomplished without so much as one glance in Webb's direction.

"You might at least have told me you were going away," he said quietly, when it was clear that Bonnie wasn't going to take the initiative and speak first.

Bonnie took her yellow crockery teapot from a shelf, along with a fresh tin of tea, and measured in several scoops of the aromatic blend. Still she didn't look at Webb. "I'm not your wife, Webb Hutcheson," she said kindly in even tones, "and I don't have to report my whereabouts to you or anyone else."

"Damn it!" Webb exploded, one hand striking the table-top with such force that Bonnie jumped, nearly dropping the yellow teapot. "Every busybody in this town is talking about you and McKutchen running off together—"

Slowly, clutching the teapot so that she wouldn't drop it, Bonnie turned and looked directly into Webb's furious blue eyes. "Don't you dare lecture me, Webb. What I do is none of their business, and none of yours."

Webb flushed, and it was clear by the white line edging his jaw that he was still angry. "By God, Bonnie, it is my business if you've been—been giving yourself to Eli Mc-Kutchen!"

Bonnie spoke softly, but she was just as furious as Webb. Maybe even more so. At that moment, she'd have loved to crown him with her teapot, but she was too fond of the piece to risk breaking it on a rock-hard skull. "Giving myself to Eli?" she echoed sweetly. "The way you give yourself to Earline Kalb, Webb? Is that what you mean?"

"Damn it all to hell, Bonnie," Webb exploded, shooting out of his chair, sending it clattering backward to the floor, "I'm a man and that makes it different!"

Of course, she could always get another teapot out of another sack of flour. Bonnie spoke with acid sweetness. "It does?"

Webb sank back into his chair, running one hand through his hair. "I know it seems unfair," he conceded generously.

Bonnie turned away, setting the teapot down on the counter with a thump, her shoulders rigid. "Only because it *is* unfair," she said evenly.

Webb's voice was hoarse, broken. "So you were with McKutchen?"

"I didn't say that," Bonnie replied. God help her, she couldn't say it, though that would have been the kindest thing to do.

Eventually the water boiled and the tea was properly brewed and Bonnie joined a despondent Webb at the kitchen table. Not a word had passed between them in several minutes.

Unable to tell Webb the painful truth, Bonnie avoided the subject of Eli, pretended that it had never come up. "There were hordes of union men on the train, Webb," she said, remembering the threats that had been made following the last article her friend had published concerning the strife at the smelter works. "They're a rough bunch."

"I saw them," Webb sighed, staring down into his tea, which was still untouched despite the fact that he had laced it with measures of sugar and milk in his careful, methodical way. He had the look of a man who needed something stronger to drink than orange pekoe. "Stay out of their way as much as you can, Bonnie."

Bonnie sat up a little straighter in her chair, ruffled by the implication that she couldn't take care of herself. "I will not be a hostage simply because a pack of ruffians are roaming the town, Webb Hutcheson."

The royal blue eyes were snapping when they rose to Bonnie's face. "You are so damnably stubborn. Sometimes I'm tempted to paddle your backside!"

Bonnie couldn't have been more surprised or more insulted if Webb had called her a name. There was no humor whatsoever in his gaze; he was totally serious. "Heaven help you if you ever try!"

Webb pushed back his chair and folded his arms across his broad chest, and that ominous glint was still clearly visible in his eyes. "I wouldn't need any help from heaven, Bonnie. I can handle the job all by myself."

Perhaps things would have been different if Bonnie hadn't lost her temper, if she hadn't openly challenged Webb with a saucy "You touch me, Webb Hutcheson, and I'll scratch your eyes out!"

The expression on his face told Bonnie that she'd pushed the man too far. She opened her mouth to apologize, but it was too late. Webb reached out and caught Bonnie by one arm and the next thing she knew, she'd been flung across his lap. She struggled, of course, but Webb scissored her thrashing legs between his own and held her motionless.

"Webb!" Bonnie cried out, in a frantic appeal to his reason. She could feel his hand poised high above her very vulnerable bottom even though she could see nothing but the floor. "Webb, you can't do this!"

"I know," Webb said, with resignation, "and yet I'm going to."

It was then, heaven be thanked, that Katie appeared in

the kitchen doorway, holding Rose's small hand in her own, and gasped, "Mr. Hutcheson, don't! Please don't."

Webb gave a long sigh and released Bonnie, who scrambled to the opposite side of the kitchen and stood with her back pressed to the sink, her teeth gnawing at her lower lip, her eyes flashing with amazement and fury.

"I'll go now," Webb said, sounding and looking distracted as he rose slowly to his feet.

"I think that would be best," Bonnie replied coldly.

When the door had closed quietly behind Webb, she turned to Katie, who looked horrified.

"I don't want to hear another word about this incident as long as I live, Katherine Ryan. Do you understand me? It never happened."

Katie swallowed. "Yes, ma'am," she said.

Bonnie lifted her chin and went about setting her valise on the table and opening its stubborn catch. The music box Eli had given her was on top, carefully wrapped in one of her petticoats. She unwrapped it and traced the beautiful painted angel on its top with a wistful motion of her index finger.

"Isn't that pretty, ma'am?" Katie cooed, admiring the box with wide eyes. "It's an angel, and she's got dark hair just like you do!"

Bonnie stiffened. An angel. Of course. She had been expecting some kind of snide attack from Eli, and she'd nearly missed it! Here it was, a subtle but effective reminder of her hurdy-gurdy days—or, more properly, nights—as the Angel.

She set the box aside, unwilling to give in to a primitive urge to send it smashing against a wall, and with a modicum of dignity brought out a small rag doll for Rose Marie and a bottle of jasmine-scented cologne for Katie.

Both girls were delighted with their gifts and, per Bonnie's decree, Webb's temporary loss of reason went unmentioned.

In the end, it was not Katie but Rose Marie who betrayed the humiliating secret. It happened the very next day, not fifteen minutes after the train from Spokane had arrived in Northridge.

CHAPTER 16

THE AFTERNOON WAS chilly and dark and the sky was heavy with rain. Because of this, Bonnie had built a busy, crackling fire in the store's potbellied stove and lit several kerosene lamps. As Katie perched on the lid of the pickle barrel, reading, and Rose sat contentedly on the floor, playing with her new doll, Bonnie was in the rear storeroom, making space for the merchandise Seth had ordered for the rebuilding of Patch Town. At the sound of the little bell over the front door, she smoothed her hair and her skirts and went out to wait on the customer.

The "customer" was Eli, who stood watching Rose with such a disapproving expression that Bonnie's attention turned instantly to her daughter.

Rose was mercilessly spanking her doll.

Eli's gaze sliced to Bonnie's pinkened face. "Is that how you discipline my daughter?" he demanded, in a quiet but nonetheless lethal tone.

Before Bonnie could answer, Katie closed her book with a snap and blurted defensively, "Of course it isn't! Our Rosie's only acting out what she saw yesterday, aren't you, sweetling?"

Rose Marie now had no interest in her doll. She struggled laboriously to her feet and toddled over to Eli, who immediately lifted her into his arms. He smiled at the child and embraced her, but there was a chill in the gaze he turned upon Bonnie.

"Go upstairs, Katie," Bonnie said calmly.

The girl hesitated. There was defiance in her manner, defiance directed not at Bonnie, but at Eli. "Shall I take the baby, too?"

Just the thought of the squall Rose Marie would put up at being separated from her beloved papa gave Bonnie the beginnings of a sick headache. "No. She's fine where she is."

Katie gave Eli one last insurgent glance and scampered up the stairs.

"What exactly did Rose see?" Eli wanted to know. There was a note of suspicion in his voice and a quiet obstinacy in his manner.

Bonnie bit her lower lip, reluctant to admit what had happened—or nearly happened—but fully aware that she had to do just that. If she didn't explain, Eli would draw his own conclusions and the result might be a terrible misunderstanding. Finally she said, "Webb l-lost his temper and—and he—"

Eli blanched. "He what? By God, if he laid a hand on my daughter, I'll—" he paused, and a knowing look flashed in his eyes. He drew in a deep breath and let it out again. "Wait a minute. It wasn't Rose that Hutcheson walloped, was it? It was you!"

"Webb didn't wallop *anyone*," Bonnie hissed, red to her ears, "Katie came in just in time to stop him. And don't you dare turn self-righteous, Eli McKutchen, because you're no better than he is! Why, just the other day, you were threatening to do the same thing!"

"Are you defending Hutcheson?"

Bonnie gripped the edge of the counter. "Certainly not," she said loftily. "I wouldn't even consider forgiving Webb, were it not for the fact that I know he didn't really mean to hurt me."

Laughter sparked in Eli's golden eyes but left his mouth unchanged. "Didn't he?" Carefully, he set Rose back on her feet, and she went back to playing with her doll, though this time in a more kindly fashion.

Bonnie sighed and averted her eyes. "I suppose he did,"

she conceded, unable to believe what had almost happened even now, after she had had a whole night to think about it.

There was a short silence and then Eli chuckled. It was a low, innately masculine sound. "How did you manage to provoke the poor bastard into losing his reason, might I ask?"

At last Bonnie was able to lift her eyes to Eli's face. She straightened her spine and raised her chin. "It was the talk, I think. Webb was upset by things he'd heard about you and me. Too, he'd ordered me to avoid those union men who came in on the train yesterday and I said I wouldn't be held hostage—" she paused, swallowed. "I guess I baited him, as well."

Eli sighed and, to his credit, there was no look of triumph about him. "I can sympathize with Hutcheson's position. At the same time, I'd like to break his neck. In fact, I mean to let him know that if he ever tries anything like that again, no matter what you've done to irk him, I'll kill him."

Eli sounded completely serious, and Bonnie shivered even though the snapping fire in the stove was keeping the store warm. "You are being most hypocritical, Eli," she said evenly. "You might have responded in just the way Webb did."

Eli shook his head in angry marvel. "You're still going to see Hutcheson, aren't you? You're going to let him suffer for a while, and then you're going to forgive him."

"I would have forgiven you," Bonnie pointed out, realizing only as she actually spoke the words that they were true.

Her former husband was not appeased. Indeed, stiff annoyance showed in every magnificent line of him. "That's generous of you," he said tightly. After a short, sour pause, he went on. "But I'm not here to talk about Hutcheson—I came in to tell you that I'm moving out of the hotel. For the time being, I'll be living at Earline's."

Earline's? Bonnie was possessed of a sudden and incomprehensible need to scream, stomp her feet and throw things, but she hid all those feelings and spoke moderately. "I'm sure that where you choose to live is none of my affair."

"I would have to agree, dear," Eli said, with a look of barely suppressed delight. "But alas, you are raising my child and if Rose needs me for any reason, I want you to know where to look." He tipped his fashionable round-brimmed hat, which he had never bothered to remove, and after a word with Rose, he left.

Bonnie was full of outraged frustration and, worse, she had no way of venting those feelings. She did note that while Eli's plan to live in Earline Kalb's rooming house made her half frantic with jealousy, Webb's residing there had never bothered her. Even learning that Earline was Webb's mistress had not ruffled her, but if Eli were to take up with that woman . . .

Bonnie gave the pickle barrel a hard kick and uttered a little cry that had more to do with bruised emotions than bruised toes. Rose looked up at her with startled McKutchen-gold eyes.

"Don't ever fall in love," Bonnie warned her daughter, with a shaking of her finger.

Rose responded with a crooked grin so reminiscent of her father that Bonnie was forced to smile. She called to Katie that it was all right to come back downstairs and returned to the task of preparing the storeroom.

Webb appeared just as she would have closed the store for the day, wearing a contrite expression and carrying a spray of soggy violets in one hand. It was raining very hard outside, and his suitcoat and hair were both dripping wet.

Shaking her head, unable to hate a man who had, for the most part, been a loyal friend, Bonnie ushered Webb over to the stove to warm up and dry off. She took the flowers, picked, no doubt, along the banks of the Columbia, and asked Katie to put them in water. As if the poor things weren't already half drowned.

"I'm sorry, Bonnie. About last night." Webb shrugged out of his sodden suitcoat, shivering a little. "Will you forgive me?"

"I shouldn't," Bonnie said. But then an angel at her shoulder reminded her that she had deliberately goaded Webb, that she hadn't been and still wasn't forthright where her feelings for Eli were concerned. "But I will forgive you, if you'll pardon me for what I did."

Poor Webb looked so relieved that Bonnie wanted to cry. It would have been so much easier if he'd stayed angry and even declared that he'd have nothing more to do with such a hellion, but easy things were rare in Bonnie's life. So rare that she didn't even bother to hope for them anymore.

There was coffee heating atop the potbellied stove, and Bonnie poured a cupful for Webb, extending it as a sort of olive branch. How she dreaded hurting him, even after the debacle beside her kitchen table. "Do you think this rain will ever stop?" she asked, just to make conversation.

Webb's shoulders, visible through his damp shirt, moved in a shrug. "I've been considering moving my presses to higher ground," he said.

Bonnie thought of the vulnerability of Patch Town and shuddered, but it was warm and cozy inside her mercantile and she quickly recovered from that moment of curious dread. "You're welcome to bring them here, Webb. There's plenty of room in the store."

"I'll think about it," Webb sniffled. The poor man had already caught cold; he was trembling and his teeth were chattering. "If anything happened to that equipment, I'd be ruined."

Bonnie thought of the toughs who had ridden into Northridge aboard yesterday's train. It was a touchy subject, but she brought it up anyway. "Have you had any more trouble, Webb? About your articles opposing the union, I mean?"

"Things have been quiet," he said, and Bonnie noticed then that he was avoiding her eyes.

"The strike hasn't ended, then."

Webb edged closer to the little stove and hugged himself against the cold. "Half the men are still out. The union leaders have been telling them that the new cabins and the shorter hours McKutchen has offered are some kind of trick. They say that Eli's just trying to keep the men from organizing, that he'll backtrack to the old way of doing things once he's gotten rid of the union."

"How can they believe that?" Bonnie asked, with rather too much spirit. "Eli does mean to build those cabins, Webb. I know because I took the orders for paint and nails and pipes and such."

Webb was still shivering so that Bonnie frowned and sent Katie upstairs to fetch a warm blanket. "Some of the men don't believe there are going to be any cabins, Bonnie. And they expect Eli to show them the road for rebelling, rather than giving them back their jobs and cutting back their hours."

When Katie returned with the blanket, Webb wrapped it around himself and gratefully sank into the chair Bonnie found for him. He sat close to the stove, with his feet on its cast-iron base.

"Those men on the train looked mean," Bonnie reflected, feeling a little cold herself. She folded her arms and drew nearer to the stove, though she kept it as a barrier between herself and Webb.

"I'm surprised none of them have been in here," Webb replied. "They're all staying next door at the hotel."

Bonnie was reminded of Eli's move to Earline's rooming house and she wondered if the overcrowding of the hotel had been the reason for it. She was, however, too proud to ask Webb if his accommodating landlady had taken in a new boarder. She could imagine how Earline would fuss over Webb's cold, and though she would have welcomed a pang of envy, she felt nothing even vaguely like it. "I'm not sure I want the trade of those odious men," she said belatedly.

Just then a small cloaked figure dashed into the store, setting the little bell ajingle. Lizbeth Simmons pushed back her rain-drenched hood and smiled broadly at Bonnie.

"I do hope you've a pot of tea brewing!" the visitor sang merrily.

Bonnie smiled. Webb had taken definite notice of Miss Simmons; he rose slowly to his feet in acknowledgment of her presence.

After introductions had been made, Bonnie apologized for not having tea prepared and offered coffee instead. Lizbeth accepted a cup with delight, lacing it generously with both cream and sugar before sitting down in the chair her hostess provided.

"I have a list," Lizbeth told Bonnie. "Please don't let me rush off without making my purchases."

So, Bonnie thought wryly, Miss Simmons has not yet been approached by a delegation from the Friday Afternoon

Community Improvement Club. "Are you staying at Genoa's?"

Lizbeth was enjoying the warmth of the stove, the coffee and Webb Hutcheson's gaze. "I am. It's most enjoyable, too. So many books, and I have use of the reed organ, as well."

"How are Susan Farley and her baby?" Bonnie asked with real interest. A part of her had been holding its breath ever since that poor little infant's birth.

"Miss Genoa says that baby gets bigger every day," Lizbeth replied happily. "He doesn't need to be kept in the oven anymore."

Webb's eyes went round. "The oven?" he echoed.

Bonnie smiled and laid both her hands on his shoulders in a reassuring gesture. "A very small baby needs help to stay warm," she said.

Lizbeth's laugh was chimelike. "Genoa told me that her brother set up an awful fuss over that baby one day, thinking that she was about to roast the little darling!"

The reminder of Eli, however amusing, dampened Bonnie's spirits. She dared not allow herself to remember their lovemaking in that elegant big-city hotel, so she tried to imagine what Eli would think of Lizbeth when—inevitably —he was introduced to her. Miss Simmons was very attractive, and she was unattached. And so was Eli.

Suddenly Bonnie wasn't so sure that she wanted this pert, laughing woman for a friend.

When Lizbeth had finished her coffee, she brought her shopping list out of her handbag and extended it to Bonnie.

Bonnie hesitated. "I don't suppose you've heard from any of the—the ladies of the town?"

Lizbeth's smile was almost blinding. "Oh, yes— indirectly. I've had several written invitations to tea." The smile faded to a look of sympathy. "Genoa told me how they treat you, Bonnie, and I don't think I want to know them. Imagine going to the bother of having one's groceries shipped in from Colville just to avoid shopping in your store!"

Bonnie was surprised and, for a moment, hopeful. But there had been other newcomers before Lizbeth, some of them initially quite friendly, but they had soon given in to

the persistent remonstrations of the Club. "You know, don't
you, that I was a hurdy-gurdy dancer at the Brass Eagle?"

Out of the corner of her eye, Bonnie saw Webb stiffen, the
back of his neck going ruddy.

Lizbeth was undaunted by this bit of scandal. "Oh, yes,
Genoa told me that, too. Here, let me see that list again—
did I forget to write down hairpins and ink?"

Bonnie surrendered the list and began gathering the items
she could remember from it. Lizbeth helped, seeking out
other necessities herself. "You ought to give those biddies a
little of their own medicine," she said cheerfully, when
Bonnie was ringing up the charges at the cash register.

Knowing that Lizbeth was referring to the members of
the Club, Bonnie frowned. "How could I do that?"

Lizbeth's pansy-black eyes danced. "Have you a big piece
of paper, by any chance, and some colored chalk?" she
countered.

Bonnie tore off a long strip of butcher paper from the roll
at the end of the counter and produced a nubbin of blue
chalk. For a time, she'd used a blackboard to post special
prices.

Spreading the large piece of paper out on the countertop,
Lizbeth bent over it, forming big letters and coloring them
in with the smidgen of blue chalk, which stained her fingers.

Curious beyond all bearing, Bonnie nonetheless went
back to the stove. Webb greeted her with a mournful look
and a rousing sneeze.

When Lizbeth had finally finished her task, she turned
around, beaming, holding the paper up for Bonnie to read.
NO MEMBERS OF THE FRIDAY AFTERNOON COMMUNITY IMPROVE-
MENT CLUB MAY TRADE IN THIS ESTABLISHMENT, the decree
proclaimed.

A slow smile spread across Webb's face, but Bonnie was
baffled. She simply stared at the paper, wondering what use
it would be to warn away shoppers who were already sworn
never to set foot inside her store.

The irrepressible Lizbeth carried the paper to the front
window and spread it out in full view, completely covering
a display of canned goods. She even went outside, without
her cloak, to read the sign through the rain-dappled glass

and gauge its effect. She was smiling, if wet, when she came back inside.

"I daresay that will put a bee in their bonnets!" she said buoyantly. "Stuffy old things!"

Bonnie was still puzzled. "I don't see how—"

Lizbeth raised the hood of her bright red plaid cloak and gathered up her carefully bundled purchases, ready to leave. "Just wait, Bonnie. Just wait." With that, the teacher made her departure, disappearing into the gray drizzle of the day.

It was closing time, and Bonnie pulled the shades and locked the doors. Katie was upstairs, preparing supper, and Rose had fallen asleep on her blanket on the floor, holding her doll close.

"Won't you stay and eat with us, Webb?" Bonnie asked, putting Lizbeth and that silly sign out of her mind. "Katie is a very good cook, you know, and she's made chicken and dumplings for dinner."

Webb looked reluctant and, at the same time, patently miserable. His finely shaped nose was red and so were his eyes, and he continued to shiver inside his blanket. "I wouldn't want to be any bother—"

Bonnie bent and lifted Rose, blanket, doll and all, into her arms. The little girl's head fell against her shoulder in sleepy abandon. "Bother? I thought we were friends, you and I. Besides, you're coming down with something and I can't send you back out into that rain without some warm food in your stomach."

Somewhat sheepishly Webb stood up. He was as tall as a mountain and yet, in that moment, huddled inside his blanket, he resembled a little boy more than a man. "Earline will have something ready—" he began, but when he saw the reaction Bonnie tried to hide, his words fell off in midsentence.

"By all means, Webb, risk your death of pneumonia," Bonnie said coolly, "but don't disappoint Earline."

Webb looked delighted. "Are you jealous?"

Bonnie turned away quickly, not wanting him to guess that she was indeed jealous, but not of his relationship with Earline. It was Eli she was worried about. "Either accept my invitation or turn it down, Webb Hutcheson," she called over one shoulder, as she carried Rose Marie up the stairs. "One way or the other, it doesn't matter to me."

Webb stayed.

The stewed chicken, topped with light dumplings, was delicious. Everyone enjoyed it except Rose Marie, who kept nodding off to sleep in her highchair. Finally Bonnie excused herself to put her daughter to bed.

When she returned to the kitchen, Katie was heating water for dishwashing and Webb was clearing the table. Bonnie paused in the doorway, strangely touched by the sight. Despite the incident that had taken place in that very room, only the night before, she knew there was no better, gentler man in all the world. What perfect good sense it would have made to marry him, tend his house and his garden, prepare his meals—but when it came to love, Bonnie had no sense.

She took a dish towel from the peg and dried bowls and spoons and cups as Katie washed them. Webb lingered at the table, drinking the coffee Bonnie had poured for him in silence.

When the dishes were all washed and put away, Katie gave Bonnie an eloquent look that clearly asked whether she should stay or go. Knowing that the girl longed to bury herself in yet another book, Bonnie nodded that she could go.

Katie cast one worried glance at Webb and left the kitchen to read in her room.

Bonnie poured coffee for herself and sat down at the table, across from Webb. One kerosene lamp flickered between them, giving the room a coziness so sweet that it tugged at Bonnie's heart.

Webb sighed, turning his coffee cup between his hands. "What I did last night—it changed things between us, didn't it, Bonnie?"

It would have been so easy to blame breaking the sham engagement on that. There would even have been a degree of justification in it, Bonnie's part in the matter aside. But she cared too much for Webb to pretend. "I'm not sure things have ever been truly right between us, Webb," she said.

"You're going to say you can't marry me, aren't you?" Webb asked gruffly, and then, poor dear, he sneezed again, with such violence that Bonnie started.

"Dear me," she hedged, as he brought out his handkerchief. "You are catching a terrible cold!"

"I don't want to talk about my cold!" Webb barked through his handkerchief. "Are you going to marry me?"

"I'm surprised you still want me, after all the talk about my trip to Spokane." Bonnie searched within herself for the courage to be honest with Webb, to hurt him this once so that he would be free to find real love with some other woman, love to last him a lifetime.

Webb wadded his handkerchief and stuffed it into his trouser pocket. "Don't be surprised," he answered, his gaze direct. So painfully direct. "I'd want you even if I caught you with McKutchen myself."

Bonnie ached. *Tell him,* demanded the still, small voice within her. *Tell him now.*

But she couldn't. "Webb, that's dreadful! You're the kind of man any woman would be proud to have as a husband, and you should have more pride!"

His eyes still held hers. "I have no pride where you're concerned, Bonnie. I'd crawl, if I had to."

Bonnie's hands were knotted together in her lap and her heart pounded in the base of her throat, all but choking her. "Don't say that!" she whispered brokenly. "I'm not worthy of that—nobody is!"

Webb was rising out of his chair, putting on his damp suitcoat. His hair was curly from the rain and the sight and scent of it gave Bonnie a pang. "I love you," he said, in that quiet way of his, and then he kissed the top of Bonnie's head and left by the kitchen door.

Bonnie laid her head in her arms and did her very best not to cry. How terribly ironic it was that she so wished she could love Webb Hutcheson and, at the same time, hoped and prayed that he would find someone else to care for.

"Things are in a fierce muddle, aren't they, ma'am?" Katie asked gently, from nearby.

Bonnie lifted her head, saw that the girl was measuring tea leaves into the yellow crockery pot. "Yes, Katie. They are."

"There was lots of talk while you were gone," Katie confided, without looking around. Her small back was stiff with indignation. "Those old hens. As if they'd ever made an effort to improve the community! Everything good's been done despite them, by Miss Genoa or Mr. McKutchen or you!"

"I haven't done anything," Bonnie sighed, wishing that she had. The misery in Patch Town might have ended long ago if she hadn't been so selfish, so caught up in the Cinderella aspects of her marriage to Eli McKutchen. How thoughtless of others she'd been then, wearing beautiful clothes, eating fabulous food, spending money as though it was her due. Why hadn't she demanded that Eli do something about Patch Town then? Had God taken Kiley away to heaven to punish her for caring so little about the people of her own class?

"You have," Katie argued forcefully. "You never deny anybody medicine or food, even though most of them can't pay."

"It's the least I can do, Katie," Bonnie sighed. Her shoulders drooped and she felt so tired, so old. "I forgot about those people when I married Eli. I abandoned them."

"What could you have done?"

"I'll tell you what I could have done," Bonnie said bitterly, furious with that thoughtless girl she had once been. "I could have demanded that Eli make Patch Town a habitable, decent place. I could have insisted—"

"Would he have paid you any mind, ma'am," Katie challenged softly, "or would he just have patted you on the head and dismissed you, like you've told me he did when you said what you thought of the war?"

The teakettle whistled on the stove and Bonnie got up to pour hot water onto the leaves of orange pekoe inside the yellow pot. Katie's words had given her pause. "I don't know," she confessed in a faraway voice.

Rain lashed at the windows and the roof, as if determined to get inside the warm kitchen and chill it, and a flash of lightning filled the room with an eerie glow. "Mr. McKutchen is a fine man," Katie observed seriously, "but he's nothing more than a man, is he? And men don't put much stock in a woman's opinion when it comes to practical

195

matters. It might be that your husband would have gone right on ignoring how things were in Patch Town, no matter what you did or said."

Bonnie carried the teapot and two cups to the table and sat down again. "Yes," she conceded, "but I didn't even try. That's what bothers me, Katie. I didn't even think to bring the subject up."

Katie poured tea for herself and for Bonnie. She was determined to lend comfort, it appeared, no matter how awesome the task might prove to be. "You can't go back and change that time, ma'am. It's gone forever, so why grieve over what you did or didn't do?"

Why, indeed? But Bonnie did grieve. And when she was alone in her bedroom, except for a soundly sleeping Rose Marie, she got out the music box Eli had given her and opened its lid. The strange melody flowed sweetly through the darkness, and Bonnie yearned for a time that would never come again. A dream time that had perhaps never really existed at all.

CHAPTER 17

EVEN THOUGH MOST of the townspeople had already endured a two-hour sermon at the First Presbyterian Church or an equally lengthy mass at St. Jude's, the Pompeii Playhouse was packed that Sunday afternoon, when the community met to hear what Eli McKutchen had to say. The union people, of course, were also present, standing at the back of the theatre and even in the aisles.

As mayor of Northridge, Bonnie demanded the right to sit on the stage, with Eli, Seth and Forbes. Forbes had apparently been reinstated as manager of the smelter works, and Bonnie observed to herself that his face was healing nicely.

The women in the audience watched Bonnie with open hostility in their countenances. It was clear enough that they considered her title a mere sham—which it undeniably was—and resented what they saw as pure presumptuousness. In truth, Bonnie only wanted an opportunity to be heard.

As Eli approached the hastily improvised lectern, however, she began to lose confidence. The mayoralty was only a token office, even when held by a man. Bonnie's appointment had been nothing more than a drunken jest, perpetrated by the town council. What was she doing, sitting up here in front of God and everybody? What could she say that Eli or Seth or even Forbes wouldn't say first?

Eli began to speak, and there was not a trace of nervousness in either his stance at the rickety packing-crate podium or in his voice. He offered a soundly built cabin to every smelter family, along with an eight-hour workday. He promised that each man could buy his cabin, if he wished to, and thus be assured of a place to live in old age. There was a stir at this announcement, for such security was almost unheard of among men who earned their living by the might of their backs and their hands.

One of the union men, the dour-faced man who had spoken from the porch of this same theatre days before, interrupted Eli to demand, "What will happen when you've successfully driven the union out of Northridge, Mr. McKutchen? Will you punish the men who've taken a stand against you by revoking the concessions you've made today?"

There was another stir, for many of the workers believed that Eli would turn on them once he'd dispensed with the labor organizers.

Eli raised his voice to be heard over the din, but he spoke evenly, without a tremor of unease. "I have nothing against unions, Mr. Denning, as I've already told you in private meetings. The men are welcome to organize if they choose, but I won't raise wages to cover the cost of dues. For now, the cabins and the shorter workday are adequate."

Genoa was sitting in the third row, and she stood up, her eyes fixed on Seth Callahan, as though to draw courage from his presence. Lizbeth, seated at Genoa's other side, rose, too.

"There is one other concession that I, as a major shareholder in McKutchen Enterprises, wish to make," Eli's sister said clearly, though her voice shook a bit. "We'll be opening a school, just for the workers and their children."

"For the *workers*, Miss McKutchen?" Mr. Denning asked pointedly, aware of Genoa's trepidation at speaking in front of so many people and determined, it seemed, to take advantage of it.

Genoa squared her skinny shoulders and swallowed visibly. In that moment Bonnie admired her more than ever. "Some of you," Genoa began, looking around at the faces surrounding her, "must want to learn to read and write. Miss Simmons and I will be available to teach you."

Bonnie noticed that some of the Patch Town women looked even more intrigued than their men. She knew that they wanted to ask if they too might attend this new school, but they were clearly hesitant to speak up. Bonnie did it for them.

"What about the wives of the workers, Miss McKutchen?" she asked. "Are they also eligible for these classes?"

Genoa was flushed with conviction and fear. "Absolutely," she said, and then, with a look of vast relief, she sat down.

There was an excited buzz in the audience as workers and their wives conferred, and scattered arguments broke out. The more prosperous ladies of the town, who were, of course, already educated, showed patent disapproval.

Forbes bounded out of his chair to stand beside Eli. "What the hell do you men have to grouse about?" he demanded hotly. "McKutchen Enterprises is willing to give your jobs back if you've been out on strike, help you own your own house, even teach you to read!"

One of the men stood up. "I'll tell you one thing we've got to bellyache about, Durrant, and that's the fact that you're managin' the smelter works again!"

There was a disturbing element of agreement in the crowd, heartily encouraged by the union leader and his throng of toughs.

Eli interceded calmly. "Mr. Durrant will be managing the smelter works again, yes. But only under the direction of Mr. Callahan here, or myself. He'll have to answer for everything he does."

"How do we know you ain't just as crooked as he is, Mr. McKutchen?" the worker persisted. "Pardon my sayin' so, but you ain't looked after us in the past, not the way your granddaddy did."

Bonnie's eyes darted to Eli, as did most everyone else's. The disgruntled man in the audience had a point; Eli had ignored the smelter people, for the most part, since his grandfather's death. The fact that the holdings of McKutchen Enterprises went far beyond that small-town smelter plant, with corresponding responsibilities attached, did not excuse his negligence.

Eli's broad shoulders were straight and his voice carried clearly through the small theatre. "I have neglected you. I admit that, and I'll make no excuses. I will say that I plan to stay in Northridge for some time, and I give you my word that when I leave, you won't be forgotten."

"What good, Mr. McKutchen, is your word?" pressed Mr. Denning, still standing. "These men have no reason to believe that you'll look after their interests in the future any more than you have in the past. They need a union!"

The outsiders in ugly suits and bowler hats cheered, and so did some of the smelter workers.

Eli waited calmly for the din to die down. "I repeat, Mr. Denning: I'm not trying to stop these men from joining your organization. In fact, I don't give a damn whether they do or not. As far as I'm concerned, you're free to recruit as many new members as you can."

Now Webb came striding down one aisle, to stand in front of the stage. "Can't you men see that these union people don't care about your rights?" he demanded. "They want to line their pockets with your dues, that's all! What more can you ask than a four-hour-a-day cutback in your shifts and a clean, dry house to live in, not only now, but in your old age? For your own sakes and the sakes of your families, go back to work while you can!"

Bonnie felt real alarm as she looked into the faces of the thugs Mr. Denning had imported to help bolster his cause. They seemed to hate Webb even more than they hated Eli.

The words "while you can" started yet another uproar.

Eli held up both his hands in an effort to quiet the crowd, but before he could say anything, Mr. Denning challenged triumphantly, "So McKutchen Enterprises is delivering an ultimatum that the men out on strike have only so long to return to their jobs!"

"The smelter is operating at half its capacity," Eli replied honestly. "The strikers have seventy-two hours to return to work. Those who do not will be replaced."

These words made the wives of the striking workers

blanch, while their husbands looked decidedly unsettled. Mr. Denning and his men, of course, were outraged.

"Seventy-two hours," Eli repeated, and then he turned from the podium and went back to his chair.

"What's Bonnie McKutchen doing up there on that stage, that's what I want to know!" a contentious female voice shouted from the audience.

Wishing that she'd sat with Genoa and Lizbeth instead of on the stage did Bonnie no good. It was too late to reconsider. Her knees shaking beneath her tasteful blue sateen skirts, she stood up and made her way to the podium.

Both her hands and her voice trembled as she forced herself to meet the challenge. "I'm a citizen of Northridge," she said firmly. "And I am your mayor, duly appointed. I realize that the office doesn't give me any authority over the rest of you, but I feel that duty compels me to—"

"Duty!" yelled another woman. Though Bonnie tried, she couldn't make out who it was that had spoken. "Listen to the Angel talking about duty!"

Everyone laughed and Bonnie was stricken with embarrassment, but she stood her ground. It was a comfort that Eli moved a step closer to her, though he kept his gaze fixed on some point at the back of the theatre.

"Stop heckling me and listen!" Bonnie shouted, suddenly full of righteous indignation and a new courage. "The issue here is not what you people think of me. The topic is your own well-being and that of your families. In the name of mercy, stop and think what Mr. McKutchen is offering you! Are your heads so full of union prattle that you won't accept the very benefits you've wanted for so long?" She paused, drew a deep breath. Bonnie didn't dare look at Eli, but she saw a certain grudging admiration in Webb's face as he looked up at her from his position in front of the stage. "Do you think these hucksters care what happens to you? They only want your money—if they had your best interests at heart, wouldn't they be telling you even now that Mr. McKutchen's proposal is eminently fair? You're sensible people—think for yourselves!"

Bonnie turned with dignity, walked back to her chair between Forbes and Seth and sat down. Forbes took her hand and gave it a subtle squeeze before releasing it again.

201

By some unspoken agreement, the meeting ended and everyone except Bonnie and Eli filed out, talking spiritedly among themselves.

Bonnie remained on the stage, her eyes downcast. She was suddenly so inexpressibly weary.

"Bonnie?"

She did not look up, even though Eli had spoken with a gentle intimacy.

Eli crouched in front of her, his hands clasping hers, and even then she wouldn't look at him.

"I made a fool of myself," she said.

"No."

A tear trickled down Bonnie's cheek and she didn't bother to dash it away. Her hands pulled themselves free of Eli's grip and knotted together in her lap. "Why do I keep fooling myself?" she fretted. "I'm not truly the mayor of this town and I had no right to say anything. Anything at all."

Eli cupped his hand under Bonnie's chin and lifted. His thumb smoothed away the traces of the single tear. "You wanted to make a difference, Bonnie. There's nothing wrong in that."

"When I had a real opportunity to change things, Eli, I didn't even try!"

He sighed. "I have regrets myself, Bonnie. But there is nothing we can do about the past. It's gone."

His words filled Bonnie with an aching sadness. She'd been bewailing her failure to persuade Eli to change things in Northridge while they were still husband and wife, but he was talking about the marriage itself. He was dismissing any possibility that they might ever find their way back to each other and, even though Bonnie thought she'd long since accepted that state of affairs, she found that she hadn't. She despaired in the face of another lost hope—a hope she hadn't consciously held.

"There are just too many sad things in this world," she said obliquely, and then she stood up and left the stage, making her way down the steps, up the aisle, out into the grayness of yet another rainy day.

Monday was every bit as dismal and glowering as Sunday had been, and Bonnie huddled in her store like a wounded animal hiding in its den. The warm fire in the potbellied stove and the lamps lighted all around did nothing to dispel her gloom.

For all the nastiness of the day, people were out and about, and many of them paused to read the sign Lizbeth had put in the window. Though Bonnie had meant to wad the silly thing into a ball and toss it into the stove, she hadn't gotten around to the deed because of the strange lethargy that possessed her.

It was midafternoon when Mrs. Sylvester Kirk, incumbent president of the Friday Afternoon Community Improvement Club, arrived with a somber and sodden delegation.

"I demand to know the meaning of that outlandish sign," she announced, her nostrils flaring in her hawkish nose, her chins quivering. She wore a knitted snood over her graying hair and a plaid cloak on her shoulders.

Bonnie's mood instantly brightened. She smiled in a cordial fashion, even though the strenuous rejection of these women and their friends had done her a deep injury. "Sign?" she echoed. "Oh, you mean the one in the window!"

"Yes," huffed Mrs. Kirk. "Do I read it correctly, may I ask? Are you presuming to bar the membership of our esteemed association from trading in this store?"

The light dawned. Suddenly Lizbeth's reasons for making the sign were clear to her. It was so simple! Why hadn't she thought of it?

"Impertinent snippet!" muttered one of the members of the Club.

Mrs. Kirk raised her hand, like an army general commanding calvary troops to come to order. "You have decided, then, to discriminate against the members of our worthy organization?"

Bonnie's smile held. "I'm not discriminating. I'm just forbidding your membership to shop in my store."

"Well, I never!" sputtered a calico soldier. "The gall!"

"Of course," Bonnie went on, remembering her humiliation in the Pompeii Playhouse the day before, during the public meeting, "it is debatable, Mrs. Kirk, whether your organization could be described as 'worthy.' You call yourselves the Friday Afternoon Community Improvement Club, and yet all you've ever done, as far as I can tell, is gather in each other's parlors and exchange gossip."

Mrs. Kirk flushed crimson. "That is not true. We have done many things to improve this town."

"Name one," challenged Bonnie.

"We gave a bake sale once," retorted Menelda Sneeder, stepping out of the ranks to glare at Bonnie. "We used the proceeds to buy hymnal covers for the church."

"Did you? I'm sure the Lord appreciated the gesture, even though there were, and still are, children going without supper just down the hill from here."

"I will not be refused trade," thundered Mrs. Kirk, apparently having done with talk of hymnal covers and hungry children, "in any establishment in this town!"

"Except here," said Bonnie.

Mrs. Kirk stomped to the shelves on the far side of the room and took down a large tin of lavender-scented talcum powder. Then—Bonnie would have sworn that the floor shook—the venerable president of the Club stomped back to the counter. "I insist upon purchasing this!" she shouted.

Her corset brigade quickly followed suit. They wanted to buy pins or rice or fresh coffee beans, and they weren't to be turned away. It was their right to trade in this store—they were American citizens!

Bonnie meekly tallied up their purchases, but when they were gone, she whirled like a ballerina. Lizbeth's clever trick had worked.

That evening the rain lifted and the storm moved on. All the rest of the week Bonnie was busy, because each day's train brought more paint, more nails, more bolts and pipes. Men on both sides of the labor controversy at the smelter were employed to build cabins in their spare time.

As Eli's seventy-two-hour dictum progressed, to the great annoyance of Mr. Denning and his imported hoodlums, every last man returned to his job at the smelter works. All was not sweetness and light, however. Some still feared that the sudden benevolence of McKutchen Enterprises would turn to vengeance when the company's purposes had been served, but there was a feeling of renewed hope abroad in the town.

And Bonnie was swamped with customers. She had not been invited to join the Friday Afternoon Community Improvement Club and had no real desire to belong to the group anyway, but the boycott on her store had apparently been lifted. The members were unfriendly when they bought eggs or milk or potatoes or hatpins, but they paid cash for their purchases and that was enough for Bonnie.

On Friday Eli came into the store and ordered more supplies for the building of the cabins. He was dressed in work clothes, and he was filthy, for though he no longer worked at the smelter, he was helping to put up the new cabins.

For the first time Bonnie was financially solvent in her own right. She closed the store early that day and hurried down the street to the dressmaker's shop, where she persuaded the proprietress to alter the one gown that remained of her extensive New York wardrobe, a pretty frock of flowered lawn, perfect for the party Genoa would be giving the next day, weather permitting.

On her way out of the little shop, she nearly collided with Tuttle O'Banyon, who looked hale and hearty, even though he was smudged with printer's ink from head to foot.

As proudly as if he'd published the whole paper by himself, he handed Bonnie a copy of the *Northridge News.* "Mr. Hutcheson told me to give you this," he said, as Bonnie unfolded the thin paper to look at the front page. "Nobody else has seen it yet."

Bonnie suffered a twinge of dread, despite the sunny weather and the lawn party Genoa planned for the following day, as she read the articles Webb had wanted her to see.

Webb had written another scathing piece about the union, congratulating the workers of Northridge on their return to work and condemning Mr. Denning and his men as "money-grubbing outsiders." Next to this was an article defending Bonnie as the town's true and only mayor.

After thanking Tuttle, Bonnie started back toward home, reading and rereading the piece touting her as a brave local political figure. "Merciful heavens," she muttered to herself, "he makes it sound as though I've had greatness thrust upon me."

Back at the store, Katie excitedly announced that they'd

all been invited to supper with Miss McKutchen. It seemed that Genoa had some sort of announcement to make, one that couldn't wait until the lawn party scheduled for the next day.

Intrigued, Bonnie wondered if Genoa's proclamation had anything to do with the way she'd been looking at Seth Callahan during the community meeting Sunday afternoon. Could it be that Miss McKutchen's days as a spinster were limited?

Bonnie smiled at the thought as she dressed herself and Rose for a pleasant evening. Genoa thoughtfully sent her carriage for the three of them, and when they arrived, she was waiting on the veranda, her face glowing.

Bonnie, carrying a squirming and impatient Rose Marie up the walk, was all but bursting with curiosity.

Genoa took Rose Marie from Bonnie and at the same time trilled, "Oh, Bonnie, I've bought a telephone and Mr. Callahan is installing it at this very moment!"

A little disappointed, Bonnie frowned. Was this the much anticipated announcement? "A telephone? But, Genoa, there is no wiring for—"

"Fiddle-faddle," Genoa chimed, flushed with something more than the delight of owning Northridge's first telephone. "When the lines are put up, I'll be ready!"

They crossed the porch and entered the grand house, Genoa leading the way, her eyes bright and her mouth forming what appeared to be a permanent smile. "Genoa McKutchen, what are you up to?" Bonnie demanded, determined to get to the bottom of things.

Genoa said nothing, but only beamed upon poor Seth, who was kneeling on the entryway floor, surrounded by tools, printed instructions and coils of wire, muttering to himself. He did have the look of a man in love.

Bonnie gave her sister-in-law an impatient and admittedly unladylike nudge. "You are being deliberately mysterious," she accused. "Admit it!"

"No wires within a hundred miles!" blustered Seth, perspiration glistening on his flushed face.

Genoa laughed gleefully, but she refused to say anything beyond "I admit it." They came to a stop in the parlor, where Susan Farley and Lizbeth were chatting over cups of tea. Susan, recovered from the birth of her son but still in mourning for her husband, smiled wanly at Bonnie.

"I mean to come and settle my account with you as soon as I'm able," the young widow said.

Bonnie removed her cloak and sat down next to Susan on the long sofa. "Don't fret about that. You just concentrate on getting your strength back."

"Susan is going to find a housekeeping job when she's a bit better," Lizbeth said, giving the statement as much importance as if the woman had been planning to run for the Senate or become the captain of an oceangoing vessel.

Susan was still quite thin and pale, though it might have been her black dress that emphasized her pallor. "I wish I'd gone to business school when I was a girl. My sister did, and now she's a typewriter."

Bonnie always wanted to giggle when she heard someone referred to as a typewriter. It sounded so odd. "You don't want to work as a housekeeper?" she asked, just to make conversation. Besides Genoa, there wasn't one other person in Northridge who employed servants, and Genoa was loyal to her efficient Martha, so the prospects of employment in domestic service weren't particularly promising.

"I wouldn't mind," Susan admitted, and her eyes shifted to the doorway of the parlor, lighting up. "Especially if I could work for a fine gentleman."

Bonnie followed Susan's gaze and blushed when she saw Eli standing just inside the spacious room, looking clean and handsome in his fresh clothes. *Over my dead body, Susan Farley,* she thought to herself, and she made a mental note to introduce the pretty widow to Webb at tomorrow's party. Webb and any other marriageable man she could catch by the scruff of the neck.

Eli's attention was all for Rose Marie, who hurled herself at him in a flurry of glee and was promptly swept up into his arms. Love for the little girl shone in his face, and Bonnie was both touched and disturbed. After all, if Eli became too close to his daughter, he might start thinking about taking her away again.

When he carried Rose Marie out of the house, through the French doors leading into Genoa's flower garden, Bonnie waited as long as she could bear and then followed after, telling herself that she was only protecting her interests as a mother.

Eli and Rose had progressed as far as the pond's edge, where they were admiring the pretty swan-shaped boats anchored to the long dock. Bonnie knew the boats had once been extravagant playthings, given to Genoa and Eli as gifts by their grandfather.

"Ride! Ride!" Rose Marie was crowing, pointing one fat little hand toward the boats.

Bonnie hung back, her heart in her throat.

Eli laughed. Unaware of Bonnie, he carried Rose along the dock. "No ride," he said. "Your aunt will be wanting you to eat your supper soon." He drew an exaggerated breath and peered into one of the two boats. "What's this?"

Rose peered, too, and immediately began to struggle in her excitement. "Doll!" she shrieked. "Doll!"

Eli bent and lifted a doll nearly as big as Rose Marie herself from inside the boat. It had golden sausage curls, Bonnie could see, and huge blue eyes that would close when it lay flat. Its dress was pink and ruffly, trimmed with sparkling silver threads.

Rose was almost feverish with delight as Eli carried her back to the grassy bank sloping toward the pond and surrendered the beautiful doll to the child before he noticed Bonnie.

"You'll spoil her," Bonnie said, unable to voice her true fear.

"It's little enough to do for my own daughter," Eli replied, and there was no challenge in his tone, only a flat statement of fact.

Bonnie was near tears, feeling that strange sensation of bereftness that nearly always came over her whenever she saw Eli and Rose Marie together, but she spoke with a smile. "She's wild for dolls. Where did you find such a pretty one?"

"I bought it in Spokane," Eli replied, his eyes caressing Bonnie, reminding her of the special time they'd shared in that city. "I had an extra day on my hands, as it happened."

Bonnie's heart was thick in her throat. "How do you like living at Earline's?" she asked, and then she could have kicked herself for inviting pain by bringing up a subject in which it was inherent.

"It's all right," Eli answered. "The food is good and, so far, Hutcheson and I have managed to get along."

"There's no reason why you shouldn't," Bonnie said, her eyes sliding from Eli's face to watch Rose Marie fussing over her new doll. "Webb's a nice man, and he does support your position regarding the union."

Eli was silent and, when Bonnie made herself look at him, she saw her own sadness mirrored in his face.

CHAPTER 18

"PRAY IT DOESN'T rain," Genoa said to Bonnie, as she handed up another Chinese lantern to be hung from one of the many wires crisscrossing her side yard.

Bonnie affixed the bright orange lantern in its proper place and smiled wryly as she got down from her stepstool and moved it ahead a few feet. Genoa had put all her guests to work; Susan and Lizbeth were placing wire hoops in the grass for croquet, while Eli and Seth carried lawn chairs and tables of various lengths into the yard. "I wouldn't worry, Genoa," Bonnie said, climbing back onto her stool, taking another paper lantern from her friend's outstretched hands and attaching it to the wire. "You know what they say. 'Red sky at night, sailor's delight.' "

Genoa assessed the crimson sunset raging in the western sky with caution. "We are not sailors," she said. Pensively she added, "The river is high, Bonnie, even for this time of year."

Everyone, Bonnie suspected, secretly worried about the rising waters of the Columbia. If the sunny spell was to continue, melting last winter's heavy snows in the mountains of Canada, and then was followed by another hard rain . . .

The determined Bonnie shook off the now familiar sense

of foreboding that came over her whenever the state of the river was mentioned. "Let's think happy thoughts," she said. "You're giving a party tomorrow, and it will be a grand one."

Genoa still seemed unsettled, though a glance in Seth's direction spawned a tentative smile. Bonnie moved her stool ahead and Genoa handed her another lantern, this one bright blue, after inserting a candle in the little holder inside it. "I have the strangest feeling," Eli's sister insisted vaguely.

Bonnie was busy trying to keep her balance on the stool and hang the lantern at the same time. "What sort of feeling?"

Genoa sighed. "'Eat, drink and be merry,'" she quoted, "'for tomorrow, we die.'"

Bonnie stopped, her hands still stretched above her head, and stared down at her friend. "My goodness, Genoa, what a somber thing to say. Are you feeling all right?"

But Genoa merely handed up another lantern.

By nightfall, all the preparations had been made—the pretty lanterns were in place, as were the tables that would hold refreshments, and the croquet hoops arched in the grass.

Bonnie joined in the conversation that followed, when everyone gathered in the larger of Genoa's two parlors to talk, but she had caught her sister-in-law's melancholy mood, and she wasn't able to concentrate. Finally she went upstairs to collect a sleeping Rose, ready to go home.

She had not noticed Eli leaving the parlor, but when Bonnie reached the room he was standing beside Rose's bed, watching his daughter sleep.

"Don't awaken her," he said, when Bonnie would have gathered the little girl into her arms.

Both Rose Marie's chubby arms were wrapped possessively around her new doll, and a sweet sadness was stirred in the depths of Bonnie's spirit, something akin to the quiet apprehension Genoa was feeling. "It's time for us to go home," she answered in a whisper.

Eli turned to face Bonnie, a hollow, reflective look in his magnificent eyes. "Where is that, Bonnie? Where, exactly, is 'home'?"

Bonnie moved to the windows before answering, pushing the lace curtain aside with one hand. She couldn't see the river for the darkness, but she had an ominous sense of its presence and its rage. "Sometimes," she sighed, "I don't think we truly have homes in this life. We light here and there, like moths, but maybe we don't really go home until we return to God."

There were patches of light glowing in the night, lamps burning in the windows of Northridge houses. Houses, Bonnie knew from experience, were not necessarily homes.

"You seem to be in a philosophical mood tonight," Eli observed quietly. "Is something wrong?"

Everything is wrong, Bonnie wanted to say, but, of course, she didn't. She turned away from the window and her thoughts of homes and rivers and managed a semblance of a smile. "Wasn't this your room when you were a boy?"

Eli folded his arms and looked around him. "Yes. Don't you remember, Bonnie? We spent our wedding night in this room."

Bonnie did remember, and the memory was traitorously sweet. She had been a virgin, at once frightened and eager, and Eli had taught her to love so gently, so patiently that her fear had soon vanished. "You were kind," she said softly.

"I was in love," Eli replied, as though that explained everything. And Bonnie supposed that it did.

Bonnie permitted herself a smile. "I was so amazed," she recalled in a faraway voice, "that you even noticed me, let alone loved me."

It seemed natural when Eli came to her, taking her upper arms gently into his hands. There was a sad sort of humor in his eyes. "To see you was to love you, Bonnie. Both Hutcheson and Durrant would probably agree."

In view of her weakness where this man was concerned, Bonnie felt a need to establish a certain emotional distance. It was all too easy, she knew, to fall under his spell. "Have you noticed the way Genoa looks at Seth? Is it just wishful thinking on my part, or is she fond of the man?"

Eli's hands were light on her bare arms now—why had she worn a sleeveless dress?—caressing her. "Seth and Genoa were very close at one time," he said. "They were engaged, in fact."

It was cool in that room, Bonnie knew that for a fact, but she felt feverish. And the palms of Eli's hands kept grazing the bare flesh of her upper arms. "Engaged? What happened?"

"My grandfather didn't approve of the match. He sent Genoa away to Europe to give things time to cool down and, as usual, he got his way."

Bonnie had known and liked Josiah McKutchen, seeing him as a benevolent benefactor, but now she felt a stirring of resentment. How different Genoa's life might have been, if the old man hadn't interfered so high-handedly! She sighed. "I had the distinct impression that Genoa was planning to make some kind of momentous announcement tonight."

Eli smiled, knowing exactly what he was doing to her with his touching and stroking, with his mere presence. "Did you? Stay with me tonight, Bonnie."

"In this house, with all these people? You must be mad!"

He bent and tasted her lips tentatively and even then, for heaven's sake, Bonnie didn't have the will or the strength to withdraw from his touch.

"There are lots of bedrooms in this house, Bonnie," he said against her mouth, "and one of them is downstairs, well away from the others—"

"No!" Bonnie hissed, even while her whole soul and body said yes.

One of Eli's arms encircled her waist, pulling her close, while his hand caressed her breast with a bold gentleness. And his lips were within a breath of hers. "Very well, but I'll give you fair warning: don't come to the party tomorrow if you don't want me to bring you inside the house and make slow—thorough—love to you—"

"You wouldn't!" Bonnie sputtered, her lips tingling in anticipation of his kiss.

"You know I would," he replied, and then he kissed her in a way that gave her a disturbing foretaste of the joys tomorrow might bring. It took all Bonnie's strength just to keep her knees from buckling, and she was breathless by the time the kiss ended.

The room was growing shadowy, with only a thin shimmer of moonlight to ease the darkness. Eli opened Bonnie's bodice and untied the ribbons that held her camisole in

213

place. Gently he bared both her breasts to the cool night air, cupping them in his hands and training their nipples to appease him with just the slightest grazings of his thumbs.

Bonnie could not speak in protest or even move, for his touch felt so good, so wholly right.

"I'll almost surely do this," he whispered, speaking of a delicious tomorrow. He bent to take tentative suckle at one well-prepared peak. "And this," he added, his breath warming Bonnie's breast.

In time Eli enjoyed Bonnie's other breast, too, and she was quite dizzy with the need of him. She'd forgotten the people downstairs, even forgotten Rose, but Eli hadn't. Satisfied, he put Bonnie's camisole right and then buttoned her dress again.

"Tomorrow," he vowed.

Bonnie was dazed, her color high. She could only stare up into Eli's shadowy face in stricken amazement.

"Unless, of course," Eli went on, in husky tones, "you want to change your mind and stay the night?"

"Never," Bonnie hissed, furious because Eli could so easily arouse need in her and then deny or fulfill that need, as he so deigned to do. Why, he was every bit as officious as his grandfather had been! "Not tonight, and not tomorrow!"

Eli chuckled and turned away to gather both Rose and her doll up into his strong arms. Had he not been holding her child, Bonnie would have crowned him over the head with the china washbasin resting on the bureau.

"I meant what I said, Eli!" she whispered furiously, as he strode along the hallway toward the stairs, Rose Marie sleeping soundly in his arms. "I am coming to that party tomorrow—nothing could make me miss it—but you'll not lay a hand on me!"

He smiled. "We'll see, darling," he said. "We'll just see."

To add insult to injury, Eli insisted on seeing Bonnie home in the carriage. She was glad that Katie was along, for the slumbering Rose was no protection.

When they arrived at the darkened store, Eli accompanied Bonnie and Katie inside, carrying Rose all the way to her crib.

Bonnie stood on the other side, gently removing Rose's

214

shoes and covering her. "You may go now," she whispered stiffly to the child's father. "You've done quite enough for one night."

Eli executed a half salute and turned to leave the bedroom. Bonnie followed him as far as the kitchen, locking the door the moment she heard his bootheels on the outside stairs.

The nerve of that man, she simmered, trying in vain to cover lingering passion in a guise of anger. Katie had already retired to her room, weary from a long night of keeping up with Rose, and Bonnie was anxious to go to bed, too. To sleep and thus to forget that Eli had sworn to seduce her the very next day.

"I won't let that man within ten feet of me," Bonnie vowed to her reflection in the bedroom mirror. Her reflection looked singularly unconvinced.

Annoyed, Bonnie blew out the lamp and undressed in the darkness. Her breasts felt heavy and their peaks throbbed, and that familiar, warm wanting was pulsing in her middle.

"Damn Eli McKutchen anyway!" she ranted, in a whisper, as she flung back the covers and crawled into bed.

Bonnie slept very badly that night.

The sunny weather held and, when Bonnie arrived at Genoa's house with Katie and Rose Marie, there were already a number of buggies and wagons parked along the driveway. There were so many, in fact, that boys were marking them with chalk numbers in order to keep track of which rig belonged to which guest.

"Miss McKutchen must have invited everyone in Northridge," Katie observed as they walked around the huge house and into the side yard, and she was glowing with a young girl's pleasure in such merry events.

The decorations did give the yard a festive look. The colored lanterns swayed in the mild breeze and there were guests everywhere, some in elegant clothes and some in the shabby calicos and cambrics of Patch Town. Bonnie had struck a diplomatic medium by wearing the summery dress of floral lawn left over from her time in New York.

A juggling clown had been recruited from the vaudeville circuit to entertain the children, and Katie took Rose Marie

215

to watch him. Just for this day, Rose had been persuaded to part with her splendid new doll.

Genoa approached, looking almost pretty in her dress of bright blue eyelet. Her wheat-gold hair was fetchingly arranged and she even wore a bit of lip rouge on her mouth. "I'm so glad you're here, Bonnie," she trilled. "I was beginning to think you weren't coming."

Bonnie had considered staying home, because of what Eli had told her the night before, but in the end she'd decided that parties such as this one were too rare and too delightful to be missed. Besides, if she'd remained in the store, Eli would probably have joined her there. "I had to have some alterations on my dress and it wasn't quite ready when I sent Katie to pick it up," she explained.

Genoa took her arm in a gloved hand. "Come and speak with Mr. Callahan," she pleaded in an odd and breathless voice.

Bonnie had been presented to Seth Callahan years before and, of course, encountered him many times since, but it would have been silly to point up so obvious a fact, so she kept her peace and allowed herself to be dragged across the lawn.

Genoa propelled her past a rousing game of croquet and four tables burdened with refreshments. "I've got to distract him," Genoa hissed. "That hussy Eva Fisher has been flirting with him ever since she arrived!"

"If you think Eva's a hussy, why did you invite her?" Bonnie asked reasonably.

"Hush!" replied Genoa, shouldering her way between the widow Fisher and Mr. Callahan and pulling Bonnie along with her. "Seth, doesn't Bonnie look wonderful today!"

The twinkle in Seth Callahan's bespectacled blue eyes told Bonnie that Genoa's tactics hadn't fooled him. Nonetheless he went through the motions of greeting Bonnie formally, even going so far as to kiss her hand. Genoa maneuvered Eva Fisher away to one of the refreshment tables, and Bonnie again puzzled over the announcement that hadn't been made.

"It's grand to be sought after," Seth confided, ruddy with self-consciousness and a certain pleasure in Genoa's obvious favor.

Bonnie smiled, but her words were serious ones. "Do be very thoughtful, Seth. Genoa is a very special woman and it would be unkind to trifle with her affections."

Seth went redder still, and his chest swelled. *Men,* Bonnie thought wryly. That scoundrel is pleased that someone considers him capable of trifling with a spinster's heart. "You may be sure, Mrs. McKutchen," he finally said in a very hoarse and earnest voice, "that I hold your sister-in-law in the very highest regard."

By this time the croquet match had caught Bonnie's eye, and she excused herself to go and watch. Lizbeth Simmons, dressed quietly but attractively in a black sateen skirt and white shirtwaist with a bib of ruffles, was being taught the proper way to swing her mallet by an attentive Forbes Durrant.

Despite the lingering discoloration of his bruises, Forbes looked handsome in his dark trousers and open-throated white shirt; he had already discarded his jacket. And how he was enjoying standing behind Lizbeth, his arms around her as they shared a grip on the mallet's handle.

Bonnie shook her head, amused at yet another display of masculine ego.

It was then that she spotted Eli, standing behind Earline Kalb and demonstrating repeated croquet strokes in the same intimate manner. This time Bonnie was not amused.

Eli must have felt her gaze, for he immediately looked up from the back of Earline's neck. The brazen wretch, he actually winked!

Bonnie turned in a whispering whirl of lawn skirts to look in vain for Webb. When she failed to find him among the many guests, she went to watch the juggler, who was really very deft, keeping no less than six rubber balls coursing through the air while balancing a seventh on the tip of his nose.

Rose Marie and all the other children were delighted by this feat, while Bonnie saw wry similarities between the juggler's act and her own hectic life. Wasn't she performing a sort of emotional sleight-of-hand, keeping everything moving?

She sighed, turned about and came up hard against a broad masculine chest.

"Care for an hour of concentrated croquet instruction?" Eli asked.

Bonnie's every nerve leaped in response to his presence, but outwardly she appeared calm, even flippant. "I already know how to play croquet," she said. "Whyever should I want instruction from you?"

Eli smiled, yet for all the merriment of the day, Bonnie knew that deep inside he was no more whole than she was. She recalled what Seth Callahan had said about her former husband's emotional state and wondered what could be done to heal him. Indeed, how could she herself be healed?

The silence lengthened and Eli's smile faded away. "About what I said last night—"

Bonnie thrust out her chin, braced to deal with an indecent proposal. "Yes?"

Eli lowered his head for a moment, as if shamed by what he'd said and what he'd done, and Bonnie was surprised to find that she had mixed feelings about his remorse.

"When it comes to you, Bonnie," he said, "I'm forever doing and saying the wrong things. I forget that you're no longer my wife and act accordingly."

Bonnie understood what Eli was saying. Intellectually, she knew that the marriage had ended. But her body and spirit seemed bonded to him, as much as if there had been no divorce. A remnant of Scripture ran through her mind. *What God hath joined together . . .*

She opened her mouth to admit to a similar failing but, before she could speak, Tuttle O'Banyon thrust himself into the invisible circle surrounding both Bonnie and Eli and squawked, "Ma'am—Mr. McKutchen—somebody's got to help—"

Eli took the gangly young man by the shoulders and gave him a gentle shake. "Calm down, boy, and tell us what's wrong."

A flush moved up Tuttle's face. "Somebody's gone and beat Mr. Hutcheson senseless! I ain't sure he's alive!"

Bonnie's knees weakened and she swayed slightly before catching herself. "Dear Lord—" she breathed, on the verge of real panic.

Eli spoke calmly. "Where is he?"

"At the office!" Tuttle cried, fitful in his despair. "The presses are turned over on their sides—"

Eli had heard enough; he was striding toward the front of the house, where horses and buggies were readily available, and Bonnie hurried behind him after a hasty word to Katie. By the time she reached the driveway, her former husband had commandeered a dapple gray gelding from someone's team and purloined a bridle from one of the wagonbeds as well.

"I suppose you want to come along," he said, extending a hand to Bonnie even as he spoke.

She took the offered hand and allowed herself to be swung up behind him. The gelding danced nervously beneath its double burden, tossing its head.

"Hold on," Eli said, and they were off at a gallop.

Bonnie clung to Eli's solid midsection, her forehead tucked between his shoulder blades, her breath sawing at her throat. She had never been a horsewoman, but this was no time to give in to fear. Reaching Webb was all that was important.

She pictured his house and the garden plot behind it, and she despaired. *Oh, Lord,* she prayed silently, as they raced through the main part of Northridge and down the great hill, *let Webb live to marry and father children.* He wanted a family so much!

Suddenly the horse came to a stop and Eli dismounted, lifting Bonnie down after him. She felt a stinging ache in the balls of her feet as they struck the ground.

The door of Webb's newspaper office stood open, as Tuttle had probably left it, and Eli bolted through the shadowy chasm. "Hutcheson?" he called.

Bonnie followed, pausing to grip the door's framework with both hands and draw a deep, steadying breath. The instant it took for her eyes to adjust to the dimness seemed like an eternity.

The presses lay on their sides, and type was scattered everywhere. Ink drenched the walls, like blood, and Eli was crouching beside a body lying prone on the floor.

"Is he dead?" Bonnie made herself ask. Her heart was pounding in her throat; she'd had to force her words past it.

Eli shook his head. "He's alive, but not by much."

Tuttle had apparently spread the word among Genoa's guests, for there were wagons approaching and Bonnie could hear men calling to each other. She moved out of the doorway and went to kneel beside Webb.

His face was streaked with blood and so battered that Bonnie could barely recognize him as the Webb she knew. His clothes were in a like state, and his skin was gray as paraffin wax.

She gently stroked his hair off his forehead, her tears falling unchecked and unheeded. "Webb? Webb, it's Bonnie —can you hear me?"

Webb groaned and stirred a little on the ink-sopped floor, but he did not open his eyes.

Just then, the men from the party burst into the small office, swearing in raucous undertones and crowding around. One of them was Doc Cowan, and Eli rose and moved aside to give the physician room.

Bonnie remained where she was, only half conscious of the townsmen, the doctor and even Eli. Webb and his dreams and hopes were all that mattered to her then—her grief was awesome—and she wondered distractedly if she did not love this man after all.

An elderly fellow, somewhat testy but very competent, Doc Cowan crouched to examine Webb, running his hands along his rib cage, checking his arms and legs for fractures.

"How bad is it?" one of the crowd of men wanted to know.

"Bad enough that we'll lose him if we aren't careful," the doctor answered. His eyes were not on his patient, but on Bonnie's face. "Webb's going to need a lot of care."

"Bring him to my place," she said, her voice little more than a whispery croak.

"It was my understanding," the doctor replied kindly, "that Webb lived over at Earline's."

"I don't want him there," Bonnie argued, rising awkwardly to her feet. She'd spoiled her last New York dress— splotched now with Webb's blood and ink and torn as well—and maybe that was fitting. That part of her life was over and done with, wasn't it? She'd tried to hold onto it, by dallying with Eli McKutchen, but the truth was that she didn't belong in that world anymore. Maybe she never had. "Bring Webb to the store."

She turned to leave, pressing her way through the throng of muttering men, gasping river-scented air when she reached the sidewalk. For a moment, she clung to a hitching rail with both hands, fearing that she would faint.

"Bonnie."

She knew the voice belonged to Eli, that he was standing beside her, but she could not look at him. It took all the strength she could muster just to keep from swooning dead away. "It's because of you," she said. "It's because you neglected the situation here for so long. If Webb hadn't taken your part—"

Eli's words were ragged, defeated ones. "Bonnie, don't."

At last Bonnie felt strong enough to let go of the hitching rail and stand unaided. Behind her, inside the ransacked office, she heard voices. "Easy there—that's it—"

"Help them, Eli," she said, without looking at the man beside her. "Help them bring Webb home."

Eli lingered for a moment, then turned away and walked back inside the newspaper office. Bonnie set her course toward the store and somehow she reached it before Doc Cowan and the other men did. She was waiting, dry-eyed, when they brought Webb to her door in the bed of a wagon, his long frame carefully balanced on an enormous slab of wood.

Eli and several other men carried the unconscious editor and publisher of the *Northridge News* through the quiet store, up the stairs and into Bonnie's apartment. She led them into her bedroom, her eyes daring any one of them, including Eli McKutchen, to comment. No one took the challenge.

At Doc Cowan's order, they placed Webb, slab and all, on Bonnie's bed. He moaned softly and then quieted as Bonnie covered him with a warm blanket.

"Tell me how to take care of him," she said, addressing the doctor.

"First thing you can do, missy," the physician immediately responded, "is get yourself out of here so I can bind Webb's rib cage and tend to some of these cuts of his. Eli, you stay right here and help me."

"I want to help!" Bonnie protested.

Doc Cowan's look was a quelling one. "I don't care what you want, young woman. Mind what I said and take yourself out of here."

"But—"

"Now!" barked the doctor.

Flushed, but still buoyed by her dignity, Bonnie went out. The men who had helped bring Webb upstairs were gone.

Making a great clatter to show her indignation at being ordered out of her own bedroom, Bonnie pumped water into a kettle and set it on the stove to boil. She rattled the stove lids as she replaced them after starting a fire inside, and she muttered words that wouldn't have been acceptable even in Patch Town.

She reached for the fat yellow teapot and, when she took it in her hands, she remembered how near she'd come to clouting Webb over the head with it. A new crop of tears spilled down her face but she set the teapot down with a thump and dried her eyes with a dish towel snatched from its peg.

Eli's voice made her backbone grow rigid, and she pulled in a deep, sniffly breath. "The doctor needs cloth for the bindings. A sheet or something."

Bonnie kept her back to Eli. "There are linens in the bottom drawer of my bureau," she said.

Eli didn't answer, merely went back to the bedroom, leaving Bonnie to stand helpless in the middle of her kitchen, wishing sorely that she'd married Webb when she had the chance. Things might have been different if only she hadn't wasted so much time fretting about love.

She thought of the pleasures she'd taken in Eli McKutchen's bed and winced. Perhaps the wages of her sin would be death. Webb's death.

CHAPTER 19

THE RAIN BEGAN sometime during the night, arriving too late to spoil Genoa's party. It hammered at the rooftops and windows of Northridge and crackled like fire upon the angry, swirling surface of the river.

Sitting beside the bed where Webb lay, still unconscious, Bonnie paid no mind to the torrential storm. The cup of tea Katie had brought to her earlier was still in her hands, cold and untouched.

She started a little as Katie pried the cup from her grip and confided, "Lord, ma'am, do you hear that rain? I declare, it's coming down hard enough to frighten Noah himself."

Bonnie looked up questioningly. "Katie?"

The young woman touched Bonnie's forehead with a cool hand. "And who else would it be?" she countered, in a voice that was, for all its brightness, full of concern.

Katie, wearing a rumpled flannel wrapper of light blue, left the room with Bonnie's cup. After a long time, she returned with fresh tea.

Thrusting the cup into Bonnie's hands, she ordered, "This time, drink up."

Bonnie took a cautious sip, her eyes fastened on Webb's

waxy, misshapen face. "Look what we've done to him," she said.

"What 'we've done,' ma'am?" Katie challenged in a quiet voice, as she sat down on the floor beside Bonnie's chair. "It was those union men that did this, if you ask me. The whole town thinks so."

Bonnie couldn't bear to explain, couldn't bear to think. "Go back to bed, Katie. It must be late."

"It is late," Katie responded but she didn't move. "Have another sip of that tea."

Obediently Bonnie lifted the cup to her lips and drank. "It's raining," she remarked.

Katie made a wry sound. "Indeed it is. Every able-bodied man in Northridge is down at the river, stacking sandbags."

At last, Bonnie came out of her stuporous reverie. Her eyes flew to Katie's pale face. "What?"

"Patch Town's going to go if they can't hold back the water, along with the railroad depot and the Brass Eagle and"—she paused, nodding toward Webb—"Mr. Hutcheson's newspaper office, too."

Bonnie's heart hammered and the teacup rattled dangerously in her hands. Quickly she set it aside on the nightstand. She rose from her chair and rushed to the window, but she could see nothing, for it was dark out and the glass was sheeted with rain.

The sound of the storm was awful: It roared like some great beast, it battered the walls and the roof and the windows of the mercantile like a barrage of bullets.

Bonnie paused to lodge a formal protest with God before turning back toward Katie. "Sandbags won't hold back that river," she said.

Katie gave her a patient look. "The men have got to try, don't they? Why, even those union devils are helping!"

"How do you know so much?" Bonnie asked suspiciously. She wasn't looking at Katie as she spoke, she was bending over the bed, smoothing back Webb's sweat-dampened hair and pulling the covers up to his chin. "You haven't been to the river, have you?"

"Mr. Seth Callahan was here a while ago, and he told me."

"Seth? What did he want?"

224

Katie shrugged. "I guess Mr. McKutchen sent him to make sure that we were all right, though it was Rose he asked after."

Bonnie straightened. She could see Eli stacking sandbags in the driving rain as clearly as if she'd been standing on the banks of the Columbia herself, hear him shouting at Seth to make sure that his daughter was safe.

The crib was gone, and Bonnie looked wildly about her. "Rose—"

Katie stemmed Bonnie's rising panic. "She's in my room, ma'am, sleeping like a little lamb. Don't you remember me moving her bed, after Miss Genoa brought us home?"

Bonnie did not remember, and that was unsettling. She put both her hands to her face for a moment, overwhelmed by the horrors of the day.

"Let me look after Mr. Hutcheson for a while, ma'am," Katie said quietly. "You go and crawl into my bed."

"I would like to look in on Rose," Bonnie said, sounding witless even to herself. She wandered into the tiny room next to hers and lingered long at the side of her daughter's crib. A string of thoughts and pictures moved, ragtag, through her head, but she couldn't catch hold of even one. Katie's narrow bed looked warm, and she slid beneath the covers, intending to rest for just a few minutes.

When she awakened, it was morning. The dark of night had gone, but the rain remained, lashing viciously at the sturdy buildings of Northridge.

Bonnie made sure that Rose was covered and then crawled to the end of Katie's bed to look out the small window. The world was gray, barely visible for the downpour, and there was a good six inches of standing water in the street, lapping in muddy waves at the steps of the Pompeii Playhouse.

With a guilty start, Bonnie remembered Webb and bounded off the bed, still wearing yesterday's dress. She hurried across the narrow hall to her own room, one hand to her throat.

Webb appeared to be sleeping normally, and Katie was curled up in the chair Bonnie had occupied during the night, her dark hair a tumble of ebony over the blue flannel of her wrapper.

225

Bonnie didn't waken her. She found fresh clothes for herself and went back to Katie's room to change. Returning to her bedroom, she unpinned her hopelessly mussed hair and gave it a quick brushing before pinning it up again in a loose arrangement that fluffed around her face.

"Katie," she whispered, taking her friend by the shoulder and shaking her gently. "Katie!"

Katie opened sleepy eyes and focused them on Bonnie's face with comical effort. "Yes, ma'am?"

"I want you to look after Rose and Mr. Hutcheson while I go out. I'll not be away long."

"Out?" Katie's blue eyes rounded. "But, ma'am, you can't go out in this weather—"

"What I can't bear to do is sit here waiting for news," Bonnie answered briskly. "Just do as I say, Katie."

The girl looked at Webb as though he might turn into a beast before her very eyes. "Suppose Mr. Hutcheson has a fit or something?"

"Webb won't have a fit, Katie. But he'll probably be in severe pain." She lifted the brown bottle of medicine Dr. Cowan had left behind and then set it down again on the bedside table. "Give him some of this if he wakes up before I get back."

Katie cast one frantic glance toward the window, where the rain pounded as if to break through the glass. "Please, don't go!" she whispered, drawing up her knees and wrapping both arms around them. "A body could drown in a storm like this!"

"You're safe here, Katie."

"It isn't me I'm worried about!"

Bonnie ignored the girl and went downstairs, helping herself to a pair of galoshes from one of the shelves. There was half an inch of water on the floorboards, and the rain was still seeping in through the space under the doors.

Shivering a little, Bonnie wondered if she'd spoken too soon. Perhaps Rose and Katie and Webb weren't safe after all, even though the store was on high ground.

She found her heaviest cloak, a plaid woolen with a hood, and put it on. Then, after drawing one deep breath in order to boost her courage, Bonnie opened the door and dashed out into the onslaught.

The rain battered Bonnie, blinding her so that she navigated the sidewalk almost by memory alone. She ran one hand along the front wall of the Union Hotel as she passed it, the wind buffeting away her breath and flinging water into her eyes.

She rounded the corner and gave a cry of horror, clutching a street lamp for support. The Columbia had swallowed Patch Town entirely, and only the upper story of the Brass Eagle Saloon and Ballroom was visible. In the gloom Bonnie saw that there were people marooned atop Forbes's roof. Webb's newspaper office and the railroad depot were under water. In fact, the muddy green river had climbed so high that men were launching rowboats from the porch of Earline Kalb's rooming house.

Still clinging to the cold iron pole of the street lamp, Bonnie squinted against the rain, watching as the rowboats moved toward the Brass Eagle. The people on the roof of the saloon waved and shouted.

By that time Bonnie was wet to the skin, but she made her way down the hill anyway, because something within her had to know who was lost and who was accounted for. Though she didn't acknowledge the fact, she needed to know that Eli McKutchen fell into the latter group and not the former.

The violent wind fought her every step of the way, making it as difficult to descend the hill as it would have been to climb the mountain looming above the town. Still Bonnie pressed on until she reached Earline's porch.

Earline was there, but she spared barely a glance for Bonnie. She was watching the people stranded on the roof of the saloon and the boats that carried their rescuers. Bonnie strained to see through the torrent of rain and spotted Eli in one of the boats, his arms and shoulders moving in a powerful rhythm as he wielded the oars.

One of Bonnie's worst fears, one she hadn't consciously acknowledged, was put to rest, and the relief was so great that she sagged against the wall of Earline's building, her hand to her heart.

"How many have been lost?" she asked, shouting to be heard over the storm. Here, near the river, the din was greater.

Earline turned around, her face bleak inside the sodden hood of her bright red cloak. "Not as many as might have been," she called back. "Most of them are either here or over at Genoa McKutchen's place." There was a minimal pause. "How's Webb?"

Bonnie felt shame for leaving Webb, but she didn't indulge it. "He's been badly hurt," she responded, "but I think he'll recover."

"You got that girl there looking after him?" Earline demanded.

Bonnie nodded and her eyes were drawn back to Eli. He had reached the Brass Eagle and was standing with one booted foot on its roof and one in the boat, his arm outstretched. Forbes was there, too, and he helped his fellow refugees into the boats before slipping down the slanted roof and landing with a splash in the angry river.

Bonnie's breath caught and her eyes widened, but Eli caught Forbes's reaching hand and hauled him into the boat.

"I thought sure he'd be washed all the way to Grand Coulee," Earline commented, standing closer to Bonnie now.

Bonnie let out her breath. She watched, mesmerized, as the rowboats drew nearer and nearer. The river swirled at her feet, nearly flush with Earline's porch, and an empty burlap sack floated by, amid twigs and tar-paper shingles and other refuse.

Suddenly Earline's shoulder struck Bonnie's as the woman strained to help haul one of the rowboats in, and Bonnie's oversized galoshes slipped on the wet boards of the porch. An instant later she felt the river water rising up around her, frigidly cold, and closing over the top of her head.

The galoshes were sucked from her feet as Bonnie struggled to the surface and managed one screaming gasp before the water filled her nose and mouth and at the same time whirled her about like a bit of flotsam. She came up again, managing a shriek as she cleared the water, and saw a huge log bearing down on her.

Desperately she grabbed for it, felt its bark tear at the skin on her arms as she held on. Too frightened to pray, Bonnie

228

clung to the piece of timber and tried to blink away the water that was blinding her. And the log spun round and round in the furious green water, as if trying to hurl Bonnie clear.

She must have been nearly a mile downriver when a head appeared over the other side of the log. She screamed before it dawned on her that this head must be attached to a living body, because it was smiling at her.

"Hang on, Bonnie," Eli shouted, clinging to the log with one arm and flinging the other over to grasp Bonnie by what he could catch: her hair.

She hadn't realized that she was slipping until Eli wrenched her head back above the water. She was too numb to feel pain, and the log was spinning crazily again. Eli hauled her up until she lay with her stomach on the log, and he held her there. All the filthy river water Bonnie had swallowed came up ingloriously and still the fallen timber turned.

Bonnie was beyond hanging on by then; it was only Eli's grip on her that kept her from slithering into the water. The fear, the cold, and the sickening revolutions of the log combined to defeat her, and she lost consciousness.

She was awakened minutes, hours or decades later by a jarring thump that would have roused a corpse. Shivering so hard that her teeth chattered, Bonnie stared into Eli's wan face and demanded, "Are we dead?"

He threw back his dripping head and shouted with laughter.

"It was a perfectly reasonable question!" Bonnie screamed. And then she looked around and saw that the log had run aground—which accounted for the impact that had jolted her back to full sensibility—and the gnarled roots of a tree were within reach.

She grasped them and hauled herself onto the muddy grass, scratching her hands in the process, but there was no pain because she was still so numb. Eli waded ashore and scrambled up the bank, giving Bonnie a look of amused exhaustion before dropping to his knees in the wet grass.

The rain showed no sign of abating, and Bonnie calculated that they must be miles and miles from Northridge. The countryside was unfamiliar.

Eli regained his breath and struggled back to his feet, his clothes plastered to his body. He held out a hand to Bonnie, who realized for the first time that she was sitting on the ground and not standing as she had thought. "Come on!" he shouted through the downpour. "We've got to find some kind of shelter."

There were no houses or barns to be seen, and the scattered pines and Douglas fir trees were too small and too far apart to offer any kind of cover. Bonnie resisted the dark vapor that threatened to rise up around her and stumbled along behind Eli, her hand locked tightly inside his.

They were about a mile from the river when they found the abandoned wagon, lying on its side. With much maneuvering, Bonnie and Eli managed to drag it up alongside the stump of a tree and brace it against that, creating a lean-to of sorts.

They crawled beneath, heedless of their sodden clothes, and drew close to each other, clinging together for warmth. Mercifully they both fell into an exhausted sleep.

Bonnie awakened first; it was the light slanting through the spaces between the slats of the wagon that roused her, touching her like a warm, teasing finger. Sunshine! With a cry of glee, Bonnie scrambled out from under Eli's protective arm and crawled into the bright light of day.

The sun was glaring down on the sodden earth, and Bonnie gloried in its rays, peeling off her wet, clammy clothes and her shoes and whirling naked in the shining heat like a pagan.

An appreciative laugh from Eli stopped her cold, and she stared at him, as shocked by what she was doing as any member of the Friday Afternoon Community Improvement Club would have been. She tried to speak, to explain that she'd only wanted to be warm, but no words would come.

Eli crawled out from under the tilted wagon that had sheltered them through the night, shivering in his damp clothes. "I think you have the right idea," he said, removing his wrinkled shirt and kicking off his boots. Having done that, he boldly removed his trousers, too, and Bonnie turned away before she could see if he was wearing anything beneath.

230

A rustling sound made her turn around again, poised to leap back under the wagon if someone was approaching, but it was only Eli, methodically draping all their clothes, his trousers included, over a row of blueberry bushes.

Bonnie blushed crimson, and even though the sunlight felt deliciously warm on her bare back and bottom, decency made her demand, "I'll have my clothes back, please."

Eli was as naked as Adam before the fall from grace, and he looked back at Bonnie over one muscular shoulder, his eyes glistening with suppressed amusement. "Not until they're dry," he said. "Doesn't that sunshine feel good?"

Bonnie covered her breasts virtuously and lifted one thigh in an attempt to hide the rest of her femininity. The odd stance made her lose her balance and topple into the damp, sun-warmed grass, and Eli was instantly beside her, kneeling on the fragrant ground.

"Thank you for coming to s-save me and b-bringing that log for us to hold on to," Bonnie said, just to make conversation. Or perhaps to forestall the inevitable.

Eli laughed again as he reached out to stroke her bare thigh, her waist, one shivering breast. "I couldn't lose you," he said after a few moments, "and I didn't bring the log. It just happened by, narrowly missing my head, I might add."

"Oh," said Bonnie. The grass was so warm and so soft and her body was arranging itself as Eli ordered. His touch felt so good, so soothing, and the sunshine framed his shoulders with a golden haze. She was lying down now.

"Sometimes," Eli whispered, "I can't bear it, you're so beautiful—"

His hand had separated Bonnie's thighs, or perhaps they had separated themselves, and she gave a cry as he found the tangle of curls and sought their secret with a soft foray of his fingers.

"Oh," Bonnie said again, feverishly, as he tampered with her so boldly, and she felt her legs moving wider still.

"We're alive," Eli observed in a gruff tone of wonderment.

Bonnie moaned, her back arching. "W-we certainly are," she agreed fitfully, as waves of heated joy flowed over her, through her, under and around her.

231

His thumb moved rhythmically to increase the delicious torment. "Now that we're agreed, what shall we do about it? Being alive, I mean?"

A soft wail rattled in Bonnie's throat and she felt her nipples go turgid as her hips and thighs seemed to undulate on a sea of rippling velvet. "Oh, my—oh—we should—we should—"

"Yes?" How could he be so calm, when Bonnie was burning before his very eyes?

"We should celebrate!" Bonnie choked out.

Eli bent and brazenly suckled at her breast, tasting it, drawing it gently between his teeth, lashing it with his tongue. "Celebrate?" he echoed. "How?"

Bonnie uttered a strangled cry of mingled passion and impatience. "You stupid man!" she cried, grabbing at his warm shoulders with her hands. "Make love to me! Oh—please—make love to me!"

For once in his life Eli obliged her instead of driving her to the very brink of madness first. He poised himself between her legs and entered her in a swift, searing stroke that made her grasp at the bare skin of his back. But then he stopped, looking down at her, his features taut with restraint.

"I love you, Bonnie," he said.

Bonnie barely heard him, her need was so great. Her body, having just escaped death, was determined to affirm life. She flung her legs around Eli, forcing him into another stroke.

Eli moaned as their joining deepened, his head thrust back, his eyes closed. Slowly, so slowly that Bonnie shuddered with need, he withdrew. His return was slow too; inch by heated inch, he again sheathed himself inside her.

Bonnie flung her arms out from her sides in a fit of wanting, clawing at the verdant ground with her fingers, her head tossing back and forth in the grass.

"Easy," Eli cautioned, in a throaty whisper, "give it time, Bonnie."

Bonnie's entire body buckled as the strokes continued, now reaching deep within her, now almost leaving her. "Time," she croaked. "Eli—you bastard—"

232

He laughed hoarsely. "What?"

Of its own accord, perhaps spurred on by Bonnie's, his body fell into a faster, fiercer rhythm.

Bonnie grasped the ground in desperation, her head thrust back, but she was flung free of the earth all the same, losing herself in the glorious burst of joy and the shuddering shout that meant Eli had reached the pinnacle, too.

They slept entwined, beneath the sloping cover of the old wagon, waking again in the late afternoon. Their stomachs were hungry, but so were their souls. Once again, Eli and Bonnie made love, but this time they were neither frantic nor fevered, and they moved together slowly, content with the gentle pace their bodies set for them.

For Bonnie, release was soft and sweet, rolling from the tips of her toes to the crown of her head in gentle swells. Eli cried out as he tensed upon her.

They fell asleep again, and when Bonnie awakened, it was dark and she was alone. She sat up so fast that she struck her head on the wagonbed and howled with pain.

From somewhere outside, she heard Eli's chuckle and the pleasant crackling of a fire. Her clothes came flying between the wagon and the stump it was balanced against, and she scrambled into them.

"I smell food!" she accused, crawling out from under the wagon on her hands and knees.

Sure enough, Eli had built a fire. He was roasting what appeared to be a chicken over the flames, having made a spit of small twigs and branches.

"Where—how—" Bonnie's body ached for food, just as passionately as it had ached earlier for Eli's thorough loving.

"There must be a farm around here somewhere," Eli said with a grin. He was fully dressed and comfortably seated by the cheery fire. "I found this chicken wandering in search of its destiny, so I—"

"Don't tell me!" Bonnie cried, but she was moving toward the fire even as she struggled into her shoes. "How did you start this magnificent blaze without matches—"

Eli shook his head. "Oh, ye of little faith. I rubbed two sticks together."

233

"Nobody really does it that way, do they?"

Eli laughed. "It might have been a spark left over from when we made love."

Bonnie was grateful for the darkness; it hid the color pounding in her cheeks. A moment later her embarrassment was displaced by worry. "Rose!" she gasped.

Eli put an arm around her, lending a solid sort of comfort. "Don't worry, Bonnie. Katie and Genoa will look after her."

"But they'll surely think we're dead!"

"In that case, our return will be a pleasant surprise," Eli said.

The chicken, spattering over the fire, smelled wonderful. Bonnie couldn't remember ever being so hungry, even during her Patch Town days. "I guess there's nothing to be gained by worrying," she said.

"There never is." Skillfully, Eli removed the chicken from the spit and tore off a huge piece for Bonnie. "We'll start back tomorrow."

Bonnie was too busy consuming roast chicken to comment, and Eli ate with comparable appetite. When they'd both washed in the river, they sat watching the fire in silence for a long time.

Bonnie had ever been an enemy of silence. She looked up at the magnificent spread of stars flung across the heavens and sighed. "Poor Genoa must be frantic."

Eli's hand cupped Bonnie's breast, which was bare beneath her stiff, sun-dried shirtwaist, and, rather than protesting, she cuddled closer to him.

"Um-hmmm," he answered.

"They'll be certain that we've drowned, you know," Bonnie went on, a little breathlessly, because Eli was still caressing her.

"Absolutely."

Bonnie shivered a delicious shiver. His thumb was brushing back and forth over her nipple, causing it to draw itself into a keenly pleasurable tautness. "Rose is too young to understand, so Genoa wouldn't say anything about our deaths yet."

"No," Eli replied hoarsely, "I'm sure she'll wait. Rose is definitely too young to understand." He moved back from the fire a way, pulling Bonnie after him, so that she knelt astraddle of his thighs.

She shivered again as he opened her blouse and bared her for his enjoyment and her own. She gave a soft sigh of contentment and tilted her head back as his mouth closed over one nipple and drew at it with growing hunger.

The stars twinkled in the black sky and Bonnie watched them as she nourished Eli, her hand moving gently at the back of his head. When it was time, she urged him to her other breast, her fingers still entwined in his hair.

She felt her skirts rising and welcomed the plundering of Eli's fingers as he prepared her for a thorough taking. When he lowered her onto himself, she trembled, and all the stars in the sky melted together into one great, shining silver light.

CHAPTER 20

ELI CAST A long look back at the overturned wagon that had served as a shelter, a wry grin lifting one corner of his mouth. "I'm going to miss this place," he said.

Bonnie, tired and dirty and vastly hungry, tried to free her hand from his. He held on and continued up the steep hill overlooking the place where they had camped, and Bonnie had no choice but to follow him.

She was consumed with guilt. Rose was probably calling for her. Genoa and Katie were no doubt making funeral arrangements at this very moment. Webb was lying on his bed of pain or, worse yet, he had already died of his injuries.

And what had Bonnie been doing while all this was going on? Making a spectacle of herself with a man she'd sworn she would never give in to again, that was what. She felt her face grow hot with self-recrimination as she navigated the rocky incline, trying to keep up with Eli.

Finally they reached the top of the hill, and Bonnie went goggle-eyed at what she saw before her. There was a small farmhouse within a stone's throw of where they stood, an occupied farmhouse with chickens scratching in the yard and laundry drying on the clothesline.

Bonnie seethed as one realization after another dawned on her. Eli had known about this farmhouse almost from

236

the first. He'd gotten the chicken they'd eaten for supper the night before and probably the matches for the fire from these people, pretending all the while that he and Bonnie were stranded. "You wretch!" she hissed, in a scathing whisper, as a sturdy-looking middle-aged man hailed them from the barn.

"Mornin'!" shouted the farmer, approaching, and Bonnie saw a slender woman with gray hair come out of the house to stand on the step. "Come on in and have some breakfast!"

The missus didn't look too thrilled with the idea of having two strangers at her table, but she said nothing.

Bonnie tried to pull her hand from Eli's and found it stuck fast. She considered kicking him to free herself and decided against it. It wouldn't do to create a scene in front of the farmer and his wife.

Minutes later they had washed up and seated themselves at the table inside Mr. and Mrs. Ezra Kinder's modest house. Bonnie was ravenous, and she consumed ham, eggs and fried potatoes accordingly.

Mrs. Kinder, a plain, angular woman with lashless eyes and thin lips, kept one hand on a battered Bible throughout the meal, as if to guard herself from the insidious spread of evil.

"Last I heard, the Northridge depot was under fifteen feet of water," Ezra Kinder imparted, through a mouthful of food.

Eli didn't seem the least bit self-conscious, even though his hair was mussed and he was wearing stiff, wrinkled clothes that he'd been swept downriver in. He might have been clad in a fine suit and dining at Delmonico's, the way he acted. "How far away is Colville? We could probably get some horses there."

Bonnie felt real despair at the thought of riding some forty miles on horseback. Dear Lord, wasn't it enough that she'd been washed away in a flood, made to sleep on the ground and seduced in the bargain? Did she have to ride all the way to Northridge on the back of some horse as well?

"Colville ain't but three miles from here. I'd borrow you a wagon, you understand," Ezra said, speaking around the biscuit he had just shoved whole into his mouth, "but I can't spare the one I've got." He sighed to show a measure of sympathy. "I figure things must be pretty bad up Northridge way."

"They were worse than bad when we left," Eli answered.

Bonnie thought his description of their departure rather colorless at best, but she said nothing to embellish it. She was too worried about Rose Marie and Webb, Genoa and Katie, to make a place for herself in the lackluster conversation.

"Water's been going down steadylike, from what I've heard," Ezra said. "Still, them tracks will need lots of fixin' and I reckon half the town's gone."

"What about the telegraph lines?" Bonnie asked, finished with her breakfast and eager to let Genoa and the others know that she and Eli were alive. Western Union was housed in the Northridge post office, which was on high ground.

Ezra looked at her with such curiosity that she was suspicious. Bonnie's gaze turned to Eli, who was studiously looking the other way.

"Thought you knew the lines were all right," the farmer answered. "Mr. McKutchen had me send off a message to his sister yesterday. Got one back right away, too." Ezra looked questioningly around the tidy kitchen. "Where's that there telegram we got back, Amanda?"

Forgetting that she'd sworn off violence, Bonnie kicked Eli beneath the table. He flinched but did not look at her, choosing to lift his coffee mug to his mouth instead.

Amanda—a pretty name, Bonnie thought, for such a dour and severe-looking woman—took a folded piece of yellow paper from beneath the cover of her Bible and tossed it toward Eli. He made to ignore the message, so Bonnie snatched it up and read it.

THANK HEAVEN, it read. ROSE AND KATIE BOTH SAFE WITH ME. WEBB BEING LOOKED AFTER. HURRY HOME. GENOA.

"It would have relieved my mind to know about this message!" Bonnie said, not caring that the Kinders were staring at her and taking in every word she said. "Eli McKutchen, how could you?"

Amanda opened her Bible and began to read silently, her thin lips moving.

238

Eli only shrugged, and that made Bonnie so mad that she wanted to slap him right across the face. Since she'd resolved not to do that, however, she had to be content with bounding out of her chair and stomping toward the door, calling an ungracious "Thank you for the food" to the Kinders as she went.

Bonnie expected Eli to follow after her in high dudgeon, but she strode almost a mile in the direction she hoped would bring her to Colville before he fell into step beside her.

"Ezra would have taken us to town in his wagon," he said, as if he hadn't taken advantage of her, as if he hadn't lied about the chicken he'd roasted and about the fire and the farmhouse as well.

Bonnie walked on, her shoes cramping her feet. "Rubbing two sticks together indeed!" she spat.

Eli laughed. "Would you really have preferred to sleep in the Kinders' barn, Bonnie? They wouldn't have put us up in the house, you know. Mrs. Kinder knows we aren't married and she considers us sinners."

"We are sinners!" Bonnie shouted, walking faster and still refusing to so much as glance in Eli's direction. "We'll both burn in hell!"

"I don't believe in hell," Eli replied reasonably, "and I don't think you do, either."

Bonnie stopped in the middle of the cowpath that served as a road, her arms folded across her bosom, her eyes snapping. She knew that her hair was matted from the dousing in the Columbia River and probably full of leaves and twigs as well. Her face was no doubt as dirty as it felt, and her clothes—a perfectly good skirt and shirtwaist—were ruined. Her best cloak had been lost and her shoes didn't even bear thinking about. "How do you know what I believe in, Eli McKutchen? You've never once in your life bothered to ask!"

His clothes looked terrible. Who would believe their fantastic story when and if they ever found their way into Colville? "All right, Bonnie," he sighed. "What do you believe?"

Bonnie was furious. Now that he'd finally asked her, she didn't know, damn it. She whirled and stomped on toward Colville, her arms swinging at her sides like a soldier's.

Once again Eli walked beside her. Rows of new corn stood along both sides of the narrow road and the smell of recent rain was pungent. A mud puddle loomed ahead, and Bonnie went right through it, while Eli skirted the small lake and joined her on the far shore.

"You found the Kinders' farm while I was sleeping yesterday!" she accused, eyes straight ahead. "You knew that farmhouse was there all the time!"

"Yes."

"I hate you, Eli McKutchen!"

"I don't believe you."

"You don't believe in hell, either. Everybody believes in hell. What do you know?"

Eli laughed. "I know that you need me as much as I need you."

"I do not!"

"Your body gives the lie to that every time I touch you, Bonnie." Eli stopped her then, made her face him. He gave a long sigh. "We have to go back."

Bonnie felt unaccountable tears stinging behind her eyes and forced them into retreat. "Why?"

"Because Colville is over there," he answered, gesturing in the opposite direction.

Again Bonnie wanted to kick him. "You might have mentioned that before I walked this far in these damnable shoes!" she yelled.

He frowned. "Do your feet hurt?"

"Yes!"

Eli bent slightly and, grasping Bonnie by the waist, flung her up onto his shoulder. After her initial shock had subsided, she doubled up her fists and hammered at his broad back.

"Put me down!"

Eli sighed and set her on her feet. "I was only trying to help," he said in a martyrly tone.

It was late morning when they reached Colville, a bustling town situated, like Northridge, on the banks of the Columbia River. The town had been spared the flood but the populace was not without sympathy for their neighbors, for there were signs everywhere urging people to donate food and money for the benefit of the victims.

Eli approached the railroad depot and climbed the steps to the ticket agent's window. Bonnie waited some distance away, praying that Ezra Kinder had been wrong, that the train would be traveling to Northridge on schedule so that she wouldn't have to travel forty miles on a horse or jostling about on the hard seat of a wagon.

Prayers are sometimes answered. When Eli turned away from the window, he was grinning and there were two tickets in his hand.

"Remind me to thank Genoa," he said. "She wired money for our fare back to Northridge."

Bonnie's relief was so great that she forgot her irritation for a moment. "Bless her," she said. But then she frowned. "Didn't Mr. Kinder say that the tracks were washed out?"

Eli shrugged. "The trains are running, so the damage couldn't have been too bad. We have a couple of hours. Do you want to check into that hotel over there and have a bath?"

"Genoa arranged for that, too?"

"My sister is a practical woman. She probably assumes that we're somewhat the worse for wear, having been washed away in a flood."

Bonnie tried not to smile, but she couldn't help it. This would certainly be a story to tell to her grandchildren, though she would leave out the part about making love in the sun, of course. Her smile faded. "Would we have separate rooms?"

Eli took her arm and ushered her toward the hotel, which was grander than the one in Northridge but not so grand as the one they'd stayed in in Spokane. "Feeling virtuous, my dear?"

Bonnie stuck out her chin. "Yes."

"Fine." They were passing a sizable mercantile, and Eli stopped abruptly on the board sidewalk. "Let's get ourselves a change of clothes."

"Without money?" Bonnie asked, longing to be clean from the skin out. It would be terrible to take a nice, hot bath and then have to put those same bedraggled garments back on.

Eli grinned. "The McKutchen name is magical," he said and, of course, he was right. The proprietor was only too happy to grant him a line of credit.

While he was selecting new trousers, a cambric shirt, stockings and boots, Bonnie outfitted herself with a simple calico dress, drawers and a camisole, shoes and stockings. She also purchased a brush and hairpins, along with a toothbrush and polish.

At the hotel, she was given a room of her own, and it came equipped with a bathtub, a sink and a commode.

Bonnie ran a hot bath for herself and sank into it, sighing contentedly as the warm water soothed her aching muscles and soaked away the worst of the grime from her adventure in and beside the river.

The tender flesh on the inside of her arms stung when the water touched it and, for the first time, Bonnie examined herself for injuries. There was a large bruise on her right hip bone and her forearms were scratched from grasping and clinging to that log. Gingerly, Bonnie lowered them into the water.

She almost fell asleep in that tub, it was so comfortable, but at the last minute she roused herself and lathered her hair with the new cake of soap provided by the hotel. Again and again she washed and rinsed, washed and rinsed, and finally she felt clean.

Bonnie got out of the tub reluctantly, drying her body and her hair with towels, and put on her new drawers and camisole. Suddenly exhausted, she collapsed crosswise on the bed and sank into an immediate, fathomless sleep.

A gentle hand on her shoulder awakened her. "It's time to board the train, Bonnie," a familiar voice said.

Bonnie sat up, blinking. Eli was standing over her in his fresh clothes, a gentle look in his eyes.

Remembering what usually happened when she found herself alone with this man, Bonnie snatched up her new calico dress and shimmied into it, permitting Eli to touch her only to do up the buttons at the back of her gown. What had possessed her to buy a dress that buttoned up the back?

"Hurry," Eli said when he'd finished. "We only have about fifteen minutes."

242

"Fifteen minutes!" Bonnie gasped, brushing her tangled hair furiously. "I'll never be ready—"

Eli's reflection smiled at her from the mirror over the bureau as she hastily did up her hair. "I wouldn't mind if we missed the train," he said.

"Well, I would!" Bonnie cried. "Rose must be scared to death and Webb—"

The name fell between them like a boulder. Eli sighed. "Yes," he said. "There's always Webb."

Bonnie's hands shook as she pinned her hair into place. "He's a fine man, Eli."

Eli might have said a lot of things, might even have reminded Bonnie that it hadn't been Webb she'd been making love with less than twenty-four hours before, but he only sighed again.

Bonnie turned to face him, but she wasn't quite able to meet his eyes. "I guess we'd better go," she said.

They had left the hotel, walked back to the depot and boarded the train before Eli spoke.

"That day in the store," he began, his gaze fixed on the clouds of steam rolling past the train windows.

Bonnie knew what day he meant, and she sat up very straight in her seat, her hands folded in her lap. "The day you were going to beat me?"

"I wasn't going to lay a hand on you, Bonnie. I was only bluffing."

Bonnie had discerned that at the time, by the twinkle in his eyes, but she didn't let on that that was so. "I see."

Eli turned from the window then, his full attention on Bonnie. "Doesn't it bother you that Hutcheson would strike you, whatever the provocation?"

Perhaps it was the lovemaking, or the joy of being on her way home, bathed and dressed in clean clothes. Bonnie didn't know what it was that made her answer so directly. "It changes everything," she said. "It isn't that I haven't forgiven Webb—after all, I did contribute to the problem, you know—but I think it was wrong for the simple reason that he's so much stronger than I am."

"It does seem like an unfair advantage."

Bonnie bit her lower lip and then repeated, "But I did—"

"I know, I know. You started the whole thing," Eli filled in, sounding exasperated.

The train tooted its whistle and began chugging toward Northridge, and Bonnie blushed because she was remembering another trip aboard this train, when she and Eli had had the passenger car all to themselves. "What would you have done?" she asked, looking down at her hands.

Eli laughed. "I don't think I would have slapped Hutcheson across the face," he replied. "I tend to prefer a right cross."

Bonnie was irritated. "That wasn't what I meant and you know it! I was asking what you would have done in Webb's place."

Out of the corner of her eye, Bonnie saw that Eli no longer looked amused.

"To be honest," he admitted, after a long time, "I don't know. I'd like to tell you that I would have been chivalrous and discussed our differences in a civilized fashion, but that might not be the truth."

Bonnie sighed. "I guess it doesn't really matter what you would have done, does it?"

"I guess not," Eli answered, and then they were silent again, each wandering in thought.

Ezra Kinder had been at least partially right; the train could go no farther than the old spur of track five miles south of Northridge, where there had once been a sawmill.

Through the window, Bonnie saw that there were wagons waiting to take on freight and passengers—there were several other people riding in the car that day—and the faces of their drivers were solemn indeed.

Eli got out of his seat without a word, and Bonnie followed him mutely down the aisle and off the train. There was a six-inch layer of mud on the ground, and Bonnie promptly sank to her ankles. She was about to swear when Genoa's voice rang out over the general gloom.

"Eli! Bonnie! Over here!"

Bonnie's spirits lifted as she looked up and saw Genoa's carriage waiting among the wagons, the lady herself bending halfway out the window and waving.

Eli chuckled affectionately and took Bonnie's hand,

wrenching her free of the mud. When she immediately sank into it again, he simply lifted her into his arms, without ceremony, and carried her to Genoa's carriage.

Bonnie was embarrassed—it would give the population of Northridge one more thing to talk about—but she was too glad to see her friend to protest. Eli deposited her inside the carriage, favored his teary-eyed sister with a grin, and climbed up into the box, beside the driver.

Genoa, seated across from Bonnie, clapped her hands together. "Tell me all about your grand adventure!" she cried.

It wasn't grand, Bonnie started to protest, but then she remembered how she'd felt in Eli's arms and stopped herself. In its way, the experience had been grand indeed. Quietly Bonnie explained how she'd slipped off the porch at the rooming house—she wasn't prepared to decide whether she'd actually slipped or Earline had pushed her—and then been carried away by the river. She told of clinging to the log with Eli's help, of being washed ashore in the driving rain. But she didn't mention the old wagon that had served as a lean-to; instead, she led Genoa to believe that she and Eli had been put up by the Kinders.

"I've been looking after Katie and Rose," Genoa said, when the tale had ended, and if she thought there had been gaps in the telling she didn't mention them. "And Susan Farley took care of Webb. I hope you don't mind her staying in your place, Bonnie—we couldn't move him and there are so many needing attention and care."

Bonnie braced herself. "How many were lost, Genoa? Does anyone know?"

"My Mr. Callahan and the marshal have been leading searches. They've found seven bodies," Genoa paused, lowering her head. "There are nine people missing, as far as anyone can tell. We thought there were eleven until Eli's wire came." The spinster produced a handkerchief from inside her sleeve and dabbed at her eyes. "Oh, Bonnie, I was so frightened, thinking that you were both lost, that poor little Rose was an orphan—"

Bonnie reached over and squeezed Genoa's hand. "I'm sorry that you were worried."

Genoa rallied herself and tucked her handkerchief back in its place. "There is much to be done, Bonnie. There is so much to be done. Northridge is a shambles."

"Has the water receded?"

Genoa sighed. "Not entirely, but I think the worst is over."

They were passing the site of the new cabins now, the carriage rolling and lurching in the mud, and Bonnie looked out to see the houses. They were merely framework, but they were surprisingly large. And there were tents, and people milling about between them, actually smiling and talking.

How resilient people are, Bonnie thought to herself, and she felt her own spirits rise. "Wherever did they get so many tents?" she asked.

Genoa smiled. "From our good neighbors to the north, in Canada. They heard of our plight over the wire, of course, and sent tents and provisions by wagon."

The carriage lumbered on, making its awkward way toward Northridge, which was indeed a shambles, at least below the hill. Before a turn in the road cut off Bonnie's view of the lower part of the town, she saw the devastation. Webb's newspaper office and Patch Town were entirely gone, while at least four feet of standing water lapped at the walls of the railroad depot and Forbes's establishment. There was no trace of the ferry or its landings.

"Forbes is devastated," Genoa said with a surprisingly wry expression curving her lips and dancing in her eyes. "He's depending rather heavily on our Lizbeth for the strength to carry on."

Despite the wreckage Bonnie had just seen, she was amused to think of Forbes Durrant falling in love with a schoolmarm. And it did sound as though he had fallen in love. "How does Lizbeth feel about the matter?"

Genoa's thin shoulders moved in a shrug, but there was still a mischievous light in her eyes. "Who can tell? Forbes is a very good-looking man, you know."

"He's also a scoundrel and a rogue," Bonnie pointed out, though not unkindly.

"They say men of that stripe make the best husbands"

was Genoa's observation. "Provided they're reformed, that is."

"I can't imagine Forbes being reformed."

Genoa laughed. "Nor can I, but love works miracles, doesn't it?"

Seth—hadn't Genoa referred to him as "my Mr. Callahan" just moments before—popped into Bonnie's mind. "Perhaps," she agreed in a reflective tone of voice. "Yes, perhaps it does."

Genoa said nothing in reply.

The days to come were busy ones for Bonnie and, indeed, for everyone else in Northridge as well.

As the water receded, the railroad authorities sent workers to repair the tracks and rebuild the depot. Supplies came by the wagonload for Bonnie's store, and she sold merchandise of every sort almost as fast as it arrived.

Webb remained in Bonnie's bed, and he proved to be an irascible patient, constantly shouting for one thing or another. Fortunately Bonnie didn't have to wait on him, at least during store hours, because Susan Farley, the young widow Genoa had so staunchly befriended, came every day to look after him. Her patience astounded Bonnie.

Susan's baby was thriving, and it was Katie who changed his diapers and took him to his mother when he needed feeding. Rose was fascinated by the infant and demanded little attention for herself, seeming content to bask in reflected glory.

Work in the smelter went on as usual, and the cabins south of town slowly sprouted roofs and windows and stoops. To the rumored annoyance of Lizbeth Simmons, Forbes reopened the Brass Eagle Saloon and Ballroom before the floors were dry. The warped billiard tables and undulating ballroom floor became local points of interest, drawing thrill seekers from every quarter of town.

Even Genoa made a pilgrimage to see the oddities. Bonnie had been too busy to go anywhere, between running the store during the daytime and coddling Webb Hutcheson at night.

She was tired of sleeping on the settee in her parlor and even wearier of plumping pillows and listening to long accountings of her patient's aches and pains. She was, in fact, very glad that she hadn't married Webb Hutcheson.

"I'm ruined," he said one night, with appropriate melodrama, when they had been discussing the flood.

Bonnie shoved a spoonful of medicine into his mouth. "Nonsense. If Forbes can start over, you can, too."

Webb looked like a little boy and, for a moment, Bonnie's heart softened. Only for a moment, for he fixed her with a petulant glare and said tragically, "Susan understands what it means to a man to lose everything he has, Bonnie."

Susan, Susan, Susan, Bonnie thought. *I'm sick to death of hearing about Susan.* "And I *don't* understand, is that it?"

"My presses are gone!" Webb thundered. "Hell, my whole damned building is gone! At least Forbes has walls and a floor to work with!"

"Hush," Bonnie said. "You'll wake Rose and Katie."

Cautiously, Webb reached out and took her hand. "I'm sorry, Bonnie. You've been so good to me, even giving up your bed, and here I am raising my voice to you."

Bonnie smiled to show that she forgave him, and subtly withdrew her hand from his. "Good night, Webb," she said, and then she blew out the lamp and left the room.

Part Three

ANGEL
ENSNARED

CHAPTER 21

"YOU SEEM TO be making a success of this place," a masculine voice observed, just as Bonnie was stretching to set a pair of new work boots on a high shelf. "At last."

Bonnie's ladder jiggled a little as she climbed down. In deference to the warm, sunny June weather, she'd left the mercantile's door open to let in fresh air. Along with the breeze and a few buzzing flies, she'd admitted Forbes Durrant.

"At last?" she echoed, smoothing the skirts of her pink and gray calico dress. "Forbes, are you complimenting me, in your own backhanded way?"

Forbes grinned, leaning indolently against the counter. As usual he was well-dressed, clad in britches of some soft, clinging fabric, high, shining black boots, a linen shirt, and a tailored jacket of lightweight wool. "I assure you that my compliment was made in all sincerity, Angel. I couldn't be more pleased to see you prospering."

Despite the warmth of the day, Bonnie felt a shiver move up her spine. Mingling with the scents of summer wafting through the open door was another smell, worse than the faint twinge of horse dung from the road. It was the smell of trouble.

Bonnie managed a businesslike smile, hiding her misgivings behind it. "How may I help you?" she asked, taking her customary place on the opposite side of the counter.

Forbes grinned, his brazen eyes taking Bonnie's measure with the same leisurely appreciation as they always had. "No doubt you're aware that your dear father left Northridge in something of a hurry a few years back? A mere two or three months before you graced us with your presence, as it happened."

Bonnie didn't bother to hide either her unease or her curiosity. If Forbes knew something important about her father's flight from this town, why hadn't he mentioned it sooner? "I'm listening, Forbes," she prompted.

"If you will remember, I was running this—store—under the auspices of McKutchen Enterprises at the time."

Bonnie felt her blood heating, rising to simmer over her cheekbones. "I remember," she said.

"You never asked why, though," Forbes went on idly, pretending an interest in the jars of colorful penny candy arrayed along the countertop. "You simply assumed that your once beloved Eli had ordered the place absorbed into his company."

"That is not exactly accurate, Forbes," Bonnie answered evenly. "Eli denied any knowledge of what had happened, and I believed him."

"Of course, you would."

"Are you telling me that he was lying?"

Forbes lifted the lid of one of the candy jars and helped himself to a stick of red licorice. "Far from it, Angel. Eli truly didn't know."

"Then what exactly are you getting at?"

Forbes gave a long sigh and then took a bite of his licorice, chewing it in a contemplative fashion. Wagons rattled past on the road, and upstairs Katie was singing, Rose was bellowing, and Webb was whining for Susan to come and straighten his pillows. A decade seemed to pass before Forbes replied, "Your father owed me money, Bonnie. A great deal of money. When he ran out on the debt, I took over the store to try and recoup some of my losses."

Bonnie's throat constricted and there was a queer sensation in the pit of her stomach. "How could my father have owed you money?"

252

Forbes's elegantly clad shoulders moved in a shrug. "It pains me to speak of such indelicate pursuits, especially to a lady like yourself," he said in polite mockery, "but nevertheless a debt is a debt. Jack Fitzpatrick drank a lot, Bonnie, and he liked his women. Even more, he liked to gamble. He ran up a sizable tab at the Brass Eagle after you'd gone off to New York with your handsome new husband. Out of the goodness of my heart, I trusted your dear papa to meet his obligations like a gentleman."

"Out of the goodness of your heart?" Bonnie repeated skeptically. "Come now, Forbes—if you granted my father any grace at all, it was because of his ties to the McKutchen family."

Again Forbes shrugged. He was enjoying this immensely, Bonnie thought, and she longed to crown him with her cash register. If only she could have lifted it.

"As you like, Angel," the saloonkeeper conceded, with a charitable sigh. "In any case, I recovered some of my money by taking over this mercantile. There is still, however, the matter of an outstanding balance."

"You can't hold me responsible for my father's debts!" Bonnie realized that she'd shouted and made a conscious effort to control her tone of voice. "Besides," she went on in an acid whisper, "how do I know that you aren't lying?"

Forbes finished off his licorice and purloined another piece before answering. "Umm," he said, chewing, "I've got papers here somewhere. Signed markers." He explored both pockets of his tailored coat and then the one inside. With great fanfare, he presented a packet of folded documents.

Bonnie was sure he'd known just where the markers were the whole time. She reached for them with a slightly tremulous hand. "I have the deed to this store," she said, after scanning the papers and seeing her father's familiar mark at the bottom of each. "I have a clear deed."

"Actually the deed is in Mr. Fitzpatrick's name, isn't it?"

Bonnie didn't need to answer. The complete dearth of color in her face—she felt it seeping away—answered for her.

"As I thought," said Forbes, going through his pockets again and finally laying a shiny copper penny on the counter to pay for the licorice he'd consumed. "You did notice, didn't you, that the markers clearly state that this establishment has been put up as legal collateral against any debts Jack Fitzpatrick incurred at the Brass Eagle?"

"Why did you wait until now to tell me all this?" Bonnie countered.

"Two reasons," Forbes replied blithely. "Number one, you didn't have the money to pay me. Number two, this place wasn't a paying proposition—at least, the way you were managing it it wasn't—and therefore it wasn't worth the bother of foreclosing."

Bonnie's frustration was great, but her self-control was greater. "Aren't you afraid of losing your job as manager of the smelter works over this, Forbes?"

Forbes laughed. "Angel, I'm surprised at you. One thing has little enough to do with the other. Of course, if you were still married to Eli, I would probably have approached him instead."

Eli's name sent Bonnie's tottering spirit plummeting. Ever since their return to Northridge, following the flood, he had been avoiding her. He still resided at the rooming house down the hill, and there were rumors to the effect that he had taken Webb's place in Earline Kalb's heart. Not to mention her bed.

"I don't want Eli to know anything about this!" Bonnie said quickly.

Forbes arched one patrician eyebrow. He needed a shave, but on him the hint of a beard was somehow attractive. "Was I right in guessing that your former husband didn't exactly approve of your father, Angel?"

"Stop calling me Angel. And, yes, you were right!" *Damn you,* Bonnie added silently.

Forbes took the time to revel in his victory and then shuffled thoughtfully through the sheaf of markers again. His lips moved as he calculated the extent of the damage. "In round figures, Bonnie, you owe me five thousand dollars," he said cheerfully.

Bonnie closed her eyes for a moment, mentally seeing the numbers in her bankbook dwindle away to nothing. When she looked at Forbes again, he was still smiling. "You're enjoying this," she accused.

"Oh, indeed I am, Bonnie. Indeed I am."

"Why?"

"Because I loved you so hopelessly for so long. Ever since you were in pigtails."

Bonnie's gaze dropped to the scarred countertop. "And this is your revenge."

"Hardly. This is business. Making you dance to my tune in the Brass Eagle was my revenge." He drew a long, audible breath and let it out with a resigned whoosh. "Tell me, Angel. Are you going to give me the store or the money?"

Bonnie swallowed. "The money. I'll have my banker draw up a draft this afternoon."

"Good," Forbes said. And then he took two peppermint sticks from their jar, plopped down another penny and swaggered out.

Bonnie rested her elbows on the counter and dropped her head into her hands. All her delightful profits had just gone winging into Forbes Durrant's pockets. Through her fingers she saw two copper pennies lying on the countertop. At least he'd left her that much.

At one o'clock that afternoon Bonnie put Katie in charge of the store and went out. Northridge's one and only bank was well down the street, toward the smelter works.

Mr. Swendenborg, the president, gave her an embarrassing lecture when she asked for her funds, but Bonnie stood her ground. When she left the bank, the draft was neatly folded and resting in her handbag.

She walked down the hill, passing Earline's rooming house on her right and the undertaker's establishment on her left. A vivid memory of the day of the flood made her shiver.

"Cold?" a masculine voice called.

Bonnie turned, shading her eyes from the sun with one hand, and looked up to see Eli leaning out of an upstairs window of the rooming house. Was that Earline's room? She found herself hoping that he would fall and crack his hard, miserable skull. "On a day like this?" she replied guilelessly.

Eli frowned. "Is the store closed?" He actually consulted his pocket watch. "It's the middle of the day."

Bonnie longed to rankle him. "Some of us can't afford to languish in our beds the whole day through," she replied.

255

"But to answer your question, the store is open. Katie is minding it while I pay a call on Forbes."

To Bonnie's enormous satisfaction, Eli bumped his head against the window sash. A string of muffled curses rent the air.

"What business could you possibly have with that—that rounder?" Eli demanded, once he'd finished swearing.

"I thought I might ask for my job back," Bonnie answered, without missing a beat. "I rather miss dancing the hurdy-gurdy." Having said this, the Angel went merrily on about her business.

"Bonnie!" the devil yelled after her from the second-story window. "Damn it, come back here!"

Bonnie walked faster.

The famous warped billiard tables were about to be replaced with new ones, Bonnie noted, as she walked boldly into the Brass Eagle Saloon and approached the bar. Indeed, she was probably paying for the set being carried in through the side doors by four red-faced and puffing laborers.

Forbes was supervising, but he turned away when he saw Bonnie, an insolent grin stretching across his face.

"You brought my money," he stated happily.

Bonnie hated handing over her hard-earned profits, and at that moment she hated Forbes, too. And her irresponsible father. "You're not getting a dime until you hand over those markers," she answered. "Furthermore, I want your written promise that there are no more debts."

Forbes offered a gentlemanly arm. "Shall we discuss this in my office?" he asked.

Bonnie's chin jutted out, but she took Forbes's arm and allowed him to escort her up the stairs and into his office. On the second floor there was very little evidence of flood damage. Forbes was a man who liked his personal comforts, and this part of the building had undoubtedly been repaired first.

There was laughter behind the doors they passed; it seemed that the Brass Eagle was doing brisk business in areas besides dancing, gambling and liquor.

"Human lust never ceases to amaze me," Forbes remarked, as he opened one of the double doors leading into his office.

"Or fatten your wallet," Bonnie added. She swept inside ahead of her escort, unable to resist a little revenge. "There are rumors that you and Lizbeth Simmons are fond of each other, you know. Of course, I don't believe a word of it."

Forbes actually flushed, but he was quick to hide his discomfort by setting his back to Bonnie and striding toward his desk. "Why don't you believe it?" he couldn't resist asking.

Bonnie sighed dramatically, as she had seen many a road-show heroine do. "A teacher has—well, you know—a certain standing in any community. Certainly Lizbeth wouldn't be foolish enough to involve herself with a—with a—"

Forbes was red in the face, and this time he was making no effort to hide the fact. His brown eyes snapped and Bonnie noted that his hands, resting on top of his desk, had closed into fists. "With a what?" he demanded.

Bonnie could not have been more delighted. It was almost worth five thousand dollars to see Forbes lose his legendary composure. "Why, with a saloonkeeper," she answered in sunny tones. "A procurer, if you will."

"I am not a procurer!" Forbes roared.

Bonnie pretended to be startled and stepped back, one hand to her throat. The dramatics did not extend to her voice, however. She spoke bluntly. "What is your word for it, Forbes?" Bonnie gestured toward the hallway. "Aren't there women behind those doors, being paid to please men?"

For once Forbes was at a complete loss. He sank into his chair and sat glaring at Bonnie, as though he'd like to see her hanged or even burned at the stake.

Bonnie opened her handbag and took out the bank draft, which represented nearly every cent she had. "The markers, if you will," she said, approaching Forbes's desk. "Along with your disclaimer, of course."

Forbes sat back in his chair, his fingers making a steeple beneath his stubbly chin. Even when the bank draft was within grasping distance, he didn't reach for it, and his brown eyes were pensive. "Lizbeth would probably never agree to marry me," he reflected, and Bonnie was taken aback. She even felt a measure of sympathy.

She recovered quickly enough. After all, she was about to turn over nearly everything she had. "You're probably right," she said. "What decent woman would want to wed herself to a whoremonger?"

Forbes's eyes shot coffee-colored fire as they climbed over Bonnie's bosom to her face. "My God, we've gotten self-righteous in recent weeks, haven't we? May I remind you, Mrs. McKutchen, that you used to be one of the biggest draws this place had?"

"I merely danced," Bonnie said airily.

"Yes, you 'merely danced.' With any man who could pay the price."

Bonnie blushed. If she lived to be nine hundred and ninety-nine, she would probably never hear the end of her stint as a hurdy-gurdy. "I needed the money, Forbes."

Incredibly Forbes smiled, but his eyes were still dark with annoyance. "And you still do, don't you?" The smile broadened measurably. "I'll tell you what I'll do, Angel. If you'll come back to the Brass Eagle and dance, I'll agree to discharge the bills your father ran up."

Coldly furious, she slapped the draft down on Forbes's blotter. "I wouldn't do that to save ten thousand dollars, or a hundred thousand, or a million!" she said, hoping that she would never have to eat those lofty words.

Forbes produced the markers from a desk drawer, along with paper and pen. "You've made your point, Angel," he said with a ragged sigh. "You've made your point."

Five minutes later Bonnie left the Brass Eagle Saloon minus five thousand dollars, but she still had her pride and her self-respect, and she had Forbes's written word that her father's debts had been paid. In no mood to deal with any more males, she passed Earline's place on the far side of the street.

When Bonnie entered the store, Eli was waiting for her. He was pretending to examine a display of sheet music, which of course didn't fool Bonnie in the least. The man couldn't carry a tune, let alone play an instrument.

"What do you want?" she demanded, snatching off her straw hat and flinging it away. It sailed over the counter and landed with a plop on the floor behind it.

Wide-eyed, Katie gathered up a fussing Rose and vanished up the stairs.

"Is that the way you greet all your customers, Mrs. McKutchen?" Eli asked, smiling.

Bonnie realized that she'd given him the upper hand and could have kicked herself for it. She yanked her white apron from its peg and slipped it on, tying the sash with wrenching motions of her hands. "Do you always waste entire days lolling about your bedroom?" she countered. Oddly enough she was more irate over Eli's place of residence than over having to pay five thousand dollars for her father's drunken pleasures.

Just then Webb bellowed something upstairs, and the sound of running feet—probably Susan's—clattered overhead.

"Speaking of lolling about in bedrooms," Eli said and, though his smile was still in place, his eyes looked distinctly angry, "how is Hutcheson?"

"He's almost fully recovered," Bonnie answered, bending her head to hide the smile that was suddenly pulling at the corners of her mouth. So that was it, she thought. Eli was staying at Earline's and stirring up as much gossip as he could because he was jealous of Webb's position in Bonnie's home.

"There is a lot of talk about you and Hutcheson, Bonnie, and I'm not sure I like it."

I'll bet you don't, Bonnie thought, but she managed to keep a straight face as she met his eyes. "That's nothing new, Eli," she said guilelessly. "People have been yammering about Webb and me from the first."

Eli did not look appeased. "Is he still in your room?"

Bonnie wondered how Eli could have known about that and then remembered that he'd been with the men who brought Webb here the day he was beaten. "Of course," she said sweetly. "Where else would he be? The only other bed in the place is Katie's, and he's much too big and muscular to lie on my rickety little settee."

The subtle, breathy emphasis Bonnie had put on the words "big and muscular" had not escaped Eli. His face went ruddy and she half expected puffs of steam to rise out

259

of his collar. For all this, he did manage to speak in moderate tones. "I believe I'll just look in on Hutcheson, see how he's feeling. If you don't mind, that is."

Just then a timid little woman floated out of the shadows, like a specter, an onion in one hand and a potato in the other. Bonnie rang up the sale, her voice chiming just as musically as the bell on the cash register. "Mind? Why, Eli, of course I don't mind. An injured man needs all the cheering up he can get."

Bonnie felt Eli's scalding glance, rather than saw it, and she smiled as his boot heels hammered up the inside stairs to the rooms above.

Tuttle entered the store, passing the onion-and-potato woman in the doorway, a cheerful grin on his face. Since the newspaper office had been destroyed, he'd been working full time helping to finish the new workers' cabins, and the job seemed to agree with him. He was tanned and he'd filled out some, looking more the man and less the awkward boy.

"Afternoon, ma'am," he said with a polite nod. "I've come for my reading lesson."

Bonnie had returned to mourning her five thousand dollars, and her smile was gone. "Katie's upstairs," she answered sharply.

Tuttle looked hurt. Night after night, for weeks now, he'd sat at her kitchen table with Katie, laboring over lessons in penmanship, grammar and reading, and the image of him working so determinedly gave Bonnie a feeling of chagrin. She made herself smile, and Tuttle immediately brightened.

When Eli came back down the stairs, he was carrying both Rose Marie and her fancy life-size doll. "This place is a circus," he said.

Bonnie did not care, at the moment, what his opinions might be. "Where do you think you're going with my daughter?"

"Rose Marie is also *my* daughter," Eli pointed out reasonably. "With your permission, I'd like to spend the evening with her."

A sudden and horrible thought possessed Bonnie and made her round the counter in a hurry. It had just come back to her that Eli lived at Earline's. "You are not taking my—our—child into that—that woman's house!"

"I had no idea you disapproved of Genoa," Eli said, pretending to puzzled injury.

Bonnie subsided. "You know very well that I wasn't talking about Genoa. I was speaking of your—paramour."

"My *what?*" The words came out of Eli's mouth as a delighted hoot.

"I do not intend to elaborate," Bonnie replied with cool disdain, "in the presence of an innocent child."

Eli's eyes lifted eloquently to the ceiling. "You don't seem to mind doing other things in the presence of an innocent child. Why not elaborate?"

His jealousy did not seem quite so amusing now. It would be just like him, Bonnie reflected, to decide that she was not providing a fit environment for Rose Marie and take steps to gain legal guardianship. "I sleep on the settee," she said lamely, her cheeks flaring. "I was only trying to nettle you before, because of what people are saying about you and Earline."

"What are people saying about Earline and me?" Eli quizzed, and there was a mischievous note in his voice that might have earned him a sound slap across the face if he hadn't been holding Bonnie's child.

When Bonnie didn't answer—sheer stubbornness kept her from it—he laughed. "I'll bring Rose back after supper," he said, and then he just walked out of the store, bold as you please, leaving Bonnie to stand staring after him in furious despair.

In a moment Eli came back. "Would you like to come along?" he asked distractedly, as though the thought had just descended upon him from on high. Perhaps it had.

Bonnie wasn't about to quibble. She was tired and she'd had to give Forbes Durrant virtually all her money and she didn't think she could bear another evening in that madhouse upstairs. Quick as a wink, she fetched her shawl, shouted to Katie that she was going out and locked up the store.

Walking along that way, with Eli carrying their daughter on one of his shoulders, gave Bonnie a good feeling. It was almost as though the three of them made up a family in the truest sense of the word.

But of course they weren't really a family. There had been

261

a divorce, after all, and Kiley's tragic death still stood between Bonnie and Eli, like a barrier. She was saddened, thinking of the little boy who should have been there with them.

"What's the matter, Bonnie?" Eli asked quietly, as they started down the hill toward Genoa's spacious house. "You look as though you're about to cry."

The whistle blew in the smelter yard, and somehow the sound added to Bonnie's lonely mood. She could not answer Eli's question honestly, though, because that would open wounds that weren't fully mended. "I'm just tired, I guess," she said. That was true enough.

Eli's next words were completely unexpected ones, and they were spoken with a shyness Bonnie would never have suspected of him. "I'd like to show you the cabins one day soon. They're almost finished now."

Bonnie's eyes slipped to Eli's face and saw a rare expression of vulnerability there. Her seeing those cabins truly mattered to him, and she found that surprising, given the attention he'd allegedly been paying Earline Kalb of late. "I'd like that, Eli," she said.

They went through Genoa's open gate and up the cobbled driveway. Rose, spotting her beloved aunt in the doorway, demanded to be set on her feet, and Eli lifted her from his shoulder with a gruff chuckle. She went barreling toward Genoa, who was laughing, her arms outstretched.

"The union men are back in town," Eli confided, as he watched his daughter and his sister embracing each other on the porch.

Bonnie stopped. Mr. Denning and his men had left after the flood and she had put them out of her mind. "I hadn't heard," she answered. "Do you think there will be more trouble?"

"There can always be more trouble, Bonnie."

"It galls me that those hooligans got away with beating poor Webb nearly to death! The marshal has gone over and over what happened, but Webb can't remember what his attackers looked like—"

Gently Eli's hands gripped Bonnie's arms. "Could we not talk about Hutcheson, please? Just this once?"

262

Bonnie smiled. Eli's touch felt as good as walking beside him had earlier. "I'm sorry."

To Bonnie's complete and utter surprise, Eli bent his head and kissed her, just softly. "For what it's worth, Bonnie," he said, when the kiss was over and his lips were lingering a fraction of an inch from hers, "the rumors aren't true."

Bonnie knew that he was referring to the gossip concerning himself and Earline Kalb. "That's good," she said. "That's very good."

Eli took her hand in his and they walked toward Genoa's house. For those few very precious moments, it was as if nothing had ever gone wrong between them.

CHAPTER 22

THE PONY STOOD nibbling at the trimmed grasses of Genoa's lawn, a creature of splendor in its decorous saddle and bridle. As Rose approached it, in cautious wonder, her hand in Eli's, the animal lifted its cocoa-brown head and neighed companionably.

Eli bent and lifted his daughter into his arms, then carried her closer to the pony. Tentatively, Rose reached out to touch the cream-colored mane, and the tiny mare nickered a greeting and tossed its head, bridle jingling.

Rose crowed with glee and clapped her hands. "Mine!" she cried.

Gently Eli set the little girl in the saddle. She looked both delighted and afraid as she gripped the pommel.

Eli took the reins in one hand and began leading the pony around and around, in an ever-widening circle. He looked every bit as enchanted as Rose did.

Bonnie stood watching with Genoa and an oddly subdued Lizbeth, and her feelings were mixed. Rose obviously loved the cocoa-brown pony, but there were other considerations —horses sometimes kicked people, or ran away with them, or threw them off into rocks or brambles. Bonnie's own fear of the beasts made her start forward, a protest forming on her lips.

264

But Genoa stopped her by extending one arm. "Rose Marie is perfectly safe, Bonnie."

Bonnie sighed. It was true. Eli was holding the reins while the pony followed docilely wherever he led. What could happen to Rose, with her father so near? "I believe I'd like a cup of tea now," Bonnie said, on a long breath.

Genoa smiled at her. They were all replete, having just eaten a marvelous supper, but one didn't have to be hungry to drink tea. "Isn't Cocoa a lovely surprise?" the spinster trilled, referring, of course, to the pony, as she led the way back through the garden and the French doors.

The parlor was pleasantly cool. Genoa immediately went to the kitchen to ask Martha to prepare tea, while Bonnie and Lizbeth settled themselves in chairs.

At first Lizbeth's reticence escaped Bonnie, for she was still thinking about the pony. Eli might have consulted her, she reflected angrily, before presenting their daughter with a potentially dangerous gift. And where would she keep a horse? Did he expect her to tether it to the privy behind the store? She sighed and determined to stop thinking about Eli and the creature, because there was nothing she could do about the actions of either.

It was then that she noticed that Lizbeth was sitting with her hands knotted together in her lap. Her normally pink and white complexion was pallorous and her pretty blond hair, though arranged as neatly as ever, seemed to droop in sympathy with her obviously flagging spirits.

"Why, Lizbeth," Bonnie whispered, "what is troubling you? You look so sorrowful."

When Lizbeth lifted her eyes to Bonnie's face, they were filled with an odd mingling of challenge and despair. "It's Forbes," she said. "Did you know that he's still obsessed with you, Bonnie?"

Bonnie had had quite enough of Forbes Durrant for one day, but she couldn't very well abandon the subject of him when it was obviously of staggering importance to her friend. "That's nonsense, Lizbeth," she said firmly. "I am not your rival."

"Oh, but you are," Lizbeth insisted, though not in an unfriendly fashion. "I suppose it doesn't really matter anyway. I could never marry a man like Forbes."

265

"I shouldn't think so," agreed Bonnie, with a primness that was out of character for her. She wondered if the prevalent attitudes of the Friday Afternoon Community Improvement Club had somehow rubbed off on her, now that the members grudgingly patronized her mercantile.

Martha, Genoa's longtime housekeeper, came in carrying a tea tray, temporarily interrupting the conversation. "Miss McKutchen has gone to the stables," the plump woman informed Bonnie and Lizbeth, without ever looking at either of them. "She begs your indulgence."

Bonnie smiled and shook her head, wondering what tangent had taken her sister-in-law as far as the stables, but her smile faded away as she took note of the misery in Lizbeth Simmons's pretty face. "Dear me, you really care for Forbes, don't you?"

Lizbeth made a fist and pounded the arm of her chair once, in a gesture of frustration. Agitated color glowed in her finely sculpted cheeks. "I do, but I could never countenance his manner of earning a living." Accusing blue eyes sliced in Bonnie's direction and pinioned her to the back of her chair. "Besides, he loves you."

"He does not," Bonnie insisted, because she didn't know what else to say. Forbes had mentioned his feelings that day, during their confrontation over Jack Fitzpatrick's debts, but he'd spoken in the past tense.

"Did you know he wept over your marriage to Eli McKutchen?" Lizbeth persisted.

Bonnie couldn't imagine Forbes weeping over anything other than financial ruin. "I find that very hard to believe. However, if Forbes confided something like that to you—and he's the only one who could possibly know—it would seem to demonstrate an amazing amount of trust on his part. Were Forbes to trust anyone with such an intimate confidence, he would certainly have to be in love with that person."

Hope leaped in Lizbeth's eyes but, before she could make any sort of reply, Genoa came bounding back into the parlor, her plain face alight. She was covered with cobwebs and dust, and her hair had bits of straw jutting out of it. If Bonnie hadn't known better, she would have suspected her sister-in-law of engaging in a romantic interlude while in the stables. She made a mental note to give Seth's person a subtle inspection for straw and dust.

"I found it!" Genoa beamed.

"Found what?" Bonnie asked quizzically.

"The pony cart, of course. The one Grandfather bought for me when I was just a little older than Rose." Genoa paused, happily shaking out her very proper black sateen skirts. "It was quite a task, pulling that cart all the way from the stables to the sideyard, but I accomplished it!"

Bonnie and Lizbeth exchanged amused looks, though Lizbeth still looked quite drawn and pale.

"You are quite as bad as your brother," Bonnie said, "when it comes to indulging Rose Marie. She'll be insufferable."

Genoa pouted girlishly as she poured herself a cup of tea and sat down in a chair. A cloud of grit hovered around her. "Pooh," she said.

Having no idea how to answer such a silly remark with dignity, Bonnie ignored it entirely and took another sip of her tea.

"I was just telling Bonnie that we'll have to place an order for school supplies very soon," Lizbeth lied brightly. "You can secure such things for us through your mercantile, can't you, Bonnie?"

Before Bonnie could answer, Genoa leaped into the conversation. "And of course we can't continue teaching the adult reading classes here," she said with happy resignation. "We'll need to send away for building supplies for the new schoolhouse. Mr. Callahan has very kindly provided the lumber, but we will require chalkboards and wiring and such. I have a list made up. Could you order the needed items right away, Bonnie?"

"I'll send for them on Monday," Bonnie replied. The light of good fortune was warm, and she allowed herself a moment to bask in it. She thought of Forbes's raid on her bank account and would have smiled, if it hadn't been for the fact that his name reminded her of Lizbeth's private heartbreak. "Thank you, Genoa," she said. And then, to make conversation, she added, "Where has Seth gotten off to? I haven't seen him since we arrived."

Incredibly Lizbeth let out a loud wail at those innocent words and fled the room in tears.

"Good heavens," said Bonnie, setting her teacup aside and standing up to follow after her friend.

"Do let her be, Bonnie," Genoa instructed gently. "There is nothing anyone can say to cheer her."

Reluctantly Bonnie sat down again. The sound of Lizbeth's grief was laced through with a mingling of father-and-daughter laughter floating in from the lawn.

"To answer your question," Genoa went on, as though nothing had happened, "Mr. Callahan is in the rear parlor, working." She paused. "By the way, Bonnie—the Club has appointed Seth director and manager of the Pompeii Playhouse, and he feels that the place has gone downhill—I agree that it needs a certain amount of restoration. Of course, he would want to buy the paint and the fixtures and such from you."

Bonnie could not hide her delight in that prospect. "You and Seth have done so much for me," she said. "I don't know how to thank you."

Genoa looked very serious all of a sudden, and she leaned forward in her chair, lowering her voice. Evidently she'd had enough talk of business. "What are your feelings toward Webb Hutcheson, dear?"

Bonnie flushed. "Why, Genoa McKutchen, shame on you! I thought you were above listening to petty gossip!"

"Well, I'm not. Things are in a dreadful tangle, you know. People are saying that you and Webb are—involved. And I don't suppose I need to tell you about the rumors concerning Eli's friendship with Earline Kalb."

A sudden and very distinct picture of Eli standing behind Earline, the day of Genoa's lawn party, loomed in Bonnie's mind. She saw his arms encircling Earline's womanly figure as he demonstrated the proper way to swing a croquet mallet. "I've heard the rumors," she said, seething behind the smile she offered Genoa.

Genoa was obviously not misled. "Bonnie, who is it that you love, truly? Eli or Webb?"

Bonnie darted a quick glance toward the French doors that were open to the pleasant scents of the garden and the expanse of newly mowed lawn beyond. She didn't want to be overheard. "I might as well confess, Genoa," she said, keeping her voice low. "I'm still as much in love with Eli as I ever was."

Genoa startled her by shooting out of her chair and proceeding to pace the room in an agitated manner. Bonnie was a little hurt, for she had expected her former sister-in-law and dearest friend to be pleased.

"Don't you want me to care for Eli?" Bonnie asked in a small voice.

Genoa stopped pacing and collapsed into her chair again. "Of course I do, Bonnie, but the man has tremendous pride and you're not helping matters by keeping Webb Hutcheson as a boarder."

"Webb was badly injured," Bonnie pointed out quietly. "I felt—obligated."

"The poor wretch expects you to marry him, doesn't he?" Genoa demanded, with what was for her uncommon stringency. "Oh, Bonnie, what can you be thinking of to lead a decent man like Webb on in such a way?"

"I'm not leading him on!" Bonnie hissed.

Genoa sneezed and a new flurry of dust swelled up around her. "Aren't you?" she sniffled, taking a handkerchief from her sleeve and dabbing at her nose. "You haven't told Webb the straight of things, have you?"

"I couldn't, Genoa. He's built that lovely house, and his ribs are broken—"

Genoa interrupted tersely. "Excuses. Think of Webb's pride, Bonnie. And Eli's."

Bonnie was insulted, and she drew herself up accordingly. "What about my pride, Genoa? Do you think I enjoy lying awake every night and wondering whether Earline and Eli are together?"

"Which do you prize more, Bonnie?" Genoa countered intrepidly. "Your pride or your happiness?"

Bonnie opened her mouth and closed it again.

"I can tell you from bitter experience," Genoa went on, suddenly deflated, "that pride of that kind is a terrible trap. I might have had children now if it hadn't been for my pride. I might have had Mr. Callahan."

Bonnie's affection for her friend was very real and very deep. She knelt in front of Genoa's chair and clasped the thin, graceful hands in her own. "Pride? I thought your grandfather stopped the marriage."

Two tears dropped from Genoa's chin and landed on Bonnie's hand. "Mr. Callahan wanted me to stand up to my grandfather, but I was afraid to—oh, Bonnie, that old man could shout to shake the rafters when he chose to, and I was never able to stand up to him the way Eli did. I went to Europe, just as Grandfather ordered me to do, but I never stopped thinking of my Seth. Not for a moment. I could have gone to him when my ship docked in New York, I could have apologized, but I was a McKutchen—too proud. I wanted Mr. Callahan to come to me, you see."

Bonnie embraced Genoa. "But he's here now, in Northridge," she reminded her friend. "You and Seth are being offered a second chance."

Genoa withdrew from the embrace and again produced her handkerchief. She was both laughing and crying as Bonnie went back to her chair. "What a silly bunch of females we are, you and Lizbeth and I! I'm trying to be young again, you're torn between two men and poor Lizbeth doesn't know up from down because she's so crazy about Forbes."

Bonnie started to protest that she wasn't "torn between two men" at all, that she loved only Eli. Fortunately she saw him coming in from the garden out of the corner of her eye and stopped herself in time. She smiled at him, and at the exhausted little girl in his arms.

"It would seem that Rose has had enough excitement for one day," she observed, and the remark sounded inane even in her own ears. "She and I had better go home."

Genoa got up from her chair and vanished.

"I want you to stay," Eli said bluntly and, though Bonnie strained to decipher it, the expression in his eyes was unreadable.

"That is ridiculous," Bonnie replied, standing up and smoothing her skirts. "Furthermore, it is improper."

She reached out to reclaim Rose, but Eli would not surrender her.

"Don't you think we've played this game long enough, Bonnie?"

Bonnie swallowed, afraid and angry and yet composed. "What game?"

"You know very well 'what game.' We should be together, making a real home for our daughter and for each other."

His words made Bonnie dizzy with hope and shock. She sank back into her chair, too overwhelmed to speak.

Eli laid Rose Marie on a window seat at the far side of the room and covered her with a colorful afghan. The child yawned and closed her eyes, and Bonnie was almost crushed by the tenderness she felt as she watched.

Finally Eli came back to sit in the chair Genoa had occupied until a few minutes before. He took Bonnie's hands in his. "I need you," he said.

Bonnie felt her face heating. "The way you needed me in Spokane," she said woodenly. "The way you needed me after the flood—"

"Yes," Eli answered, with stunning honesty.

Bonnie wanted so much more. She wanted him to love her. She wanted him to value her opinions and, for once, share his life with her. "You have Earline Kalb for that!" she spat, in her disappointment and her pain. She tried to turn away, but Eli caught her chin in one hand and made her look at him.

"I'm not involved with Earline. I've already told you that."

Bonnie willed herself not to cry. "Why should I believe you? You betrayed me in New York, when you were still my husband. Why would you be faithful now?"

Eli lowered his head for a moment and, when he spoke, his voice was gruff. "I guess we're going to have to talk about New York sooner or later, aren't we?"

Bonnie pulled her hands free. She wasn't sure she could bear to discuss Kiley's death and Eli's reactions to it. It would be like reliving the nightmare. "I'll just get Rose and go home, if you don't mind."

"I do mind, Bonnie." The golden eyes were looking into hers now, holding her prisoner in her chair. "You're not going anywhere until we've talked things through."

Bonnie braced herself against the inevitable pain. "If you're going to tell me about your mistresses, Eli McKutchen, I don't want to hear it."

Eli sighed. "I don't deny that there were other women, Bonnie."

For the first time Bonnie realized how much she'd wanted him to do just that. She'd wanted him to deny everything. She closed her eyes and stiffened, doing her best not to cry. "Of course you don't," she said.

"Bonnie, look at me."

She looked, but she remained stubbornly silent.

"Those women—I didn't love them—"

"They didn't mean anything to you," Bonnie said, feeling and sounding like a marionette being worked by some unseen puppeteer. "Isn't that what errant husbands always say, Eli?"

"In my case, it happens to be true."

"I don't care anymore, Eli," Bonnie lied in self-defense. "One way or the other, I don't care!"

"You don't want to care, I'll give you that. But you do, Bonnie, and so do I."

"No!" Bonnie whispered wildly. Painful wounds would be opened if they talked about those women and about Kiley, and she hadn't the strength to endure it.

"Yes," Eli insisted. "Bonnie, help me."

Bonnie remembered holding a lifeless Kiley in her arms, remembered the funeral and the despair, remembered how her husband had failed her when she'd needed him the most. "I said that to you once," she reminded Eli in an odd, hollow voice. "You turned away. You left me."

"I'm trying to apologize for that, Bonnie."

"Apologize!" Bonnie spat the word and bolted out of her chair, moving to stand behind it and make a barrier between herself and the only man in the world who had the power to hurt her. "Do you think your pitiful apologies make up for what you did, Eli? Do you think you can just say 'I'm sorry' and mollify me? I'm not Rose—you can't win me with presents and pretty words!"

On the other side of the room, Rose began to whimper and call out, "Mama!"

Bonnie swept over to the window seat and gathered her fretful daughter up in her arms. "There, there, darling," she fussed. "Mama's right here. We'll go home now, where we belong."

Eli made a raspy sound of frustration and ran one hand through his hair. "I will repeat myself once and only once, Bonnie," he said. "You're not going anywhere until we've talked."

"I defy you to stop me!"

"That would be very unwise. We both know that I can stop you, and I will if I have to, Bonnie. I swear I will."

Moving like a sleepwalker, Bonnie went back to the window seat and laid Rose upon it, covering her as gently as Eli had. "Just close your eyes and sleep, sweetheart," she said, bending to kiss the child's forehead. "Mama will be right here. And there won't be any more fighting, I promise."

Rose yawned expansively and closed her eyes, and it was a long moment before Bonnie could bring herself to turn and face Eli again.

When she did, it was only to find that he was standing in front of the fireplace, his back to the room, his powerful hands braced against the mantelpiece and white at the knuckles. Someone had closed both French doors leading into the garden, as well as those that opened onto the main hallway.

The room was spacious and airy, and yet Bonnie felt as though she'd been closed up in a tomb. "You should have consulted me before buying a pony for Rose Marie," she said, desperate to forestall the topics she knew Eli meant to work through.

Eli did not turn around, and because his head was lowered, Bonnie could see only the top of his head reflected in the mirror above the mantel. "Our son is dead," he said, in a voice that, for all its softness, throbbed with grief.

Bonnie clasped the back of a chair for support, tears slipping unheeded down her face. "Eli, please—"

Suddenly he whirled around, his features taut with an anguish that had been part of him for far too long. "Kiley is dead," he repeated, measuring the words, drawing them out, flinging them at Bonnie like stones.

She closed her eyes, but still the tears came. "Don't make me go through this, Eli. Not again. I've done my grieving."

"Well, I haven't!" he retorted. For Rose's sake, his words were spoken softly, but they had the impact of a scream of agony. "I haven't!"

Bonnie swayed, still gripping the chair back, and her eyes flew open when Eli grasped her arm in one hand and dragged her toward the French doors. He opened one of them and fairly flung Bonnie through it into the garden, but he was a long time closing the door again and turning to face her.

When he did, his eyes were haunted. Eli didn't seem to see Bonnie at all. "God in heaven," he said hoarsely, his face ravaged, "nothing has ever hurt me as badly as feeling my son's life slip away and not being able to help."

Bonnie's knees wouldn't support her. She sank to one of the marble benches set about the garden, looking at the pink buds on Genoa's favorite rose tree but not really seeing them. She was seeing herself in New York, hurrying in from the cold, full of the comedy revue she'd just seen at her favorite theatre.

The housekeeper, Mrs. Perkins, had met her in the middle of the staircase, and Bonnie had known instantly that something was dreadfully wrong. She'd run past Emma Perkins, past the room she shared with Eli, into the nursery.

And Eli had been there. He'd been sitting in the wicker rocking chair, holding the baby, rocking back and forth. Endlessly back and forth. When his eyes had lifted to Bonnie's face, they'd been empty of any expression at all.

"Where have you been?" Eli had demanded in a voice as empty as his eyes.

Bonnie hadn't answered; she'd been too stricken. When she'd reached out for her son, Eli had withheld him from her.

Now, almost three years later, sitting on a bench in a beautiful, fragrant garden, Bonnie could hear her own scream, feel it tearing at her throat. She swallowed hard and wiped away her tears with one sleeve of her calico dress.

The sense of Eli's controlled grief was crushing. She watched helplessly as he struggled to contain emotions that refused to be held in check any longer.

He began to pace back and forth on the stones of the patio, fighting. Fighting. But Eli's face was contorted, he was losing the battle.

Finally he stopped pacing. He threw back his head and a cry of tormented rage, throaty and primitive, rent the gathering twilight. It was as though Kiley had just then died in his arms.

Without thinking, Bonnie rose from the garden bench and made her way toward Eli. When she reached him, she gathered him into an embrace and held him as he wept. In silence and utter misery, Bonnie shared his pain.

A long time later, when Eli's sorrow had lost its shuddering violence and become a healing quietness, they walked, arm in arm, toward the pond. Though darkness had fallen, there was a full moon and a path of silver lit their way.

It was Eli who broke the silence that had arisen between them, and his voice was still raw, still broken. "I can't lose Rose," he said.

They were standing beneath a whispering willow tree, and the shadows of its tiny leaves moved against Eli's face. Bonnie felt a deep and terrible sadness. "She's a very healthy child—"

"That isn't what I mean, Bonnie." The golden eyes were the eyes of a stranger, just as they had been that terrible December night, nearly three years before. "I want my daughter to live under my roof."

Bonnie's hand slipped lifelessly from Eli's arm and she stared at the rippling waves of darkness and light moving across the pond. "There's no use pretending that I can stop you. We both know that any judge in the country would side with you."

"I don't think you understand, Bonnie." Eli's voice was still ragged, but his strength and his dignity were clearly returning.

Bonnie's temper flared. She'd lost one child and now she was about to lose another. Her fists clenched at her side, she glared up into Eli's shadowed face. "Damn you, Eli, don't patronize me! I know a threat when I hear one!"

"A threat?!"

"Yes! You blamed me for Kiley's death—you made my life unbearable—and now you're trying to punish me again by taking Rose away! Oh, God, Eli, how can you be so cruel?"

Eli's face, a picture of bewilderment, slowly hardened into an expression of cold, bitter fury. "Is that what you think? That I'm trying to punish you?"

Bonnie was desolate, and she turned away, unable to bear the look on Eli's face. "I know that's what you're doing," she said.

"You actually believe that, after all that's happened between us since I came back to Northridge?"

Bonnie tilted her head back and looked up at the stars. "Yes," she said. She remembered another night under the stars, near a flooded river, and added out of pride, "Don't you see? I was only using you, the same way you were using me. I wanted a lover, and I took one."

Eli swore, then wrenched Bonnie around with such force that she collided with his chest. His lips were drawn taut across his teeth and his eyes flashed in the moonlight like those of some dangerous beast. "In that case," he breathed furiously, "you might like my terms. One way or another, Bonnie, I'm going to raise Rose as my daughter. But she needs a mother and for that reason, and that reason alone, I'm willing to marry you."

"You're willing?!" Bonnie had never been so insulted in all her life. "Why, you pompous, arrogant, insufferable ass! I wouldn't marry you again for anything in the world!"

Eli's face was rigid with loathing. "I think you will. Because you don't want to lose your daughter."

"Do you know how reprehensible you are?" Bonnie bit out, proud even in her defeat. Finally, she was forced to say, "I'll marry you, because of Rose, but I'll never be a wife to you, Eli. I swear I'll never share a bed with you!"

Eli laughed and turned to walk away. "I'll bed you whenever I want to," he promised over one shoulder, as Bonnie's face burned. "Of course, Earline will be fulfilling some of your duties, so you needn't worry too much."

Livid, Bonnie crouched, searching the bank of the pond for a rock. By the time she found one suitable for doing murder, Eli was safe inside the house.

CHAPTER 23

BONNIE STOOD A long time beside the moonlit pond, turning an impossible dilemma over and over in her mind. How might she take Rose home to the mercantile without first going inside the McKutchen house to fetch her?

There seemed to be no answer but to slip inside the parlor and pray that Eli would not be there, waiting to prevent her from slipping away with her daughter.

Cautiously Bonnie approached the house through the garden. Light from the parlor windows fell across the shrubbery and flowers in golden bars, and she took great care to keep to the shadows between. The French doors were unlocked.

Bonnie peered inside, hoping to see a clear track between herself and the little girl sleeping peacefully on the window seat. Instead she saw Seth and Eli standing in the center of the room, arguing in hushed voices, while Rose was nowhere in sight. She closed her eyes for a moment, trying to think, and when she'd calmed herself she was able to hear parts of the discussion going on between Eli and his friend.

Seth was red in the face and so agitated that he actually tore off his jacket and flung it away. Then, incredibly, he even loosened his celluloid collar. "—Inexcusable behavior —I won't be a party to such a thing—"

Bonnie carefully opened one of the French doors in order to listen. Eli's words, though spoken quietly, carried into the cool, fragrant shadows of the garden.

"I've tried everything else, Seth. Everything."

"This is coercion!" Seth answered forcefully. He looked ready to engage in fisticuffs, should matters come to such a pass. His eyes shifted suddenly toward the French doors, and Bonnie, realizing that she had been seen, ducked away to crouch behind a forsythia bush.

She heard no more, but that didn't matter, because Bonnie knew all too well what the altercation between Eli and his lawyer was about. Eli had related his plan to force Bonnie into a sham marriage and Seth, a decent, upstanding man, was adamantly opposed to the idea.

Aware that few people defied Eli McKutchen with any success, Bonnie offered a silent prayer that the argument in the parlor would last for a few more minutes, then dashed around the back of the house and through the kitchen door. "Don't either of you dare give me away!" she whispered to Genoa and Lizbeth, who were having a cup of tea at the table. Before anyone could answer, she raced up the rear stairs to the second floor.

There were a number of rooms where Rose might have been put to bed, but Bonnie, operating on intuition, went straight to the master bedroom, which, despite his long absence from Northridge, had been considered Eli's private domain ever since his twenty-first birthday.

Rose was nowhere in sight, but the door to the small sitting room adjoining the bedchamber stood open, a faint glow of moonlight shining within. Bonnie slipped through the doorway.

The sitting room had always been an inviolably masculine place. Eli, like his grandfather before him, had often retreated to this room to think. There were still books on the shelves, and the familiar chair and settee, both upholstered in rich Moroccan leather, remained, but a subtle transformation had begun. A brass daybed had been brought in from Genoa's room—Rose slept upon it now—and the covering at the windows, somber velvet draperies as Bonnie remembered, had been replaced with white eyelet curtains.

Bonnie lit a lamp and looked about her with a growing sense of betrayal. An elaborate dollhouse, some eight feet long and fully furnished down to tiny coal scuttles and china dishes—a relic of Genoa's privileged childhood—sat where Eli's desk had been, waiting to enchant Rose in the morning —as the pony had already enchanted her and, before that, the magnificent doll.

Approaching the dollhouse, Bonnie ran a trembling hand over its roof of tiny shingles. There was a library, with infinitesimal books on minuscule shelves, and wee crystal chandeliers hung from ceilings with intricate moldings of rosettes and cherubs, making fairy music in the draft. With a sigh, Bonnie straightened.

It wasn't the fact that she could never give such toys to Rose Marie on her own that hurt so much. She knew that love was what children thrived on, not ponies, not beautiful dolls, not dollhouses fit for display in the world's finest museums. No, what gave Bonnie pain was knowing that Genoa, heretofore her staunchest friend, had been a party to Eli's plan. She must know that the brass daybed had been brought here from her own room, and unpacking all the precious furnishings of the dollhouse, not to mention putting them in place, would have taken hours. It was a task too delicate for clumsy masculine fingers.

Numb, Bonnie blew out the lamp and turned away, leaving her daughter to sleep, undisturbed. On entering Eli's room, she was only mildly surprised to find Genoa there, sitting on the edge of the first bed that Bonnie had ever shared with her husband.

Genoa had the good grace to look sheepish. "I know what you must be thinking—"

"I'm sure you do," Bonnie agreed. "How could you, Genoa? For so long, you were the only friend I had, the only person I could really trust—" Her voice fell away, and she leaned back against the framework of the doorway to the sitting room, her arms folded. "Rose Marie is far too young to play with such a dollhouse," she went on after a long silence. "She's likely to eat everything that will fit into her mouth."

The lamp flickering on Eli's bedside table splashed Genoa's McKutchen-blond hair with golden light. She let Bonnie's remark about the dollhouse furnishings pass. "Rose belongs in this house, Bonnie. Just as you do."

Bonnie smiled, even though amusement was the last thing she felt. She supposed it was some sort of hysterical reaction, her smiling like that, for the expression felt foreign and awkward on her mouth. "You must feel very strongly indeed, Genoa, to betray me this way."

"Eli said there'd be no reasoning with you," Genoa sighed. "I should have listened to him, I guess."

"By all means," Bonnie replied tartly, "listen to Eli. He's a man, so he must know best!"

Genoa sniffed. "You are being deliberately difficult, Bonnie McKutchen! You love Eli—you admitted as much to me only a few hours ago—and yet you refuse to cooperate with him in any way!"

"I may have loved Eli then, but I hate him now. He's put me in an impossible position—I can either live with him as his wife or lose custody of my child. That's some choice, isn't it?"

Genoa went pale. "Are you going to agree to his terms, Bonnie?" she asked in a small voice. "Or will you run away?"

"If I were going to run away—and I can't think where I could go to get out of his reach—I certainly wouldn't confide in you, Genoa. I'm going to marry Eli, and then I'm going to make him wish to high heaven that he'd never been born."

Looking as though she'd been slapped, Genoa stood up and walked toward the door. There she paused, her thin back rigid, her hand on the knob. "Martha's boy has gone for the reverend. I could have the carriage brought round if you want to go home and fetch something suitable to wear."

Bonnie looked down at her plain calico dress. "Considering the circumstances, this will do just fine," she answered coldly.

Genoa flinched as though a snowball had struck her back, then walked out.

Twenty minutes later, in the main parlor, with Genoa, Lizbeth and Susan Farley for witnesses—Seth had apparently stuck by his resolution to have no part in the debacle

—Reverend Beam remarried *Bonnie* to Eli McKutchen. The elderly clergyman had performed the first wedding ceremony as well, and he read the holy words in a stern voice, his white eyebrows bobbing up and down when he came to the part about letting no man put asunder what God has joined together.

When it came time for the customary kiss, Bonnie turned toward Eli with a resigned sigh. She had decided to permit her reprehensible groom this one kiss, just for the sake of appearances.

Eli made no effort to kiss her, however. He turned away instead and signed the waiting marriage license with a grim flourish. More than a little embarrassed, Bonnie signed, too.

Lizbeth was looking on with bewilderment, while Genoa would obviously have preferred to be anywhere but in that room. The Reverend Beam hastened away as soon as he'd been paid and Eli looked blatantly restless.

In fact, of the wedding party, Susan Farley was the only one who looked truly happy.

"Well," Eli said expansively, to everyone in general and no one in particular, "I'm off to celebrate. It isn't every day a man gets married."

Bonnie gaped, watching in disbelief as Eli checked his cufflinks and tugged at the sleeves of his suitcoat. Both Genoa and Lizbeth wore stunned faces, but Susan Farley piped up, "There won't be anyone to look after Webb tonight, except for that flighty Katie. Would you mind much, Mr. McKutchen, if little Samuel and me went as far as the mercantile with you?"

Eli smiled, every inch the accommodating gentleman. "I'll hitch up the buggy and meet you out front," he answered cheerfully. One would never have guessed that he'd just taken a bride, and Bonnie didn't know whether to be relieved or furious. With dignity, she walked out of the parlor, across the entry hall and up the stairs.

Susan Farley was right behind her, collecting her infant son from the room they shared. She was humming happily as she prepared to rush back to Webb.

Enlightened, Bonnie silently wished the young widow Godspeed and made her own martyrlike way into the master bedroom. She looked in on Rose, and then got ready for bed. Genoa—thoughtful creature—had set out a tooth-brush and a tin of polishing powder on the bureau for her. Carrying these to the bathroom down the hall, Bonnie took her sweet time brushing her teeth and washing her face, but the inevitable could only be delayed for so long, and she finally returned to the bedroom.

She had half expected Eli to be waiting for her there, ready to demand his conjugal rights, and Bonnie had been rehearsing her refusal, but the room was empty.

With a sigh, Bonnie took off her calico wedding dress, turned back the covers and climbed into her lonely marriage bed. Hands cupped behind her head, she stared up at the ceiling and waited.

After an hour or so, the lamp on the bedside table began to flicker and smoke. Bonnie sat up, lifted the china globe and blew out the flame.

When she was settled again, her mind immediately filled with memories of the first night she'd spent in this very bed. She'd been a virgin bride, full of love and anticipation and fear, and Eli had taken great care in deflowering her. Deliberately, thoroughly, he'd taught her pleasure, and she'd been in such a fevered state of joy by the time he entered her that the pain passed almost unnoticed . . .

Now, once again a bride but no longer a cherished virgin, Bonnie lay alone in the darkness, her heart as sore as her pride. Sure, she'd told Eli that she wouldn't let him so much as touch her if he forced her into this disastrous marriage, but there was a part of her that hadn't meant those words, a part that craved his caresses and his possession.

An invisible clock on an invisible mantelpiece ticked away the minutes, and Bonnie tried her best to go to sleep, but the war between her pride and her love for Eli Mc-Kutchen kept her awake, tossing and turning. The clock chimed eleven and then twelve and then one.

Finally Bonnie fell into a fitful sleep. She dreamed that she and Eli were making love on a warm bed of grass, beside a river that had nearly claimed their lives, and awakened in a state of heated misery to find that it was morning.

Eli's side of the bed was empty.

Muttering because she knew that if she let go of her anger

for so much as a moment she would cry enough tears to flood the Columbia River all over again, Bonnie got out of her bed and dressed hastily.

A quick peek into the adjoining room revealed that Rose Marie was already up, probably having breakfast with her doting Aunt Genoa.

Seething, Bonnie brushed her hair and pinned it up, washed her face and rinsed her mouth, then stomped down the rear stairs to the kitchen. Only Martha was there. "Good morning, Mrs. McKutchen," she said, busy at the stove. "Miss Genoa and Miss Rose Marie are in the garden, enjoying the sunshine."

Miss Genoa and Miss Rose Marie are in the garden, enjoying the sunshine. How normal those words sounded, and how horribly abnormal Eli had made this untenable situation by staying out all night long.

Not, of course, that Bonnie had wanted him to share her bed, the wretch. And if he could be contrary and difficult, so could she.

"I won't be having breakfast, Martha," she said loftily. "Please tell my sister-in-law that I've got business to attend to at the mercantile."

Servants in Northridge were not like their counterparts in New York. "Tell her yourself, Miss Big Britches," Martha replied amiably.

Blushing, Bonnie stormed out of the kitchen, through the dining room and the parlor and out into the garden.

"Good morning, Bonnie!" Genoa sang happily. Bonnie would have given her a set down, and a proper one, but Seth was there and she didn't want to make a scene in front of him.

Bonnie lifted a squirming Rose into her arms and gave her a hug and a kiss before responding with a "good morning" of her own.

Genoa looked so relieved that Bonnie was ashamed of bearing a grudge against the woman, but bear it she did. "I've got to go and open the mercantile," she said. "I'll give Rose breakfast there."

"Open the mercantile?" Genoa parroted, openly shocked. Mr. Callahan, seated on the marble bench beside her, discreetly looked away, pretending an interest in that year's colorful crop of marigolds and zinnias.

"Certainly. I have a business to run, Genoa. And I must speak with Katie and Mr. Hutcheson."

Rose was kicking—even as an infant she had not liked being held—and Bonnie was forced to set her down. The child scampered off across the lawn in pursuit of a butterfly, and an obviously relieved Seth followed to make sure she didn't go too near the pond.

Genoa was pale as alabaster. "I can understand why you would want to inform Katie and Webb of the—the marriage, but surely you know that you needn't earn your own living any longer. Why, you're the mistress of this house!"

Bonnie folded her arms. "You, Genoa, are the mistress of this house. I'm merely a fixture."

As quickly as she'd paled, Genoa flushed. Her eyes danced with sweet secrets, and incredibly she smiled. "Mr. Callahan and I will be announcing our engagement within the next few weeks," she confided, in a girlish rush of pure glee, holding out her left hand to display a very respectable diamond.

Bonnie couldn't help softening toward her sister-in-law. Misguided as the effort had been, she knew that Genoa had only been trying to mend her brother's broken family. No betrayal had been intended. "If I weren't furious enough to wring your neck, Genoa McKutchen, I'd be happy for you!"

Genoa laughed, and her eyes were bright with joyous tears. "Oh, do be happy for me, Bonnie. It will spoil things if you stay angry."

Bonnie sat down on the bench beside Genoa and hugged her. She was delighted for her sister-in-law, of course, but she was also sad. "Northridge won't be the same without you. I don't know how I'll cope."

Genoa sniffled. "Goose. I'm not leaving Northridge permanently—Seth and I are going to build a house just down the road from this one. It should be ready by the time we return from our honeymoon trip."

Dreamily Bonnie sighed. Unless one counted the train trip across country to New York, she and Eli had never taken a honeymoon after their first wedding. Their second was only a pretense, of course, so there would be no romantic journeys to celebrate it. "Where will you go?" she asked somewhat sadly.

Genoa took Bonnie's left hand in hers. "We're going to a marvelous hotel in Canada," she confided in a delighted whisper. "Oh, Bonnie—a bride at my age! You can't imagine how nervous I am!"

Bonnie was looking down at her own hand, the hand Genoa still held, and she was near tears. She'd been married in a calico dress and Eli hadn't given her so much as a wedding band. "I envy you, Genoa," she confessed. "Oh, I do envy you."

Genoa patted her hand. "Things will work out for you and Eli, Bonnie. Just you wait and see."

Bonnie sighed. "I wish I had your confidence," she said. She wanted to tell Genoa that Eli hadn't come back to the house the night before, but her pride prevented such an admission, even though Genoa probably knew the truth already.

Seth returned just then, beaming and carrying Rose on his back. Bonnie wondered if the Callahans would have children of their own and smiled at the thought.

"Do let Rose Marie stay here with us today, Bonnie," Genoa pleaded. "She's such a joy."

The coming confrontation with Webb would probably not be a pleasant one. It would be better, Bonnie decided, if Rose weren't there. She kissed her daughter's plump cheek. "You be good while I'm gone, sweetness. I'll bring your dolly when I come home."

Rose approved of the plan. "Bye-bye, Mama," she chimed, waving.

Bonnie turned away so fast that she nearly walked into a lilac bush. For some reason, her vision was blurred.

The walk to the store was all too short. Within mere minutes, Bonnie was letting herself in at the front door.

The familiar goods on the familiar shelves were a comfort to Bonnie. She might be trapped in an empty marriage, but at least she still had Rose Marie and she still had this store.

"Katie?" she called, climbing the inner stairs.

There was no answer.

"Katie?" Bonnie repeated.

Susan came out of Bonnie's bedroom, cheeks aglow, eyes

downcast. "Katie isn't here, Mrs. McKutchen. She's packed her things and gone."

"Gone?" Bonnie echoed, stunned. "Where?"

Susan shrugged and rushed into an entirely new subject. "Isn't it wonderful! The doctor's just been and he's given Webb—Mr. Hutcheson—a pair of crutches to get around with!"

Still trying to guess where Katie would have gone without saying a word of farewell, Bonnie walked around Susan to enter her bedroom. Webb was indeed out of bed, his big frame balanced on crutches, struggling into his shirt.

"Are you sure you're strong enough—" Bonnie began, noting the dearth of color in Webb's face and the tautness of his jaw.

His blue eyes pinioned Bonnie, accusing and desolate. "I'm strong enough," he answered in a raspy voice.

"You've heard, then?" Bonnie queried softly.

"About your wedding?" Webb's voice was harsh and hostile, the voice of a stranger. "You might have told me that you'd changed your mind, Bonnie."

Bonnie lowered her head for a moment, lingering in the doorway, her hands clasping the woodwork on either side. Her position was indefensible; she'd changed her mind a long time before Eli had forced her hand, and she'd put off telling Webb the truth. "I'm sorry."

"Don't be. I should have listened when people implied that you were warming Eli McKutchen's bed. I should have been prepared for this." Webb was hobbling toward the door, forcing Bonnie to step back out of his way.

She stared at him, appalled and furious, even though Webb's inference was basically true. "Warming—"

"Susan!" Webb roared, determined to ignore Bonnie.

Susan came out of Katie's room, carrying her baby and wearing a straw bonnet. Patches of pink stained her cheeks and she was very careful not to meet Bonnie's eyes. "Mr. Hutcheson's asked me to keep house for him, while he's on the mend and all. It will give Samuel and me a real home."

Bonnie's words were for Webb, who stood with his broad back turned to her. "I hope you'll be happy," she said in a small and sincere voice. Her eyes moved to Susan's face. "Webb has a beautiful house and it will be a pleasure to

286

tend. He also has a talent for newspaper work, Susan, and I hope you won't let him give up on his life's work."

There was a silence during which Bonnie looked from Susan to Webb and neither of them looked at her.

"As soon as I can walk without these blasted sticks," Webb replied in raw, distant tones, "there will be a newspaper again."

Knowing that Webb wouldn't be able to navigate the stairs without help, Bonnie held out her arms for the baby so that Susan would have her hands free to aid Webb. Even then, the descent was slow and laborious.

A wagon—Susan had probably gone out to arrange for it earlier—was waiting in front of the store. One of the ferryman's sons was at the reins, and he tipped his stained hat to Bonnie and grinned. "Mornin', ma'am," he called.

Bonnie, surrendering little Samuel to his mother, wondered what Rob Fenwick knew that was making him grin like that and then decided he was probably just flirting. None of Hem's boys were known for their brilliance. "Has your father got the ferry back in working order?" she asked.

"Yes, ma'am," was the reply. That rascal was definitely smirking. "Hear you and your man done tied the knot again."

Bonnie swallowed and closed her eyes for a moment, ready to duck back inside the store. "Where did you hear that?" she retorted, smiling for all she was worth.

Young Fenwick was helping an awkward and roundly cursing Webb into the back of the wagon. "Mr. McKutchen told us all this mornin' at breakfast. Peculiar thing, him stayin' at Earline's on his own weddin' night, ain't it?"

Webb shot a stunned, questioning gaze at Bonnie and she thought she'd die of humiliation, right there in the doorway of her mercantile. Trust one of the Fenwick boys to shout out her personal problems to all of Northridge. Soon enough, the story would be all over town.

Bonnie groaned inwardly, her smile fixed on her face, and Webb made his torturous way out of the wagon, the bottoms of his crutches making an angry thump-thump sound on the wooden sidewalk as he approached the doorway of the mercantile.

"What the hell is going on here?" Webb demanded,

287

standing nose to nose with Bonnie, and blessedly making an effort to keep his voice down. "You did marry McKutchen last night, didn't you?"

Bonnie didn't trust herself to speak. She bit her lower lip and nodded.

"And he left you alone?"

Again Bonnie nodded. There were tears in her eyes, as if she hadn't already had enough public disgrace for one day.

Webb looked full to bursting of righteous wrath, and his ears turned bright red. "Of all the—I ought to find that son of a bitch and break his neck!"

Bonnie made an attempt at humor. "It wouldn't be much of a match, would it, with you on crutches and weak from being flat on your back all this time?"

Ignoring Susan and Hem's son and all the passersby on the street, Webb cleared his throat. "Bonnie, if there's still a chance for us—"

Bonnie wouldn't have imagined that there could be such pain in being loved and not returning that love. Her throat closed tight and she shook her head once, then slipped back inside the store and closed the door.

She stood with her head down until she heard the wagon rattling away, and then she raised the shades that had covered the windows. The store was officially open.

The first customer wasn't a customer at all, but a very agitated Tuttle O'Banyon. The boy's Adam's apple was riding up and down his neck and his eyes were round as pancakes. "Mrs. McKutchen, ma'am, you've got to do somethin'—"

Bonnie was alarmed. What more could happen on this awful day? So much of it still stretched out ahead. "Don't run on, Tuttle," she said firmly. "Just tell me what's the matter."

"It's Katie—she's gone and got herself a job in the Brass Eagle, that's what she's done!" Tuttle wailed, crushing his big cap in his hands. "I tried to reason with her, ma'am, I really did, but she's bound and determined she's goin' to be a hurdy-gurdy and make her fortune! She figures by the time we're old enough to get married right and proper, she'll be ready to buy us a house!"

"Oh, Lord," Bonnie wailed, rubbing aching temples between thumb and forefinger. "What next?"

"What are we gonna do?" Tuttle demanded, in adolescent hysteria.

Bonnie stomped over to the windows and wrenched down one shade and then the other. She turned the sign in the door from OPEN to CLOSED and stood waiting half inside and half out, the brass key in her hand. "I'll tell you what I'm going to do," she said, biting off every word. "For a start, I'm going to snatch Forbes Durrant bald-headed!"

Tuttle just stood there, probably trying to imagine Forbes with no more hair than one of his billiard balls.

Bonnie gestured angrily. "For heaven's sake, Tuttle, stop standing there like a scarecrow in a pea patch and come along!"

Tuttle's legs were long, but that day he had to hurry to keep up with Bonnie. Bent on rescuing a lamb from a wolf, she was moving at roughly the same speed as the five o'clock train to Colville and generating almost as much steam.

Part Four

ANGEL
OF LIGHT

CHAPTER 24

BONNIE BARELY NOTICED the stream of people falling in behind as she and a gulping Tuttle O'Banyon made their way down the hill. They passed the undertaker's and Earline's rooming house and the wreckage of Webb's newspaper office to climb the mud-stained front steps of the Brass Eagle Saloon and Ballroom.

The double doors stood open to the warm June weather, and inside the sound of hammers and saws produced an industrious cacophony. Forbes, alerted to impending trouble by some mysterious means of his own, stood waiting just inside the entryway, an indulgent grin on his face, thumbs tucked into the pockets of his embossed satin vest.

"I've been expecting you, Angel," he said companionably. His brash brown gaze slipped momentarily to Tuttle, who stood gasping for breath at Bonnie's side, and just as quickly dismissed him as harmless. "Permit me to offer congratulations on your second attempt at marital bliss, by the way."

"Your congratulations," Bonnie ground out, "mean nothing to me. I'm here to bring Katie home and you know it, you degenerate!"

Forbes smiled harder and rocked back on the heels of his

costly leather boots. "Ah, yes. The erstwhile nanny. Sorry, my beloved, but you're too late."

"I'd damned well better not be too late, Forbes," Bonnie vowed, in a scathing undertone. "Where is she?"

"Upstairs," Forbes answered blithely. "She's being fitted for—"

Bonnie was only too aware of what Katie was being fitted for, and it wasn't just the silken gowns Forbes had been about to allude to. "That girl is *fourteen years old,*" she said, starting around her former employer to mount the flood-warped stairs.

Forbes halted her progress with a surprisingly forceful grip on her left elbow. Bonnie was now fully conscious of the crowd of lookers-on clogging the doorway behind her, and the hammers and saws had been stilled as well. Doubtless the confrontation taking place at the base of the stairway was more interesting than the task of laying a new floor in the ballroom.

"Not so fast, sweet thing." Though Forbes spoke the words in cordial tones, they nonetheless carried a distinct note of warning. "You no longer have the run of this place, and if I have to throw you out bodily," he paused, smiling dreamily, unable to resist relishing the prospect for a moment, "I'll do it."

"Eli wouldn't like that," counseled some yokel, from the doorway.

"Somebody go up to Earline's quick, and fetch Mr. McKutchen," put in yet another small-town sage.

Bonnie flinched and her reward for the involuntary reaction to Eli's name and scandalous place of residence was a slow smile spreading across Forbes Durrant's eminently slappable face.

"Our Mr. McKutchen has more forbearance than I would ever have given him credit for," breathed Forbes. "Imagine having a legal and moral right to your bed and still managing to resist. The man is either a saint or an idiot."

"Amen!" shouted one of the spectators.

Various other daring souls shouted out their singular opinions as to whether Eli classified as a saint or an idiot. The final tally was a draw, give or take an idiot or two.

By some miracle Bonnie had managed to recover her composure. She lifted her chin and at the same time wrenched her arm free of Forbes's grasp. After giving him one defiant look, she shouted, "Katie!"

"It won't do you any good to reason with her," Forbes said easily. It was obvious that he was enjoying his part in the sideshow, though there was still a certain snapping rancor visible in his eyes. "She's disillusioned with you, Angel, and the money she can earn dancing the hurdy-gurdy looks good to her. Damned good."

Bonnie knew that Katie was far too young and too idealistic to deal with the likes of Forbes Durrant and come out of the skirmish with her virtue intact. For all her book learning, the girl was woefully ignorant of the world and its ways.

This was apparent when the child appeared at the top of the stairs, dressed in a skimpy bit of blue taffeta and wearing a feather boa. As she glared down at Bonnie and jutted out her chin, Bonnie was reminded of her own willfulness at the age of fourteen.

Katie examined her fingernails, making a show of sophisticated nonchalance. Probably because of her theatrical training, a trace of boredom was thrown in for good measure. "What's all the fuss about?" she asked, almost yawning the words.

Bonnie wasn't about to give a lecture on the perils of working in a place like the Brass Eagle; she knew that would be a waste of breath. Katie was caught up in the false glamour and the promise of making her fortune, and there was only one way to stop her from plunging headlong into a situation she simply wasn't mature enough to handle. Fortuitously, the plan brewing in Bonnie's mind would serve another purpose as well.

Forbes was watching Bonnie's face and his expression shifted from one of smugness to one of watchful concern. "Get back to work," he muttered distractedly to the men who were supposed to be replacing the ballroom floor. His worried gaze moved past Bonnie to the multitude pressing into the doorway. "You people—either buy beer or get the hell out of here."

Grudgingly the spectators went away, and in the ball-room, the hammers thumped and the saws made their rhythmic, slicing sound.

Katie remained on the upper landing, leaning indolently against the balustrade, but she didn't look quite so blasé now. "You might have invited me to your wedding, ma'am!" she complained. "It wasn't as though we weren't friends—"

So that was it. Inwardly Bonnie sighed. "I'm sorry, Katie—I didn't mean to exclude you from the ceremony. It's just that everything happened so fast—"

At last Tuttle spoke. "Get back in your regular clothes, Katherine," he ordered, no less forcefully for the adolescent catch in his voice. "You look like a hussy in that getup!"

Katie flushed and made her way down the warped stairs, moving very slowly. "Do you know how much money I can earn in two years, Tuttle O'Banyon? Why, enough to buy a house—"

Bonnie turned to face Forbes squarely, leaving Katie and Tuttle to work out their argument on their own.

"I have a proposition for you," she said.

Forbes assumed a look of blissful mockery. "Angel, Angel—how I've yearned to hear those words tripping from your lips."

"Don't push your luck, Forbes," Bonnie hissed in an undertone. "I'm offering to come back here and dance the hurdy-gurdy in Katie's place."

Forbes's eyebrows almost disappeared beneath the rakish lock of caramel hair that had fallen across his forehead. "You must think I'm touched in the head, Angel. I don't need that kind of trouble."

Bonnie batted her eyelashes and looked up at Forbes with an innocent smile. "Why, what kind of trouble is that, Mr. Durrant?" she asked sweetly.

Forbes gave her an ironic look and turned on one heel, striding purposefully into the saloon. Bonnie followed, watched with carefully hidden triumph as he rounded the fancy new bar and helped himself to a glass and a bottle of prime scotch. "Damn it, Bonnie," he snapped, his reflection glaring at her from the long, ornately framed mirror behind

296

the bar, "do you think I was born yesterday? I know what you're up to, so spare me the simpering histrionics!"

Bonnie bit back a smile. Years before, in the Patch Town days, she'd been able to charm Forbes out of everything from pencils to penny sweets in just this way—it was amazing that such silly tactics could still work. She leaned against the bar, bracing herself with her forearms. "Are you afraid of what Eli will do? Is that it?"

"You bet your sweet bustle I'm afraid of what Eli will do!" Forbes hissed, slamming down the bottle of scotch and the glass in a furious motion of both hands. He uncorked the bottle, sloshed a healthy dose of whisky into the glass and tossed it back. He made a choking sound before going on. "I don't know what the hell's going on between you two—maybe Eli is availing himself of Earline Kalb's singular talents and maybe he isn't—but I can guarantee you this, Angel: I'm not going to help you avenge yourself!"

"Think of the money you could make, Forbes, if I were dancing again."

Forbes scowled and poured himself another double shot of scotch. "I'm making more by managing the smelter works, and I don't plan to get myself sent packing again just so you can make a point, sugarplum."

"Eli would never dismiss you for that, Forbes," Bonnie persisted softly. "He doesn't think in those terms. You should know by now that my husband keeps his personal life separate from his business life."

"See this?" Forbes pointed to a small scar beneath his right eye. "This is a remnant of the *last* time I got on the wrong side of Eli McKutchen!"

"I think it adds to your roguish charm," Bonnie said, and somehow she managed to keep a straight face. She even reached out and touched the tiny scar with the tip of one index finger. "I want to dance again, Forbes. Please?"

Forbes was sipping his second drink thoughtfully. "I'll grant you that I've lost a lot of customers since you left, but you're kidding yourself if you think McKutchen will look the other way and let his wife dance with every man jack who can ante up a silver dollar. He'll go through the ceiling."

"Maybe."

Forbes was leaning against the opposite side of the bar now, and his tone was comically plaintive. "Why do you want to do this, Bonnie? Are you tired of living, or what?"

Bonnie sighed. "You were right when you said I wanted to avenge myself. That's it, pure and simple, and there's no use denying it."

Forbes looked pleased. He did enjoy being right about things. "All right, Angel, we'll do this your way. But be advised of this: When McKutchen comes busting through those doors out there, I'm not going to lift a finger to protect you. Furthermore, I'll send you the bill for any damages."

"What about Katie? She's too young to work here, Forbes."

Forbes stared off into space for a few moments, probably calculating possible profits. "She's a beautiful girl, Bonnie. She might even bring in as many customers as you did."

Bonnie played her trump card. "What do you think Lizbeth will say, Forbes, when I tell her the whole sordid story of how you're willing to sacrifice a young girl's innocence for profit?"

Forbes went pale as death.

"On the other hand," Bonnie went cheerfully on, "one act of good conscience might sway Miss Simmons to overlook a few other—failings."

"Nothing short of my putting a torch to this place and building a honeymoon cottage over the ruins will sway that woman," Forbes muttered with enlightening gravity.

There was no ulterior motive behind Bonnie's response. "You really love Lizbeth, don't you, Forbes?"

For a moment it looked as though Forbes might turn away or even walk out, but in the end he gave a heavy sigh and answered, "Yes. It came as something of a surprise, given my lifelong habit of loving you."

Bonnie ignored the reference to Forbes's enduring ardor. "What are you going to do?"

Forbes looked so miserable that Bonnie actually felt sorry for him. "I'm hoping it will pass," he said.

"Maybe it won't," Bonnie felt honor-bound to point out.

The time for intimate confidences had clearly passed.

Forbes gave Bonnie a mocking grin and lifted his glass in a toast. "Here's to you, Angel. May you live to tell your grandchildren the stirring story of your return to the Brass Eagle Ballroom."

Bonnie tossed her head slightly, in lieu of an answering toast. "May you live to have grandchildren," she retorted, and then she turned to go.

"Wait a minute, Bonnie."

She stopped, but did not turn around. "Yes?"

"Your gowns were ruined in the flood. You'd better go upstairs and see if the dressmaker can alter something Katie would have worn."

Bonnie nodded. "Shall I tell Katie that you want to see her?"

"Hell, no," Forbes replied, and once again Bonnie heard the clink of the bottle's rim against the glass. "Tell her to go home and embroider tea towels for her hope chest."

Smiling, Bonnie looked back over one shoulder at her longtime friend-enemy. "Thanks, Forbes."

Forbes drained his glass before answering sardonically, "Any time, Angel. Any time."

Eli sat astraddle one of the cabin roofs, shirtless in the sun, nailing shingles into place with a force well in excess of that required by the task. He smashed his left thumb and cursed.

Just then Seth's head popped into view over the edge of the roof, his red muttonchop whiskers wriggling with suppressed amusement. The lawyer's expression immediately turned serious when the ladder beneath his feet threatened to topple.

Eli spoke around the side of his injured thumb, which ached fiercely. "I suppose I owe the pleasure of this visit to your continuing fascination with my stupidity?"

Seth grappled worriedly with the ladder for a moment and then scrambled up onto the roof. He was clearly sweltering in his woolen suit, and he tugged at his starched collar with one finger. "Your stupidity does seem fathomless, I must agree," he said, gaining his footing with some difficulty and then gripping his lapels in a sporting fashion.

Seth looked like a mountain climber who had just conquered a peak, and Eli would have laughed if his thumb hadn't been throbbing with pain.

"Did you climb all the way up here, risking life and limb, I might add, to discuss my regrettable lack of intelligence?"

Seth seemed to be enjoying his manly pose. He pushed back the sides of his suitcoat and thrust his thumbs into his vest pockets. If his red hair hadn't been so wiry, the wind would no doubt have ruffled it in a dashing manner. "I've made my opinions on that quite clear, I daresay," he finally got around to answering. "My purpose in making this death-defying ascent was simply to tell you that the union people are demanding another meeting with you. Immediately. Please take your thumb out of your mouth—I find that mannerism most distracting."

Eli stopped pandering to his injured digit and frowned. "Another meeting?" he muttered, with a complete lack of enthusiasm. "You'd think those goons would have gone on to greener pastures by now."

"They will remain in Northridge, I think, until they have gotten what they want," Seth replied. "They're a tenacious lot, I'll say that for them."

Eli took another batch of nails from the carpenter's apron he wore, holding them in his lips the way a tailor would hold pins. He thought of the beating Webb Hutcheson had taken for his stand against the Brotherhood of American Workers and scowled. God knew he had no special fondness for Hutcheson, but an injustice was an injustice, and the bastards behind the attack had gotten off scot free—so far. Eli spoke around the nails jutting out of his mouth. "I don't understand why they want to meet with me again. I've stated my terms and, if they have any business, it has to be with the men themselves."

Seth cleared his throat in a way that Eli had come to regard as ominous. "I've told them that repeatedly. Still they persist." The lawyer paused and his color heightened. "Eli, the Brotherhood has implied that there might be more violence if you don't agree to meet with them. Frankly, I'm afraid for your family."

Eli let the nails fall from his lips and they rolled down the half-shingled roof, forgotten. "They made an actual threat?"

Seth slipped a little and then righted himself. He was no longer making any effort to appear debonair. "Not directly. But reference was made to—well, Mr. Denning inquired after Bonnie and Rose Marie, and my own Genoa as well—in a manner I didn't quite like."

"What kind of manner?" Eli demanded in a low voice.

Seth sighed. "It was all very solicitous and polite. Nonetheless, it was my impression—and I confess that it is a subjective impression—that we were being warned. Reminded, perhaps, that the delegation from the Brotherhood is lodging at the Union Hotel and that the proximity of that establishment to Mrs. McKutchen's mercantile allows them to monitor her activities with some degree of accuracy."

Eli reached behind him for his shirt and struggled into it. He saw red as he made his way swiftly down the ladder, and he paced as he waited for Seth to follow, his fingers fumbling over the buttons of his shirt as he moved.

"Calm down," Seth admonished, when he too had reached the ground. "I may have misunderstood, you know. Mr. Denning might not have meant to threaten anyone."

Eli ran a hand through his sweat-dampened hair and let out a long breath. "So help me, if those pockmarked sons of bitches so much as approach my family—"

Seth was annoyed and he didn't bother to hide the fact. "Your concern is somewhat belated, isn't it? You married Bonnie last night, after all, and then you ignited a virtual holocaust of gossip by spending the night—"

"Are we back on that?!" Eli shouted, striding past gaping workers and their wives toward the buggy Seth had brought to the building site. He sprang into the seat, and the rig was already moving when the lawyer managed to climb inside.

"Yes!" Seth bellowed back, taking out his handkerchief and mopping his brow. "You saw fit to force Bonnie into marriage and then you subjected her to a public humiliation that was, in my view, most uncalled for!"

"I don't give a damn about your view!" Eli roared, as the buggy careened onto the road leading into Northridge proper.

301

"Mrs. McKutchen in no way deserved—"

Eli stood up in the buggy, like a Roman in a chariot, and promptly smacked his head against the metal framework supporting the rig's bonnet. He sat down again, cursing, and tried to come to terms with the fact that the nag hitched to the buggy was no racer. "I don't need you to tell me what I've done wrong, Seth," he said in a somewhat calmer tone of voice. "Believe me, I had all night to think about it."

"I wouldn't blame Bonnie if she never spoke to you again!" Seth railed, his eyes fixed on the rutted road ahead. "Indiscretions in a city the size of New York are one thing—in a backwater burg such as this, they are quite another!"

Despite his anxiety to reach the Union Hotel and personally throttle one Mr. Denning, Eli drew back on the reins and brought the horse and buggy to an ominous halt. "My wife seems to have quite a champion in you, my friend," he said evenly. "Is there some point in this sermon of yours or are you just enjoying the sound of your own voice?"

"Blast!" bellowed Seth. "Sometimes I think your skull must be made of iron ore!"

Eli was seething, though he gave the reins a conservative snap and drove at a much more sedate pace. "It's none of your business, Seth," he said, through teeth clenched so tightly that his jaws ached, "but I'll tell you anyway. I didn't marry one woman and then spend the night rolling around in the hay with another. Is that clear?"

Seth was struggling to regain his composure. He checked both cufflinks and tugged at his insufferably neat suitcoat. "No one would ever guess that from your behavior," he said indignantly. "Least of all Mrs. McKutchen herself."

Eli had a headache, a sudden pounding headache. He had been a fool and he'd spent the night suffering for it, but he would have towed Hem Fenwick's ferry across the river by his teeth before admitting that to Seth. Inwardly he sighed. Only one person's opinion mattered to him, and that was Bonnie's. He would have to swallow his pride and apologize to her if he ever hoped to have any peace.

Right now there was no time to think up pretty words of contrition. He had the Brotherhood to deal with. By sheer strength of will, Eli forced his headache into remission and drove all thoughts of Bonnie from his mind.

Upon reaching the Union Hotel, he left the horse and buggy to Seth and strode across the wooden porch and in through the open doorway. At the desk, he demanded Mr. Denning's room number and was informed by a nervous clerk that the official was having a late breakfast in the dining room.

Eli turned and stormed into that spacious chamber, his eyes sweeping the room and finally coming to rest on the face he sought. Mr. Denning sat at a table near the front windows, surrounded by a half dozen of his compatriots.

With a smile, he dabbed his mouth with a linen table napkin and then stood up. "Mr. McKutchen. This is a pleasant surprise."

Eli crossed the room in a few strides, his hands itching to grasp Denning by the lapels and shake the bastard until his teeth rattled. Luckily, Seth materialized at his side and injected a pleasant "Remember your temper, Eli."

The trained apes sitting around the table looked eager for a fight, and Eli longed to oblige them, but he knew that he needed to keep his wits about him. If Seth's instincts were right, and they usually were, Bonnie, Genoa and Rose Marie might be in very real danger.

"Sit down, sit down," enjoined Denning, as though he and Eli were old and dear friends.

Eli suppressed an urge to hurl the offered chair through the bay windows and sat down in it instead. Seth appropriated a chair from a nearby table and took a seat beside his employer.

"You wanted a meeting, Denning," Eli said. "Here I am."

Denning smiled warmly, though the expression in his eyes was as cold as a polar bear's ass. He took a fat cigar from the inside pocket of his suitcoat and bit off the tip. "Cuban," he said, as if he thought Eli gave a damn.

Eli scowled, impatient.

"Like Consolata Torrez," Denning added, almost as an afterthought.

Eli hadn't thought of Consolata in months; it was Seth who saw that bank drafts were sent to her with discreet regularity. The reminder of the girl who some years earlier had risked her life and probably saved his came as a stunning surprise.

"According to my research," Denning went on pleasantly, "Miss Torrez is now enrolled in a convent school in Havana, having been disowned by her uncle. How old is she? Seventeen? Eighteen?"

Eli closed his eyes.

Seth had regained his equilibrium. "I fail to see what Miss Torrez has to do with your efforts to enlist our workers in your organization," he said evenly.

Denning gave a long and highly dramatic sigh and then completely ignored what Seth had said. "She saw you through a bout of yellow fever—am I correct, Mr. McKutchen? At considerable risk to her own safety, in fact, she protected you from the Spanish forces until you could be taken to an American field hospital and then transported back to the United States. Of course, it goes without saying that a wealthy and influential man such as yourself, Mr. McKutchen, would be deeply—grateful."

The goons seated around the table snickered into their coffee cups.

"I repeat my question, Mr. Denning," Seth said forcefully. "What does Miss Torrez's kindness have to do with the Brotherhood of American Workers?"

A waitress brought coffee for both Seth and Eli. Eli had no memory of ordering the stuff and simply stared at it, making no move to lift the cup to his mouth.

"Oh, I think Miss Torrez has everything to do with our cause, Mr.—Callahan, wasn't it?" Denning was in fine form. At Seth's irritated nod, he went on. "Mr. McKutchen was in fact so grateful to the young lady—"

"Enough," Eli broke in, his voice a low rumble that grated in his throat. "You've made your point, Denning."

"That's good, Mr. McKutchen. I would certainly hate to see your second marriage to the lovely Bonnie go the way of the first. Since things are already somewhat shaky between you, if rumor is correct—"

Eli's hold on his temper was tenuous, though his grasp on Denning's lapels was anything but. Glaring into the mournful, moon-shaped face, ignoring angry mutterings among

304

the man's cohorts, Eli issued his warning with deceptive softness. "Persuade my men to join your union if you can, Mr. Denning. Tell the world about what happened in Cuba. But mark my words, you smarmy bastard: If any harm comes to my wife, my daughter or my sister, I will find you, as God is my witness, and when I'm through with you, you won't be fit for anything beyond singing soprano in a church choir."

Denning paled, then went ruddy with stifled rage.

Eli smiled poisonously, released his hold on Denning's coat, and stood up. Furious, the bruisers in bowler hats rose from their chairs, too, all six of them spoiling for battle.

Much to Eli's disappointment, Denning ordered them to sit down again.

CHAPTER 25

KATIE WATCHED RESENTFULLY as the dressmaker took Bonnie's measurements for a gown of scarlet silk. The fabric lay, resplendent and quite out of place, across the top of Forbes Durrant's new desk.

"I don't see what's so wrong in my dancing the hurdy-gurdy," the girl complained, her chin cupped in her hands. "If it's proper for you, why is it improper for me?"

Bonnie sighed. "We've been all over that, haven't we?"

The dressmaker finished her measuring and held a length of the scarlet fabric across Bonnie's bodice, muttering and shaking her head. "Not your color, though some would say scarlet is fitting—"

Bonnie fixed the seamstress with a withering glare. "Indeed?" she challenged.

The plump woman averted her eyes. Apparently she did not wish to pursue the point. "I'll do my best to have this done by tonight, but I can't guarantee a proper fit."

Bonnie, who had stripped to her underclothes for the measuring, hastened back into her own modest dress. She wished that she'd just dragged Katie out of the Brass Eagle by the hair, if it had come to that, and never agreed to take the girl's place among the hurdy-gurdies. Repaying Eli for the humiliation of having the whole town know he'd spent his wedding night with Earline Kalb didn't seem quite so important now. In fact, it seemed downright pointless.

"You seem so sad, ma'am," Katie commiserated with real concern, as she buttoned up the back of Bonnie's dress. "A bride should be happy."

The dressmaker wound the scarlet silk into a bulky bolt and left Forbes's office, and the moment she'd closed the door behind her, Katie gave a gasp and turned white as milk. "A bride! Oh, ma'am, what's Mr. McKutchen going to say about all this? Surely he'll not want his own wife dancing—"

Bonnie didn't know whether to laugh or cry. The whole situation was a horrible muddle. "I'm not sure he'll care one way or the other," she confided quietly.

"Not care?" Katie echoed. "Mr. McKutchen? Why, his eyes just about burn holes in his face whenever he looks at you, ma'am. And he married you again, didn't he?"

"It wasn't a marriage in the true sense of the word, Katie," Bonnie said with as much dignity as she could manage, and somewhere inside herself she found a spare smile. "None of this need concern you, in any case. You'll like living at Genoa's house on a permanent basis, won't you?"

Katie's lovely face lit up. "I hadn't thought of that! Will I be allowed to play the concert roller organ and have my pick of the books?"

This burst of girlish innocence bolstered Bonnie's spirits; she'd done one right thing, at least. She'd gotten Katie to forget all about dancing the hurdy-gurdy in the Brass Eagle Ballroom. "Of course you will," she answered softly. "Now, let's go back to the mercantile and pack our things."

When Eli returned to the site of the new Patch Town, where some families were living in tents and others were already camping inside unfinished cabins, he found Genoa and Lizbeth Simmons there, conducting informal reading classes on a grassy slope overlooking the framework of the new schoolhouse.

Genoa listened as a young woman struggled painfully through a page of McGuffey's *Second Eclectic Reader.* Apparently neither the teachers nor their students were concerned with the fact that Rose Marie was running from one group to another, wearing a feathered headdress and whooping like an Indian.

Eli scooped the child up into his arms, then shifted her to his back, where she continued to emit earsplitting war cries. "Where the hell is Bonnie?"

Genoa looked up and smiled bewilderedly in the face of her brother's annoyance and her niece's delighted shrieks. "Bonnie?"

"Your sister-in-law," Eli prompted, in an angry whisper. "My wife." He reached back to clap one hand over Rose's mouth. "Geronimo's mother!"

"Oh," Genoa said fondly. "Bonnie. Well, when last I saw her, dear, she was off to the mercantile to sell buttons and potatoes and all those things. Isn't Rose's headdress just the sweetest thing you've ever seen? Mr. Callahan sent away for it."

"Remind me to have him scalped," Eli replied succinctly. At least two dozen pairs of eyes were looking at him over the tops of reading primers and he was suddenly self-conscious. "I'll take the Indian home," he said, striding off toward the buggy.

Seth had taken the reins, and he smiled at Rose's colorful feathers and emitted a witless "How, big chief!"

Rose chortled and started to whoop again.

Eli groaned and sank back into the seat, content to let Seth drive the rig. In the distance, a train whistle shrilled.

"There's the four-fifteen," observed Seth cheerfully. "Right on time!"

Rose was still carrying on like an Apache and Eli's head was pounding. Not only would he have to apologize to Bonnie for abandoning her on their wedding night—and in the process convince her that he hadn't slept with Earline—he was going to have to explain all about Consolata Torrez in the bargain. His jaw tightened. "Rose Marie McKutchen," he said evenly, "shut up."

Rose Marie was mercifully quiet during the ride into Northridge, which ended, by tacit agreement between Eli and Seth, in front of Bonnie's mercantile.

The shades were drawn and there was a CLOSED sign hanging on the door. Grimly, Eli left his daughter in Seth's care and bounded up the outside stairs to let himself into Bonnie's kitchen.

Because of his headache and only because of his headache, he called her name in a reasonable tone of voice.

She immediately entered the kitchen, her eyes wide. "You might have knocked," she said somewhat nervously, keeping her distance.

"And you might have looked after our daughter instead of leaving her with Genoa all day," Eli countered, "but we'll talk about that later. Right now, there are some other things we need to discuss."

Bonnie looked wan and very reluctant. "I quite agree, but I don't have time just now," she said, and it seemed to Eli that she was being careful to keep her distance.

"What the hell do you mean you haven't got time? This is important!"

"So is a wedding, Eli McKutchen, but you certainly didn't let ours interfere with your busy schedule, did you?"

Eli rubbed the back of his neck with one hand, unable to hide his frustration. "I'm trying to tell you—"

Bonnie's chin rose and, though there was still no color in her cheeks, her smoky violet eyes snapped with defiance. "Like you, Eli," she said coldly, "I have things to do. If you'll excuse me—"

She would have walked right out and left him standing there in the kitchen like a fool, if he hadn't grasped her arm and forced her to face him again. "I won't excuse you," he bit out, and suddenly, for all his anger, the wanting of her ground painfully within him. "What things do you have to do that are more important than taking care of your daughter or talking to your husband?"

Bonnie looked as though she'd like nothing better than to spit in his face, but even she didn't have quite that much courage. She did wrench her arm free of his hand and step back, though, and her eyes were still shooting fire. "I have always taken care of my daughter," she said evenly. "In fact, Rose Marie is the only reason I was willing to marry you."

The words had the bracing effect of a sound slap across the face. "I suppose I deserved that," Eli conceded with a ragged sigh. "Last night, when we talked about Kiley, I—"

She turned away suddenly, wrapping her arms around herself. "Please go."

Eli tilted his head back and closed his eyes for a moment. Sometimes he wondered if the fire this woman had ignited in his spirit and his body was worth all the frustration she caused him. He began again, because Bonnie was worth any amount of frustration. "Last night, when I said I wanted Rose Marie to live under my roof as my daughter, I wasn't threatening you, Bonnie. I was proposing."

Bonnie turned slowly back to face him, cautious questions in her eyes. "But—"

Eli held up one hand. "Let me finish, Bonnie," he said hoarsely. "I was trying to tell you that I love you. That I need you. It was an emotional time for both of us and things got out of hand—" He paused, at a loss for words, but Bonnie waited in silence for him to go on and finally he did. "When you jumped to the conclusion that I was using Rose to force you into marrying me, I lost my reason for a little while."

She looked as though she wanted to believe him, and that was a start at least. "You spent the night at the rooming house," she said woodenly. "With Earline."

"I wasn't with Earline. Not in the way you think."

Bonnie lowered her eyes. "I'd like to believe that, Eli."

He approached her cautiously, bent his head to give her a brief, innocuous kiss. "Go ahead and believe it, because it's true. Come home with me, Bonnie. There are so many things I have to explain."

There were tears glistening in her eyes when she looked up at him. "God help me, I'd like nothing better than to go home with you, but—"

Eli was instantly on his guard, though he tried not to show it. "But?"

"You're not going to like it," Bonnie said, half as a confession and half as a challenge.

Eli was in no mood for either, but he knew that too often he reacted to the things this woman said and did without thinking first. The results were invariably disastrous. He spoke in carefully impassive tones. "I'll be the judge of that, if you don't mind."

Bonnie's throat moved slightly as she swallowed, and her

gaze skirted his for a moment. "I told Forbes that I would dance again."

Eli felt an explosion brewing within him and swayed with the effort of stemming it. "Why?"

There was a long silence, during which Bonnie looked as though she'd like to be anywhere but in that kitchen. "He'd hired Katie to take my place. She's fourteen and she's gullible and I don't think I need to tell you what would have happened."

Eli drew a chair back from the table and sank into it. This had been one hell of a day, and he was determined not to make it worse. When he spoke again, it was with a moderation he wouldn't have thought himself capable of attaining. "I do believe you could have saved Katie from a sordid fate without sacrificing yourself in her place," he said, careful to keep his eyes fixed on the linoleum.

"I wanted to embarrass you," Bonnie replied, with that cold-water forthrightness that generally came just when a man was preparing himself to deal with evasion tactics. "I was—and continue to be—very angry."

"About my alleged tryst with Earline," Eli threw out on a weary sigh.

"It was a very cruel thing to do, Eli," Bonnie insisted softly, still standing and still keeping her distance.

He looked up at her face then, unable to hide the peculiar combination of vulnerability and amusement he felt. "You made it quite clear that you wouldn't welcome me in your bed, Bonnie."

Two patches of bright pink outrage blossomed on her fine cheekbones. "So you just found another bed," she retorted.

"Yes. My bed." Eli stood up, very near the tattered ends of his emotional rope. "My single, solitary, empty bed. Which happens to be in Earline's rooming house."

"How convenient, Eli, not only for you, but for Earline," Bonnie said with quiet contempt.

He caught her proud little chin in his hand, gently, and forced her to meet his eyes. "I will repeat myself just once, Bonnie, so listen carefully. I did not break my wedding vows with Earline Kalb or anyone else."

A tremor went through her small, shapely body, though whether it was born of anger or of pain, Eli could not discern. Silently he cursed himself for throwing away Bonnie's trust during their first marriage. And then there was Consolata.

Bonnie opened her mouth to speak, but before she could get a word out, someone knocked at the kitchen door, while there was a simultaneous pounding at the one downstairs.

Slowly Bonnie reached up and removed Eli's hand from her face. "Katie?" she called back over one shoulder, as she rounded Eli to answer the knock at the kitchen door.

"I'll see who's downstairs, ma'am," the young girl sang out in reply.

Eli closed his eyes and muttered an exasperated curse. Was he never going to have Bonnie to himself long enough to say the things that had to be said?

Seth was standing on the outside landing, wearing a ridiculous feathered headdress and holding Rose Marie in one arm. The sight of him provided just the touch of humor Bonnie needed to keep herself from shattering into bits, and she smiled even as tears welled in her eyes.

"Beg pardon, Mrs. McKutchen," Seth said kindly, "but Miss Rose seems to be needing her supper and perhaps a nap."

Bonnie reached out for her grumpy daughter and held her close for a moment, trying to regain her composure. It seemed important that she speak normally. "Thank you, Seth," she said. "Won't you come in?"

Seth peered past Bonnie to Eli, and hastily removed the colorful toy headdress. He looked self-conscious and very sympathetic, and Bonnie silently begged the lawyer not to comment on the obvious climate of emotional tension. "That will depend, of course," he answered, pausing once to clear his throat. "Are you ready to leave now, Mr. McKutchen?"

Eli's words were hollow, and for all their softness they echoed in the kitchen. "No, Seth," he replied. "I am not ready to leave. But I would like you to take Rose Marie and the girl—Katie—back to Genoa's house."

"Of course," Seth agreed, "I'll just—"

Before he could complete his sentence, there was a clatter

312

on the inside stairs and Bonnie turned, wondering what Katie could be in such a hurry about. Not in her wildest dreams, she was to reflect later, could she have guessed what was about to happen.

Katie's beautiful eyes were very round and her color was high. After shy glances at both Eli and Seth, she burst out, "Ma'am, you'll never believe it! Your own dear father is downstairs, come all the way from Ireland!"

Fearing to drop her, Bonnie set Rose Marie on her feet and then sank into the chair Eli had occupied only minutes before. Rose toddled immediately to Katie, looking for pampering.

"Ma'am?" Katie prompted, somewhat worriedly, even as she took a whimpering Rose into her arms.

Eli spat a swearword and stormed out of the kitchen without a word of farewell. Bonnie heard his boot heels clattering on the outside stairs and covered her face with both hands.

"I gather this isn't a happy reunion," Seth observed tentatively from somewhere behind Bonnie. "Is there anything I can do, Mrs. McKutchen?"

Bonnie lowered her hands, sat up very straight in her chair and spoke calmly. "Please see Katie and Rose back to Genoa's, if you would."

Katie hesitated. "Ma'am, you're sure you want me to go?"

"Yes," Bonnie answered, staring at the inside doorway and waiting for her father to appear in it. "Everything is all right, Katie. Please go with Mr. Callahan."

She heard the door close behind her, then footsteps on the stairs outside. She stood up, smoothed her hair and her skirts and then Jack Fitzpatrick made his entrance. He was still a handsome man, though his dark hair was thinning and the reddened veins in his nose were more pronounced.

"You've taken good care of the store, miss," he said by way of a greeting. "I'm thankful for that."

Bonnie was at a loss for words. She'd never really been close to her father, though she'd felt honor bound to send him money after his curious departure for the Old Sod. Shameful as it was, all she could think of was that she was about to lose the mercantile. After all the work and the tears and the struggles to keep the enterprise afloat, she was going to have to hand it over, lock, stock and pickle barrel. "I wasn't expecting you," she finally managed to say.

Jack Fitzpatrick laughed. He was wearing an ill-fitting suit, somewhat the worse for travel and, even though he couldn't have been in Northridge for more than half an hour, he reeked of liquor. "From the looks of you, you'd sooner I'd stayed away," he commented, making himself comfortable at the table without so much as a by-your-leave. "I'm some hungry, daughter, so if you wouldn't mind—"

Bonnie minded, oh, she minded indeed, but she got out a skillet and set it on the stove, built up the fire and cracked a half dozen eggs into the pan.

"There's a good girl," her father said approvingly, and Bonnie's back stiffened as she sprinkled salt and pepper over the eggs. Once they'd begun to sizzle, she turned to face Jack Fitzpatrick.

"You're back to stay, then?" she asked.

Jack smiled again and nodded. He needed a shave and, from the smell of him, a bath. "Seems to me that you're not very glad of that, girl."

Bonnie was seething. "I wasn't very glad of paying your gambling debts at the Brass Eagle," she said, taking a plate from the shelf and slamming it down on the table in front of her father. "It took five thousand dollars!"

"Five thousand dollars that you earned selling my goods in my store," Jack Fitzpatrick pointed out dryly, thus dispensing, to his mind, with the whole matter. "I'll be takin' myself a wife soon. Settlin' in."

Bonnie set a knife and fork on the table, along with bread and butter, and put a lid on the skillet. Her father liked his eggs cooked clear through. "Have you anyone in mind? To become your wife, I mean?"

"Oh, there's always a widow or two willin' to tie the knot with a man of business. I don't imagine I'll have much trouble findin' myself a bride."

With furious motions, Bonnie measured tea leaves into the yellow crockery pot. She considered crowning her dear father with it and then decided that violence was not the answer. "That's it, then? After all this time, you're just going to waltz in here and take this store away from me, and never mind all I've done to keep it going?"

Busy masculine eyebrows arched in a frankly dissipated face. "You're a married woman with a man to look after you. A rich man, at that. What do you want with a mercantile anyway?"

Bonnie wasn't about to go into detail. The story was too complicated and too personal. "A lot has happened that you know nothing about."

"Little wonder, that," complained Jack Fitzpatrick. "Not a word from you since you wrote me that the boyo passed on."

Any mention of Kiley, however indirect, could be counted on to take the starch out of Bonnie. She took the plate from the table and began filling it with fried eggs. "I'll wager it was the money you missed, rather than my letters."

Her father looked truly hurt when she met his gaze. So hurt that Bonnie turned away to the sink and pumped water into the teakettle with more industry than the task required.

"Daughter."

Bonnie set the teakettle on the stove with a clatter and whirled to face her father, her eyes snapping with a rage she could barely contain. "Don't you speak to me as though I were still a ten-year-old in a patched dress and pigtails! I'm a grown woman and I've kept this store going single-handedly. You owe me more than a 'thank-you-very-much,' damn you!"

Jack was tucking into his eggs, but his eyes danced when they stole sidelong glances at Bonnie's pink face. "I'm glad to see that nothin's broken your fine Irish spirit, girl. Glad indeed. Eli McKutchen would've had me to deal with if you weren't in such fine fettle."

Brave words, she thought, but she said nothing. Her spirit was not in such "fine fettle" as her father seemed to think. With a sigh, she sat down at the table.

"Where is Mr. McKutchen anyway?" Jack asked through a mouthful of fried eggs and fresh bread. "And how did it happen that he allowed his wife to stoop to keepin' store?"

Bonnie set her elbow on the table and rested her chin in her hand. "I left him after Kiley died, Da. We were divorced."

Jack Fitzpatrick choked on his dinner, probably thinking that now he'd have a grown daughter on his hands, and him seeking a wife. "Divorced?" he croaked.

"Oh, don't worry. We were married again last night. And you have a granddaughter."

Jack looked wildly about for something to wash down the food lodged in his throat. "Fast work, that," he said, after Bonnie had mercifully provided him with a glass of water.

She smiled but made no effort to clarify matters. Let Jack Fitzpatrick hear the story piecemeal from the town gossips. "I'm sure you're tired," she said, opening the kitchen door to leave. "I'll leave you to rest yourself."

"Bonnie—"

She stepped outside and closed the door behind her. The dressmaker was waiting at the base of the stairs, a large box in her arms.

Bonnie took the box containing her scarlet silk dancing gown, said a gracious "thank you" and walked away. Unable to face the crowd at Genoa's house, most notably Eli, she followed an impulse that led her in the opposite direction.

Earline was waiting when she got as far as the rooming house, leaning lazily against the recently added railing of her porch. "Going back to the Brass Eagle already?" the woman crooned.

Bonnie stopped, clutching the cumbersome box in both hands. "I can't think why that should interest you, Earline," she said sweetly, her gaze fixed straight ahead, on the green-gray width of the river.

"I hope you didn't lie awake worrying about your man last night," Earline went on. "I took real good care of him."

The box containing the scarlet dancing dress thumped to the wooden sidewalk and Bonnie left it there. "I'm so grateful," she drawled, "that I could positively spit."

Earline laughed. She looked voluptuous and womanly in her summery dress, and Bonnie could imagine her taking good care of Eli. All too well. "A man shouldn't be lonely on his own wedding night, now should he?"

Bonnie drew in a deep breath and mentally counted to ten. "I'm sure you think I'm heartbroken," she was finally able to say. "To be perfectly frank, though, I was relieved that you took him off my hands. You see, ours is a marriage in name only."

Earline looked smugly unconvinced. "Sure it is, Bonnie. That must be why you're about to climb over this railing and tear my hair out by the roots."

There was no way Bonnie could deny those words without being damned to hell for an outright liar. She bent, with as much dignity as she could muster, and picked up the box she'd dropped to the sidewalk. "You've lost Webb Hutcheson once and for all, Earline—I truly think he's going to marry Susan Farley before the summer is out—and tormenting me isn't going to change anything."

"It's going to make me feel better," Earline answered. "Not that making love to Eli McKutchen is such a terrible chore. He's all man, that one."

To think I've made my way all this time, Bonnie marveled to herself, *dancing the hurdy-gurdy, running the mercantile, getting myself appointed mayor. And all to be hanged for cold-blooded murder.*

She let the box fall again and started up the steps of Earline's porch, only to be restrained from behind by strong hands that came out of nowhere and gripped her upper arms.

"Angel, Angel," Forbes's voice scolded, flowing past her ear, smooth as warm brandy with sugar and cream. "Surely you don't want to fight with Earline." He paused and then added thoughtfully, "She must outweigh you by forty pounds."

Earline's face went crimson. She forgot all about Bonnie in her indignation over Forbes's remark and stormed into her house, slamming the screened door behind her.

Bonnie calmed herself and turned to look into those familiar, impudent brown eyes. "It pains me to say it, but thank you, Forbes. I'm afraid I was about to disgrace myself."

Forbes reached down for the bulky dress box. "I was merely protecting my investment. That she-cat would have torn you to shreds and what good would you be then?"

Suddenly Bonnie was angry all over again. "You simply cannot bear to be accused of kindness, can you, Forbes?"

He smiled, tucking the dress box under one arm and using the other to propel Bonnie onward, over a sidewalk warped by the floodwaters. "Is that what I'm being accused of? How refreshing."

"You are really every kind of scoundrel!" Bonnie amended in a hiss, trying to dig in her heels and finding herself ushered along at an even brisker pace for her troubles.

Forbes laughed. "That's more like it," he replied.

CHAPTER 26

THEY HAD REACHED the front steps of the Brass Eagle before Bonnie could get Forbes to listen to her. "I've changed my mind—about dancing, I mean."

Forbes's eyebrows arched. He opened one of the doors and steered Bonnie through the entryway into the saloon itself, and they were in the kitchen before he answered. "That, as they say, is a fine how-do-you-do, considering that I was generous enough to agree to your outlandish terms." He tossed the dress box onto the long trestle table in the middle of the room, and it made a resounding thump, but for all that Forbes did not look angry.

Bonnie peered at him quizzically and then sat down on one of the long benches that stretched along either side of the table. Normally this room was a busy place, but that afternoon it was empty except for herself and Forbes. "I expected an explosion at the very least," Bonnie admitted.

Forbes swung one leg over the bench and sat astraddle, facing Bonnie. "Oh, we're a pair, you and I." He set one elbow on the table's edge and disconsolately propped his head in his hand. "You love Eli, I love Lizbeth. And yet we seem to devote ourselves to driving them away. Why do you suppose that is, Bonnie?"

Bonnie's mouth was open. She had expected such honesty

319

from Forbes about as much as she had expected her father to appear out of nowhere and take back the mercantile. In either case, she'd sooner have looked for God to part the Columbia River Tuesday after next, just for something to do. She sighed. "I don't know about you," she confessed miserably, "but I think I'm afraid."

"Afraid? Of what?"

Bonnie shrugged. "I'm not sure. Eli just scares me, that's all. Maybe because it's so easy for me to let my happiness depend on what he says or does or thinks."

Forbes took Bonnie's hand and squeezed it, and there was a gentle smile on his lips. "You, the Angel? The mayor of Northridge? Depending on someone else for happiness? I'll believe it when I see it."

Bonnie made no effort to remove her hand from Forbes's. Their friendship might have been a contradictory alliance, but it was an old one and it was real. "Believe it, Forbes," she said, "because you're seeing it. If Eli really has been unfaithful to me again, I'm not going to be able to stand it."

"Again?" Forbes prompted, bending his head in an endearingly boyish way to look directly into Bonnie's eyes. "What do you mean 'again'?"

In for a dime, in for a dollar, Bonnie thought dismally. "After our little boy died, Eli turned into a complete stranger. He wanted nothing to do with me." She paused, remembering the way Eli had wept in the garden the night before, and her throat constricted into a burning knot. Forbes's grasp on her hand tightened reassuringly. "There were other women."

Forbes's dark eyes betrayed a quiet fury. "Go on."

Bonnie only shook her head, unable, for the moment, to speak.

Again Forbes surprised her. He let her hand go and took a tender hold on her chin, making her look at him. "For what it's worth, Angel," he said huskily, "men usually don't deal well with grief. We're expected to be rock-ribbed and all that and keep our deeper feelings to ourselves. It's possible that McKutchen did his mourning in the only way that he could manage at the time."

A single tear streaked down Bonnie's face, and at the

same time she smiled. "Are you admitting to deep feelings, Forbes Durrant?"

He rubbed his stubbly chin with one hand. How he contrived to look unkempt and damnably attractive at the same time was a mystery best left to greater minds than Bonnie's. "Oh, yes, Angel," he said, with a husky sort of reflection, "I am. The night you married McKutchen—for the first time—I hurt so badly that I thought I was going to die of it."

Bonnie felt chagrin. "I'm sorry," she said, averting her eyes again. "I never meant—"

Gently Forbes cupped Bonnie's face in his hands, one thumb brushing away the traces of the tear. He kissed her, not passionately, but in a tender way that was almost experimental. It felt very nice, that kiss, though it didn't set Bonnie's toes to tingling the way Eli's kisses did.

"I'll be damned," Forbes muttered a moment or so after the fact with a wistful shake of his head. "I really am in love with Lizbeth."

Bonnie laughed. "How am I supposed to take that remark, Forbes?"

One of his hands lingered on her face, the thumb moving in a feather-light caress, but his smile was the brazen, mischievous one that Bonnie was used to seeing. "As a compliment, Angel. As a compliment. Loving you has been such a habit with me that I guess I half expected to forget my name or something—when I finally got to kiss you, I mean."

"Do you forget your name when you kiss Lizbeth?" she asked mischievously.

Forbes groaned. "Yes. Among other things, like how to breathe and where I live."

His misery made Bonnie happy in a bittersweet and poignant sort of way. "Then I guess you'd better marry her. Next, you'll be forgetting your bank balance."

Forbes looked pleasantly horrified. "That *would* be serious," he agreed.

Bonnie stood up, resigned. "For my part," she said, "I'm through beating around the bush. I'm going home and talk to my husband."

"I could get my buggy and drive you there," Forbes offered.

Bonnie stood on tiptoe to kiss his whisker-rough cheek. "Thank you, but walking helps me think, and I've got a lot of thinking to do."

Forbes touched her hair, in a fleeting, tentative motion of one hand. "Good-bye, Bonnie," he said gruffly. "And good luck."

"The same to you," Bonnie replied quietly, filled with a feeling of sweet sadness. *Who would have thought,* she asked herself, as she left the kitchen by the rear door, *that there could be pain in the ending of something that had never begun?*

Genoa's house was quiet, though Bonnie could hear faint sounds of merriment coming from the direction of the garden. On such fine evenings, supper was often served outside.

It was just as well, Bonnie thought, as she started up the wide stairway leading to the second floor. Her walk across town had done little to clear her mind and she simply wasn't up to dealing with anyone except Eli. All her emotions, all her instincts were driving her toward him.

Bonnie found her husband in the master bedroom, as she had somehow known that she would, sitting disconsolately on the edge of the bed. His head was resting in his strong, work-roughened hands, his fingers splayed in his rumpled hair, and he did not look up when Bonnie entered.

She closed the door behind her and leaned back against it for a long moment, her upper lip caught between her teeth.

Eli still didn't raise his head. "I thought you would be spending the evening with your father."

"No," Bonnie said with a sigh. "I don't believe I'll be up to having a chat with Jack Fitzpatrick for a while. I went to the Brass Eagle to see Forbes."

"Oh," Eli said. That was all, just "oh."

Bonnie felt fiery disappointment. She'd expected a grand and passionate rage at the very least. Didn't Eli care whether she danced the hurdy-gurdy in a scarlet dress? She was silent for a long time, not trusting herself to speak.

Eli lowered his hands, but he had yet to so much as look

in Bonnie's direction. His magnificent shoulders were stooped, she noticed now and, in the last fierce rays of daylight pouring in through the windows above the bed, he looked drawn and strangely hopeless.

At last Bonnie overcame the odd shyness she felt and approached the bed. Standing at its foot, she asked, "Eli, what is it? What's the matter?"

He turned his gaze to Bonnie with an effort, and she was stunned at the anguish in the depths of his eyes. "There isn't any easy way to say this, Bonnie," he said in a voice as ravaged as his face.

Bonnie's heart threatened to stop beating, and she put one hand to it. He was going to say that he'd lied before, that he'd shared Earline's bed after all. She just knew it. Maybe he had even decided to have this second marriage annulled . . .

"Sit down," he said with an attempt at a smile, his hand patting the nubby white bedspread.

Bonnie obeyed, mostly because she couldn't trust her knees to support her, but she didn't say anything because it was taking all the energy she had just to keep herself from crying.

"There was a woman in Cuba," he said. While Bonnie's mind reeled, he uttered a sound meant to resemble a laugh, but falling far short. "Consolata was a girl, really—she must have been about eighteen when I knew her."

Bonnie reached out blindly for the bedpost and held on. She still couldn't speak, but she'd given up the effort at holding back the tears that streamed down her cheeks.

Eli made no move to touch Bonnie and that was a kindness, for she couldn't have borne it, but he went on talking, his voice taut with controlled emotion. "I liked playing soldier, Bonnie, and when I was asked to carry a dispatch to the southern part of the island, I jumped at the chance. I'd been in Santiago de Cuba all of six hours when I collapsed in a cantina—"

"You had yellow fever," Bonnie said stupidly, still gripping the bedpost. She remembered the day Genoa had showed her a letter from Seth, explaining that Eli had contracted the disease.

Eli's hand touched hers and then drew back to run

through his hair. "A young girl named Consolata Torrez took care of me. I was out of my head most of the time and I don't remember much even now, beyond cracked walls and a crucifix and the godawful heat."

Bonnie cleared her throat. "And Consolata?" she prompted miserably.

Eli stood then, facing Bonnie. He pried her fingers loose from the bedpost and crouched before her, catching both her hands together in both of his. "I know you're not going to believe me, Bonnie, but I wouldn't recognize Consolata if I met her on the street. The only woman I remember seeing is you."

Bonnie had not intended to look at Eli again, but her eyes sliced to his face. She trembled with sudden fury, wanting to kick and scratch and scream. "You must think I'm every kind of fool, ready to believe any outlandish lie—"

Eli closed his eyes for a moment. "No."

"You made love to that woman, didn't you?" Bonnie spat, struggling in vain to free her hands from his. "You made love to Consolata Torrez and now you're trying to say that you were so delirious with fever that you thought she was me!"

"It began that way, Bonnie," Eli said brokenly. "I swear it did."

Bonnie spoke archly, for all that she was sobbing by then. "And how did it end, Eli?"

Eli might have been an actor, had he not been born to an industrial empire. He looked at Bonnie as though she'd run him through with a sword. "According to Consolata and her uncle," he said after a long time, "it ended in disgrace."

Bonnie had managed to free her hands, but she clasped them together in her lap, afraid of the violence she wanted to do. "I can imagine your horror," she mocked, sniffling, "when you realized that you'd just taken your pleasure with someone other than me!"

Eli rose to his full height and then sat down beside Bonnie again on the bed. The sunlight had faded away and the room was dim. There was a long, torturous silence.

"Did you make her pregnant?" Bonnie whispered, when she couldn't hold the question inside her any longer.

Eli grasped Bonnie's shoulders in a sudden motion and there was true and startling anger in his face. As well as in his rasped "No, damn you, I didn't make her pregnant, but I ruined her for any other man, at least the way her uncle tells it, and I've been supporting her ever since! Are you happy now, or do you want to torment us both by asking to hear every last detail?"

Somehow Bonnie broke free of his grasp and shot to her feet. She'd already slapped Eli—her hand throbbed with the force of the blow—before she even became conscious of the impulse to make him hurt the way she was hurting.

He made no attempt to retaliate, to restrain Bonnie, or even to rise off the edge of the bed.

"Why did you tell me this?" she whispered, her hands clasping each other. "Why, Eli, after all this time, did you tell me?"

"Someone found out about Consolata and tried to use the information to blackmail me. I didn't want you to hear the story from anyone else."

Bonnie felt sick and covered her mouth with one hand for a moment, before going on. "Who? Who was blackmailing you?"

The look Eli gave her was at once scornful and wry. "It wasn't Durrant or Hutcheson," he ground out, "so don't worry. Your circle of admirers is unbroken, Bonnie."

"I can always ask Seth."

He stretched out on the bed then with a weary sigh, his hands cupped behind his head, his golden eyes closed. "If it's that important to you, Bonnie, you go right ahead and ask him."

At that moment Bonnie was fairly convulsed with rage. She flung herself at Eli like a furious animal, all claws and teeth, and all the while she was sobbing because the pain was beyond bearing.

Eli grappled with Bonnie for several seconds and then subdued her by clasping her wrists in his hands and flinging her onto her back beside him. Still she struggled, kicking as hard as she could, and Eli finally pinned both of her legs beneath one of his own. There were long, angry scratches on his face and tears in his eyes.

"I'm sorry, Bonnie," he choked out. "I'm sorry."

Eli's hands were still holding her wrists and she arched her back in an effort to be free of him, curses she didn't remember learning hissing past her lips. The shock was a jolting one when he kissed her, and the sensation was not all rage.

She squirmed, now more furious with herself than with Eli, but he subdued her by stretching out upon her, the kiss unbroken.

His weight was crushing, and yet Bonnie no longer sought to be free of it. Eli had released her wrists and, in a last-ditch effort to save her pride, she tangled her fingers in his hair, fully intending to pull it out in hanks. Instead she took frightening pleasure in the silky texture, pressing Eli deeper into the kiss.

With a groan that made Bonnie's embattled tongue and the whole inside of her mouth quiver, Eli ground his hips against hers. Through skirts and petticoats and drawers, Bonnie felt the awesome, heated length of him and her body raged to be appeased.

Gasping, Eli escaped the kiss, and Bonnie saw bewilderment in his eyes, along with a nearly ungovernable passion. Her hands meshed in his wheat-gold hair, she forced him back to her, meaning to consume him in her anger and her love. She wasn't thinking, only functioning on the most primal level of her femininity, and there was no pain, for that had been thrust aside by the fury that drove her to take and be taken.

A violent tensing of muscles as hard as tamarack told Bonnie that Eli was not going to be conquered willingly; he was too used to conquering. He tore his mouth from hers and rolled onto his back, his chest heaving as he fought to breathe. "Bonnie—" he said in a rasping attempt at reason.

She knelt beside him, slowly unbuttoning his shirt, her hands hungry for the warm feel of his chest. His eyes aglitter with warning, he clasped her wrists in his hands, but she freed them easily and bared him to her touch.

Bonnie's palms tingled as they made soft, fevered circles on his flesh, brushing over the mat of golden maple hair glistening there.

326

She bent her head to tempt one masculine nipple with the tip of her tongue and Eli tensed, groaning. He tried valiantly to resist the sensations Bonnie was creating with her fingers and her mouth, but at last his formidable will was broken. His hands grasped Bonnie's hips and he thrust her onto her back in a single fierce motion.

If she hadn't been driven beyond good sense already, Bonnie would have been frightened by the look in his eyes. Kneeling astraddle her like a furious Viking, he ripped her dress from neckline to waist, and then he did the same with the camisole beneath. Her breasts swelled proudly, defiantly in his hands.

"You wanted this, Bonnie," he ground out. "Remember that when it's over and you're back to hating me."

Bonnie heard Eli's words and at some level of her consciousness they registered, but she was consumed by her own aching need for the full and thorough loving of this one man. He moved sinuously into a position of interwoven subservience and mastery, and Bonnie gasped with pleasure as she felt his mouth close over her breast. Instinctively her fingers entangled themselves in his glossy, toasted-gold hair, caressing. He drew at her, now hungrily, now with a tormenting tenderness, until he'd taken his fill at both her nipples, and then he sat back on his haunches. His breathing was deep and uneven and his eyes were closed.

Bonnie, still caught between his powerful thighs, shinnied upward until she was half reclining and half sitting up. A visible tremor went through Eli's body as she undid his belt buckle and then the buttons of his trousers. He endured her caresses as long as he could and then lunged off the bed, pulling Bonnie after him.

Glaring at her all the while, he finished removing his clothes and then proceeded to divest Bonnie of hers. They stood facing each other, like naked warriors about to do battle.

Eli lifted Bonnie by her waist, setting her firmly upon his manhood. She wrapped her arms around his neck and tilted her head back in glorious submission as he glided slowly inside her.

* * *

327

The room had long been dark, but there was no lamp burning. Bonnie feigned sleep when Eli left the bed, breathing evenly and keeping her eyes tightly closed. There was moisture along her lashes, but he couldn't know that.

Eli dressed quietly; she heard the jingle of his belt buckle, the change in his breathing that meant he was pulling on his boots. When the doorknob turned, Bonnie could no longer keep up the pretense.

"Eli, wait," she said, through the wall of pride that was threatening to smother her.

He was silent, but Bonnie sensed that she wasn't the only one struggling to hold dangerous emotions in check. She sat up in bed, drawing the covers over her breasts even though the room was pitch dark.

"Where will you go?"

Eli sighed raggedly. "San Francisco, I think," he answered. "There's a shipyard there that I might buy."

Bonnie was ever so glad that he couldn't see her face in the gloom. She needed to hide her despair and her hurt and her shattered pride. She would always love Eli McKutchen, right or wrong. For all of this, her words were a flippant taunt. "So you're tired of the smelter works already. I guess the challenge is gone now, isn't it, Eli? It's time for a new toy."

There was a muffled curse as he left the door and collided with the footboard of the bed, and then a match flared. His face grim in the crimson flicker, Eli lifted the globe of the lamp on the bedside table and lit the wick.

The springs creaked as he sat down on the side of the bed and ran one hand through his hair in a typical gesture of frustration. Bonnie used those brief moments to gather her dignity.

She needn't have worried that he'd see her reddened eyes, for Eli was studiously looking in the other direction. "That's what you think the smelter is to me? A toy?"

Bonnie was breaking apart inside, but she shrugged and her voice was light. "It was broken, you fixed it, and now it's time to play with a shipyard."

The pale amber eyes sliced to her face, menacing and despondent. Bonnie knew then that Eli had told her the truth about Consolata Torrez and about Earline, but it was too late for forgiving. Too late for loving. The damage was probably irreparable.

"I think it would be better if Rose Marie stayed here with you."

Bonnie settled back on her pillows and closed her eyes. *Please God,* she prayed silently, *don't let me cry again.*

"All right," she said, for there seemed no point in telling Eli that she'd never have let Rose Marie go without a fight.

She felt the mattress shift, and Eli's lips brushed hers. "I don't want you to dance at the Brass Eagle," he breathed against her mouth, "and I don't want you to be mayor of Northridge."

Bonnie's eyes flew open. "You're coming back?" she asked, before she could stop herself.

Eli nodded. "And I'd better not find you up to mischief when I do," he said.

Blood flowed into Bonnie's face. "Here I sat, Eli Mc-Kutchen, with my heart breaking right in two, and all you were meaning to do was go on a business trip?"

"That's all."

"And you're forbidding me to dance or serve as mayor, out of hand? Just like that?"

"I am."

"You have your nerve," Bonnie flared. "After all you've done!"

"Ah, but you forgave me." He arched one eyebrow. "Didn't you?"

"I couldn't help it," Bonnie admitted, dropping her eyes for a moment. "I love you, Eli, and that's a fact."

He kissed her, lingeringly, sweetly. "And I love you. But I won't have you working for Forbes, Bonnie, and I mean that."

Her cheeks throbbed. Pride, she found, was a hard thing to swallow. "I'd already made up my mind not to dance again," she said petulantly. "I didn't need you to tell me. And what does my being mayor mean, anyway? I've called twelve meetings of the town council and nobody came to a one of them."

Eli chuckled. "Then you won't mind resigning."

"I'm not about to resign! I'm the mayor of this town until November, and that's that!"

Grinning now, Eli shook his head and moved to stand up. Bonnie caught his hand in hers and made him sit down again.

"Stay," she said.

"Why?"

Bonnie bristled again. "Because there's no train leaving Northridge before tomorrow afternoon, that's why!"

Eli drew the blankets down slowly, baring Bonnie's breasts to his full view. She shivered but made no attempt to cover herself, and when he raised one hand to caress her, she sighed and closed her eyes. The feeling was lovely.

He fondled her gently, but Bonnie started when his hand moved beneath the covers to move over her belly in an ever-widening, unbearably tantalizing circle.

With his free hand, Eli pressed her back onto the pillows. "You said it yourself," he teased. "We have until tomorrow afternoon."

"Oh, but—we've already—" Bonnie arched her back as his fingers trailed down her abdomen. She clenched her teeth together, but a whining sound got past them all the same as he teased her.

"I'll expect you to stay close to this house while I'm gone," he said distractedly. "I don't trust those union people."

Bonnie was gasping for breath. "Oh!" she cried. "Oh, Eli—we've missed dinner and I'm—I'm hungry—"

Eli looked concerned, but not overly so. "You'll probably survive," he said.

Bonnie's knees had parted and she was looking up at the ceiling now. "At least—put out the lamp!" she pleaded.

Eli laughed and shook his head. "Why would I want to do that? It's so much fun to look at you."

"You're—enjoying this!" Bonnie sputtered frantically.

"Aren't you?" Eli purred solicitously.

"No!"

"You are a liar, Mayor McKutchen." He stopped tormenting Bonnie just long enough to fling back the covers, so that she was entirely revealed to him. "A very beautiful liar."

"Eli, please—the lamp—my supper—truly I'm so very h-hungry!"

"So am I," he said, slipping to his knees beside the bed. "In fact, I'm ravenous."

Bonnie felt his fingers part her for pleasuring and shivered in anticipation. A wave of heat passed through her as she watched him bend his head toward her. His touch wrung a cry of lust from her throat and the lamp blazed on the bedside table, quite forgotten.

CHAPTER 27

THE DAYS FOLLOWING Eli's departure for San Francisco were blessedly busy ones for Bonnie, even though she no longer had her store to work in and worry about. Preparations for Genoa's wedding had begun in earnest, and she spent entire mornings addressing invitations and helping to plan for the reception that would follow the marriage ceremony.

The cabins and the schoolhouse were nearly finished, and Genoa had decided that a celebration was in order. She and Seth planned to combine the formal announcement of their engagement with a grand picnic and a dance to follow. Everyone in Northridge, from the pot tenders at the smelter to the members of the town council, was to be invited, and the festivities would be held in the grassy clearing behind the cabins.

A dance floor was built, fiddlers were hired, food of every sort was ordered through Jack Fitzpatrick's mercantile. An air of busy anticipation overtook the entire town, and while Bonnie shared in the excitement, she also felt a certain disquiet, reminiscent of those rainy days preceding the flood.

Of all the people she knew, only Lizbeth Simmons seemed to share her uneasiness. Bonnie was pragmatic enough to know that the pretty teacher's wistful sighs and general absentmindedness had more to do with Forbes Durrant than any sense of impending doom. And she was sympathetic, missing Eli the way she did.

Standing in the brand-new schoolhouse, with its shiny unscratched desks, its indoor bathroom, its fresh blackboards and wonderful books, Bonnie looked at Lizbeth's forlorn face and decided to meddle.

"It's a good thing the world doesn't turn quite so fast as you're spinning that globe, Lizbeth, or we'd all be flung past the Big Dipper."

Lizbeth looked up from the beautifully detailed model of Earth that stood behind her desk and smiled thinly, her lovely face coloring with embarrassment. "I'm sorry—I should be outside helping with the decorating."

Bonnie sat down in a chair at the back of the room near the potbellied stove. She wasn't above giving a weary sigh. "We've finished all that," she said. "The Chinese lanterns are hung and the refreshment tables are set out and, according to Mr. Callahan, the fireworks will do quite nicely."

Lizbeth caught her lower lip in her teeth. "What an Independence Day this will be," she reflected absently. "A picnic, a dance, fireworks." Suddenly Miss Simmons burst into tears. "And an engagement!" she wailed.

Bonnie stood up quickly and went to enfold her friend in an embrace. "Oh, Lizbeth," she said, patting the young woman's trembling back. "Love really hurts sometimes, doesn't it?"

Lizbeth backed away, sniffling. "Of all the men in this world, of all the decent and substantial men, I had to choose Forbes!"

It was a strange feeling, this wanting to defend Forbes Durrant. "Forbes is decent, Lizbeth," Bonnie pointed out quietly. "And if the ability to provide well for a family is what you mean by 'substantial,' he's that, too."

Lizbeth dashed at her tears with the heel of one palm. She was trembling again, this time with the obvious effort to control her anger. "He's a saloonkeeper, Bonnie! A whoremaster!"

"I'm not sure there is anything so terrible about keeping a

saloon," Bonnie said. "Perhaps if you were willing to tolerate that much, Forbes would give ground on the other."

"I don't know that I could do that," Lizbeth whispered. "Forbes is an admitted rounder, a rogue. What kind of husband would he be?"

Bonnie remembered the tenderness Forbes had shown her that day in the kitchen of the Brass Eagle Saloon and Ballroom. She remembered his kiss, too, though of course she didn't mention it. "A very interesting one, I think. And certainly a passionate one."

Lizbeth's cheeks went crimson, a good indication that she knew Forbes to be passionate, perhaps even from experience. "I love him so much, Bonnie," she said after a long time. "I don't want to need him, but I do."

Bonnie recalled what Forbes had told her about forgetting his name when he kissed Lizbeth and smiled. "Does Forbes feel the same way you do?" she asked, even though she already knew the answer.

"He says he does."

Thinking of the time she'd wasted because of her pride, time that might have been spent with Eli, Bonnie went to the front of the room and gave the globe a perfunctory spin. "Did Genoa ever tell you about her first engagement to Seth Callahan?" she asked.

There was a long pause. "Yes."

Bonnie turned and met her friend's gaze directly. "She's lucky to have a second chance at happiness, Lizbeth. And I don't say that lightly—I made a similar mistake myself. Take a lesson, teacher, and spare yourself a great deal of grief. Pride makes for very poor company in the lonely hours of the night."

Lizbeth was looking at Bonnie very closely. "You sound almost as though you think you've lost Eli for good," she probed softly. "It was my understanding that he was only away on business—Genoa expects him back any day."

Bonnie bit her lower lip. Eli had been gone nearly two weeks, not a long time considering the distance between Northridge and San Francisco. He had sent neither a letter nor a wire, but that wasn't unusual, either, for Eli had never been inclined toward such gentle amenities. In the end it all came back to that strange, nebulous feeling Bonnie had that something was very, very wrong. Somewhere. She sighed and spread her hands.

"Where Eli is concerned," she said, thinking of his time in Cuba with Consolata Torrez, "the old saw sometimes applies—out of sight, out of mind."

Lizbeth paled slightly at the implication inherent in Bonnie's words. She probably had similar doubts about Forbes's ability to be faithful to any one woman, and that was understandable. "Not even a minute ago, Bonnie McKutchen," she scolded gently, "you were telling me that you regretted the time you've lost."

"I do," Bonnie said. "More than ever, I do."

"If you could turn the clock back, what would you do differently?"

Bonnie thought of those terrible days and nights following Kiley's death, of Eli's coldness and his betrayals, of his soldiering in Cuba. "I would fight," she said, with certainty. "Somehow I would pass through my own pain and grief and into Eli's and force him to face his sorrow directly. And if he still insisted on chasing off to Cuba, I would wait for him. I would be there when he came to his senses."

"My stars," Lizbeth breathed, "you do love that man, don't you?"

"More than my life," Bonnie replied, without hesitation, "and certainly more than my pride." She started toward the door, for it was time and past to go home, to be with Rose Marie, to have a hot bath and tumble into bed and sleep. In the doorway she paused. "Unless you want to lose Forbes—and I assure you, Lizbeth, there are plenty of women in this world who would be more than happy to bind his wounds and soothe his brow—fight for him."

Lizbeth lit a lamp, for the last of the light was nearly gone, and in the glow her face looked hopeful and determined. She started toward the rear door of the schoolhouse, which led into small but comfortable living quarters provided for her use and the use of those who would inevitably come after her. "Good night, Bonnie," she said. "And thank you."

Bonnie smiled and stepped out into the twilight. Genoa had already left, but Seth, thoughtful, quietly valiant Seth, was waiting patiently in the seat of Eli's buggy.

Without waiting for help, Bonnie climbed up into the seat beside him and settled herself with a sigh. Seth was not a man to make small talk, and on this night Bonnie was grateful for that trait. They drove to Genoa's brightly lit home in comfortable silence.

The enormous clock in the entryway was chiming eight as Bonnie and Seth came in, and Bonnie sighed again. It was always later than she thought, she reflected. Katie would have long since given Rose Marie her supper and her bath and tucked her into bed.

Disappointed, Bonnie said good night to Seth and climbed wearily up the stairs. Spending a happy hour or two with her daughter would have given her spirits a lift they sorely needed.

Bonnie entered the master bedroom quietly, meaning to get a nightgown, a wrapper and slippers and then go back to the bathroom and sink into a hot, relaxing tub of water. A lamp flickered on one of the nightstands and the covers on the bed had been turned back, probably by the efficient if sometimes tart-tongued housekeeper, Martha. Bonnie took a gown of lightweight flannel from a bureau drawer and opened the wardrobe to pull out her favorite wrapper, a worn robe of dark blue corduroy trimmed in white piping.

With both these garments over one arm, Bonnie crept toward the adjoining study-turned-nursery, hungry for at least a glimpse of her sleeping daughter. There would be no wild sessions of tickling this night, no hugs and no stories told, but at least she could look at Rose for a while. She could kiss her forehead or her cheek and make sure that the child hadn't kicked away her covers . . .

Bonnie entered the nursery and stopped between one step and the next, her breath caught in her throat. Eli was sitting beside Rose's bed, in a leather barrelback chair, his chin resting flush with his chest, his long legs stretched out and crossed at the ankles. Silvery moonlight flowed into the room, giving his wheat-gold hair an ethereal and completely misleading halo effect.

A smile curved Bonnie's lips and she was able to breathe again, able to move. She went to Rose's bedside and saw that her daughter was sleeping soundly, her covers in place, and she bent to kiss her forehead. Eli chose exactly that moment to awaken, and being a man to take advantage of opportunity whenever it presented itself, he gave Bonnie's bottom a mischievous pinch.

She gasped and straightened, at once insulted and very, very glad that Eli was home again. "Cad!" she accused in a saucy whisper.

Eli stood up and smoothly lifted Bonnie off her feet. The wrapper and nightgown she'd carried had long since fallen to the floor, forgotten. Chuckling to himself, Eli carried his wife into their bedroom and set her on her feet. Turning her so that she faced the bed—and the delicious fate that awaited her there—he began unfastening the buttons of her dress.

Strangely flustered, her heart fluttering against her rib cage, Bonnie searched her mind for something to say. Something reasonable and ordinary. "Did you buy the shipyard?" she blurted at last.

Eli had finished unbuttoning Bonnie's dress, and his hands were warm on her bare shoulders as she shrugged free of the garment. He laughed and the sound was husky and warm and very, very masculine. "We'll discuss the shipyard later. Right now, my love, I need you."

He turned Bonnie to face him and finished divesting her of her dress, leaving her to stand before him in her camisole and petticoats and drawers. She blushed, feeling just as nervous and bridelike as she had that long-ago night after their first wedding, when Eli introduced her so tenderly to the sweet mysteries of her own womanhood.

Now his warm and deft fingers were undoing the wispy pink ribbons that held Bonnie's camisole closed. She caught his hands in her own, half dizzy with the awesome power he exerted over her.

"How long have you been home?" she asked. "The train came in hours ago—"

Eli's fingers, stopped by her touch, began their slow and gentle work again. "I've been back for a week," he said, his golden eyes smiling at Bonnie's mouth, just her mouth, as her tongue whisked once over her dry lips. "We'll talk about that later, too."

"A week?" Bonnie gasped, stepping back. "Eli McKutchen, you didn't go to San Francisco at all! What—"

337

He drew her close again, his hands on her quivering shoulders, and kissed her. Bonnie forgot all the questions she wanted to ask and, moments later, when the lamp had been extinguished and Eli lowered her to the bed and stretched out beside her, she forgot her name.

Mary. Jane. Elizabeth. She smiled as her husband groaned and tensed upon her, in the final throes of a passion that had already driven her into a maddened state of whimpering and thrashing about, and finally the sweet satiation her body had hungered for. Bonnie, that was it. Her name was Bonnie.

The fingers of her right hand entwined themselves in Eli's hair as he sank to her, appeased, while the fingers of her left explored the moist hollow between his shoulder blades. "I love you," she said, laughing softly. Or was she crying?

Whatever Eli said in reply was rendered insensible by the muffling of his face in the pillows.

Bonnie giggled, purely happy. When Eli lifted his head, she caressed his cheek, rough and strong and exactly right, exactly wonderful.

Still struggling to breathe properly, he gave her a brief kiss. "Woman," he said, his lips moving softly against her mouth, "do you have any idea how badly—and how often —I need you?"

"A vague one," Bonnie teased. "In eight months, twenty-nine days and fifteen minutes, I'll probably have triplets as well."

His grin was benevolently wicked. "That would be fine with me. Ummm, let's sleep this way all night. I like being inside you."

"Thank you very much, sir," Bonnie retorted, kissing his stubbly chin, "I like having you. But the sad truth is that you weigh as much as a horse and you're squashing me."

Considerately he braced himself on his elbows, relieving Bonnie of his weight but not his swelling manhood. His face, barely visible in the moonlight, was suddenly serious. "I didn't go to San Francisco," he confessed gravely.

Bonnie wriggled for the sheer pleasure of feeling him grow to straining magnificence within her. "I'd already guessed that. Where were you?"

"In Spokane, for the first few days anyway."

"And somewhere in Northridge for the past week," Bonnie concluded archly. "How did you manage to come back to the gossip capital of the world without being noticed?"

"I took the train as far as Colville and rode from there on horseback."

"Arriving under cover of darkness, no doubt. Such mystery. And heaven help you, Eli McKutchen, if you've been under Earline Kalb's roof all this time."

He groaned, caught between the renewed demands of his body and an obvious need to tell Bonnie what he'd been up to for the past two weeks. He moved slowly, involuntarily upon her, and she moved with him, purposely making his predicament worse. "I haven't—oh, God, Bonnie, don't do that—"

Her hands coursed up and down the powerful expanse of his naked back and she smiled, enjoying her triumph while it lasted. "Go on," she teased primly, though her heart was beating faster and it was difficult to breathe properly.

Eli shuddered and delved deeper, in an effective exertion of mastery. "You little witch," he gasped. "You like— tormenting me this way—"

"I love tormenting you this way," Bonnie gulped out. "Oh, especially this way."

"I was—in your father's—" Eli sucked in a hard breath. "You heartless—little hellion—how am I supposed to tell you anything—"

Bonnie gave a strangling, fevered laugh and caught both her hands behind his head, dragging him into a kiss that muffled a long moan that might have been his and might have been her own.

Weaker now, but wiser, Eli rolled to the far side of the bed when the loving was over, and held the blankets firmly in place over his thighs even while he was stretching to light the lamp.

Bonnie thought this was outrageously funny and shook with secret laughter.

In the flickering light of the lamp, Eli scowled at her. "Don't you dare touch me again," he warned righteously, "until I tell you what I've been doing!"

Bonnie's laughter escaped as a series of muffled giggles. "Yes, sir!" she said, into the covers pressed to her mouth.

Eli glared her into wide-eyed silence and then told her how he'd spent the past week hiding out in her father's spare bedroom at the mercantile during the daytime and following the union delegation at night. Before that, he'd been in Spokane, checking into the Brotherhood of American Workers, and he'd learned some disturbing things about their tactics. As he might have expected from their tenacity, they didn't accept defeat gracefully.

Bonnie now understood why she'd been so on edge since Eli's departure a fortnight before. She sat up in bed. "But the smelter workers took a vote—just a day or so after you left—"

"Yes," Eli broke in. "And almost to a man, they voted against the Brotherhood. They want a union, but one of their own choosing. Jack told me all that."

Bonnie wondered how Jack Fitzpatrick, a man Eli had always quietly disliked, had suddenly become a confidant and trusted ally. He had invariably been spoken of, with controlled disdain, as "your father." Now, he was "Jack"? It didn't make sense. "Why did you choose my father to help you, instead of Seth or Forbes or even Webb?"

"Seth and Forbes knew what I was doing, of course." Eli looked damnably smug. "And as for Webb—well, the whole thing was his idea. Bright man, Hutcheson—did you know he plans to run for mayor?"

"I'm certainly glad you felt you could trust everyone in this damned town except me!" Bonnie flared in a furious hiss.

Eli grinned and reached out to caress Bonnie's cheek at the same time. "I trust you completely," he said after a moment, looking serious again. "But in this case it was safer for you to believe that I was in San Francisco. The Brotherhood was watching you, and that wistful, bewildered expression on your face convinced them that the cat was away and the mice could play."

Bonnie was outraged. "'Wistful, bewildered expression'?!" Angry tears filled her eyes and she slammed him with her pillow. "Eli McKutchen, you beast! I really believed that you would go to San Francisco and become so engrossed in resurrecting some failing shipyard that you'd forget all about me!"

He settled back in his pillows and sighed contentedly, then grinned up at the ceiling. "I could never forget you, Bonnie. Never. But I've got to admit that it was good to know that you missed me."

"You bastard," she said, but with less spirit than such rash words called for. "You were watching me pine away like some sappy character in a melodrama, weren't you?"

"Yes. A couple of times, I even came into this room to watch you sleep. You cannot possibly imagine how hard it was not to wake you up and make sound, thorough love to you." Again that mischievous grin tilted one corner of his mouth, though he was still staring up at the ceiling. "Speaking of that, Bonnie, I think you'd better prepare yourself for a new stepmother. I heard some things while I was hiding out over the mercantile that lead me to believe your dear father thinks it would be better, scripturally speaking, to marry than to burn."

Bonnie was out from under the covers and on her knees in the middle of Eli's belly before he had a chance to protect himself. "Who is he going to marry? You'd better tell me, Eli, and right now, or I swear—"

Eli groaned, and this time not with passion. "You're not going to like the answer," he said, grasping her shoulders in his hands and prying her off his stomach.

"Tell me!"

Suddenly Eli roared with laughter. He made to scramble out of the bed and thus to safety, but Bonnie prevented his escape by flinging herself at him and wrapping both arms around his middle. "Do you think you'll be able to call Earline 'Mama'?" he asked, his eyes dancing.

Bonnie covered her mouth with both hands, staring at Eli in abject horror, but then the irony of the thing dawned on her and she gave a giggling squeal. Would she be able to call Earline "Mama"? She would make a point of it!

Eli's smile faded. "Bonnie," he said seriously, pulling her into his arms and holding her against his chest as if to keep her safe from invading armies. "Listen to me."

Bonnie could feel the beat of his heart against her cheek, along with the pleasant cushion of brown-sugar hair on his chest. "I'm listening."

"The Brotherhood is planning to dynamite the smelter sometime tonight or early in the morning. I've got to see that it doesn't happen, and I want your promise that you'll wait here."

Bonnie tensed. If Eli was going to be in danger, she wanted to be with him. She grasped at the only excuse that came to mind. "I'm the mayor of this town!"

He eased out from beneath her and began putting on his clothes. "I've got plenty of help, Bonnie—I don't need a woman underfoot." Eli shook one finger at her. "Don't mistake this for an idle threat, because I mean it. If I see you anywhere near that smelter, tonight at least," he vowed, glowering at Bonnie as he buttoned his trousers, "you'll be the first mayor in history to be publicly spanked."

Bonnie was too frightened to be angry. She would be angry later, when and if Eli survived this night. "But I'll be so worried—"

The expression on Eli's face was as cold and hard as granite. He clearly meant what he said, and there was going to be no reasoning with him. Pleading and crying would do no good either. There was only one way to get past his unreasonable decree, and that was by pretending to comply with it.

Meekly Bonnie settled back in bed. She gave a docile sigh and even closed her eyes. "Very well, then," she said. "I'll see you in the morning."

Eli cursed roundly and then his hand clamped over Bonnie's mouth. She stared up at him, trying to writhe free, but he not only restrained her, he assured her silence by gagging her with her own camisole. Then, to add insult to injury, he caught her hands together at the wrists and bound her to the bedpost with his belt.

Bonnie struggled helplessly, but the gag prevented a shout for help and the belt, though not secured tightly enough to hurt, held her hands fast to the bedpost above her head.

Grinning, Eli kissed her forehead. "Sorry, my love," he said lightly, "but I'm afraid this is the only way I can be sure you'll stay put. I'll be back as soon as I can."

Bonnie squirmed, making a pleading sound behind the bunched muslin of her camisole, but Eli shook his head regretfully, blew out the lamp and left the room.

"Sleep well, Mayor McKutchen," he said from the doorway, then the door closed crisply behind him and he was gone.

For what seemed like hours, Bonnie fought in vain to free herself. She had never felt so furious, so helpless or so afraid for Eli. Eventually she fell into an exhausted, fitful sleep.

The explosion rocked the house and rattled the windows, and Bonnie awakened with screams locked in her throat. She flailed wildly at the belt that bound her hands and made a desperate humming sound behind her gag when there was an anxious knock at the bedroom door.

Bless her forever, Bonnie thought, as her sister-in-law burst into the room, wearing a wrapper and a nightgown. Genoa's hair was rumpled and her eyes were puffy from sleep, and she looked aghast as she hurried toward the bed.

"I knew you two were passionate," she fretted as she fumbled to undo the belt that kept Bonnie's hands immobile, "but this is just silly!"

Bonnie tore away the gag, just as a second explosion sounded, scrambling out of bed and frantically plundering the bureau drawers for underclothes.

"What on earth?!" Genoa cried, as she rushed to the bedroom window to look out. "Where is Eli and why were you tied up that way?"

Bonnie had no time for explanations. She shimmied into a dress just as Rose Marie came out of the nursery crying, and Katie bounded through the open doorway of the bedroom. "Mercy! What's that noise?"

"It's the smelter!" Bonnie choked out, wrenching on her stockings and then her shoes. Katie had lifted Rose into her arms and calmed her, but Bonnie gave her daughter a hasty kiss on the cheek all the same. "You must stay right here in this house, all of you!"

"Poppycock!" Genoa cried, rushing off toward her room. "You wait for me, Bonnie McKutchen," she called from the hallway, "because I'm going with you!"

Bonnie didn't wait. She ran for all she was worth toward the smelter, praying that there was something left of it.

Specifically its bullheaded and overbearing owner! *Oh, God,* she pleaded earnestly, *please don't let him be dead. Please, please, don't let Eli be dead.*

There were a hundred men outside the smelter works—the brick smokestack had fallen and the dust of its mortar was still hovering against a blue Independence Day sky—but Bonnie fought her way through. Eli was standing with Forbes and Seth, watching as a dozen of the union men were flung, one by one, into the back of a wagon, their hands and feet securely tied.

For a moment Bonnie was so relieved that she couldn't breathe or move. She just stood there, on the edge of the crowd, staring at Eli's torn, soot-covered clothes, at his bruised and filthy face.

Forbes, every bit as dirty as Eli, was the first to notice her. His teeth flashed in a grin remarkably white against his sooty face, and he nudged his employer and pointed, saying something Bonnie couldn't hear.

Eli didn't smile, and his eyes were fiery with annoyance. Bonnie remembered his threat to assign her a most unfavorable place in history and swallowed hard as he strode toward her.

But he was alive. Tears streamed down Bonnie's face and she laughed with joy. Eli was alive! His scowl dissolved into a grin when he reached her, and he lifted her clear of the ground and brazenly kissed her, right there in front of a hundred cheering men. When he set her down again, he gave her a smart slap on the bottom, and that brought even more cheers.

Bonnie was indignant, and her face burned with embarrassment. She drew back one foot, kicked Eli McKutchen hard in the shin. The onlookers howled with laughter and Eli howled with pain.

"I thank the good Lord you're not dead, Eli McKutchen," Bonnie screamed, "for now I can kill you myself! Tie me up like a heifer about to be branded, will you?!" She started for him and he backed away from her, holding out both hands and grinning nervously.

"Now, Bonnie, calm down—"

"Calm down? I'll calm down! As soon as I've torn out your gizzard, you execrable no-account!"

344

Eli shouted with laughter and, to the delight of his men, ran for his life.

Love seemed to be everywhere.

Genoa and Seth were spooning near the ice cream table, and Webb Hutcheson and his Susan were sitting in the grass, laughing and feeding each other from plates heaped with fried chicken and potato salad and sour dill pickles. Lizbeth was standing with her back to the whitewashed wall of the new schoolhouse, gazing up into Forbes's face. He stood braced against the wall, his palms flush with the wood, Lizbeth willingly trapped between his arms.

And then there was Bonnie's own father, making a public fool of himself by following a pleased Earline all over the picnic grounds. He brought her lemonade, he brought her ice cream, he even put his suitcoat on the grass so she wouldn't spoil her new gingham dress when she sat down to watch the foot races.

It was disgusting.

The musicians began tuning their fiddles as twilight fell, talking and laughing beside the enormous wooden dancing platform. Bonnie hadn't seen Eli since morning, when she'd chased him down Main Street in front of half the town. Leaning back against a birch tree, she sighed. He'd deserved that kick in the shin and every name she'd called him as well, she told herself.

The fiddlers began to play and Bonnie watched sadly as men and women joined in the first lively round of dancing, their laughter mingling with the music. Bonnie felt lonely enough to cry, though she was damned if she would. She'd shed enough tears over Eli McKutchen as it was. He simply wasn't worth it.

Her throat went tight as the first song ended and the fiddlers began to play a waltz. Oh, yes, her heart argued, Eli was worth that much and more. And now he'd probably left her, boarded the afternoon train for parts unknown.

When a gentle hand took her elbow, she started and looked up to see Eli standing there beside her, grinning. He looked so obnoxiously handsome that Bonnie almost wanted to kick him again.

"Where have you been?" she whispered, as he propelled

345

her toward the dance floor. The moon was faintly visible in the darkening sky, and so were the first twinkling stars.

"Sleeping," he answered. "It's an exhausting job, being married to you."

Bonnie looked up at Eli, with her heart in her eyes. "Are you thinking of resigning?"

He led her to the middle of the floor and they might have been alone there, with just the stars and the music and the clean evening breeze, for all the attention either of them paid to the people whirling around them.

Eli's golden eyes glowed with warm laughter as he studied her face and the new lawn dress she'd bought that afternoon. She'd selected the delectable concoction for the express purpose of impressing her husband, should she ever see him again.

"I love you," she said softly.

Eli acknowledged the words with a bow of his head and a sparkle in his eyes. He drew Bonnie into his arms as the strains of another waltz wafted toward the sky. "Does it still cost a dollar to dance with an Angel?"

Bonnie smiled up at him through a shimmering mist of pure joy. "For you," she replied crisply, "it's two dollars."